Girls Who Wear Glasses

JENNIFER INGLIS

CHAMPAGNE BOOK GROUP

Girls Who Wear Glasses

This is a work of fiction. The characters, incidents and dialogues in this book are of the author's imagination and are not to be construed as real. Any resemblance to actual events or persons, living or dead, is completely coincidental.

Published by Champagne Book Group
2373 NE Evergreen Avenue, Albany OR 97321 U.S.A.

~~~

First Edition 2020

pISBN: 979-8-676384777

Cover Art by Erin Inglis

www.champagnebooks.com

Version_1

For my mother, Jane Inglis.

Chapter One

Rachel Simon's hand shook as she read the email on her phone.
Congratulations!

She blinked a few times before continuing.

We discovered your blog, and we love your voice...

She sat at her desk and pushed the potluck Bundt cake away. This is not what she had in mind. It was just for fun...

"So, are you going to meet *him*?"

Rachel gave a start at the male voice. Brennan Donaldson leaned against the doorframe of Rachel's college classroom, posing like Marlene Dietrich, one hand on his chest, the other holding an imaginary cigarette.

"Didn't mean to startle you. Are you okay?" He entered the classroom and sat on her desk.

Rachel held out her cell phone. "It's hit the fan, my friend."

Brennan's face got brighter as he scrolled through the email.

"This is amazing!" he said. "*Charmé* magazine loves your blog and wants you to write a bimonthly column for them! And you thought no one would want to read it."

"Keep going. There's more."

In addition to the column, we'd like to honor you as one of our Women to Watch at our yearly gala, where we invite you to give an acceptance speech. Please call our editor, Brittany Ekberg, so we can set up a time to meet with you and go over the particulars...

"Oh my god, Rachel, this is too cool! What're you going to wear?" He handed her phone back as it pinged with an incoming text.

"Well, in addition to me not actually wanting to do any of that, there's a reason I can't..." Rachel glanced at her phone.

The text was from Lisa, her best friend. She knew what Lisa wanted, and was hoping to avoid her a little longer.

Rachel Adelaide Simon, I have just the man I want you to meet!

Not my middle name. Rachel shook her phone at Brennan. "Is this what you meant by *him*? How do you know about this?"

"Gay GPS. I can tell when someone is having man problems." Brennan shifted his weight and moved a copy *of Wuthering Heights* further down her paper-strewn desk. "Yes, I'm being a stereotype." He paused. "Plus, Lisa texted me. Like, eight times. I'm here to strong-arm you into saying yes."

"*You're* her ace-in-the-hole? You couldn't strong-arm a starving man into a steak dinner." Rachel nudged the Bundt cake toward him.

The English department chair's assistant had foisted it on her after today's potluck lunch. Rachel knew, with her size sixteen waistline, that she was an easy target for leftovers. There was no way she'd throw away a perfectly good cake, because of the starving children in whatever country her mother used to guilt her with when she was a child.

She stared at the dessert like she was having a one-way wild west showdown.

"Hello?" Brennan waved at her. "Thinking deep thoughts again?"

"I'm debating cake."

"I'm assuming you're *pro*."

"I shouldn't have it."

"Rachel Morgana Simon, a piece of cake is like a man. Both have to be a little bad for you to be any good." Brennan smiled.

Rachel thought her young friend to be quite wise, although he didn't know her middle name either.

"You want it? I'd dump the whole thing in my trash bin, but I'm not entirely sure I wouldn't do a culinary search and rescue the moment you left." She stared at the cake. "I think it's mocking me."

"I'm good." Brennan toyed with the stack of papers on her desk. "Would you like to get coffee? I'm done with classes for the day, and I think we have a ton to talk about."

Rachel inhaled the rich aroma of vanilla and cinnamon, and then gently placed the leftover Bundt in her trashcan. Bolstered by her tiny show of bravery, she smiled and nodded.

Although she didn't want to talk about either the magazine or the potential blind date disaster, coffee with Brennan was one of her favorite things. He always had the barista blend two of the featured flavors and add just enough milk to smooth it out, qualifying him as a java genius. He was also caught up on the latest campus gossip, which Rachel appreciated since she minded her own business and no one ever told her anything, anyway.

And to top it off, as a CPA and accounting instructor, he did her taxes for free. Rachel was hoping he'd find a way to add her cat, Lindsey, as a dependent.

"I thought you were covering Dr. Martin's statistics class,"

Rachel said.

"Nah," Brennan said. "Can't bear the thought. Last time, I dealt with a student who thought statistics was, *did you know that no two snowflakes are alike?*"

"Sounds like we share students. Most of mine think Shakespeare wrote in Islamic pentameter."

"Serves you right for teaching English." He shuddered as he glanced at the posters of famous writers hanging on her classroom walls. "They look like a fun bunch."

"They are. At least sixty-two percent of them could be considered legitimate hoots." She smiled. "And don't try to play the nerd card with me. Don't you have an abacus on your desk?"

"Yes, but I display it ironically." He zipped his jacket. "C'mon, let's go get overpriced coffee."

"Yay!" Rachel waved two highlighters in the air like pom-poms.

She collected the rest of her things, and they headed to the quad. The leaves were changing, a sure sign that autumn, as well as the school year, was fully underway. It was her favorite time of year. Sweater weather, her mother used to call it, yet still managed to admonish Rachel because of the baggy sweaters she favored. Never mind that it was the style.

To Ruth, it was schlubby, and there were few worse sins. Her mother was a stickler for fashion and presentation, a trait she hadn't passed on to her daughter. But on this bright, crisp afternoon, Rachel's sweater was appropriately loose. Soon everyone would be wearing jackets, and the plethora of flip-flop wearers would relent and put on actual shoes. Now if only she could do something about those who insisted on wearing pajamas to class. She frowned and shook her head.

"How's Ruth?" Brennan said.

"How did you know I was thinking about my mother?"

"You've got the 'mom divot' between your eyebrows."

Rachel stopped and rubbed her forehead. "She's fine. Why?"

"I thought maybe I'd call her and ask her to nag you about going on that blind date."

Rachel quickened her pace.

"Give it up, Bren. It's not happening."

"Can't you try one more time?" Brennan hurried along beside her. "Boy, for an old gal, you sure can hustle—"

"For the last time, no. I've spent my whole life being rejected and hurt. At this point I can't face it anymore."

"What would Ruth say?"

"Oh, she says a lot. Believe me. I just stopped listening."

Brennan put a hand on shoulder, slowing her pace.

"But—"

"Brennan, I'm done. The world has spoken. I must've been absent on the day they distributed the *How to Find a Man* brochure, because I never got the hang of it. I'm perfectly fine living my life the way it is. There's no lid for this pot, no peanut butter to my jelly. I appreciate the concern, but I just can't. Please."

He turned her to face him.

"Okay," he said, "I'll leave it. It's just that I love you and I want you to be happy." He cupped her cheek. "Or at least get you laid. How long has it been?"

"I...ummm..." Rachel gazed at the sky, hoping for divine intervention. "Well..."

"If you have to think about it, it's been too long."

Rachel slapped his hand away and punched him on the arm. "Knock it off. Now you're paying for the coffee."

"Just don't spill it. I'm not paying for the dry cleaning, too."

First day, junior year of college. Intro to Linguistics. Rachel entered the lecture hall as the bell rang, coffee in hand. The large room was full, the students pulling out their notebooks as the professor wrote his name on the board. Spotting a single seat in the back row, she hurried up the narrow stairs, fumbled the cup, and spilled coffee down her front.

"Here," a male voice whispered. "Use this."

Rachel glanced up from her mocha-latte-stained sweater as a pair of blue eyes blinked at her. He smiled and pulled a towel from his gym bag.

"Don't worry, it's clean."

She accepted the towel, sat in the empty chair next to Blue Eyes, and dabbed her sweater.

"I do that all the time," he said.

"Really?"

"Nah, I was trying to make you feel better. That was kinda damn funny."

"Thanks. That's what I was going for." She held up the towel. "I'll wash this." She put it on the floor next to her book bag and screwed up the courage to introduce herself to Blue Eyes. "My name is Rachel."

"Alex Hunter." He extended his hand. "You know, if we got married, your name would be Rachel Hunter. Like the supermodel." He brushed a stray curl from her forehead.

Rachel let out a flustered giggle and squirmed in her chair. They spent the rest of the class whispering back and forth, Alex telling jokes in her ear each time the professor paused. As she took notes, he drew caricatures of their fellow students in his notebook and made her laugh when she was trying to pay attention to the lecture. After class they went to the school store, where he bought Rachel her first travel coffee mug.

"Spill proof," he said.

"And then he said, 'Not with that jacket, you won't!'" Brennan paused. "Hey, where'd you go?"

Rachel gave a start. "Oh…er…I was thinking about the cake again."

"It was probably dry. You wouldn't have eaten it."

"Ha. Compulsive eaters know no bounds."

They strolled in silence for a bit, enjoying the sun. Brennan unzipped his jacket and put his hands in his pockets.

Rachel's phone rang. She dug around in her bag, and without taking it out, checked the caller ID. It was her friend, Joanie, video calling her. Rachel and Brennan stopped to sit on a wooden bench. Walking and talking wasn't one of her strengths.

"Joanie," she said.

Brennan's eyes widened with joy.

"It's the duchess? Lemme talk, lemme talk." He reached for the phone.

Rachel swatted him away, then hit accept, and her friend's rumpled visage appeared on her cell phone screen.

"This book says I'm supposed to beat the sauce with a whisk," Joanie said, dispensing with the usual pleasantries. "What is that, and am I supposed to own one?"

"You must have one," Rachel replied. "It's kitchen standard-issue. How do you make eggs?"

"Make…eggs?" Joanie blinked.

"She's trying to cook?" He seized Rachel's phone. "Duchess, are you mad?"

Duchess wasn't an official title, of course. Rachel had given her the nickname after auditing one of her classes at the college. An instructor in the theater department, Joanie Lawson's courses were popular and energetic, just like her. Only her wild, curly red hair matched her over-the-top personality and her dramatic arm gestures, which needed to be dodged like a weapon if she was excited about something. She was part royal lady, part badass, and part cartoon.

Plus, with a husband and a thirteen-year-old son, she was the only person in Rachel's inner circle with a functioning adult relationship.

"I'm trying to make coq au vin. I fear I might have lost control at some point." Joanie turned her phone around to give a panoramic view of her kitchen.

"Holy mother of Liza!" Brennan examined the footage. "Did you have a frat party in there?"

Rachel had never seen Joanie's kitchen in such a state. Pots and pans were strewn about, boxes and milk bottles were knocked on the counter, and what appeared to be a colander of cherry tomatoes was upended on the black and white marbled floor.

"Yes, it's a bit *ungapatchket.*" Joanie sighed.

"Messy?" Rachel translated the Yiddish word. "Yeah, just a little."

"Have you been binge-watching the food channel again?" Brennan said. "Also, there are no eggs in coq au vin."

"I should have played to my strengths and ordered takeout."

"It would have eliminated the need for a hazmat suit," Rachel said.

"What're you doing now?" Joanie said. "You're outside. You hate the outside."

"Brennan and I are grabbing coffee. Want to meet up with us?"

"Better not. I have to figure out this kitchen situation."

Rachel's phone dinged.

"I bet that's Lisa," Joanie said. "She's been texting me about her new beau. Sounds like she's in love again."

"Ostensibly. She used the word *magical.*"

"How have we decided to react to this?" Brennan said.

"We've decided to remain supportive," Rachel replied.

"Noted," Joanie said. "Boy, I like Lisa, but she can be a bit much."

"That's kind of like the pot calling the kettle high maintenance, wouldn't you say?" Rachel winked. "She's one of my oldest friends. Yes, she's a bit much sometimes, but she means well. And if I survived living with her in college—"

"I just hope it works out with this new guy. She does tend to put you through the ringer when it doesn't. You could ignore her."

"Then she'd start calling you."

"Never mind," Joanie said. "All right, hon, I better go. Enjoy the coffee." She glanced away from the camera. "Jason! Come help me clean the kitchen!" She turned back to Rachel. "I'll see you later, okay? I'll fill you in on how dinner went." She ended the call and the screen went blank.

Rachel put her phone back in her purse and stood. "All right, onward and upward."

"There's a fix for your issues," Brennan said.

Rachel stared him square in the face. "Could you be more specific?"

"This whole self-image thing. You just need to boost your confidence. It would really help. You could wear contact lenses. Or get laser surgery. As Dorothy Parker used to say, *Men seldom make passes at girls who wear glasses.*" He chuckled to himself.

Rachel furrowed her brow until she felt it pressing into her skull. She pushed her glasses higher on her nose and adjusted the sides on her ears.

"Yeah, well, they also don't make them at girls with fat asses. So, I'm kind of screwed on both points. Besides, I have contacts. But why bother?" She pointed to the street ahead of them. "Can we go?"

"Yes. I'm in the mood for something sweet. I'm a bit peckish. How about you?"

"Always. As long as I eat it there. Don't want to bring anything home for later."

The last thing a thirty-eight-year-old English professor with a compulsive overeating issue needed was leftover baked goods in the house. Not that there was ever much in the way of leftovers. She grocery shopped, but not all the food would make it home.

After one particularly bad day, she ate half a loaf of bread on the way home from school. She'd eaten crackers and half a mini cheese plate in the parking lot after a volatile faculty meeting. She could even eat pudding cups in her car if there were enough stoplights.

Ten minutes later, they arrived at the coffee shop. The Java Hut was two blocks from campus, and Rachel originally avoided it because she thought students would overrun it. It turned out they preferred brand name coffee, so it became a de facto faculty and staff place. Rachel and Brennan got in the short line, and she studied the menu—pointless, since she always ordered the same thing.

"Medium non-fat latte with two pumps of sugar-free vanilla syrup, please," she said to Linda, the young lady who usually worked the counter in the afternoons.

Linda accepted the order with a sigh and an eye roll only achievable in those under the age of twenty-five.

After paying for their drinks, they sat at their usual table, in the front of the café on the right-hand side. It gave a good view of the joint without being too obtrusive—close enough to the door so they could make a dash for it if it got too crowded, but not so close that they were bobbing and weaving whenever it opened or closed. She sipped her coffee and Brennan picked the cranberries from his mixed-berry scone, purchased along with a cinnamon muffin.

This magazine thing threw her for a loop. *Why on earth would they want me? I'm not their type.*

She retreated inward. Everyone had a part of themselves they kept hidden away. They kept the hurt and pain and disappointment in a box, because if anyone saw it, they would love them less. Often love seemed conditional, offered when one looked a certain way or behaved a certain way. Or love offered itself, until one day it went away. So you kept a smile on your face and did what you needed to do to keep everything running smoothly.

"I need to ask you a favor," Brennan said.

"Get in line."

"No, seriously. Would you come home with me over Thanksgiving?"

"Why?"

Brennan poked at his scone. "To be honest, I need a beard. My family doesn't know I'm gay, and they think I have a girlfriend."

"Why do they think you have a girlfriend?"

"Because I told them I had a girlfriend."

"Makes sense. Why me?"

"We'd have fun."

"This is true. But how is this possible? Have they met you? I mean, if you typed in *gay* on Google Earth, it zooms in on a street view of *you*."

"So how about it? We can do a spa day. My treat."

"Let me think on it."

"It will be like research for you. You could write a book about the experience—*Goyim Like Me.*"

"Intriguing." Rachel picked at the cranberries piling on Brennan's napkin. "Are you coming over tonight?"

"I will if you tell me why you're so freaked out about that email."

She sighed. There was no getting away from this.

"You know my blog? The one I write for fun?"

"You take characters from classic literature and analyze them using current fashion trends. Like Jane Eyre would totally be a Ralph Lauren gal."

"Well, there's more to it."

"Yes, feminist stuff and women's choices today versus back

then, blah blah blah. Fun as hell, though. Needs more Colin Firth."

"Everything does. The thing is, I wrote it for me. I never thought more than maybe you, Joanie, Lisa, and my mom would read it."

"But it's great it caught the eye of *Charmé*. You're a good writer, and you deserve the recognition."

"That's the problem, though. I don't think they're recognizing *me*." She brought up the blog page on her phone, clicked on the biography, and handed it to him. "This is the picture I used."

Brennan furrowed his brow and handed the phone back. "That's a picture of Lisa. Ohhhh…"

"Yep. They think I'm her. That's why they want me. She fits the mold."

Brennan popped a large piece of scone in his mouth. "Why didn't you use your own picture? You weren't worried about the college, were you?"

Rachel sipped her coffee. "No, it wasn't that." She sighed. "Even though I thought no one would see it, I figured the few people who did wouldn't buy me as a fashion authority. It was easier to hide behind Lisa."

"And now they want to meet you…"

"And they're expecting Lisa. Thin, blonde, beautiful, fashionable. Yup." She placed her coffee cup on the table. "You see why I can't do this. It would be one thing if I could do this remotely—they'd never see me. But a meeting? And an *awards ceremony with a speech*? No. Not happening."

Brennan opened his mouth to protest, but Rachel's phone dinged. She held up her finger to silence him, then put it down.

"Sorry. Didn't mean to give you 'the finger.'"

"It's Lisa, isn't it?"

"Yes. She's nagging me about that blind date thing. She is nothing if not persistent." Rachel glanced back at the phone. "She also says her boyfriend wants to take her on a weekend getaway." She sighed. "Such problems she has."

"Sounds like it's getting serious," Brennan said, with his mouth full of the last piece of scone.

"Yeah. She's only three dates away from buying a stack of bridal magazines. So are you coming over tonight or not?"

"I'll be there. This is significant."

"Bring snacks."

Rachel had experienced enough to know how it would play out for Lisa and her new man. Her friend would be blissfully happy for three months, regaling Rachel with all the wonderful things Mr. Right did and said, how he brought her gifts, told her how gorgeous and amazing she was. She'd get text messages that would describe how amazing the clouds were, or how the flowers she'd received smelled so sweet.

But at some point, the other shoe would drop, and Lisa would start complaining that *he doesn't call me as much,* or that *he's being withdrawn,* or in one case, how *he's asked me to post bail.* Then Rachel was in for at least three weeks of Lisa crying, taking her friend on therapeutic shoe shopping excursions, and phone calls at one in the morning. There might be seven stages of grief, but Lisa had six stages of the breakup.

Brennan's gaze locked on a man entering the café. "Speaking of snacks…"

Rachel followed Brennan's gaze.

Wow.

She didn't notice men anymore. She wasn't blind; she just didn't have her radar up. A few years ago, Lisa decided they'd missed the first round and they'd have to wait for the divorces to start, at which point Rachel shrugged and ate a sandwich. But this man was different. He was tall, handsome, though not aggressively so, with a squarish face, a nose that flattened slightly on the bridge, and a strong jaw.

His eyes are probably sparkly, too.

The man walked up to Linda, still behind the counter, and gave his order.

Wait. Did I think his eyes sparkled? I sound like one of my student's metaphors—his eyes sparkled like a sparkly sparkler.

Rachel inwardly gagged. Linda apparently liked his eyes, too, because as he ordered his coffee, she relaxed, abandoning the dour, pursed-lipped face she reserved for everyone else. His brown hair was ruffled in a natural way—not in an I-spent-half-an-hour-and-a-large-goop-of-hair-gel-to-appear-like-my-hair-does-this-on-its-own kind of way. He wore a brown tweed blazer, and grownup shoes—brown lace-ups, not hipster vegan sneakers made from recycled tires and hemp.

Rachel couldn't take her eyes off him. Mr. Good Shoes smiled at her. Brennan squeezed her knee under the table.

"*Himself* is looking at you!" he whispered.

"What? I mean…ow!" As Rachel brushed Brennan's hand from her knee, she banged her elbow on the table, hitting her funny bone.

Her coffee cup hiccupped from the vibration and nearly tipped before she managed to catch it.

"Hot!" she yelped.

"Careful there." Mr. Good Shoes passed their table.

Heat flushed over Rachel's face. She hadn't blushed like this since she was seventeen and Greg Awesome said her curly hair no longer resembled a Brillo pad.

"Hi-aya, ha-ha, thanks!"

Mr. Good Shoes waved as he exited the shop.

"Bye!" She gulped.

Brennan leaned over. "Why are you yelling?"

"I don't know!"

"Okay, Miss Shouty. You're gaining an audience here."

Rachel's face froze. "Sorry," she mumbled.

"That was...I don't know what the hell that was."

She laid her forehead on her hands. "I'm thirty-eight..."

"Yes."

"I should have developed some poise by now."

"Some, yes."

"That wasn't it."

"No." Brennan patted her hand. "No, it wasn't."

"I'm going to need a moment here."

"Take your time." He pushed the cup away from the edge of the table and bit into his muffin.

Rachel sat with her head down for a minute or two. She could stand in front of large groups of college students with no issues. There, she was confident. She could determine the difference between Henry David Thoreau and Ralph Waldo Emerson, and she never uttered *OMG*.

But one handsome guy smiles at me and I become Captain Nerd Girl. She went to the counter, bought a croissant, and downed it in three bites, all while visualizing the calories making a beeline for her ass.

"We're not done talking about this magazine thing," Brennan said, as they packed to leave. "We. Are. Not. Done." He kissed her on the cheek and waved as he marched out the door.

Heading back to the campus to pick up her car, she replayed the scene with Mr. Good Shoes again and again.

Crud. I am not cool. That is not how adult women behave. I shouldn't beat myself up, but good Lord. And I'm supposed to meet these magazine people, too? I'll be laughed right out of the building.

By the time she got home, she was drained. She changed into her sweats and headed for the kitchen. She wasn't hungry, but she noticed those old familiar pangs that needed to be squelched. She tried to resist the emptiness, the at-a-loss moments when she didn't quite know what to do with herself. She needed something, anything, to fill the void. Or maybe she just *needed*. She wanted to leave herself, to avoid the realness of it all. She needed something to do.

She made toast.

It was a distraction for a few minutes, an avoidance of the void, and it calmed her brain until the food was gone and she was left with the shame of food-medicating again. It was the place she went when the hole in her soul became too great. It wasn't healthy, but it was her. It's the place she took solace when she was bullied. When she wasn't invited. When Mom was upset and Dad was absent and she was sure it was her fault. Food was pain and food was life. Sometimes it was all she had.

Today something great happened—someone liked her work. But she couldn't celebrate because it was a fallacy. And a man she didn't even know talked to her, but she couldn't hold it together enough to say hello, because on some level she couldn't figure out why he was saying hi to *her*.

Men seldom make passes...

After the toast was gone, she ate a bowl of cereal. As she chewed and chewed, the events of the day slipped away.

Food: one. Chubby girl: zero.

Chapter Two

Later that evening, the duchess stood in the doorway of Rachel's kitchen, formidable in her gray sequined tracksuit. Rachel was busy at the stove, pouring freshly made popcorn into a bowl.

"Smells amazing!" Joanie said. "So much better than microwaved."

"Please. With whom do you think you're dealing?" Rachel feigned offense. "I even put real butter on it. None of that butter spray, which by the way, we totally can believe it isn't." Rachel sprinkled sea salt over the kernels for good measure.

"I want mine plain, please!" Lisa shouted from the living room.

"Tell her it's the spray," Rachel whispered. "It won't kill her. She'll work it off tomorrow at the gym."

Brennan materialized by the duchess's side.

"I love her," he said, "but if I have to look at one more bridal magazine, I'm going all Jessica Lange as Frances Farmer on her." He stretched his arms, attempting to touch the top of the door arch, then smoothed the front of his University of Michigan T-shirt.

"We'll be right in," Rachel said. "Stay strong."

"I will. Bring vodka." Brennan took the popcorn, spun on his heels, and headed back to the living room. "Snacks!" he shouted. "Magazines down!"

"I think she's getting ahead of herself again." Joanie sounded irritated. She opened a cabinet door and removed a glass. "She's all, *Ooh, dinner with Bruce at Casa de Pretentious. Then jazz at a cute little club no one's heard of.* She might as well be having crumpets and champagne with Prince Charming. One of us needs to talk her down."

"I'm in the trenches every day," Rachel said. "I'm tired. You're the married lady. You give it a go."

"I'll try. But if she finds an ugly-ass bridesmaid dress and insists it would look fabulous on me, I'm out. I'm too old for that *mishegoss.*"

"Fair enough."

Joanie sipped her drink. "Has Mr. Wonderful, you know, *proposed* yet?"

"No." Rachel returned the salt to the pantry. "She's just

planning ahead."

"Oh, boy."

"Yep."

Rachel futzed with the butter dish, pushing the stick back and forth over the ceramic image of a cow.

She had to hand it to Lisa. She certainly was determined to make this happen. As always, she jumped into the relationship with both feet, blindfolded, and without a shred of doubt that this would be *The One*. It was most likely to end in hurt and tears, but part of her was jealous. Lisa believed in herself and what she wanted. Rachel found it admirable.

Although, with Lisa's supermodel guise, there was a seemingly endless stream of potential suitors ready to help pick up the pieces. It wasn't a cure-all from heartbreak, but it must have lessened the sting.

Over the years, Lisa had tried to instill her confidence in her friend, though she couldn't pierce Rachel's innate shield. *I believe in you,* she'd repeat. But Rachel couldn't share her friend's enthusiasm, as her appeal had a narrow scope. *Nope. Never good enough, still fat,* she'd say, always silently.

Rachel placed the butter-covered cow dish back into the refrigerator. She got more glasses from the cabinet, placed them on a tray, and poured the drinks. The duchess grabbed a second one. She sipped it and made a show of trying to swallow.

"What is this shit?" She frowned.

"Cranberry juice," Rachel said.

"It tastes weird."

"There's no vodka in it."

"Ah. That's it." Joanie turned and called to Brennan. "Brennan? Come here, please?"

He appeared in the kitchen doorway. "You bellowed?"

"Go get me my purse, love."

"Why, do you have a flask in there?"

"Yes."

"You're badass, Aunt Gladys."

"Get the booze, Judy."

When Brennan left to get Joanie's bag, Rachel leveled her gaze at her friend. "So? How did it go?"

"What, dinner? We had Thai. It was fine."

Rachel intensified her stare, implying that she wasn't letting her off the hook.

"Okay, fine. I made dinner because I wanted to butter-up Hank before I dropped a bomb. Didn't want him to get mad."

"You're married to the nicest guy in the Chicagoland area. I can't see him flying off the handle. Especially with you."

Joanie blew a strand of hair from her face, leaned against the counter, and stared at her sequined shoes. "I got cast in a show in Chicago. It's not a big part, but it's a good one."

"How wonderful!"

"The thing is, Hank and I discussed me taking a break from acting. Just for a while."

Brennan returned and poured a splash of the flask's contents into Joanie's drink.

"What'd I miss?"

Joanie finished her newly fortified beverage in one gulp. "Hetero marriage drama."

"Ah." Brennan seated himself at the table. "Continue."

"I've been waiting forever for a break like this, but I don't want to feel like I'm ignoring my family."

"I can't tell you what to do," Rachel said. "I'm no relationship expert. I don't even think my cat and I are on speaking terms."

Joanie sat at her kitchen table. "It will work itself out. I mean, doesn't he want me to be happy? Working makes me happy. An actor acts." She cleared her throat.

Brennan rose, stood behind Joanie, and wrapped his arms around her. "Don't worry. You always get what you want, right? And remember, divas got to diva." He paused. "I don't know why I said that."

They joined Lisa in the living room, popcorn, and drinks in hand. Rachel was on one end of the couch, Duchess Joanie on the other, with Brennan's head in her lap, while Lisa had strewn pillows on the floor in front of the television and set up camp there. Rachel opened the DVD player, but Brennan stopped her.

"We're not doing that now." He put the movie down.

"You don't want to watch it?"

"We have another activity planned," Joanie said. "It has come to our attention that you will be giving a presentation at a swanky awards gala, and of course, you will be bringing us as your plus one. Well, two." She gestured to Brennan.

"And although you are an accomplished lecturer," Brennan said, "much respected in the academic world, this is vastly different. You need a little polish."

"I'm not doing it. I told you, they don't want me. They want Lisa."

"What did I do?" Lisa perked up at the sound of her name.

"Rachel used your picture on her biography for her blog," Brennan said. "She thinks they won't want her as is."

"Why?" Lisa said. "You're perfectly lovely."

Rachel was cornered. Her heart rate accelerated, and she wanted to send everyone home and eat leftover meatloaf. And the rest of the popcorn. She could hear her mother's voice in her head. *Stand up straight. Are you really wearing that? Would it kill you to wear a little lipstick? Do you really need that second helping of dinner?* Rachel shook it off and faced the group, who looked at her with expectant faces.

"Say, for the sake of argument, that I agree to this. What do you have in mind?"

"I've prepared something for you to practice on." Brennan leapt from the couch and dashed into the front hall. He returned a moment later with a stack of large tagboard pieces "Here. Take a glance at these."

"When did you have time to do this?" Rachel took the tagboards and flipped through them.

"Honey, for something as big as this, I'll *make* the time," he said. "Okay, give them back to me. So I'm going to stand there," he gestured to the back of the room, "and I want you to pretend we're at the awards. Dazzle me."

Rachel stood in front of her friends and tried to control her breathing. She'd given countless lectures and presentations to the English department. How different could it be?

"Will she be wearing heels?" Lisa said.

"No," Rachel said.

"Yes," Joanie and Brennan said, in unison.

"First of all, you're standing wrong," Lisa said. "Angle your hips toward the audience a bit and put one foot a touch in front of the other."

Rachel did as she was told and wobbled.

"You'll need to practice that. Now put one hand on your hip."

"Nope, too pageantry," Joanie said.

Rachel put her arm by her side. "Anything else?"

"Smile," Brennan said. "Be open and inviting. Make people want to lean in to hear what you have to say."

Rachel plastered her best enthusiastic grin on her face. Her cheeks felt frozen and hot at the same time.

"Good Lord, that's terrifying," Brennan said. "Take it down about twelve notches."

Rachel relaxed her face. She blinked at Brennan's cue cards

and felt like she had six arms. "Can I just start?"

"Give it a go, sweetie. You can do it," Lisa said.

"Hello, and welcome to my presentation. I am honored to be here, accepting your annual Ladies to Look For Award." Rachel turned to Brennan. "Women to Watch. Did you write this on your own?"

"Well, I don't know specifically what you'll want to talk about, so I winged it." He looked at Joanie. "Is that right? Winged? Wanged? Have wung? I don't know." He threw up his hands. "Besides, you can deal with the substance. We're here to help with style."

"Continue," Joanie said.

"All women can be their own fashion icons if they try hard enough…really, Brennan?"

"Just go with it."

"And in this age of superficiality…"

"Now gesture to the audience," Joanie said.

Rachel made a broad gesture, from one end of the couch to the other.

"A human gesture, please," Brennan said.

"…we must seek the Goddess within, appealing to the pages of classic literature…"

"Now take a few steps stage left," Joanie said.

Rachel took two steps to the left, faltered, then took four steps to the right. She squinted at the cue cards.

"Just pick a direction, hon," Joanie said.

"And in the names of Virginia Woolfe, JK Rowling, and the Bronte sisters…seriously? I accept this award humbly and say that now, right now, you like me, you really like me." Rachel ended with both arms outstretched and did jazz hands to show she was finished. She paused and curtseyed.

"Nice touch," Brennan said. "But, no."

Rachel flopped on the couch. "I told you it would be a disaster. Even here in my own living room, reading what you wrote."

Joanie scooted down the couch and patted her knee. "You can do this. I'll send you a few breathing exercises just in case. And keep practicing. How good was your first lecture at the college?"

Rachel sighed. "Excellent."

"Sure it was. Just practice what you want to say, come up with a few appropriate gestures to drive home your point, and don't forget to breathe."

"I got it. Can we watch the movie now? I need time to forget," Rachel gestured vaguely around the room, "about whatever the hell this just was."

After the movie, they gathered the bowls and glasses, and headed into the kitchen for drink refills. Rachel put on her yellow rubber gloves and did the dishes, while the others stood around the table.

"Do you have to do that now?" Lisa said.

"It's just a few things. I hate having them laying around."

"Rachel is trying to keep herself distracted," Brennan said. "She met a boy today."

"Oooooh!" Lisa and Joanie chimed.

"I did *not* meet anyone today. I saw a cute guy at the coffee shop, and he said hi to me." Rachel paused. "That didn't sound any better."

"What did you say?" Lisa was intrigued.

"Well, I, uh…"

"She squeaked, yelled at him, and spilled her coffee," Brennan said.

Rachel glared at him as if he had betrayed a deep, dark secret.

"Oh, c'mon, you did," he said.

"Did you get his number?" Lisa said.

"Oh, yeah," Rachel replied. "And I used his sleeve to wipe up the latte."

"I can't believe we've been friends for twenty years, and you've learned nothing."

"I'm sure you weren't as awkward as you felt," Joanie said.

"Yeah, she was," Brennan replied.

Rachel put the last of the bowls in the dishwasher, placed the rubber gloves on the edge of the sink, and took a coffee cake from the fridge. "Can we change the subject? Does anyone want cake?" she said, without turning around. "Maybe something from Joanie's flask?"

"No, I want to hear more about this man!" Lisa said.

"There's nothing to else to say. Some random guy said hi to me after buying a coffee. No big deal. He probably said hello to six people before me, and twelve people after."

"Those are oddly specific numbers," Brennan said.

"Whatever. Besides, I'll never see him again. Thank goodness." Rachel pulled a piece of paper towel from the roll and wiped the excess water from the counter.

"You never know." Joanie put her arm around Rachel's shoulders. "There must be a reason you had such an, *ahem*, strong reaction. Maybe it's *beshert*."

Lisa and Brennan cocked their heads in unison.

"'Meant to be,'" Rachel said. "And, no." She directed her gaze to Joanie. "No." She turned back to the counter.

Lisa said, "Maybe if you just…"

Rachel was uncomfortable, exposed, and she didn't want to go down the road again, especially after what was a Big Nothing event.

She spun around. "Brennan's family doesn't know he's gay!" she blurted.

"Yes, they do, dear." Joanie patted his arm. "They do. Trust me."

"How do they not know?" Lisa said.

"We're WASPs," he said. "We never discuss the six-hundred-pound pink gorilla in the room."

"See? He's not the only one with avoidance issues." Rachel leaned against the sink and folded her arms. This game of dodge the question was getting exhausting.

"Rachel won't meet a friend of Bruce's!" Lisa said.

Rachel pulled a roll of plastic wrap from the cabinet and placed a piece over the cake.

"They know," she said. "I'm surprised my Aunt Sadie hasn't called me about it."

"He's smart and successful," Lisa said. "I think she'd like him. One measly blind date. Is that too much to ask?"

"Don't try the guilt thing on me. I grew up with it. I am immune." Rachel wrapped the cake in plastic. "Besides, he won't be interested in me. I've got a track record of not being most men's cup of tea."

"You forgot to put toothpicks in the cake. It'll cling." Brennan pointed at the dessert.

Rachel narrowed her eyes.

"Oh, please, please, please!" Lisa ran to Rachel and embraced her, rocking back and forth.

Rachel held the cake plate in one hand, the other arm fixed at her side.

"Please do me this favor," Lisa said. "Bruce has been trying to set up his friend, and I promised him I'd find someone. You're the best person I know. Pleeeeeease?" She squeezed Rachel tighter.

Help me out here? Rachel mouthed to the others.

They shook their heads.

"I'll think about it." Rachel acquiesced with a sigh.

Brennan and Joanie applauded, a forced golf clap.

"I said, *think*. No guarantees."

"Rachel Luella Simon, you are the best!" Lisa hugged her.

"Yes, I know. I'm fabulous. Not my middle name. Now get off

me."

"What would I do without you?" Lisa kissed her friend on the cheek and let her go. "I'm going to call Bruce right now and tell him it's a maybe."

She grabbed her cell phone and headed to Rachel's bedroom to make the plans. As she got to the edge of the kitchen, she stopped and turned on her heel.

"Guys, I have a good feeling about this. I think Bruce might be *the one*."

"I'm sure he is," Rachel replied.

Lisa flashed her megawatt smile, gave a little hop, and ran upstairs.

Rachel nodded at Joanie and Brennan. "Listen up, gruesome twosome. If this goes as badly as I think it will, I will blame you."

"The charges will never stick." Brennan lifted the plastic from the cake and picked walnuts from the top.

"Stop being so dramatic," Joanie said. "It's not the end of the world. It's a blind date."

"Yeah," Brennan said. "Maybe he'll be cool. It could happen."

Rachel handed them both a slice of cake after batting away Brennan's fingers from the plastic wrap.

"Just go out," Joanie said, between mouthfuls. "And hey, it's a free meal, right?"

"Not necessarily." Rachel speared the edge of the dessert with a fork. "The last guy she set me up with made me pay for both of our dinners and his parking because he considered himself a feminist." She placed a chunk of cake in her mouth.

"That's one…"

Rachel swallowed, the cake turning into lump in her throat. "And then there was Ricky, the one who, halfway through the meal, got up to leave because he couldn't deal with *this*." She gestured up and down her body. "And how about the one who took one look at me and turned around and left?" She took another bite, chewing more thoughtfully.

"It only takes one good one," Brennan said. "And you have to say yes eventually, or Lisa will have a nervous breakdown. Besides, it will make a great story to tell over coffee. We can compare notes. I'm seeing that new guy, Jon, next Thursday."

"Trade ya," Rachel said.

"Ha, ha, ha, no."

"Worth a shot."

Lisa came bounding down the stairs with the energy of a wired toddler, three necklaces clenched in her fist.

"Bruce is so sweet. He said take your time making your decision, but he looks forward to meeting you." She held out the jewelry. "How have I never seen these?"

Rachel removed them from her grasp and placed them on the counter. "Secret stash."

"Some secret stash," Joanie whispered to Brennan. "Most people have porn in theirs."

Rachel spun around to face them. "I heard that."

"Meant you to!" Brennan said.

"Oh, I can't wait for you to meet Bruce," Lisa said. "I know the other setups were kind of nuts, but he's said nothing but nice things about Jerry. I'm sure you'll have fun this time." Her voice was inching up the vocal scale, and she hugged Rachel again with a finalizing squeeze. "You deserve fun."

"We're excited. I'm sure it will be a total love connection." Joanie leaned into Brennan. "Do people still make that reference?"

Brennan patted her arm. "Not since the early nineties, dear."

"Ah, well. Time to hit the road," Joanie said. "I have to make sure the boy goes to bed at a decent hour." She placed her empty plate in the sink and brushed off the crumbs. "Courage," she whispered.

"I'd better go, too," Brennan said. "I get tired in my old age. You heading out, Lisa?"

"Nope, Rachel and I have to plan outfits for the thing." She dashed out of the kitchen and up the stairs.

Rachel faked a smile and mimed cheering.

"All right, we're off," Joanie said. "Walk me to my car, handsome. You can protect me from marauders."

"Sure. I'll use my marauder-be-gone spray and hit him with your purse." Brennan gathered his coat and helped the duchess on with hers. "Bye!"

"Bye, guys," Rachel said, as they were leaving. "Joanie, please keep me in the loop, okay?

After getting assurances from Joanie that she would indeed keep her informed about her unfolding drama regarding her theater role, Rachel closed the door and headed back into the kitchen. Lindsey, her cat, decided to make an appearance after the to-do died down, and followed Rachel around, making her *feed me now* meow. Rachel scratched her kitty on the head and refreshed the dry kibble in her bowl. The cat ate her meal, her tiny mouth crunching the round bits.

She eats when she's hungry. And when she's not, she doesn't. Wonder what that's like.

"Don't you have anything without an elastic waist on it?" Lisa yelled from the bedroom.

Sighing, Rachel left the cat to her snack and trudged upstairs. She found Lisa sitting on the bed, holding a purple neckroll pillow in her arms.

"I knew that would get you here," she said. "You really don't want to go on this blind date, do you?"

"Gee, you think?" Rachel hovered in the doorway and pressed her hands against the oak trim as if she were trying to widen the entrance by force of will.

"I think it will be good for you, though."

"You said that about kale. I remain unconvinced."

"I think you need a kick in the ass from time to time."

Rachel dropped her arms to her side. "Do I ever complain about being single? Joke, yes, but complain?"

"No." Lisa spun the tube-shaped pillow between her fingers. "No, you don't."

"Then it's kind of your problem, not mine."

Rachel sat next to her on the bed, removed the pillow from Lisa's hands, then squeezed it like an accordion. She was sure her friends found this routine of hers tiring. She tried to give not even the merest hint of the *poor me* thing, but there were times they threatened to smack her in the head. But at the same time, Rachel was the one who had to live her life, not them. Even her mother had backed off, and she was the Queen Nudge. Rachel couldn't understand why everyone cared about her single status. Maybe it made them uncomfortable, as if she were challenging what they were *supposed* to be doing.

I'm not trying to be a rebel. I'm just trying to avoid the pain.

"You'll never get anywhere without taking chances occasionally," Lisa said.

"I had a mullet in the late '80s. I've taken risks."

"Let's pick out an outfit for you to wear. You'll feel better about the whole thing once you're fashion coordinated."

"It's like you don't know me at all."

"C'mon." Lisa grabbed Rachel's hand and dragged her to the closet, pulling her along like a bag of wet laundry. "You've got nice things in here."

"Most of it doesn't fit."

"We'll find something. Ooh, this is cute!" Lisa held up a magenta halter dress.

"That's yours."

Lisa sighed. "Pants or skirt?"

"Pants."

"Are you sure? You have such nice legs."

Rachel glared at her. Surely Lisa wasn't talking about the lumps of clay Rachel called her calves. She shook her head.

"Pants it is," Lisa said.

"How about this?" Rachel picked a pair of black trousers from the side of the closet. "And…this?" Black blouse, black shoes.

"Another selection from the Johnny Cash collection? Uh, not again. And nothing with cats on it."

"I have a cat. I don't wear cats. Please."

"It's a slippery slope."

"Yeah, it really isn't."

Rachel spotted what she thought was her best bet—a blue top with a ballerina neckline. It still had the tags on it.

"That could be cute," Lisa said. "Not bad at all. Pair it with dangly earrings. It will show off your pretty eyes." She put it back in the closet. "So that's a *maybe.*"

"I have a pair. Got them a few months ago. On clearance, even."

"Sexy."

"Hey, I'm trying here."

"Sorry. Do you own any makeup?"

"I'm wearing makeup right now."

"Oh. Of course. It's very nice. Maybe a tad more oomph? A little glamour?"

"I will wear lipstick."

"Cherry Chapstick doesn't count."

"For someone trying to get me to do them a favor," Rachel leaned one hand against the closet door, "you're kind of digging yourself into a hole."

Lisa held up her palms and laughed. "All right, all right." She hung the clothing back in the closet and shut the doors, then shifted her attention to Rachel's jewelry box. "Let's see if there's anything in there I can borrow." She rummaged around, picking up pieces and inspecting them like a seasoned jeweler. "Ooh, I like this one." She took out a chunky gold bead necklace.

Once she had it fastened it around her neck, she checked her reflection in the mirror. Her blonde hair, cut in a shoulder-length bob, set off the piece beautifully, and the gold in the necklace enhanced the gold flecks in her large blue eyes.

"This is it," Lisa said.

Rachel thought it was stunning on her, musing that her jewelry went on more adventures than she did.

Because rich, handsome businessmen ask her out. You get flustered when the cute barista at the coffee place calls you ma'am.

Lisa chose a gray silk blouse from the closet. "You're wearing this."

"Whoa, whoa. I haven't said yes yet."

"Oh, you just have to." Lisa's eyes were round and pleading.

"I'll tell you what. I'll go on this date if you will pretend to be me for the magazine."

"What? I can't do that. It's your blog. You're the writer. It's you they want."

Rachel paused and inhaled deeply. "Lisa, I can't give this speech. Or meet with them in their office. They're going to think I'm a fraud. Or best case scenario, change their minds and decide they don't want to give a job at a fashion magazine to someone who looks like a marshmallow in a cardigan."

"That's not true."

"It is. They're expecting champagne, and they're going to be disappointed in a bottle of Mogen David." Rachel sat on the bed. "I need to call in every favor I've ever done for you, every chit I have out. I need you to be me. At the meeting and at the awards. I'll do the work—I'll prepare what you'll say to them, and I'll write your acceptance speech. You'll go out there and be my face."

Lisa chewed her lip. "This is a big favor to ask. What if they find out?"

"They won't. We're just giving them what they want. Besides, it's a freelance, remote writing position they're offering. I'll never have to set foot in the office again."

"And if I do this, you'll go out with Bruce's friend?"

"If you do this, I will…" Rachel let out a measured stream of breath, "go out with Bruce's friend. Yes."

Lisa enveloped her friend in a bear hug and rocked her back and forth. She let Rachel go and held her at arm's length.

"Okay, let's go over the list of approved topics of conversation when we go out."

Rachel held up her hand to stop the lecture. "You're doing me a huge favor, and I appreciate it. In return, I'm going on this *thing* with you. I will wear high heels, and I will put on makeup. I will be as charming as my personality allows, laugh at appropriate times, nod when this guy is telling a boring story, and look interested. I will not correct his grammar or order anything with spaghetti sauce, as it would probably wind up on my front. I will refrain from telling the story about how your underpants fell off at Macy's, or that time I was in New York and chased Sting down the street for three blocks before I realized it was just the hot dog guy. And because of all this, you will take a breath and back the heck off."

Lisa frowned as much as the Botox would permit and chewed her lip. "All right, I get it. I love you, Rachel Beulah Simon." She turned, pulled her phone out of her pocket, crossed the room in three strides, sat on the bed again, and texted Bruce.

Don't any of my friends know my middle name?

Rachel opened the closet door and rearranged what had been taken out. On the dresser she spied a woven leather bracelet, a gift that had been stashed in the back of her jewelry box, underneath the green button earrings her mother gave her, and the brooch she made in the fourth grade. She picked it up and ran her fingers over it.

"Is this the low-fat stuff?" Alex was sprawled on the couch in Rachel's tiny college apartment, his bare feet hanging over the armrest.

"Never. Why bother?" Rachel entered the living room with two bowls of ice cream, vanilla fudge in one hand, chocolate marshmallow in the other, and held them both out. "What kind do you want?"

"Surprise me"

She handed him the vanilla fudge, the spoon hanging from the side. He sat up, straightened his form-fitting U2 shirt, and accepted the bowl from her outstretched hand, all while flexing his well-developed biceps.

"I like that you don't worry about that stuff. Not like other girls." Alex winked and flashed his mischievous grin.

"Life is too short for low fat."

"Amen to that." He patted her on the behind.

She sat on the couch next to Alex. He'd been spending more and more time at Rachel's place—watching movies, talking about books, music, or the meaning of life. Mostly, though, they talked about Alex.

He was between girlfriends, and although Rachel liked to think she was being supportive, she was probably more like an amateur therapist, boosting his confidence and reaffirming that it was the girls' problem, not his. Whatever the reason, she didn't care.

She was slightly uncomfortable with his handsomeness, worried that she paled in comparison and that people would notice this difference. They rarely went out in public, though, and she was able to convince herself that he saw the real her. That was all that was important.

"Oh, this is awesome. You have to try it." Alex lifted his spoon, heavy with the sweet treat, and held it in front of Rachel's mouth.

Of course, she knew what it tasted like, but she couldn't resist the offer. She took the bite, closing her eyes in bliss as it melted on her tongue, then swallowed.

"Wait, wait!" Alex leaned in close. "I want to try that." He kissed her, sampling the taste of fudge on her lips.

It was a short kiss, sweet and tender, the resulting headiness a combination of it and the sugar buzz. For a moment, he was hers, his blue eyes tracking her. His fingers, cold from the bowl, traced a line on her jaw. She shivered.

"Hey." He pinched her on the hip. "Better not have too much of this stuff." He put the bowl on the table and went into the kitchen, his feet padding on the clean linoleum as he got a pitcher of water from the refrigerator. "Did you see that hot redhead sitting in the front row of psych class yesterday? Think she's seeing anyone?" He poured himself a glass, flopped back onto the couch, and picked up the remote.

Rachel finished her ice cream in silence as Alex continued on about the redhead. The rest of the pint would be gone shortly after he left.

As Rachel put the bracelet back in the box, Lisa put her phone in her pocket and smiled at Rachel.

Such opposites we are. The Bennet Sisters. Jo and Amy March. Anne Shirley and Diana Barry. Monica and Rachel. And during one particularly interesting weekend, Patsy and Edina.

Rachel loved her friend, mixed with a dropperful of begrudging admiration and a soupçon of envy. There had been times she tried to end their friendship, weighted by moments of melancholy, but Lisa refused to budge. She held Rachel's hand as she worked through the gray clouds, sticking by, fueling herself with Rachel's depth of thought and dark wit.

Rachel once asked her what she got out of their bond, the yin and yang of themselves often threatening to overwhelm.

"You make me better," Lisa had replied. *"And I keep you from sinking too far."*

After Lisa went home, Rachel went downstairs, grabbed the coffee cake, and sat at her kitchen table, enjoying the quiet. No music, no TV, nothing. She just sat. She regretted saying yes to Lisa, but she had to make the deal. Outwardly her protest was about her blind date's possible shortcomings, but inside it was about her. She feared the apathy, the out-of-hand dismissal. The fear that twenty minutes into the evening, she'd no longer be enough and he'd be checking out the *talent* at the bar, embarrassed to be seen with her. It wouldn't matter if Rachel didn't like him either. His rejection would come and she'd feel like a zero.

Lindsey crept into the kitchen, winding herself around Rachel's feet. Purring, she jumped into Rachel's lap, and she scratched the cat's velvety ears. The cat's purr became louder and she closed her emerald eyes, reveling in the attention and pleasure of a well-practiced head rub. Rachel closed her eyes, too, alone with the sound of purring and an occasional feline *mip!*

"You get it, don't you, sweet pea?" Rachel picked up the cat and gave her a quick kiss on the top of her head. "Aren't you a good girl? Yes, you are."

Lindsey settled in, curling up in Rachel's lap and tucking her head under her paw. Rachel ripped a chunk from the coffee cake and put it in her mouth, the walnuts crunchy, though covered in glaze. She leaned over, stretched out her arm, shut off the kitchen light, and closed her eyes again.

Chapter Three

The following Friday afternoon, Rachel stood in front of her English 292 class, ready to wrap things up for the day. A few more minutes and class would be over. *The tick-tick-tick* of the clock on the wall grew louder with each passing second. The room was full, especially for a Friday, with the usual amount of shuffling and pencil tapping. Her Emily Dickenson poster was starting to peel away on the upper left-hand side, as if she were also ready to make a break for it.

"Remember your assignment, due Wednesday," Rachel announced, quieting the murmurs. "You'll need to answer questions one through four in your study packet. Read those with me now. Describe the setting of *Great Expectations and* note how it contributes to the mood of the novel. Number two, provide brief but precise analyses of the main and secondary characters. These are listed. I won't read them out loud. And for three and four, please note the key plot developments in the first two stages of Pip's expectations. The first stage includes chapters one through nineteen, and the second stage is chapters twenty through thirty-nine. We'll hit the rest of the chapters next week, and power on through Victorian England. Please wear comfortable shoes."

A few students chuckled.

"This is a lot of work, so please don't leave it until Tuesday night. Any questions?"

A young man in the back row raised his hand. The elastic around the wristband of his green hoodie was stretched, and his thin arm was pale and dry. "How many points is this worth?"

"Refer to your syllabus."

Another student raised her hand, the other appendage occupied with checking a text.

"Yes, Miss Miller?"

"What will happen if we don't finish this assignment? Will we, like, fail?"

"It's a slippery slope, Miss Miller. At the bottom of which is the place where you explain to your parents why you're wasting their hard-earned money because you can't put down the phone and pick up a book."

A few students mumbled amongst themselves, and Rachel could hear the word *harsh* being bandied about.

"Life is harsh, my friends. Anyone who says otherwise is trying to sell you something."

She often resorted to paraphrasing *The Princess Bride* in class. The students didn't know the film, and it made her feel cleverer than she was.

"All right, it's Friday and I'm feeling generous, so I'll dismiss a few minutes early. Have a good weekend."

The volume in the room increased by several notches as the students packed their backpacks and various sundries. Raves, keggers, and marathon video game sessions were being planned with the precision and intensity of the Rose Bowl parade, although the odds were good that the students' evenings would end with a much higher amount of vomit.

Rachel envied them.

Tonight was the blind date. She had run numerous scenarios in her head. None of them turned out well.

As the students filed out of the room, a few of them waved goodbye, and she responded in kind. She packed her own things, placing manila class folders into her brown leather briefcase and tucking her pen into the zippered flap—her Montblanc pen, a gift from her father when she earned her Ph.D. eight years ago. She fastened the main closure on the briefcase with a click.

The classroom door closed behind her with a heavy *thunk*. She plodded down the hall, balancing her coat and briefcase. She had to sidestep various students who were oblivious to their surroundings and blocking the way. There was a faint, musty odor in the hallway, one that surfaced in the Humanities building after a strong rain but was now giving equal time to dry days. She pushed through the front door of the building, glad to be free from the smells of hairspray, body spray, and young adult angst.

She loved teaching, but sometimes she encountered one eye-roll too many. Plus it was difficult to convince eighteen-year-olds that *Pride and Prejudice* could compete with *Fifty Shades of Gray*. She was pretty sure Mr. Darcy had never owned a ball gag. If she were to be honest, there were times she found Jane Austin unappealing, too. However, she did appreciate that her works kept Colin Firth gainfully employed in films for several years, and Ms. Austin would always have Rachel's gratitude for that.

The air was warmer than she'd expected, so she decided to forgo her coat, and instead enjoyed the sun on her arms. It was one of those glorious autumn afternoons which, if they occurred with more frequency, would probably encourage too many people to relocate to the Chicago area, despite the harsh winters, ungodly humid summers, and near-constant road construction.

Keys in hand, Rachel headed to the faculty parking lot, then stopped. *I'm not ready to go home. I need a scone. Or three.* She pivoted and walked toward the quad. It was a nice shortcut to the coffee place, and she could use the exercise.

The wind picked up, and she put her coat on, juggling her heavy briefcase, and she wondered why she hadn't dumped it in the car. *I'll have something to do when I'm sitting alone at the coffee shop, that's why. A woman sitting alone looks sad. A woman sitting and reading looks worldly and self-sufficient. Yeah, let's go with that.*

Rachel kept a brisk pace, the thought of a hot vanilla latte spurring her on. Out of the corner of her eye, she spotted a familiar head of copper red hair.

Oh, no. Not now.

The woman waved her arm.

Just keep walking.

The wave stopped and the woman started a light jog, perfect hair swinging.

Maybe it's not her...

"Dr. Simon? Dr. Simon!"

Cindy McPherson, the petite, Bundt-foisting administrative assistant, caught up with Rachel and matched her stride.

Crap.

"Oh, hey, Cindy. I didn't see you there."

"You did seem lost in your own little world, like always. How was the cake?"

You mean the one I threw out because I didn't want it? "Oh, fine, thanks."

"Good. I knew you were the right person to give it to. I didn't want it to go to waste."

Bitch. "Do you need something? I was on my way to...out."

"I'm helping organize the cocktail reception next Friday at Dr. Collier's house, and I need to get a head count. Will you be bringing a plus-one?"

The party at the department chair's house. Rachel had forgotten about it. Tiny food on sticks, martinis, and too many Poe puns. For the last three years, she'd worked to get out of attending, to no avail. One year she pulled a *Bartleby, the Scrivener,* and simply RSVP'd *I'd prefer not to,* but Cindy had assumed Rachel was being clever and put her down as bringing cups to what turned out to be an ill-advised *The Great Gatsby*-themed potluck.

"Yeah, I'm not sure," Rachel said. "Can I get back to you?"

"Haven't scared up a date yet, huh?" Cindy's faux sympathy bordered on absurd. "That's all right. No one will care."

"No, no, it's not that," Rachel replied, flustered. "I don't want to commit without my calendar in front of me."

"You don't keep that on your phone? How retro." Cindy gave the ample flesh on Rachel's bicep a gentle squeeze. "Don't worry. There's no shame in flying solo."

"I'm not ashamed, I just…"

Cindy regarded Rachel as one might a turtle that came in dead last in a foot race. "You'll find someone. Just hang in there."

It took every fiber of Rachel's being to not grab Cindy by her perfectly coiffed head and swing her around like a kettlebell. Instead, she inhaled and smiled.

"Thanks, Cindy. Let you know about the plus-one on Monday?"

"Of course. But no later than. Hey, maybe you'll meet Prince Charming this weekend."

"Only if he's delivering my pizza."

Cindy laughed and gave her a patronizing pat on the shoulder. "Oh, you! Always the jokester." She took off in the other direction, her heels clackety-clacking on the pavement. "See you Monday!"

Not on purpose!

Taking another cleansing breath, Rachel continued on her trek for a scone and coffee. After walking past the science building and turning left on 4th Street, she had the sidewalk to herself. She liked being able to stop and window shop without fear of getting in the way.

She scanned the block and decided to stop at a shoe store and check out the display. A pair of black satin strappy heels caught her eye. They sported a delicate ankle strap and a few gems attached to a dangle on the instep. They were pretty and impractical. Where would she wear them? To the grocery store? Faculty meeting? Those were definitely shoes Lisa would wear. Or the women at *Charmé.*

She regarded the display on the other side of the entrance. Now *there* were shoes that were more her speed. Brown flats with a wide toe box and ergonomic footbed. Much better for tooling around campus and being on one's feet all day. If she bought those, however, Lisa would beat her to death with a pair of Jimmy Choo's. And she was pretty sure if she wore them to the meeting at *Charmé*, the security guard wouldn't let her past the main desk. Good thing Lisa was going in her place.

The next store was a shop full of cute, much-too-expensive clothes. She'd never been inside. The name *Keska Say* was an obvious play on the French *Qu'est-ce que c'est?* which meant, *What is that?* The displays were nice, though. Coordinating scarves and hats, pleated skirts, and blouses that appeared to be held together with a wish and a prayer.

She glanced at her watch. She had time before she needed to be home. She decided to check the place out, just to see. Lisa's birthday was approaching, and maybe there was something in here that would make a nice gift.

Rachel pushed open the door, stepped inside, and was overcome with the scent of lavender and vanilla. Walls were covered with cubby-style shelving, filled with sweaters and knit tops in a rainbow of colors. She browsed the nearest rack. There were skinny jeans with cuffs around the ankle, and she rifled through the sizes. Zero, zero, two, four, six. Was there nothing above a six? Did they think people disappeared after that size?

The larger we are, the harder we are to see.

Rachel wandered to a rack of tops. Extra small, extra small…

Walking her fingers over the hangers to check the sizes, she sensed the gaze of the salesgirl following her. Finally she approached, her proximity announced by the rustle of her tulle mini-skirt.

"Can I…" She paused, as if trying to find the right words. "Help you?" She gave Rachel the up-and-down and raised an eyebrow.

"No, I was just looking." Rachel became aware of her rumpled coat and glanced at the door.

"I don't think you'll find what you need over *here*," the salesgirl said. "Perhaps you might be able to find a pair of gloves that would suit you. Or socks."

"Thanks, no. Like I said, just looking. I go past this place all the time, and thought I'd stop in to see what it was. *Qu'est-ce que c'est?*"

"Huh?"

"Never mind. Thanks." Rachel adjusted her coat and exited the store.

The shop bell tinkled as she left—a sad, out-of-tune tinkle. Her shoes made a light *clump, clump* as she walked down the sidewalk, and she imagined the ways to exact revenge on the size zero shop girl. Letter-writing campaign. Strongly worded op-ed in *The New Yorker*. She wasn't good at revenge planning but thought of sending Joanie in there to make the girl cry.

Rachel quickened her pace for the last two blocks, eager to have a warm cup of coffee in her hands, and a few minutes to enjoy her book. The chimes rang as she opened the coffee shop door, as if to say, *Welcome to your happy place.* The shop was packed. She noticed a placard in the side window, *Fresh Hot Scone's! Free today only!* That explained it.

Her first instinct was to go reprimand the person responsible for the flagrant misuse of the apostrophe in that sign, but her priority was the coffee. She found herself in line behind a couple of chatty twenty-somethings, eager to share their adventures in romance with their girlfriends.

"And he hasn't called in six days, but he's been super busy with work and helping his brother move…"

Yeah, he's not going to call you.

"Oh, he's totally into you. You're a hottie."

Not as hot as the girl who works the juice bar at his gym.

"He'll call you. Don't worry."

Who he's probably already sleeping with.

"Give him time. He'll see you're the one for him."

Nope.

"I mean, you do everything for him. Who bought him that amazing suit for his interview? He'll propose. I mean it."

Thanks for playing. Here are some lovely parting gifts.

Rachel was sure the first girl wasn't persuaded by her friend's assurance, because by the time they got to the counter to order, she accepted her free scone, plus two orders of banana bread, and a piece of cake on a stick.

I feel ya, sister. Stay strong.

Eventually it was Rachel's turn to order. Linda was there, even more dour than usual. Her brow was furrowed, and she had a divot between her eyebrows Rachel was sure wasn't there last week. It was just Linda behind the counter with a new girl whose nametag read, *Be nice to me—I'm in training.* Not the best time for a scone promotion.

Rachel rattled off her order, ending with what she hoped was a sympathetic smile.

"Free scone?" Linda sighed. "We have blueberry, coconut, banana coconut, plain, chocolate chip, razzleberry…" Her voice trailed off, as if the sheer variety of scones was too much to bear.

"No, thanks. Just the coffee."

Linda handed the order off to the trainee, who seemed glad to have a low-maintenance customer.

"Busy day, huh?" Rachel said to Linda.

She regretted that comment the moment it passed her lips. Linda narrowed her eyes, and Rachel hoped she wouldn't spit in her latte.

"Your order'll be ready in a minute," Linda droned. "Next!"

Rachel went to the accessories counter, picking up packets of artificial sweeter and a wooden stirrer. She'd fix it at a table, assuming she got one. She didn't want to be one of those folks who spent a half-hour doing major surgery on their coffee, sprinkling a dab of cinnamon and a whisper of nutmeg, slowly stirring in one and a half packets of raw sugar, being careful not to make the steamed milk collapse, while other people waited for straws and napkins.

"Medium nonfat latté!"

The trainee's chirp was starting to grate on Rachel, and she'd only been there a few minutes. That certainly explained Linda's divot.

"Did you get your free scone?"

"Nope. None for me, thanks."

"Ya sure? They're awesome."

"I'm good."

With her drink on one hand, and a couple sweeteners balanced on the top of the cup, Rachel scanned the room for a seat. There was a young couple by the mug display, oblivious to everyone else. They weren't going anywhere. Three older ladies at another table sat there like they had no other place they needed to be. Two teenage boys making a fort out of used stirrers. And a young woman with a baby.

That was promising. The baby was starting to squirm and make urps and squeals. Focusing her sights on that table, Rachel gambled that the baby would start fussing. His smooth, round cheeks grew pink, and he rubbed his eyes with his tiny fists. There would be liftoff in five…four…three…two…

Bingo!

His high-pitched wail was his mother's signal to get him home. Trying not to hover, Rachel inched over. As the mother pushed the stroller past the table, Rachel made her move. She swooped in as gracefully as her size and full hands would allow and plopped in the chair with a sigh that made her sound like a leaky bike tire.

Placing the coffee gently on the table, she put her bag on the seat next to her and removed her coat. She noticed that Miss Cake-on-a-Stick was giving her a look.

Sorry, honey, I need this more than you do.

On some level, the girl appeared to understand, because she and her friends headed out the door, no doubt gathering strength for another round of man-rationalizing.

"Should I text him again or…" Their hopeful young voices trailed off into the afternoon.

Chuckling, Rachel shook the packets of sweetener a few times, ripped them open, and poured them on top of the frothy milk. She attempted to fold it into the foam, wondering why they filled them so close to the top. She was glad to get her money's worth, but people needed stirring room. She decided to sip her drink so it didn't spill. She raised the cup to her lips, and the warm foam enveloped her tongue. It was the best sip of coffee she'd ever had.

"Do you mind if I sit here?"

Rachel was shaken out of her java-induced reverie by a male voice. She glanced up and nearly spewed froth out of her nose.

Mr. Good Shoes. Please don't let me have milk on my lip.

Dumbfounded, she stared at him.

He pointed at her briefcase. "Do you mind if I…"

Rachel realized he was not, in fact, speaking Swahili, and the words sunk in. She placed her briefcase on the floor and smiled.

He slid into the seat. "Is it usually this crowded in here?"

"No," she replied, finding her voice. "Friday afternoons are generally pretty dead. I guess people love a free scone." She brushed the grains of sweetener off the table. "Stirring mishap."

"They do fill the cups to the brim, don't they?" he said. "You kind of have to stab the sugar into the coffee."

"Et tu, brew-tus?"

He grinned, his eyes crinkling at the corners. "That's funny." He offered Rachel his hand. "I'm Nathan Fletcher."

"Rachel Simon."

He had a firm handshake, not one of those half-hands where the shaker couldn't commit.

"So." Nathan licked the foam off his stirrer and removed a scone from the white paper bag he'd placed on the table. "Come here often?" He glanced sheepishly at the table. "I can't believe I just said that. *Do you come here often?* Who am I? Burt Reynolds?"

"I can't believe you referenced Burt Reynolds."

"It's the mustache. It was pretty epic."

So was he. His dark green eyes had the faintest hint of lines around them, the kind that appear in one's late thirties and indicate a lot of smiling. There was something about him that made the muscles in Rachel's shoulders relax and made her want to tell him her life story.

"…so what do you think?"

Rachel had no idea what he was talking about.

"Well, it's a complicated issue…"

"You don't want half of this scone?"

Busted.

"No, thank you. Gee, I guess that wasn't complicated." Rachel's ears felt hot.

The crowd in the café thinned out and the noise level died down. The smells of freshly ground coffee and cinnamon hung heavy in the air. She expected Nathan to excuse himself and find his own table, but he remained sitting, sipping his coffee.

"That's a pretty impressive briefcase." He pointed to the leather monstrosity on the floor. "What do you do? Lawyer? Plumber? Prop comic?"

She laughed. "I teach English lit at Oakton College. Exposing the young people of today to the classics, even though there are no zombies in them."

"I love James Joyce." He slapped his hand on the table. "*Finnegan's Wake* is my favorite book of all time."

Rachel stared at him as if he had grown a third ear. "Seriously?"

"Oh, God, no." He laughed. "I've attempted it three times." He cocked his head. "Does he even write in English?"

"Barely. He pretty much made up his own language. Lots of neologisms, multilingual puns, and portmanteau words. Totally stream of consciousness. Some scholars even believe he wrote it as a hoax. Personally my money's on *he lost a bar bet.*"

"I believe it." He bit into his scone.

"I haven't touched it since grad school," Rachel said, quickly. "These days, I prefer things like *Harry Potter*. But don't tell my students. What do you do?" She lifted the coffee cup to her lips.

"Prop comic."

Rachel laughed mid-swallow, then sputtered and reached for a napkin. Thankfully the coffee went down, and not out, as she'd feared. She coughed one last time, sending her napkin fluttering to the floor. They both reached for it, and as Rachel picked it up, she noticed Nathan's socks were mismatched.

"Wow," Nathan said, as they sat up. "I don't usually have that effect on people."

"No worries. Excellently timed. You and George Carlin are the only ones who ever *almost* made a beverage come out of my nose."

"I'm honored. And about the socks…" He grinned, sheepishly. "I have a habit of getting dressed before I put in my contact lenses, and I always forget to check." He passed Rachel another napkin, his hand brushing hers. "Sometimes I'm like an overgrown seven-year-old."

Rachel's face flushed warm as she spotted the clock on the wall, one of those black and white plastic cats where the eyes click back and forth with the second hand. Was it 4:30 already? She wiped her mouth again with the napkin and reached for her coat. Nathan was quicker, handing it to her as she stood, leaving her coffee on the table.

"Hey, there's a photography exhibit in River Park tonight, about Chicago architecture after the Great Fire. Would you be interested in going?" He searched her face.

"Normally, yes, but I've, um, got a pile of work to do this evening. Do you have friends going, too?"

"Nope, just me."

"Have a good time. Should be an interesting show."

Nathan furrowed his brow. "Okay, sure."

Rachel held her briefcase in a death-grip, the leather creaking as she worked the handle back and forth. He held the door for her as they exited.

"Here's my card," Nathan said. "Maybe we can find a James Joyce book reading sometime."

She accepted the card and tucked in into the front pocket of her briefcase. "If you have time between comedy gigs, you mean."

"Of course."

"It was nice meeting you." She slung the strap over her shoulder. "It was fun. Hope to see you around soon."

"Me, too." Nathan touched her elbow and caught her strap as it slid down her arm.

Sparks danced down her neck, and she pulled her arm close to her side and gave him a fleeting smile.

"So, okay. Have a good evening," she said, with a slight squeak.

They turned at the same time, heading in opposite directions. Rachel glanced back at Nathan, only to find him looking back at her. She quickly turned her head forward, the heat in her cheeks returning.

Be cool, Rachel. Cripes.

She couldn't resist one more stolen glance as he was opening his car door. He waved and smiled. Not having a free hand, she nodded, and hurried on her way. She needed to return home with enough time to get ready for dinner tonight. *Ugh.* She turned the first corner on the way back to the faculty parking lot, then stopped dead in her tracks. *Did I just get asked out on a date?*

The giggling of two co-eds passing by alerted her that she was standing in the middle of a crosswalk. Shifting her briefcase off her shoulder and into her right hand, she managed to put one foot in front of the other, her knees like lead as she lifted them over the crumbling curb. Her pace remained steady, as if the cool air ignited the caffeine pulsing through her bloodstream. Her scalp prickled, and her shoulders crept closer to her ears. She jammed her free hand into her pocket, ripping an old tissue within into tiny, fluffy bits.

No. Guys like that don't date girls who look like me. He was just being nice. Maybe he wants to be friends. Yes, that's it. Friends.

The faculty lot was almost empty, with only a few cars left in a hopscotch pattern. She opened the worn leather pocket of her case and fished for her keychain. She tossed the bag in the back seat, missing the cushion. The briefcase landed on the floor, upending itself, but she let it be.

Rachel grabbed the handle of the driver's side door, opening it just enough that it slammed shut before she could get in, then seized the handle again with more force, and the door opened full swing, waved on the hinges twice, then slammed shut, the gray cloth interior disappearing into a wall of red. She grasped for the handle a third time, and it opened.

"Stay." She pointed at the metal frame.

She sat, her body hitting the seat with a *pwomp*. After shutting the door, she gripped the steering wheel with both hands and stared blankly at the dashboard. As she let out a steady stream of breath, the air rushed past her dry lips and released a tiny bit of the chaos in her brain. The tension in her forehead crept back, and she looked in the mirror at the deepening creases, about which Lisa insisted she needed to talk to Dr. Bowman.

If you never see him again, don't be disappointed. You know how this goes.

Rachel started the car and backed out of the parking spot. After shifting into drive, she placed her foot on the accelerator and listened to the hum of the engine as she made the familiar drive home. The sun was low in the sky, though it was capable of sending the last of its bright rays into her eyes.

She picked up her sunglasses from the passenger seat—the ones that Joanie called her *old lady cataract glasses*—and put them on. As she drove home and then pulled into her driveway, a sense of relaxation washed over her, the new knot in her left shoulder beginning to release. After she shut off the engine, her cell phone beeped, indicating a new text. She removed the phone from her bag and saw a message from Lisa.

Don't forget to wear Spanx!

The dinner. Of course. Rachel gathered her things from the car and trudged up the front stairs of her house, the newly fallen leaves crunching beneath her feet. Going out was the last thing she wanted to do. Still, a promise was a promise, and faking the plague wasn't an option.

She let herself in, closed the door behind her, and locked the bolt. Lindsey wandered over, good cat that she was, rubbing her head on Rachel's ankles. She leaned down to pet the cat's ears, and Lindsey meowed, staring at Rachel with her big green eyes and tilting her head.

"Just don't sit on my blouse, okay?"

Rachel went upstairs, formulating a plan of attack to make herself look acceptable. It was going to be a long evening.

Chapter Four

Rachel met Lisa under a street lamp in front of the restaurant.

"Are we going in?" Rachel said.

Lisa tapped her platform-pump-clad foot on the sidewalk. "Do you have lipstick on your teeth?"

"No, I don't have lipstick on my teeth."

"Here, let me check." Lisa adjusted the delicate chain on her designer bag so it sat higher on her shoulder, then held Rachel's chin. "Show me your teeth."

Rachel pulled away. "Stop it. I'm fine."

"Okay, but at least go like this." Lisa bared her teeth.

"I'm not going like that."

"Can you please try to have a good time tonight?" Lisa pushed open the restaurant door and held it for Rachel. "Relax. Be Zen. Follow my lead."

"Are you kidding? *You're* Zen? I've seen students strung out on energy drinks the night before finals who are more relaxed than you." Rachel sniffed. "Bruce already likes you. Take a breath before something pops." She blinked a few times to allow her eyes to adjust to the low lighting.

Lisa stared at the floor and chewed her lip as the light from a passing car flickered through the glass doors.

"It's important that Bruce likes my friends. Hopefully, we'll be spending a lot of time together in the future. I don't want to drift apart like we used to when…you know."

The women checked their coats and waited at the maître d' stand.

"What about Brennan and Joanie? When are they going to meet him?"

Lisa met Rachel's gaze. "One step at a time. I don't think he's ready for the *Aunt Gladys and Judy* show."

"Sissy." Rachel kicked the parquet floor with the toe of her shoe.

She could smell marinara sauce wafting by, and decided she was hungry. She wistfully thought of the free scone.

"Ladies?" The maître d' caught their attention. "Your table is ready. Would you like to be seated while you wait for the rest of your party?"

"Yes!"

Rachel must've sounded too eager because Lisa did a double-take at her change of heart.

"This will give us time to settle in and look fabulous before they get here," Rachel said.

They followed the host to their table. It was a nice place, not too large, with the typical red-checkered tablecloths and candlesticks made out of empty Chianti bottles. The red brick walls were worn in places, as if they'd gotten jostled during their journey from Naples.

Glasses clinked, forks scraped the plates, and spicy aromas floated through the air—good, homey smells, and one could imagine the kitchen doors opening to reveal someone's *nonna* in a headscarf, making meatballs and insisting you stay for seconds. Rachel resisted the urge to peek inside to check.

The clientele was eclectic. Old ladies with fur coats slung over the backs of their chairs because they didn't trust the coat check girl. Middle-aged couples arguing about the entrees, because no matter what she ordered, his wife would wind up eating off his plate anyway. A nervous teen boy, eager to impress his young lady, sweating under his older brother's blazer and tallying the potential bill in his head, wondering if he had enough to order food for himself, too.

All bathed in the semi-glow of candlelight and dimmed fluorescent bulbs. It was like being on the set of a 1950s movie. Rachel wondered if their waiter would sing the evening dinner specials.

Rachel followed Lisa into the semi-circular booth, sliding over the buttery red leather bench. While Lisa smoothed imaginary wrinkles in her floral dress, Rachel pulled a breadstick from the basket and gnawed on it like a cranky beaver in a twig-buffet.

Midway through her second stick, she caught a glimpse of a brown tweed sports jacket and a head of artfully tousled brown hair. She inhaled the breadcrumbs, hacking and coughing before taking a swig from her water glass to wash it all down.

"Are you all right?" Lisa patted Rachel on the back.

"Yeah, yeah, I'm fine. I thought I saw…someone."

"Who would make you react like that? Wait, is Colin Firth here?" Lisa craned her neck to scan the joint.

"What? No! Why would Colin Firth be *here*?"

"Maybe he heard the lasagna is good."

Rachel paused, wondering if she should open this can of worms. "I thought it was this guy I met today. Well, met for the second time."

"Ooh, who? Where?"

"At the Java Hut. Mr. Good Shoes. Nathan."

"Get out of here! What did he say?" Lisa lowered her chin and gazed levelly at Rachel. "What did you *do*?"

"I didn't spill anything, if that's what you're asking. We just talked. I think he…asked me out."

"He asked you out?"

"Could you keep it down, please? People are staring." Rachel sipped her water again. "I think he did. I'm not one hundred percent on that."

"What did you say?"

"I asked who else was going, and then said I was busy."

"What?" Lisa banged on the table, jarring the silverware.

"Is everything all right, ladies?" A waiter side-eyed them, balancing his tray of tiramisu.

"Yes, we're fine, thanks. My friend here heard you serve Apple Brown Betty. It's her favorite dessert." Rachel smiled and patted Lisa on the arm.

"I don't even know what that is, Rachel," Lisa hissed.

"Kind of not the point, Lisa," Rachel whispered.

The waiter cocked his head, obviously deciding not to tangle with the crazy women. He swooped to his intended table and set the tray on the stand. The older ladies squealed with delight as he dusted extra cocoa powder over their desserts.

"May I remind you," Rachel said, "that I was busy doing *this* tonight. Besides, I got his card. No big deal. I'm sure I misread the whole thing."

"This is potentially wonderful. I'm so excited for you. We'll have to talk later—oh… here they are!" Lisa spotted Bruce and his companion. "Don't slouch."

Rachel gave her a pinch.

"I'm kidding. You're fine." Lisa giggled. "Tits out."

"There's my gorgeous girl." Bruce sidled up to the table, leaned in, and kissed Lisa on the cheek. "Have you been waiting long?"

"Two breadsticks worth," Rachel said.

"You must be Rachel. Very nice to meet you. Ladies, this is my colleague, Jerry Slidell. Jerry, you remember Lisa. And this is her friend, Rachel Stone."

"Simon."

Jerry stuck out his hand. "Simon Says shake hands."

"What?"

"Simon Says. Like the game?"

"Oh, yes, of course." Rachel shook his hand.

He had one of those clammy, limp handshakes, and she couldn't get her hand back fast enough. She discretely wiped her palm on her pant leg.

"Shall we sit?" Bruce slid into the booth next to Lisa, his black striped suit, tailored and obviously expensive, barely creasing as he landed. His hair was handsomely salt and peppered, his dark eyes alert, and his hands manicured. It was easy to see why Lisa was enamored. Lisa giggled as she cozied up to Bruce. Jerry sat next to Rachel, rounding out the foursome. Glancing under the table, Rachel noticed that his socks matched.

How disappointing.

Jerry picked up a glass of water and downed it in one gulp. "*Ugh.* Obviously tap water."

"How can you tell?" Rachel said.

"I just *know*. It's a gift." He sniffed and scratched his ear.

Rachel couldn't help but notice the difference in the two men. Bruce was coolly elegant, while Jerry appeared to have taken a correspondence course in *How to Look Suave*. He wore a gray suit, no tie, and a gold cross around his neck. There was too much product in his spiked, dark blond hair, and he had it arranged in what he probably hoped was an effortless fauxhawk. It was much too young of a style for a man who appeared to be in his mid-forties. Not unhandsome, he had an elusive quality as if he was looking for the next big thing, scanning the room between conversational sound bites. His heavily applied cologne made Rachel's eyes water, and she felt like sneezing.

"Shall we order wine?" Bruce said.

Lisa beamed. "Bruce did a wine tour of Italy a few years ago. He's fantastically knowledgeable."

"It's all red to me, bro." Jerry picked up his water glass, noticed it was empty, and set it back down. "But if you're paying, I'm drinking."

How are these two men friends?

Bruce signaled to the waiter with a wave of his hand. The server arrived immediately, as if he knew this guy meant business.

"I'd like a bottle of the 2002 Burlotto Monvigliero, *por favore.* And four glasses.

"Just three. None for me, thanks." Rachel wasn't much of a drinker, and she had to drive home later.

The waiter scribbled on his pad. "Excellent. I will be back in a few minutes to take the rest of your order."

Rachel scanned the menu. Even with her contact lenses, she had trouble with up-close reading. She removed her dark purple reading glasses from her purse. Lisa scooted over, tapped her on the thigh, and held her mouth to Rachel's ear.

"Put those away," she whispered.

"What, the glasses? I need them to read the menu."

"They make you look like Granny Clampett."

"They're brand new."

"Just. Put. Them. Away." Lisa slid back to Bruce, who was also wearing reading glasses, but she didn't have a problem with that.

Rachel placed her glasses back in the case and stuffed them in her purse. She picked up the menu, moving it closer and further away from her face, willing her eyes to focus on the minute print. She didn't understand why Lisa was freaking out.

Bruce was obviously enamored. Men were always falling over themselves for Lisa. In college there was a steady stream of young men parading through their apartment, most of whom were content to do things for her.

"This is Andy. He's helping me with calculus."

Bye, Andy.

"This is Steven. He's going to hook up the stereo."

Nice knowing you, Steve.

"Rachel, meet Bjorn. He's going to paint the kitchen."

Seriously?

Maybe Lisa enjoyed flirting, or maybe she was genuinely unaware of her effect on men. Either way, the girls always had in-person tech support, and they always got their security deposit back when they moved.

"Bruce tells me you're an English teacher." Jerry's voice jarred Rachel back to the present.

"Professor, actually. Associate Professor. English literature."

"And she's an extremely talented writer," Lisa said. "An *award*-winning writer." She leaned in to whisper again in Rachel's ear. "Remember that, please, and make good choices."

"Wow, smart lady," Jerry said. "I'm a money guy, myself. Manage several large accounts at the firm. Set to be head of accounts in a couple years. Then I'll be sitting pretty."

"Fascinating." Rachel was squinting at the menu.

She decided to have ravioli. There was always ravioli on the menu in places like this. She placed the menu on the crisp tablecloth, taking care to avoid the lit candles. She tried to ask Lisa what she was having, but she was busy being nibbled on. Rachel turned back to her companion and placed her chin on her fist.

"I like Gertrude Stein." Jerry straightened his shoulders, trying to appear casually erudite. *"The Autobiography of Alice B. Toklas* was cool. I've always been intrigued by lesbians."

"Is that so." Rachel held her water glass, the ice cubes clinking as she gently swirled the glass.

"What did she say? *A rose is a rose is a rose,*" he quoted.

Rachel was impressed. Maybe she was judging him a bit harshly. She raised the glass to take a sip.

"I guess that's why she made those flower paintings," Jerry said.

The sip of water got caught in Rachel's throat, as if it was mounting a protest that it couldn't make it any further. She swallowed with great difficulty. "Uh, what?"

"The flower paintings. The ones that you think are flowers but are actually vaginas. I can get into that."

She stared at him, squinting like he was the *side order* section of the menu. "You're thinking of Georgia O'Keefe."

"Isn't that the girl from *Gone With The Wind?"*

"That's Scarlett O'Hara."

"Oh, yeah. Right. So Stein didn't paint? Let me check that out." Jerry whipped out his smartphone, hoping to prove Rachel wrong.

His thick finger tapped and tapped, hovering over the keypad, waiting for the pages to load. When he found his answer, he waggled his eyebrows in surprise.

"Hmm. What do you know? Two different people. But the flowers are still vaginas, right?"

Rachel flagged down a passing waiter. "Another wine glass, please."

Jerry drummed his fingers on the table.

"Yes, they're still vaginas," she said.

Unable to top that train of conversation, they sat in silence. She reached for another breadstick, and Jerry ogled the young women at a nearby table putting on their coats. His eyebrow rose as the blonde stretched her arm into her light blue satin sleeve, her back arching. Rachel had no idea what to say to this man, and he didn't appear to care either way.

Their awkwardness was broken by the waiter's reappearance. He stood before them in his crisp, white apron, like a culinary angel of mercy.

"You folks ready to order?"

"Oh, God, yes," Rachel said, quickly.

"We have a couple of nice specials tonight. First, *Coscia Alla Scarpariello*, which is a bone-in chicken thigh sautéed with homemade sausage, garlic, vinegar, and lemon..."

Rachel could hear Jerry snicker under his breath at the words *bone-in*.

"We also have *Filetto Al Rosmarino*," the waiter continued, "which is a ten-ounce medallion of filet mignon sautéed in a fresh rosemary garlic sauce. And a *Ravioli Casalinga*—homemade, of course—filled with potato, leeks, and Romano cheese, and covered in pesto sauce."

"Oh, it all sounds so good!" Lisa scanned the menu again. "I think I'll have the grilled chicken." She handed her menu to the waiter.

"And you, sir?"

"I'll have the filet. Medium-well, please," said Bruce.

"Very good. And you, miss?"

Rachel handed him the menu. "I'll have the ravioli special."

"You think that's a good idea?" Jerry said.

"I like ravioli."

Jerry gave Rachel the once-and-down with his eyes. "Okay, you're the boss. I'll have the pork loin. No starch on the side." He regarded her coolly. "Carbs. Nasty stuff. Gotta stay in fighting shape."

The waiter removed the rest of the menus and departed. Rachel shifted in her seat, and Jerry drummed his fingers. She felt as if she were taking up much more space than before, aware of her hips and thighs spreading on the seat like cheap margarine.

"I'll be over in ten minutes." Alex's voice sounded sexy and warm.

Rachel hung up the phone and went into panic mode. She ran around her college apartment, simultaneously trying to zip her new dress and dust the surfaces of the living room with a rag. While picking up Lisa's stuff from the floor, drips of sweat collected at Rachel's hairline, threatening to smear the sultry evening look she'd created and convert her smoky eye into one ruined by water damage. She'd been anticipating this party for weeks, hoping to make a good impression on Alex's friends, most of whom she hadn't met yet.

The doorbell rang, and she shoved the dust rag under a couch cushion. She opened the door and struck a pose.

"Wow," Alex said. "Fancy."

He brushed past her and draped his coat over the back of a dinette chair and put his portfolio on the table.

"I'm ready to go if you are," Rachel said.

"Go? Go where?"

"To Dave's party. You told me last week we were going."

Alex stared at the floor. "Oh, yeah, that. You know, I'm not up for a party tonight. I thought we'd stay here and hang out."

"Are you kidding? You've been talking about it all week how epic this party was going to be. Your friends, their girlfriends, a live band..."

He approached her and put one hand on her waist, the other on her cheek.

"C'mon, sweets, don't be like that." He gazed at Rachel intently, scanning her face with his navy blue eyes. "I want you to myself, that's all."

Rachel's insides melted under his gaze, but she pressed on. "I was looking forward to meeting your friends."

He pulled her close. "Nah, you don't want to meet them. They're a bunch of numb-nuts. We don't need them."

"Is it me? Do you not want them to know me?"

Alex knotted his brow. He cleared his throat and lightly kissed her on the lips. "Forget them. Let's enjoy our night here. I have new photographs I want to get your opinion on before I submit them for a grade." He kissed her again and squeezed her arm. "You've got such a good eye." He picked up his portfolio and sat on the couch, patting the cushion next to him. "C'mon. I need you." He smiled, the corner of his lips turning up, and brushed a stray black hair off his forehead.

"All right." Rachel sighed, kicking off her shoes. "Show me what you've got."

"Rachel?" Lisa tapped her on her shoulder. "Want to go to the ladies' room with me?" Her voice sounded shrill.

"No, I'm fine."

"I think you need to go to the ladies' room with me. Let's go."

She gave Rachel a nudge to get out of the booth, and Jerry let them out. Rachel straightened her blouse, and Lisa scooted out in a much more ladylike fashion.

"Don't spend too much time talking about us."

Jerry's smugness was beginning to grate on Rachel's nerves. His actual appeal was in indirect proportion to his sense of self-worth.

"Oh, we won't. Trust me," she said.

Lisa gripped her elbow and led her to the women's bathroom. She wasn't messing around. They were two steps into the lavatory when she spun Rachel around. "What are you doing?"

"I thought you had to pee."

"I have to talk to you. Actually, I do have to pee, but I want to do this first."

Rachel shrugged. "Your bladder."

"Why are you being mean to Jerry?"

"Mean? I'm not being mean. The man is a narcissistic idiot. I think I'm showing a great deal of restraint."

"He's a nice-looking, single man with a good job."

"Which is meaningless if I don't like him!"

The toilet in the third stall flushed, and Lisa and Rachel fell silent as an old lady hesitantly emerged. She made her way to the row of pink ceramic sinks and regarded Rachel from the corner of her eye, warily.

"Hi, how are you?" Rachel nodded.

The lady finished washing her hands, and Lisa handed her a paper towel.

Before exiting, she stopped and patted Rachel on the hand. "Honey, maybe you should consider settling." She threw the paper towel in the can and walked out.

Lisa gestured toward the lady, as if giving tacit approval.

"Could you just try a little?" Lisa's voice sounded urgent.

"Why is this so important to you? You haven't fixed me up in years. And I can't imagine Bruce and Jerry are best buds. This may not be worth having you impersonate me at *Charmé*. Maybe I should go home."

"No! Please stay. It will be worth it, I promise. I think things are getting serious with Bruce, and I want to show him that our friends can blend. Our lives can blend." Lisa turned to the mirror and held on to the sides of the sink with both hands.

She lowered her head, her blonde hair partially covering her fine features.

Rachel stepped toward her, gently touching her on the back. "We can blend, Lisa. Don't be silly. We don't need to be a foursome, okay? Relax."

Lisa brushed her hair across her forehead and tucked a few stray pieces behind her ear.

"You're right. I'm being nutso. I just get worked up over Bruce sometimes." She inhaled sharply. "I'm going to pee now."

"Okay."

Lisa went into a stall and closed the door. "Are you waiting for me?"

"Yes. I don't want to be at the table without you. Bruce is fine, but if Jerry starts talking about his abs, I might have to stab myself in the hand with a fork."

After Lisa washed her hands, they made their way back to the booth to find the men and the meals waiting for them. Rachel thought her ravioli was appetizing, the plate filled with pasta and cheese, covered in a thick, green pesto sauce. It smelled heavily of garlic, but she was happy to indulge since she was certain Jerry wouldn't try for a goodnight kiss.

They settled into their seats, and Jerry raised an eyebrow when Rachel attacked the first ravioli with gusto, but she paid no notice. She even ate two more breadsticks to annoy him.

"Boy, you're lucky you don't worry about what you eat," he said. "Must be nice. Me, I would be spending an hour on the treadmill to work that off."

Lisa leaned in and whispered in Rachel's ear, "I get it now. You have my permission to stick a breadstick up his nose."

The rest of the meal went without further incident. Once Rachel stopped worrying what Jerry thought of her, she found that Bruce was pretty interesting. He told a funny story about the concierge at a hotel in Taiwan and a translation gone horribly wrong, and Lisa hung on his every word. She laughed in her charming and melodic way, touching his arm affectionately.

Rachel thought she seemed genuinely happy, happier than she'd seen her in a long time. Maybe he really was The One.

The bill came, and Bruce paid like a gentleman. Rachel thanked him for the meal, and he responded with a warm smile.

"It was my pleasure, Rachel. I'm glad my Lisa has such a good friend."

Rachel felt goosebumps form on her arms.

The man is charming. That's for sure.

After putting on their coats in the restaurant lobby, they paused for goodbyes. Jerry slipped on his black leather gloves, the kind that snapped at the wrist and had holes over the knuckles.

Rachel stuck out her hand, preemptively. "Nice to have met you, Jerry. Have a good evening."

He shook her hand, giving her the impression of a limp fish in a leather vest.

"You too." He handed her his card. "Call me if you ever want me to take a look at your stock portfolio. Oh, and I'll email you an article I read, about how they think Shakespeare didn't write his plays. Like he was just a spokesmodel or something."

Rachel resisted the urge to roll her eyes. "I look forward to reading it."

Bruce held the door for the women as they went out into the cool night.

She buttoned the top button of her coat to ward off the chill. "Goodnight, everyone!"

"I'll call you tomorrow, okay? We'll talk about the meeting." Lisa hugged her. "Thank you."

"Thank *you*," Rachel replied. "Fair's fair."

Bruce handed his ticket to the valet, who ran off to retrieve the car.

Maybe Jerry's not so bad. He has a good job, and he's not unhandsome. Maybe I am too judgmental.

Then he flipped off the driver of the passing cab who honked at him for jaywalking.

Yeah, never mind.

Rachel drove home in silence, cracking the window for some fresh air. She thought how she would much rather have spent the evening with Nathan, discussing books and art and Burt Reynolds movies. He wouldn't have eyeballed her choice of dinner, or make disparaging, passive-aggressive comments about her weight. Rachel was projecting—she didn't even know him. But she wanted to.

Just as friends, though. That's the best I can hope for. Let's not get crazy here. Put down the fantasy, and no one gets hurt.

Chapter Five

"Rachel! Over here!" The duchess waved her bejeweled hand from across the faculty cafeteria.

Rachel speared a wedge of lemon for her iced tea and made her way to the table. Joanie was difficult to miss, with her red hair and sequined emerald green tunic. Brennan was next to her, mouthing *stop waving,* but Joanie's bangle bracelets must have gained momentum, because she kept it up until Rachel arrived at the table. Brennan was decked out in his teaching attire, or what he referred to as *accountant chic*—argyle sweater vest, bow tie, chinos, and loafers.

Rachel had a sudden flash of the movie *Auntie Mame* but decided to keep this information to herself. She feared one or both of them liable to break into song.

As she settled into her chair, she came to a profound realization. She was at the cool kids table, relatively speaking.

The nice thing about Mondays, Wednesdays, and Fridays was that she, Brennan, and Joanie were free for lunch at the same time. The food was classic crapola, as Brennan colorfully pointed out, end-of-the-week refitted leftovers disguised as tater tot casserole.

"Glad you made it," Brennan said. "Gossip. Now."

"About what?" Joanie replied. "This is Oakton College. Nothing happens. I think maybe Professor Macintosh overwatered her fichus last week. Woo."

"It was a big deal," Rachel said. "It made the faculty newsletter." She tapped her straw on the table to strip off the paper sleeve.

The cafeteria was quiet today. A few groups were scattered around the room, some digging away at the baked mystery casserole, a few covering their empty plates with their napkins, like a tiny food funeral. There weren't many pictures on the wall, apart from the one from the fifties depicting the four food groups, and a faded poster demonstrating the Heimlich maneuver. There was a corkboard by the door, where someone had been advertising the same 1988 Ford Fiesta for sale for the last year and a half, and a flyer indicating a roommate was wanted—*Extremely liberal attitude required. Clothing optional.* Rachel often marveled how the college cafeteria wasn't that different from its typical high school counterpart.

Cliques were evident, from the math types in one corner, laughing about the abacus joke, to the sports coaches in another, making up the jock's table, to the physics folks at their regular spot by the window, who on at least two occasions nearly blew up a folding chair. Departments generally kept to themselves, the sciences never deigning to sit with the liberal arts. Nobody wanted to sit with the psych department. Joanie, Brennan, and Rachel were one of the only examples of departmental co-mingling. They were the rebels, with bow ties and bangles.

Rachel plucked a paper napkin from its metal container and spread it on her lap. She took two more for good measure since she was having vegetable soup and wanted to be prepared. Brennan was halfway through a turkey on pumpernickel, and Joanie was picking at a Caesar salad topped with a few sad croutons.

Aren't we the gourmands? Julia Child would be proud.

"Starting tomorrow, I'm bringing my own lunch." Rachel placed her spoon on her tray.

"Did you hear from Lisa over the weekend?" Joanie examined a piece of lettuce. "How is Madame?"

"She texted me Saturday. Bruce whisked her away for a romantic weekend in Lake Geneva."

"What is a weekend?" Joanie said, in her best upper-crust English accent. "No, seriously, what is it? I spent my Saturday and Sunday cleaning up after Jason and avoiding Hank."

"You still haven't told him about the show? You've been in rehearsals for a week." Brennan had no concerns regarding his sandwich and took a large bite. "Where have you told him you've been?" he said, chewing.

"Pilates."

"How long do you think you can keep that up?" Rachel said. "Isn't he going to notice you don't look any different after all that *exercise*?"

"I'm not sure he knows what Pilates is," Joanie said.

Brennan wiped his mouth. "So you're in a play. What can he do?"

"He could leave me. Pack up the house and take Jason, leaving me with only a hot plate, a carton of expired milk, and the memory of my youth."

"At least you're not being dramatic or anything," Brennan said.

Rachel decided to give the hot soup a try. As she raised the spoon to her lips, she glanced at the main door to find Nathan standing there. Her spoon missed her mouth by an eighth of an inch, spilling broth and two cubes of carrot down her front.

Brennan handed her the third napkin. "Wow, slurp much?"

"Nathan," she whispered.

"Who?" Brennan said.

"Mr. Good Shoes."

"Where?" Joanie and Brennan chimed in unison, craning their necks.

"Don't both look at once," Rachel hissed, dabbing at her sweater.

She was glad she'd worn one with a pattern. The carrot blended in. "I ran into him at the coffee place on Friday. We chatted. He may have asked me out."

"*May* have?" Joanie said.

"We have people looking into it," Brennan replied.

"It's no big deal. I'm sure he just meant it in a friendly way."

"How do you ask someone out in a *friendly* way?" Brennan said.

"I don't know, with hand puppets? Can we talk about this later?" Rachel said. "Oh, shoot, he sees us. Um…hide!"

"Where are we supposed to go?" Brennan glanced around the cafeteria, then nodded at the drink station. "Duck behind the ice maker?"

Nathan waved as he zig-zagged between the tables, and Joanie and Brennan waved back enthusiastically. Nathan grinned as he approached, his cheeks flushed, as if he'd just come in from outside.

"I found you!"

"I didn't know you were looking for me."

"Good thing you got here when you did," Brennan said. "Fifteen minutes ago she was crouched behind the salad bar."

Rachel kicked him under the table.

"I wound up going back to the coffee shop thirty seconds after I left on Friday," Nathan said. "I thought I lost my reading glasses. Turns out they were in my inside jacket pocket. At least they weren't on my head, right? Done that before. Anyway, as I was leaving, I saw this." He placed Rachel's Montblanc pen on the table. "This must've fallen out of your briefcase when you were packing up. Looks expensive. Thought you might be missing it."

Her eyes widened. "Goodness, yes." Then she squinted. "How did you find me?"

"I remembered that you said you taught here, and I was driving by. Thought I'd check if you were around."

"And you had a hunch I'd be here?"

"It's lunchtime. It's where the food is," Joanie whispered.

"I did a bit of wandering first. Asked a few students on the quad. You're, um, well-known."

"I'll bet," Rachel replied.

"They suggested the library or English office. That secretary, Cindy, said you'd probably be here. And here you are. Easy peasy, lemon breezy."

"How very *thorough* of you." Brennan winced after Rachel kicked him again.

"Too creepy?" Nathan lowered his head and raised his eyebrows.

"I think it's adorable." Joanie stuck out her hand. "Appropriate level of creep. I'm Joanie. Theater Arts."

Nathan shook her hand. "Nathan. Not a stalker."

"Don't pay any attention to her," Rachel said.

"I'm pretty certain that's impossible," he replied, as Joanie reluctantly let go of his hand. "Mind if I sit?"

Brennan pulled out a chair. "Sit next to me. Brennan. Accounting."

Nathan sat, wedged between Brennan and the duchess. He crossed and uncrossed his legs, then cleared his throat, but his rigid posture said he knew he was being sized-up.

"So Nathan, what do you think of our little corner of heaven?" Joanie rested her chin on her fist and gazed at him.

"It's a nice campus. Reminds me of where I went to school. Monmouth. Small private college in northern New Jersey."

"Is that where you're from?" Joanie said.

"Yes. Just moved here, in fact. How's the coffee in this place?"

"Terrible. I'll get you a cup." Brennan popped from his chair like he had been on the receiving end of a tiny electric shock.

"No, that's all right. I'll get it my—well, he's gone."

"And what is it that you do, Nathan?" Joanie leaned in.

"Technical writer."

"How fascinating! Rachel, did you hear that? Technical writer."

"I heard. I'm right here. You don't have any idea what a technical writer does, do you?"

"No," Joanie replied. "Although I'm sure it's *fascinating*." She toyed with her bracelets, twisting them on her wrist. "And you're single? Any kids? Pets? Outstanding warrants?"

"Joanie!"

"Where is Brennan with that coffee?" Nathan peered around the cafeteria. Brennan was at the cash register, and he raised the coffee cup in salute.

"Don't worry," Rachel said, nervously. "They're harmless."

Brennan swooped into his chair, placing the lidded cup in front of Nathan. "I didn't know what you liked in your coffee, so I brought one of everything." He dumped a handful of sugar packets, creamers, and artificial sweeteners in blue, pink, and yellow packets.

"Wow, thanks. How efficient." Nathan poured a creamer into his drink.

"You just moved here from New Jersey?" Rachel said, glad to get a word in.

"Yes. Only been here a few weeks. I'm pretty much settled into my place. I've met a few folks through my job, but I mostly work from home, so it's hard to socialize."

"It's tough to make friends when you're an adult. I was lucky to find Joanie and Brennan."

Joanie and Brennan smiled.

"It's easy when you're a kid, isn't it?" Nathan's eyes crinkled when he smiled. "It's like, *Hey, do you like bikes? I like bikes. Let's be best friends.*" He sipped his coffee. "You're right. This is terrible." He took a second sip and shrugged. "I guess that's why I wanted to find you. You seemed really nice the other day. And interesting."

"Thanks. You, too. And you got my Julius Caesar joke."

"Rachel is very smart like that," Brennan said. "You should see what she can do with *Richard III.* It's Hi-larious."

"I'm sure. Is there a lot to do around here?" Nathan's gaze remained on Rachel.

"You mean, on campus?"

"On campus or in town. I know about the art museum."

"There's a ton to do," Joanie said. "Independent and foreign-type films at The Bijou, good music at several of the downtown bars, and of course, if you're willing to travel outside city limits, some *wonderful* theater in Chicago. *Ahem, ahem.*"

"Yes, and Chicago is within a reasonable driving distance, too." Rachel said.

"Or...if you want something more intellectual," Brennan winked, "you could go with Rachel to a faculty gathering this Friday. I'm sure she'd love for you to go. Right, Rach?" He turned back to Nathan. "Drinks, tiny food on sticks, and all the Shakespeare puns you can handle."

Rachel fully expected Nathan to make a bolt for the exit. The cafeteria had cleared out, so he'd have a straight shot to the door. Joanie and Brennan were in rare form, raking him over the coals, putting him in the hot seat, or whatever metaphor one uses when they want to ensure they never ever see that person again. She wondered if they had an evil plot afoot.

"I'm sure Nathan has no interest in a boring faculty party," Rachel said.

"Honestly that sounds kind of interesting. I mean, if that's okay with you, Rachel."

Brennan leaned in and whispered in her ear, "He said yes."

Rachel smacked him on the leg, under the table. "Uh, all right. Yes, sure, that would be fine."

"I'd love to hang out sooner if you have the time. Maybe lunch on Wednesday? Not here. We can do better." Nathan peeled the lid off the coffee cup and peered at its contents.

"Um, yeah, all right."

"Here's her card with her cell number." Joanie magically whisked a card from her tote bag, like the neighborhood yenta. "Give her a call to figure out a place to meet."

Nathan chuckled and placed the card in his jacket pocket. "Well, I'd better get back to work." He rose, brushing the creases from his jeans. "It was nice meeting you. I'm sure we'll become good friends. Brennan, Joanie." He patted Rachel's hand. "I'll call. Do you like Asian-Irish fusion cuisine?"

"I can't imagine I do."

"Me neither. This place sent me a menu, and it sounds dreadful. We'll find something else. See you."

Nathan left, straightening his jacket and running his hand through his hair.

"Boy, he looks as good leaving as arriving, doesn't he?" Brennan sighed dramatically.

"And our Miss Rachel Ethel Simon has a date." Joanie paused. "Two dates!"

"I do not have two dates. And not my middle name."

"I beg to differ," Brennan said. "You have a date to the faculty party."

"Because *you* asked him."

"And then he asked you on a lunch date," Joanie said. "That's two."

"No, he asked me to *hang out*. Completely different thing."

"You're going out with a cute boy," Joanie sing-songed.

Rachel cleaned the napkins and sugar packets from the table.

"Nothing in his demeanor said *date*. He was cornered. He's just trying to make friends. He even said it—*I'm sure we'll be great friends*."

"Rachel..."

Ignoring Brennan, she got up to throw away the trash and return her tray. She was irritated, like they had pounced on him and forced his hand. He was probably too nice a person to back out in front of them. There was no way on God's green earth that Nathan Fletcher wanted to date her.

I'm not the type men are attracted to. I wish they hadn't put me in that situation.

They exited the cafeteria in silence. Rachel thought maybe they were gearing up for an apology. She gave Joanie a moment to prepare her *mea culpa*. She and Brennan were both glued to their phones.

"I texted Lisa," Joanie said. "She's taking you dress shopping on Thursday."

"And I made a reservation for you at McMurty's," Brennan said. "Great burgers, real casual. Perfect." He puffed out his chest and smiled.

There was no arguing with these two. Joanie and Brennan both gave her a goodbye kiss on the cheek and disappeared into the crowd. She spotted Brennan chatting up a few students, one taking out a calculator and notebook to show him his latest assignment. Except for his bow tie, Brennan could be one of them, his boyish charm allowing him an easy camaraderie that Rachel could never quite master.

Rachel left the cafeteria and strode across the lawn to the humanities building. The air was bracing, refreshing, and good for clearing her head. When she arrived at the door of her classroom, she paused and realized she needed to focus on the class. She opened the door and entered. It was the same, although for a split second she expected it to be different. She sat at her desk and reviewed her notes for the upcoming lesson.

No, I shouldn't let myself get too excited. It's no big deal. I made a new friend.

But her stomach fluttered.

Knock it off.

As she got up, she noticed the Emily Dickenson poster hanging forlornly on the wall.

You had the right idea, Em. Be a recluse and write poems.

As the students filtered in and took their seats, Rachel gave one last passing thought to Nathan. He was awfully nice, and she liked him. She wouldn't ruin it by building it into something it wasn't.

You've been here before.

As the clock struck one o'clock, she turned her attention to her class and the task at hand. This she could do.

When the class was finished, Rachel was excited for quiet work time in her office, until she remembered she had important papers to bring to the department office, and that she needed to check her mailbox.

Shoot. So much for that.

She got her coat, slung her bag over her shoulder, and headed downstairs to the department office. It was a nice space, consisting of Collier's private office, a conference room, a kitchenette where they ostensibly kept refills of tea and coffee but were always out, and…the assistant's desk. There was Cindy, typing away on her laptop, cradling the phone receiver between her neck and shoulder. Rachel hoped that if she was quiet, she wouldn't be noticed.

"Dr. Simon. Almost missed you, there."

Crap! So close.

"Hi, Cindy. Just putting these papers in Collier's mailbox." The muscles in her neck tensed, and she casually inched to the wall of mail cubbies.

Cindy hung up the phone and glanced around the office, getting only halfway out of her chair to pick up stack of papers. Her copper hair was pinned in a neat bun, and her white blouse and pinstripe pencil skirt gave her the appearance of a secretary in a Rock Hudson and Doris Day movie.

"Hey, I need your RSVP for Dr. Collier's party on Friday. You'll be there, I assume."

"I will."

"And will there be a plus-one?" Her voice was too cheery for Rachel's comfort.

"Yes, there will be."

"Wow! So, you got yourself a boyfriend over the weekend?" Her eyes widened, bordering on caricature.

"Yes. I mean, no. He's coming as my date, but it's not like a date-date." Rachel leaned on the edge of Cindy's half-cubicle, gripping the black laminate, willing the conversation to end.

"That's all right. We've all had imaginary boyfriends." Cindy patted Rachel's hand "Should I put down a plus-one, or should I just pretend to, and you'll tell everyone there that he got called out of town at the last minute?" she whispered conspiratorially.

Rachel's shoulders rose to the level of her earlobes, and she stuffed her fists in her pockets, clenching them. She would not take the bait. She took a deep breath, wanting to punch Cindy's pert nose. She let the breath out and attempted to channel some Zen.

"No, he's real, and he'll be there. Put him down."

"Will do!" Cindy sat back at her desk, opened a spreadsheet, and typed in a few numbers.

Rachel wondered if Cindy knew how grating she found her. Maybe she did and didn't care. She could be one of those people who relished passive-aggressive relationships.

Rachel headed for the mailroom as Cindy addressed Pam Wolsey, the creative writing instructor.

"Pam! Wow! I wish I could be brave like you and wear such *comfortable* outfits."

Yeah, she's a bitch. Rachel exchanged knowing glances with Pam as they passed.

When Rachel got to her car, she threw her bag onto the passenger seat. As she sat, her cell phone pinged, alerting her to a new text. She had not one, but seven new texts. The first two were from Joanie.

You're welcome!

Matchmaker, matchmaker, la la la.

Then Brennan.

You're welcome! (The duchess made me say that.)

Then six in rapid succession from Lisa.

Isn't life wonderful? :-)

All of a sudden, the lyrics from My Heart Will Go On *are so much less sappy.*

I LOVE Celine.

Bruce bought me a bracelet!

I'll meet you at your house in half an hour so we can drive to the meeting together.

Wear Spanx.

Rachel was surprised by her friends' persistence. She wouldn't call it a date, but maybe the party would be fun. He did track her down. On purpose. It's not like she stole his wallet. Maybe he'd think she was great. Maybe he'd see past her outside, and like the inside.

Maybe, maybe, maybe.

The drive to her house was a blur. A hundred scenarios were running through her head. Having lunch and going to the party with Nathan. The meeting at *Charmé.* Pretending Lisa was the author of the blog they loved, and Rachel was, what? Her assistant? Her proofreader? As she parked in her driveway, her stomach fluttered again.

So much can go wrong. Very, very wrong.

The realization made her gasp, and a familiar pang hit her solar plexus. She couldn't let herself get too excited. She mustn't get her hopes too high. About anything.

As she turned the key in her front door, Lisa's car pulled into the driveway. She had just enough time to run in, drop off her bag, and pick up her meeting materials. She waved to Lisa and went inside, making a side trip to the kitchen for a snack. Or several snacks. Maybe a bag full.

~ * ~

Rachel rustled around in her bag, searching for her notes. Reading in the car made her feel ill, but she was willing to risk the expected nausea to make sure Lisa was prepared for the meeting.

Lisa gripped the wheel of her BMW, taking her job as driver seriously. Her normal put-together business look had been taken up a notch, with her hair freshly blown-out and makeup a touch heavier than usual.

At last, Rachel located her portfolio and flipped it open. "Did you finish the reading list I gave you?"

"I tried, but I got busy. I focused on the fashion aspect. Besides, that's your area."

"What if they ask you about the literature portion of the essays?"

"I'll tell them you're in charge of research. It'll be fine. Relax."

That would be next to impossible. Brittany Ekberg, the editor at *Charmé* who found her site, balked when Lisa asked to bring a guest. Lisa was the main attraction they were seeking, not her schlubby assistant. But she had to go along. If they grilled Lisa on the literary portion of her piece, the jig would most definitely be up. They needed to get in, take the meeting, and get out. She'd deal with the awards banquet later.

They got on the elevator in the large steel and glass building, in the middle of the business section of Chicago. Far from the ivy-lined campus of Oakton, these people moved fast and held no deference for Rachel if they bumped shoulders. They rode in silence, Rachel furiously rehearsing the scene in her head, while Lisa touched up her lip gloss.

The elevator doors opened, and Rachel felt like Dorothy from *The Wizard of Oz* when she stepped out of her old wooden house and into Munchkinland. The floor was polished marble, the furniture in the lobby shiny and expensive. Everyone was tall, thin, and wore sleek and elegant clothes. There were pots of orchids—most likely the real thing, not silk—on either side of the reception desk. Lisa strode toward the receptionist, while Rachel trailed behind her, feeling conspicuous in her boxy suede jacket and low-heeled shoes.

"Lisa Hanson. I have an appointment…"

Rachel gave her friend a nudge in the ribs, as the receptionist typed her name into the computer.

"I mean, Rachel Simon. Of course, Rachel Simon. Because that's who I am."

The receptionist gave a long sigh and slumped her shoulders as she clicked the keys on the keyboard.

"Yes, here you are. Two o'clock." She gave Rachel—the real Rachel—the up and down and raised her eyebrow. "Have a seat. I'll let your party know you're here."

"Party? Do we get funny hats and noisemakers?" Rachel said.

The receptionist glared at her and sighed again.

"Don't do that," Lisa whispered.

"Rough crowd."

"Have a seat over there." The receptionist waved vaguely. "Brittany and her people will be right with you. They're talking to Oscar's people."

"The Grouch?" Rachel said.

The receptionist gazed at her levelly. "De. La. Renta."

Lisa and Rachel retreated to the seats in the waiting area.

"Don't do that," Lisa whispered again.

"I won't. She did *not* find that funny." Rachel stopped in front of the chairs. "Sorry. I'm nervous."

"It'll be fine. Just sit and relax." Lisa gracefully lowered herself into the chair, which looked like a waffled velvet hammock.

"You've got to be kidding me," Rachel said, trying to do the calculus that was obviously necessary to figure out how to get herself into this chair without her knees going up her nose.

"Nope, nope, nope—" Rachel lost her footing as she was lowering herself into the chair and landed with her feet splayed out in front of her. "This is comfy." She rested her hands on her bag, which was now chin-level.

"Sit on the edge," Lisa said. "You kind of have to perch." She tried to give Rachel an assist, then got up and grasped Rachel's hands, hoisting her out of the seat. "There. Just stand. I'm going to go to the ladies' room to freshen up. I'll be right back. Don't…touch anything."

"For Pete's sake, Lisa, I have a PhD. I'm not going to embarrass myself."

Lisa glanced at the chair and raised her eyebrows.

"Okay, fine. But they need to make those more visitor-friendly," Rachel said.

Lisa turned on her heel and headed for the restroom.

Rachel glanced around, wondering how many people noticed her clumsy attempt at sitting. Fortunately, no one seemed to have noticed, and she took a deep breath.

"Excuse me," she called to the receptionist. "Do you have any water?"

The receptionist sighed mightily and reached below her desk.

"Oh, that's cool. A fridge right there. I should do that at my job. I'd save a ton at the vending machine."

The receptionist's heels clicked on the floor as she brought Rachel the water and handed her a clear plastic pod.

"Um, what's this?"

"You asked for a water."

"This looks like a detergent packet."

The receptionist sighed again. Rachel was surprised she hadn't hyperventilated yet from those deep breaths.

"It's an edible hydration pod."

Rachel held it up in her hand. "Do I get a straw?"

The receptionist ignored her request and went back to her desk. Rachel discretely placed the pod in an orchid planter.

"Still waiting?" Lisa tapped her on the shoulder.

"Yes. Hopefully any minute. Don't ask for water."

"What?"

"Never mind. Oh, I think that's her." Rachel indicated a young woman walking toward them.

"Rachel Simon! Hello." The young brunette extended her hand as she approached them. "I'm Brittney Ekberg. It's nice to meet you in person." She took Lisa's hand and shook it delicately. "And you must be her assistant, Lisa." Brittany made the attempt to put her hand out, then dropped it as if she'd suddenly lost interest. "Let's head back to the conference room. Everyone is excited to meet you."

"Everyone?" Lisa said.

"A few of the fashion staffers, plus our editor-in-chief decided she wanted to sit in. She adores your take on feminism in fashion."

"It's not really feminism per se…" Rachel said.

"Whatever. She likes it, I like it, so here you are." Brittany gave Lisa the side-eye. "I love your outfit. Marc Jacobs?"

"Vintage Chanel," Lisa said.

Rachel decided it best that she not mention her own outfit came from Target.

They arrived at the conference room, and Brittany opened the glass doors and ushered them in. There were two seats open at the end, and she gestured for her guests to sit.

Brittany slid into her seat. "Welcome. Let me introduce you. This is Anita, Jorge, and Stella. They're associate fashion editors. And on the other side, we have Madeleine, Olivia, and Brent. They work in Features. And of course, our editor-in-chief, Elizabeth Burns."

Lisa and Rachel acknowledged everyone in the room, then sat in the padded leather chairs. There were various untouched pastries on the table, and a pitcher of water in the center. Each person had his or her own various beverages, from coffee to something green in a sport bottle. Rachel's mouth went dry. She wanted to pour herself a glass of water, although she was fearful it would appear obvious and awkward.

"Rachel, we're glad you're here, and that you brought your assistant." Brittany shifted in her chair. "We're such fans of your blog. It's smart and offers such a fresh take on fashion and the modern young woman. We think you'll be a big hit with our readers, too."

"And of course, your picture will go with your column, showing readers that you walk the walk, too." Jorge cleared his throat. "In four-inch Christian Lacroix, of course." He smiled.

"She definitely fits the *Charmé* ideal," Brittany said. "You and I have chatted via email several times, but why don't you tell the others what inspired you to write these pieces in your blog?" She turned to her colleagues. "It's fascinating."

Lisa squirmed in her seat. "Well, you know, there's always *fashion*, and of course, literature. And many of these characters were quite well-dressed. And, you know, for the time, and, uh, I thought people should, um, put them in modern day…"

"What Rachel means to say is that the characters she writes about were very much of their time, and she draws a parallel to modern-day counterparts and how these classic characters would have fared in twenty-first century Western culture." Rachel patted Lisa's hand.

"I think that speaks to the level of literacy of our reader," Elizabeth Burns said, as the staff collectively rotated to give the editor their full attention. "I've always believed we should be more than clothing and accessories. If we can get them to read widely, especially our younger audience, we can raise the level of discourse in other areas of their lives." She put her palms on the reddish wood table. "And that's where you come in, Rachel."

"I'm flattered," Rachel said. "I mean, we're flattered."

"Lisa does a lot of the basic research for me. I don't know what I'd do without her." Lisa smiled.

"How nice." Elizabeth nodded. "Of course, we have staff here who could help you with that."

Brittany regarded Rachel, her perfectly arched eyebrows raised. Rachel disappeared with each passing moment, like she was blending into the polished finish of the table. She resisted the urge to wipe her hand across her forehead, certain a fine sheen of perspiration had collected there, and focused instead on the sudden gnawing in her stomach.

"Of course, as you discussed with Brittany, we'd like to offer you a column with us. We'd start with bi-monthly to see what kind of feedback we get. And if it goes well, we'd start you as a regular early next year. How does that sound?" Elizabeth rested her chin on her fist, her lips pursed in a confident smile as she waited.

"I think that sounds amazing." Lisa's voice sounded clear and bright as she placed her hand on her chest.

"She can do this remotely, correct?" Rachel folded her hands and squeezed her fingers together. "She doesn't want to give up her job at the college."

"Of course," Elizabeth said. "That's what makes you our expert in the field." She glanced at Rachel, then rose slowly and regarded Lisa. "Brittany will show you around the office, let you know where everything is, and what resources are available to you."

"This is a dream come true." Lisa stood and shook Elizabeth's extended hand. "Really. Thank you so much."

"And you, Lisa." Elizabeth nodded at Rachel. "Good helpers are hard to find. I'm sure you'll find another assignment soon." She tilted her head. "Do you write?"

Rachel choked on her spit. "Uh, no. I mean, yes. Sort of. You know, stuff and whatnot."

"Of course," Elizabeth said, without breaking eye contact. "You're quite knowledgeable."

"How about that tour?" Lisa said.

"Yes. Indeed. It was nice meting you two. I look forward to seeing you again at the awards gala this winter. Perhaps, if you ask nicely, Jorge will let you borrow a gown from The Closet."

Lisa's eyes widened, and Elizabeth smiled warmly.

"Brittany, don't keep them too long. I'll need to send Rachel's info to the event coordinators this afternoon." She swept out of the room, leaving the scent of Armani perfume in her wake.

"Let's get started," Brittany said, as the others cleared the room. "Rachel, let me take you around and introduce you." She tilted her chin. "Lisa, why don't you wait in the reception area? You'll be comfortable there."

"Should be easy to do in those shoes," said Stella, who had been gathering the folders.

Brittany waved her off. "We'll give Rachel the short tour."

Lisa squeezed Rachel's arm. "Wait for me there, okay, *Lisa?*"

Rachel agreed and headed back to the reception desk while Brittany and Lisa sashayed away. Their heels clicked in unison as they marched down the hallway to the main offices, through the iced glass doors, and into the fold of the genetically gifted.

Rachel bent to lower herself into one of the hammock chairs, then thought better of it. She stared at the orchids in the large pots, thumbing the leaves absentmindedly. The sun shone through the large windows, casting a large shadow as it hit the side of the reception desk. The receptionist sighed again, closed the blinds halfway with her remote control, and misted her face with water that smelled of roses.

"They're fake, you know."

Rachel jumped at the voice behind her

"Whoops. Didn't mean to startle you."

Rachel turned to find a lovely, plump young woman in a dark green skirt and plaid blouse. She had her hair piled high on her head, and she wore wire-rimmed glasses, similar to a pair Rachel had sported in college.

The girl smiled. "Yeah, fake. Like a lot of things here. But it's a living." She handed the receptionist a pile of interoffice envelopes. "Got anything for me?"

"You could have sent those with Suzie. *She's* approved to be here."

"And miss a chance to see my BFF? It would be like a day without sunshine." The younger woman turned back to Rachel with a wide grin and scurried to her side. "One of these days she'll call security, I'm sure." She leaned in. "They don't enjoy seeing the likes of me." She thumbed conspiratorially at the glass doors. "But they don't realize how many of their readers look like us. I've seen the research."

Rachel smiled, afraid to say anything that would blow her cover. "I'm waiting for a friend. She's getting a tour."

"Ooh, special. I'm Amy, by the way. Banished to the basement mailroom. I got the job because the editor-in-chief is my aunt, but personnel keeps me out of sight most of the time." Amy glanced at her watch and gave a start. "Whoops, better go. Nice talking to a normal person." She waved as she jogged to the elevator.

Rachel gave her a vague wave in return, taken aback that a person in this place had spoken to her voluntarily. She glanced at the hammock chairs, put her bag down, and positioned herself on the edge of the seat. Not the most comfortable spot, but it would have to do given the lack of options.

She picked up one of the magazines on the table in front of her and thumbed through it. Page after page of idealization, hopes, and dreams, reminding her of the magazines her mother used to buy to encourage her daughter. Rather, though, it sent her young mind reeling with the ways she could never measure up—arms too short, neck too thick, hair too curly, size too large.

The models on the page, even the ones in the so-called teen mags, were too perfect to be real. They were like aliens from a far-off, exotic planet, who came here to make others feel bad about themselves. Rachel shut the magazine and tossed it on the table.

They like your brain. Too bad it doesn't come in the right package.

And it was all about the packaging. Everyone likes things that come in pretty packages, or cool boxes, or that have an exotic name. Even prunes became hip when they were rebranded as dried plums. The plain girl in the movie takes off her glasses and lets down her hair, and the leading man exclaims, *Goodness, Janet, I've never noticed you before.*

Except it wasn't true. Prunes, at the very heart of it, were still prunes, and a name change and clever marketing wouldn't change that they were wrinkly and sticky. And Rachel could swipe on a new lipstick or lose a pound or forty, and she'd still be a prune.

A dried plum by any other name…

She was zapped back into the moment by the sound of Lisa's laughter down the hall of the magazine's inner sanctum.

"Okay, thanks. Talk soon. Bye!" Lisa waved behind her.

She searched for her companion, and Rachel was met by a huge grin.

"I got a goodie bag." She held up a lavender and silver package. "Such amazing stuff. It's going to be so cool to work here."

"You mean, for me."

"Of course. You. I just assumed you'd pass along any freebies."

"How did it go? I'm guessing you didn't blow our cover."

"Not at all. The column didn't come up much. We talked shoes and this new facialist Brittany found. Stuff you don't care about." Lisa paused. "Let me get a water for the ride home."

"Wait, those things are weird. You might spill it on your…"

Lisa bit into the corner and placed the whole pod in her mouth and swallowed, neat as a pin. "What?"

"Never mind. You want to show me how to sit in that chair again?" Rachel pointed to the purple hammock.

"Hover, align, descend." She demonstrated, sitting delicately in the difficult chair.

"Got it. Let's go."

"I think this will work out. I know this world," Lisa said, gesturing. "You do the writing, and I'll make you look good."

"You always do. You hungry?"

"No, I think that water pod filled me up."

"I *do* need to get you out of here. I'll buy you a sandwich."

They walked to the elevator. Rachel wanted to give the receptionist a high-five or the finger guns before they left, but she was afraid the young woman's head might explode. The elevator car was empty as it opened on their floor, and they stepped on in unison.

"Ooh, you have that thing tomorrow with that guy," Lisa said. "Norman?"

"Nathan. Yeah. It's not a thing, though. It's just lunch."

"Oooh, Rachel has a date," Lisa sing-songed. The elevator hummed quietly.

"It's not a date."

"You don't like him?"

"He's nice."

"But you're just friends?" Lisa lifted an eyebrow.

The elevator doors opened into the lobby, a sudden rush of sound and street noises confronting them. Rachel worked to avoid the people intent on bumping into her, either because they were overly committed to their trajectory, or more likely, because they didn't notice her, which at her height and size she always found odd.

Just friends, she mouthed, as they navigated the revolving door. "Seriously."

"One can never have too many friends," Lisa said, once Rachel joined her on the sidewalk. "Let's get a salad." She pointed to a café across the street. "We'll eat fast and head home, okay?"

"Did they show you The Closet?" Rachel said, as they crossed at the stoplight. "I heard they have a pair of Manolo Blahniks the public hasn't seen yet. Oh, and Jimmy Hoffa. Is Jimmy Hoffa in there?"

They entered the café for a quick lunch, and as Rachel listened to Lisa describe her experience at the magazine, Rachel made a mental list of concerns. This was going to fall apart; she just knew it. Then they'd expose her as a talentless fraud, and things would most definitely not be okay.

Chapter Six

It was four minutes until noon and Rachel was panicking.

She'd arrived at McMurty's to meet Nathan for lunch and couldn't find a place to park. On her third lap around the block, tiny beads of sweat were forming on the back of her neck. She swung around to the next block, cursing street parking in general.

Finding a spot two blocks away, she did her best to parallel park—tough to do without her father standing on the curb yelling, *Now turn the wheel. Turn it. Turn it!* She eased into the spot and used the blotting papers Joanie gave her. The papers, however, did not erase the abject terror at that moment, which was 12:04.

She hated being late. Being late robbed her of the opportunity to compose herself and to formulate amusing anecdotes. If she was lucky, Nathan would be late too, and they could have a laugh over their lunchtime follies.

Or maybe he wouldn't even show up.

Rachel spotted Nathan's car parked directly in front of the pub. *Lucky bastard.* She pulled the large gold door handles and went inside. The place was dim and smelled of beer and French fries. The light jazz saxophone playing over the speakers wasn't too loud, and the place wasn't too crowded.

It's like the Goldilocks of bars. Good job, Brennan.

"How many in your party, miss?" The young lady at the host's stand smiled, her pencil poised over the reservation book. Her nametag said *Sandi*, and she was cute, had light brown hair, and a dimple in her left cheek.

"I'm meeting someone." Rachel got on her tiptoes to scan over the booths, and did a waist-tilt to the left, where there was a dark wood pillar with posters of local bands splashed across them.

"I have a book club sitting near the bar." Sandi pointed them out.

"You have a book club? Are they open to new—never mind. It's just one person I'm meeting."

"Is it that handsome guy with the brown hair and tweed blazer? Name is Nathan?"

"Yup, that's him."

"Yowza. Good for you. Let me show you to your table." Sandi picked up a menu from the stand.

Nathan waved from a booth. He'd ordered a beer already and was holding a menu.

"It's okay, I see him." Rachel took the menu. "Thank you."

"Hey, you made it," Nathan said. "Didn't know if you'd see me here."

"I did. I described you to the hostess. Said I was meeting Captain Elbow Patches. She knew immediately who you were."

Nathan lifted both elbows. "Good call. It's a look." He sipped his beer. "Hope you don't mind that I ordered myself a drink already."

"No, no problem. I'll order something when the waitress comes back." Rachel slid into the booth, praying the leather didn't make a rude noise.

"What's good here?" He browsed the menu, casually adjusting the collar of his striped shirt.

"I have no idea. Never been."

"It'll be an adventure, then." He winked.

Rachel felt her face get warm, evaporating any remaining sweat. She opened her menu and pretended to read it. "So…you're a technical writer? That must be interesting."

"It's a living. I did a lot of freelance work, reporting on news and trends for computer journals and magazines. I moved out here to do contract work for TruTech."

"The software company?" She was impressed.

"Yeah, I work with them to create online help files, and write and edit their online documentation—user guides, how-to manuals, and the like."

"So when I can't understand how to get software to load, you're the one to blame?"

"Pretty much. It's not like I'm writing the next Great American Novel, but the pay is good, I can work from home, and I work on a bunch of different projects."

"Sounds great to me. Do you have a background in computers?"

"I majored in computer science in college, with a minor in journalism. Odd combination, but it's worked out well." He picked up his beer. "Wow, I'm talking a lot. I need to stop now."

The waitress arrived at the table and took an order pad out of her red and green plaid apron.

"Can I get you something to drink?" she said, her voice perky and energetic.

"Iced tea, please. Lemon on the side." Rachel smiled.

"Dr. Simon?" the waitress said. "Oh, my goodness. What a surprise. I'm Mary Hooper. I was in your English 201 class last year."

"Mary. Of course. How are you?"

"Doing great. Working here part-time, and still going to Oakton. I have to tell you, your class was tough, but I got a lot out of it. You helped me learn to write better, to really think deeper about my topic."

"I'm glad to hear that, Mary." Rachel glanced at Nathan, who appeared suitably impressed.

"A few kids thought you were mean. What was the word they used? Battle ax?"

Nathan choked on his drink.

"I knew you just wanted to challenge us."

He hid his face behind his menu.

"Anyway, I'll go get your iced tea. Be right back."

"That was awesome," he said. "Did you plan that?"

"Uh, no."

"Still impressive. I'm starting to get a better image of you as a teacher."

"I promise I'm not the *Nurse Ratched* of higher education."

"I bet there's no standing on desks or shouting *carpe diem*, though.*"

"There is not. I'd probably fall over. Better safe than sorry."

Mary returned with the iced tea, lemon on the side. Rachel sipped it, appreciating that it tasted fresh-brewed as it soothed her dry throat.

"Ready to order?" Mary asked.

"I'm still thinking," Nathan said. "Are you ready?"

"Yes," Rachel replied. "I'll have the turkey sandwich. No mayo, no cheese, please."

"Soup or salad?"

"Yes. Oh, I have to choose? Okay. Salad. Italian dressing on the side."

"Chips or fries?"

"Can I have fruit?"

"I think we have some." Mary wrote the addition on the pad.

"You don't like French fries?" Nathan said.

"Love them. But they don't love me. We've decided on a mutual *détente*."

"And you, sir?" Mary's eyes lit up as she waited for Nathan to order.

He placed his chin on his fist and regarded her intently. "What would you recommend?"

"If you like burgers, the BBQ Ranch Burger is super good. Not at all greasy." She glanced at her feet, then back at him.

"Then that is what I shall have. No soup or salad, and I'll have the fries. We're on speaking terms."

"I'll put your order in right away." Mary took their menus and left for the kitchen, stopping on her way to give another table a few more napkins.

Rachel looked around the room, taking in the dark wood tables and the brass accents on the bar. Sunlight streamed in through the large windows, the rays hitting the comfortably worn leather chairs.

Nathan glanced at the table placard of daily dessert specials. Usually she was nervous or self-conscious around men like him, but he had a certain way that put her at ease. He was self-assured without being arrogant, and he was handsome, but he didn't feel the need to point it out to everyone he met. Plus he had a little trouble matching his clothes, which Rachel found endearing.

"Do you have any brothers or sisters?" she said.

"Ah, sibling listing. Yes, one sister. Two years older."

"Are you close?"

"I guess. Our parents worked a lot when we were growing up, so we helped each other out."

"Makes you grow up quicker, too, I think."

"Also, Kelly had a few physical issues. Nothing life-threatening—she wore leg braces for a while due to muscular problems, and it was challenging." He paused, gazing out the window across the room. "I'll always be in her debt, though."

"Saved you from bullies?"

"Nah. Her best friend was the girl who gave me my first kiss. She was a dead ringer for Sophia Loren. Curves for days." He looked at Rachel. "My sister had the bully problem. She got made fun of at school, and I always felt I needed to stand up for her. She was a great person, but a lot of people couldn't see past all that metal."

"I had a friend in junior high who wore headgear. She used to tape tinsel on it. She liked the way it glittered in the breeze when she walked."

"How about you?" Nathan said.

"I wore orthopedic shoes when I was three—"

"I mean, brothers or sisters."

"Oh. No siblings. Just me. Dad was an executive for an insurance firm. Now retired. And Mom is a lawyer. And I have an uncle and a couple cousins in the city. They own a magic store."

"That's cool. Do you see them a lot?"

"The cousins, from time to time. I'm not close to my parents. Dad was always a bit distant, even in the best of times. And Mom…she means well, but she can be a bit…much."

"A tad overbearing?"

"Not overbearing. It's just that…Mom was quite glamorous in her day. Still is, actually. And a total ball-buster. Which is a real one-two punch in her line of work. She's proud of what I do, but I think she's disappointed that I don't take after her. In more ways than one."

"It's tough to live up to our parents' expectations."

"True. When Mom was young, she was good at everything, and had the awards to show for it. Student government, cheerleading, academics, you name it. She just seemed to have the magic touch. Me, I never won anything except for those ribbons they give out to everyone at day camp, the ones that were orange and said, *You participated!* They may as well have said, *You didn't fall down!* or *You're not the biggest dork!*"

Rachel paused for a moment, wondering if she should mention an actual award she was getting.

Another time. Too complicated.

"I have two trophies," Nathan said. "One for taking third place in a junior-level church bowling league, and one that my dad made for me out of paper towel rolls that he sprayed painted gold. He gave it to me when I stopped wetting the bed."

"That's sweet." Rachel took another sip of tea. "How old were you?"

"Twenty-three."

She laughed and pinched her nostrils to keep the tea from shooting out of them.

Mary arrived with their lunch—dishes arranged on a large, round tray that was wider than she was tall.

"Let me know if you need anything else," she chirped, placing the plates in front of them.

Rachel and Nathan thanked her, and she moved on to check her other tables.

"I was kind of hoping she'd spin the plates," Rachel said.

He snort-laughed and reached for a napkin.

She appraised her meal. The sandwich was appealing, the fruit pieces large and plentiful. His lunch was imposing, the hulking burger taking up most of the plate. It had to have been at least five inches high. He was staring at it as if formulating a plan of attack.

"Would you think less of me if I ate this with a knife and fork?" He wrinkled his nose.

"I would think more of you. Unless you're part boa constrictor, you're not getting that whole thing in your mouth."

"Challenge accepted. Just kidding. This is insane."

After unrolling his utensils from the napkin, he removed the top bun and the vegetables, placed them on the side of his plate, and cut them into bite-sized pieces. He then shifted his attention to the burger, slicing one piece and piercing it with his fork, then spearing pieces of lettuces and tomato before taking a bite.

"You are a professional," Rachel said.

"I have a system," Nathan said, after swallowing. "This was a good choice. Remind me to thank Brennan."

"He'd love to hear it, I'm sure." She took a bite of her sandwich, dripping mustard on her shirt. "Oh, darn. Can't take me anywhere." Her cell phone beeped, indicating a text. "Excuse me. Speak of the devil's aunt. It's from Joanie."

Please, please call me ASAP. Very important!

"I'm sorry, Nathan. This is horribly rude, but she's beside herself. Do you mind if I call her really quick?" Rachel inched down the seat.

"You don't have to go. I don't mind if you make the call here. If you don't mind me hearing, that is."

"Thank you. It shouldn't take more than a minute."

Joanie picked up the call on the first ring. "Rachel!" Her voice sounded strained.

"What's going on?"

"Hank's gone!"

"What do you mean, he's gone? Was he abducted?"

Nathan raised his eyebrows in concern.

"No, no, he left! He left me. Rachel, what am I going to do?"

"Wait a minute. Define *left you*. Did he move out? Or is it like that time he went on a business trip to Las Vegas without you?"

"He packed a bag and stormed out. I don't know where he is."

"Where's Jason?"

"Holed up in his room. He's freaked out."

"Don't do anything right now," Rachel said, hoping she sounded calming and soothing. "I'll be right over. We'll figure it out."

"Okay."

"Take a breath. I'll be there as soon as I can." Rachel hung up and placed the phone back in her bag.

"Is everything all right?" Nathan said.

"Joanie and her husband are having issues. He stormed out." Rachel removed the napkin off her lap and set it on the table. "I have to go there right now. She's a wreck."

"Is there anything I can do? Do you want me to come with you?"

"That's very nice, but I better go alone. I need to get to the bottom of this. It's not like Hank." She took a twenty from her wallet and put it on the table.

"You don't have to do that." Nathan pushed the money back to her.

"It's all right. I like to go Dutch. I hope that's enough."

"It's fine. Go to your friend. Call me if you need anything."

"Thank you. I appreciate you being so nice."

"You're a good friend. I admire that." He smiled. "Now go. I'll call you later about Friday."

She smiled back, holding his gaze for a moment.

Friday! I forgot about Friday.

She slung her bag over her shoulder and dashed for the door. The duchess was now a damsel in distress. She had to be exaggerating. She was prone to the melodramatic, like the time Hank forgot her birthday and she took to her bed for three days.

With clammy hands, Rachel drove to Joanie's house. When she pulled into the driveway, the house's cream-colored siding seemed washed out and there were one or two bricks on the steps in need of repair that she'd never noticed before. In the window, Joanie peeped through the vertical blinds, snapping them shut as Rachel climbed the front steps.

Before she could knock, Joanie yanked the door open. Her eyes and nose were red, and she was pale and drawn. Despite her general disdain for the practice, Rachel wanted to hug her close and pat her hair. She entered and followed her friend to the living room.

Joanie plopped on the couch and brought her legs to her chest. She came across as fragile and small. She removed a tissue from her sleeve and dabbed her nose, then handed it to Rachel, who held it by the edge and placed it on the coffee table.

"I came home from school early today," Joanie said. "I thought I'd surprise him with lunch."

"Was he with another woman?"

"What? No, God no. He was in our room, throwing stuff into a duffel bag. He looked right at me and blew past without saying a word. Slammed the door and took off."

"Wow. Did Jason see this?"

"Unfortunately. He had a half-day at school, so he was home. Saw the whole thing. Apparently he even tried to talk his dad out of leaving. Can you imagine that? He's in his room. Poor kid won't talk about it either."

"Take some time. Let Hank cool down. He loves you. This is a bump in the road."

"More like a mountain."

"Mountains can be climbed. You'll get over it." Rachel placed her hand on Joanie's shoulder and brought her close.

Then she said the words her friend wanted to hear, though she wasn't sure were true. "It'll be fine."

Joanie relaxed into the hug, as if releasing a ball of fear that she'd been holding onto for hours.

She sat up and wiped her nose on her sleeve. "I need wine."

"That's my girl. Listen, can I use your bathroom? I just noticed I've got mustard on my shirt, and I'd like to wipe it off before I start sucking on it."

"I'll meet you back here." Joanie got up to retrieve two glasses from the kitchen.

Taking wet wipes from her purse and putting her phone in her pocket, Rachel headed to Joanie's powder room down the hall, and closed the door behind her. She dabbed at the fabric, smearing the sauce, pulled tissue from the roll, and held it under the water to soak the stain away. She considered trying the guest soaps when she heard the front door open and slam shut.

"Hank? Is that you?" Joanie called from the kitchen. "Are you back?" Her footsteps were in the hall now, right outside the bathroom.

"I'm not back, Joan. I have a few things I needed to say." Hank's voice was low and modulated, much different than his usual affable cadence. "I can't do this anymore. I just can't."

"What you mean, you can't? Can't what?"

"It's the show. You promised me you'd take a break after the last one, that we'd have time for us. You lied to me."

Rachel was trapped, and she desperately wanted to escape.

"I didn't lie. It was an amazing opportunity that came out of the blue. It was too good to pass up."

"To good to pass up?" Hank's voice cracked. "My God! I feel like you're cheating on me with the theater." His voice rose a couple octaves. "I asked you not to take any more jobs, and you went behind my back."

"I didn't go behind your back. I…told you about it."

"Only after I saw a copy of the script on the table."

"I thought…"

"You thought I'd roll over, let you do whatever you wanted? It's always about you, isn't it?"

Rachel's cell phone rang, and she snatched it out of her pocket to stifle the sound, but out of habit accepted the call instead of declining.

Shit!

"Hello?" she whispered.

"It's Nathan," he whispered back. "Is everything okay?"

"No, it's…wait, why are *you* whispering?" She sat on the toilet seat lid.

"I thought it was just something we were doing. What's going on?"

"Joanie and Hank are arguing, and I'm trapped in the bathroom."

"I thought he left."

"He came back and now they're fighting outside the bathroom. I don't know what to do. Do I stay? Do I edge past them, say hello, and make a run for it? What's the protocol here?" Rachel hissed.

"I think you better stay put and let them ride it out. Don't get involved."

The noise outside the bathroom stopped, and she froze. The door swung open and Joanie and Hank stared at her as she sat hunched on the toilet seat lid, her hand cupped over her mouth.

"I think I just got involved."

"Is that Nathan?" Joanie snatched the phone before Rachel could respond. "Nathan, we need a man's opinion here—"

"Oh, for Christ's sake, Joanie." Hank slapped his forehead.

She marched down the hall, relating her version of events in a non-stop monologue. Hank stood in place, blinking at Rachel. She looked up at him from her seat in the powder room.

"Sooo, how've you been?" He let out his breath in a swift stream.

"Fine, fine." She pointed to the vanity. "That's nice. Is it new?"

"Yep, yep. Just put it in last month." He shoved his hands in his pockets and rocked back on his heels. He let out a quiet hum. "Three trips to the hardware store."

"Isn't that always the way?" She drummed her fingers on her knee.

He stared at his shoes, and she examined the ceiling.

Joanie came back up the hall, nodding and listening intently to Nathan's response. She stopped in front of the bathroom doorway and handed Rachel the phone.

"He said he doesn't want to get involved, especially since he doesn't actually know us."

Rachel put the phone to her ear. "Nathan? Sorry about that. I'll call you later?"

"I think Joanie hates me now."

"No, she doesn't hate you." She regarded Joanie. "I think she just wanted a second opinion. Or third." She sat back down on the toilet lid.

"Good luck. Bye," Nathan said.

Rachel ended the call and closed the bathroom door.

"I'm done, Joanie," Hank said.

"What does that mean?" Joanie's voice got fainter as she followed him down the hall.

"It means I'm leaving."

"Hank, c'mon, you'll get over this. I'm your little star, remember?"

"No more. I'm going to my sister's. Jason can call me whenever he wants."

"Hank, please!"

The front door slammed behind him.

Rachel waited a few seconds before poking her head out, then followed Joanie back to the living room.

Joanie handed her a glass of wine, then sat on the couch, focused on her own glass, and swirled the wine around as the light played on the surface. Her tears had stopped, but she was a million miles away.

"I can't quit the play," she muttered. "We're too far into rehearsals. Recasting my role would be too disruptive." She took two long sips of wine. "And to be honest, Rachel, I don't *want* to quit. It's an amazing company. This role is a dream, especially for an actress my age, and I feel like I'd be letting myself down. But Hank..." Her eyes welled. "Hank is my life." She put the glass on the table and leaned back. "He wants me to give up on who I am. He knew this about me when we married. Why now?" She covered her eyes with her hands.

Rachel was at a loss. Joanie had been an actress her whole life, teaching theater, and directing. She was always working on a project, and Hank appeared to be fine with sharing her with her art. Even Jason got a kick out of his *drama queen mom*, playing backstage when Joanie would take him to rehearsals as a small boy.

But for Hank to up and leave was far outside of Rachel's advice wheelhouse. She sat with Joanie, handing her tissues from her purse. Nothing she could say would fix this. It was between Joanie and her husband, and as close as she was to her friend, she was not a part of it.

"Do you and Jason want to stay at my house tonight? So you don't have to be alone. Or I could stay here? I'd just have to run back and put food out for the cat."

"Thank you, but I'm fine. You don't have to stay. I'm going to keep trying to get a hold of Hank. I need to talk to him some more. And besides," she managed a smile, "I have to call Brennan. He's texted me twelve times this afternoon, and if I go more than three minutes without responding he threatens to get me one of those Life Alert buttons." She held Rachel's hand and squeezed it gently. "I'm glad you came. Sorry you got trapped."

Rachel squeezed back. "Me, too. About both things."

"Wow." Joanie brushed hair off her face. "Real life sucks, huh?" Her eyes rimmed with tears. "*Gaaahhhhrrr!*"

"Do you want to eat? Do you have…like, food here?"

"Not much. Haven't had time to shop. We might have tortilla chips somewhere."

Rachel went to the kitchen and found the chips. She sliced cheese and put it on a plate, then brought it to the living room.

"Has Jason eaten?" Rachel said, as they sat on the couch nibbling the snacks.

"I put a PB and J in front of his door. He'll come out later, I'm sure."

They polished off the chips and cheese, drank the sparkling water they had switched to after the wine, and burped loudly. As Rachel rummaged through her bag for an antacid, Joanie turned to her with a start.

"You were having lunch with Nathan, weren't you? That's why he was on the phone."

Rachel tilted her head, wiping the salt from her hands.

"Oh, my God, I made you leave," Joanie said.

"It's fine. You needed me. No big deal."

"It *is* a big deal. Nathan must have been disappointed."

"He'll survive. Didn't he sound fine when you accosted him on the phone?"

"I appreciate you, hon. And tell Nathan I'm sorry about the ambush."

Rachel glanced at her watch. "I hate to do this, but I've got to get back to campus. I left papers in my office. I'll call you later, all right?" She hugged Joanie again.

Once Rachel made it back to her office, she sat, slumped at her desk, and opened her laptop. It was a good time to write. She had no appointments, and though a student could come by, experience told her that none would.

She opened her laptop, and as she held her fingers over the keyboard, she let her mind wander, drifting though thoughts of food, and love, and how people judge others. How different Nathan was than other men. When she was with him, she wasn't overly conscious of her padded hips, nor did she need to position her head at just the right angle to avoid a double chin. She felt she could be herself, and that was okay. She could just *be.*

It was a new experience for her, one she was eager to have again. But this realization came with a side order of trepidation. She could barely peek over her emotional wall before having to put her head down. She had to be careful, lest she leave herself open to the pain—something she couldn't survive again. There had been a lifetime of a thousand little cuts, building over time into one big wound.

And she had a feeling Nathan could do some serious damage if she let him.

Chapter Seven

Lisa held up two dresses. "Do you like the green or the blue?"

"The blue. Too much green makes me feel like Santa's chubby elf."

As promised, Lisa had dragged Rachel shopping to find an outfit for the awards ceremony, despite it being more than a month away. She also had to agree to attend as her plus-one. Lisa was working hard, making it her personal mission to make Rachel look fashionable, and not, as Lisa so lovingly put it, eighty.

She put the green dress back on the rack and continued to rifle through the size fourteen through sixteen section. Rachel held the blue dress in one hand, tapping her foot to the too-loud overhead music, and wishing she could do this online. Her friend was in the moment, putting together ensembles with belts and necklaces and cuff bracelets, as if she could style Rachel through sheer force of will.

Lisa lived for fashion, always having the air of someone who'd just stepped out of an editorial spread in *Vogue*. Or *Charmé*. Except for the gym, she always wore heels, and even her warm-up suits were couture. This was why *Charmé* loved her.

Rachel thumbed through a rack of leggings and stopped when she came across a pair that would offend her friend. She brought it to her, grinning like the cat that ate the canary.

Lisa tilted her head, looked Rachel in the eye, took the item from her and put it back on the rack.

"Friends don't let friends wear leopard-print yoga pants," Lisa said.

"They have sequins on the butt," Rachel replied. "They're snazzy."

Lisa laughed. "Yes, they are. But that's not quite what we're going for. This is the Women to Watch awards, not senior jazzercise."

"Wait! I forgot my support garment. We won't get a good idea of how the dresses hang on me. Oh, well. Guess we have to leave now." Rachel threw up her hands and walked away.

Lisa snagged her by her jacket collar. "You're not going anywhere, Rachel Celestia Simon. We'll get an idea without them. You can just suck it in."

"You can just suck it in," Rachel muttered.

"What was that?" Lisa said, from the other side of the rack.

"Nothing! Love you!"

Rachel let Lisa get back to work, and out of the corner of her eye she spotted a familiar figure. Brennan came into focus, weaving through the racks of misses dresses, holding a large Bavarian pretzel. He leaped the last two or three steps, landing next to Rachel with grace.

"You're not supposed to have that in here." She motioned toward the pretzel. "Here, let me dispose of it for you—"

"Hands off. They won't kick me out. They just care about sales." He offered the pretzel. "Want a bite?"

"God, yes. I could wear a dress made from *these*." She handed the remainder to Brennan.

"Have you spoken to Joanie today?" he said, his voice uncharacteristically muted. "I can't believe what's going on."

"I haven't, no, other than in passing at school. She finally got a hold of Hank, but I don't know if progress has been made."

"Does Lisa know about all this?"

"Yes, but she hasn't said anything. I think she's setting up camp in Bruceville. She's so happy it's like she can't deal with anyone else's unhappiness."

Lisa appeared out of nowhere, giving Brennan and Rachel a start.

"Brennan. Good, you're here. I need a cocktail dress, size sixteen, no shoulder pads, no glitter." She shooed him off. "And no birds."

"What makes you think I know anything about fashion?" Brennan said. "Stereotype much?"

"You're here, you're an extra set of hands, and if I send this one," she pointed at Rachel, "I'll find her in the food court getting one of *those*." She pointed to the pretzel.

Brennan indicated his agreement and set off like a Bloodhound searching for a scent.

Rachel crinkled her nose. "Birds?"

"For some reason designers think that women above size twelve love parrots on their clothes. I don't know why."

Within two minutes Brennan was back. He had two dresses and the same pair of yoga pants Rachel had earlier. As Lisa sent him to put the pants away, Rachel sat next to the dressing room, tired from all the standing around. Her only company was a washed-out older man holding a purse. He sank into the chair like it was his job, his gray windbreaker bunched around his ears, his back rounded, and he appeared like he would have given up his retirement fund to be at the nearest bar watching the game. Any game. Rachel gave him a sympathetic nod.

The smell of Chloé perfume wafted past. Lisa was looming like one of the giant trees in *Lord of the Rings*. This Ent was carrying six different dresses, followed by Brennan with two. Rachel's time had come.

"Okay, soldier. Up and at 'em." Lisa grasped Rachel's elbow to pull her out of the chair, and appraised Brennan's selections. "I said no shoulder pads."

As Lisa and Brennan discussed the merits of the exaggerated shoulder—*it makes the waist appear smaller! But she'll look like a linebacker!*—Rachel spied another familiar form. Salt and pepper hair, mid-fifties, tan blazer slung over his shoulder. From a distance she thought it was Bruce but dismissed the thought.

The man appeared to be following an elegantly dressed woman wearing lots of jewelry, with her black hair in a chignon. Maybe it *is* Bruce. But he's shopping with his sister? Cousin? Youthful aunt?

Her heart beat faster and she darted her gaze around the store, trying to erase what she wasn't even sure she was seeing.

"Rachel? Rachel!" Lisa's voice snapped her back into the moment. "Start with these two, and we'll pass you the other ones."

Rachel took the two dresses into a dressing room. The white slatted doors closed behind her, the tight springs latching the sides into place. She hung the dresses on the back of the door, removed her jacket and slung it over the bench.

Staring into the mirror, her eyes widened as she saw herself in the full-length mirror under the fluorescent lighting. Were those circles under her eyes? And pores so big one could park a truck in them? The store should have a poster with the number of a dressing room support hotline.

She disrobed and placed her clothes over her jacket on the bench. Despite averting her gaze, she managed to get a clear view of herself in the mirror. Her waist, although narrower than her hips, felt soft and mushy, like an under-baked dinner roll. She ran her hands over her thighs, feeling the pitted surface and the lumps that sat on each side like handles below her dowdy underwear. She felt old and tired, like someone she barely recognized.

Is that where my ass is located now? It looks like it's trying to hide behind my knees.

She was never slender, never lithe. But this?

She couldn't breathe. She removed the red dress off the hanger and pulled it over her head. It zipped, barely. The light fabric crisscrossed over the bust and gathered at the waist. The skirt swished back and forth as she rotated her torso like an oscillating fan. The dress was pretty, feminine, and so very wrong. Rachel felt like a party favor.

"Which one do you have on?" Lisa called from the other side of the door.

Rachel cleared her throat and wiped her eyes. "The red. It's a bit too tight."

"Do you want me to get the next size?"

"No. I mean, I think it's too fancy. I'll try the gray."

She shed the red dress, exchanging it for the more comfortable gray. It was a heavy jersey knit, cut in a wrap style. It was plain but flattering, and Rachel had jewelry that would go with it. It was a definite maybe.

She passed the red one over the door, trading it for two more. This time she made sure not to check the mirror. It was easier than fighting back more tears.

The next two were much worse. They cut her off in the bust in the wrong place. Tight in odd places, or loose in others. They seemed like things a seventy-year-old woman on a cruise ship would wear. She figured Lisa had run out of options and was flinging outfits at her in the hopes of tiring her out and getting her to agree to something. An item of clothing slid down the back of the door. Something slinky, sparkly, and way too shiny.

"Keep an open mind," Brennan whispered, through the slats. "I want to see it on you."

Rachel held up the hanger. It was a red sequin jumpsuit with a halter-top and plunging neckline.

You have got to be kidding me.

"Are you trying it on?"

"Bren, I don't have time to indulge in one of your Liza fantasies right now."

"Please? For me?"

"If you break into a chorus of *New York, New York,* I will never speak to you again."

"Fine…"

She shimmied into the spangly concoction, hoisting the straps over her head and contorting her arms to get the back zipped.

I look like a Liberace museum tour guide.

She popped open the doors to her dressing room, revealing Brennan with a huge grin.

"What do you think?" he said. "Is it great, or am I barking up the wrong tree?"

"It's insane. Now back up before I birch slap you."

Brennan laughed and clicked her picture with his iPhone before she could protest further.

"Now one with us together. It will be my Christmas card picture. Do jazz hands." He took their picture.

"You're buying me coffee for six weeks."

"Totally worth it." Brennan kissed her on the cheek.

After spending the next few minutes posing in front of the mirror, doing their best *Fosse* moves, there was a noise outside the dressing room. Loud voices, a man and a woman, clearly arguing, though Rachel and Brennan couldn't hear what they were saying.

"Maybe it's that older couple," Rachel whispered. "The man in the chair looked like he was planning an escape route."

It wasn't the older couple. The woman's voice belonged to Lisa.

Brennan's eyes widened, and he mouthed, *Oh. My. God!*

"You're *married?*" Lisa screeched.

Brennan and Rachel dashed out of the dressing room. The elegant brunette woman from earlier followed them, exiting from an adjacent stall, her coat on, dragging her purse behind her. They found Lisa and Bruce standing toe-to-toe, in front of the three-way mirror. She dropped the remaining dresses on the ground. Bruce was trying to console her, but she backed away as if he were electrically charged.

"What's going on here?" The woman glanced back and forth between Lisa and Bruce.

"Is this her?" Lisa said. "Is this your wife?"

"Yes, I'm his wife." The woman pointed a finger in Lisa's face. "Who are *you?*"

The color drained from Lisa's face, and her eyes were glassy, as if all the air had been let out of her lungs. She stumbled and Brennan caught her. "I can't believe it. Why didn't you tell me?"

"I was going to. I just—"

"Liar!" She shrieked again. "You were never going to tell me. Were you just using me?"

Bruce grasped Lisa's elbow to pull her to the side. "It's not the time to talk about this."

"Bruce?" His wife went to his side and tentatively touched his shoulder.

Her eyes were dark and intent as if she was searching for a clue that her husband was innocent, that this woman was crazy and making up a story.

"Does she know about me, Bruce?" Lisa addressed his wife. "Did he tell you we've been seeing each other for four months? That he told me he wanted to marry me, to take me anywhere I wanted? Did you, Bruce?"

He studied his black leather loafers, unable to meet Lisa's gaze.

"I can't believe this. I was ready to give up everything for you. And you're nothing but a liar!" Her voice grew louder and shriller.

She turned away, burying her face in Brennan's shoulder. He held her in his arms, stroking her hair as she sobbed.

The store manager approached, accompanied by a security guard. "Is there a problem here?" she said, cautiously.

"Yes, there is a problem," Bruce's wife said. "My husband is a cheater. Do you have a department that carries divorce lawyers?" She glared at Bruce. "Don't bother coming home. We're done. Again." She spun on her heel and strode out of the store.

He said nothing, rocking back on his heels as his wife stormed out. Lisa was crushed, standing in a pile of dresses and weeping as if she would never stop. A fire started in Rachel's chest, the embers stoked by the silent man in the ironed khakis.

The manager's forehead relaxed, and posture straightened when it was obvious that it would not come to blows.

"Why don't we take her in the back and get her some water," she said. "Would you like that, honey?"

Lisa didn't respond, but she didn't resist either. Brennan led her to the back of the store, following the manager and murmuring assurances that she'd be okay. As they left, Rachel noticed Bruce still standing there like he had almost been hit by a truck.

"You're a real jerk, you know that?"

It wasn't the strongest opening, but it was the best she could come up with on the spot.

"It's complicated."

"No, it's not."

"Maybe if you minded your own business…"

"Yeah, that's not going to happen. She loved you, and you shit all over her. Were you ever going to leave your wife?"

"Yes." He paused. "I don't know."

"Of course you weren't. Would've cost you too much money. You figured you could have it all. What kind of a man lies to a woman's face and calls it love?"

"I really did—"

"Stop. I don't want to hear it. You disgust me. Truly. You hurt my best friend. That is inexcusable. And gross."

"I can make this right. I'll be free soon, and—"

"Leave her alone. Don't call her. Don't contact her in any way. You've done enough damage." Rachel glanced at her Liza outfit, the halter top digging into her sides. She spun around. "Now unzip me, please, and then get the hell out of here."

Bruce paused for a second and unzipped the top of her jumpsuit.

"Thank you. Now go."

He opened his mouth as if he was going to protest, but then changed his mind and left the store like a man defeated, his formerly elegant frame now saddled with shame.

What kind of man treats a woman like that?

She noticed that she had an audience.

"Performances at two and four o'clock, folks." She gestured to the shoppers staring at the remnants of the completed drama and slunk back into the dressing room to change into her old clothes.

She left the outfits on the dressing room bench.

First Joanie, then Lisa. It's a good thing Brennan doesn't have a boyfriend. I'd probably be useless if that relationship tanked, too.

She was glad, in a way, that she didn't have to deal with this sort of thing personally. She'd rather have a relationship with a freshly baked loaf of bread. Or a piece of lasagna. People hurt you. People leave. Food never does. She patted her left hip.

Yup, still there.

Lisa and Brennan came out of the back room with a bottle of water and a bunch of wadded tissues. Brennan had his arm around her, and Lisa was no hurry to leave his side.

Rachel cradled Lisa's cheek in her hand. "I'm sorry."

Lisa kissed Rachel's palm. "You should get the gray dress. I bet that looks lovely on you. You'll have to model it for me when we get home." She wiped her cheek.

"Staying over?"

"Yes, please."

"You could at least be an ugly crier," Brennan said. "Doesn't seem fair."

Lisa managed a laugh and took out her wallet. "Let's all buy something. It's on Bruce. I still have his credit card."

"We need cinnamon rolls," Rachel said. "Those are on me. No arguments. I bet your blood sugar is low."

They left the store, arm in arm—three sad, tired musketeers. The pastry would fortify their spirits for now. Time would take care of the rest. It had been a hell of an afternoon.

Chapter Eight

Lisa sat on the edge of Rachel's bed, holding a glass of wine, her pink yoga pants matching the pastel flowers on the bedspread. Even Lindsey the cat joined her therapy team, curling up next to Lisa and purring. Lisa had called in sick to work that day, but she hadn't been idle. Rachel came home at lunch to find her closet organized, her living room vacuumed, the *tchotchkes* rearranged, and the towels in the linen closet refolded. She had also baked cookies, and Lisa and Rachel spent the afternoon eating and watching courtroom reality shows. It was like they were back in college.

"I came up with a list of topics for our *Charmé* column." Lisa handed Rachel a yellow legal pad.

"My column."

"Of course. Given that I'm the face, though, I thought I might make myself useful by contributing some brain, too."

Lisa had completely invested herself in the charade. It was partly due to the breakup and trying to channel her energies. She wondered if Lisa was starting to believe this was her project.

But wasn't it? At least a bit?

It was Rachel who decided to hide behind Lisa's image. She made it a partnership the moment she talked Lisa into going along. It was her idea, her writing, her work, and Lisa taking partial credit made her uneasy.

Never mind. It's your own doing. It's for the best.

Later in the afternoon, Rachel got ready for the department party. Lisa was supervising like a seasoned foreman on a construction site. After makeup was applied under Lisa's strict tutelage, Rachel got dressed and sat on the edge of the bed for inspection. Lisa grasped her chin, tilting it this way and that. She had Rachel close her eyes, suck in her cheeks, and she checked Rachel's teeth for errant lipstick.

"Now go like this." Lisa crossed her eyes and made beaver teeth.

"I'm not doing that."

"Well, you look lovely, anyway." Lisa chuckled.

"It takes a village."

She plopped down next to Rachel on the bed. "Tell me about

this Ned guy. Brennan says he's gorgeous."

"Nathan. He's nice."

"And he likes you!" Lisa sounded like a junior high school cheerleader.

"Okay, take it down a notch. I guess so. I mean, he agreed to go to this God-awful gathering with me."

"No, I mean he likes-you-likes-you."

Maybe they were back in junior high.

"We're friends. New friends. I'm not thinking any further ahead than that."

"Why not?" Lisa raised her eyebrows.

"I've been down this road before."

"You mean Alex, don't you?" Lisa's voice modulated to its normal pitch. "He was a real shit, Rae. That doesn't mean Nathan is, too."

"I know. And you know it wasn't just Alex. I meant I cannot, will not, set any expectations. I will not wrap all my hopes on this one guy and have my life come crumbling apart when he doesn't love me back."

Lisa stared at her pink fuzzy slipper-clad feet. "Harsh."

"Oh, that's not what I meant. Bruce did have feelings for you, obviously. He was just a lying scumbag."

Lisa flopped backward on the bed. "I sure can pick 'em. He was my perfect type and old enough I thought he wouldn't play games."

"So it turned out he was the starting quarterback for the Chicago Adulterers. Maybe you should find a new type."

Lisa held Rachel's hand and stared at the ceiling, hypnotized by the rotation of the fan. Rachel lay next to her, her head leaning against Lisa's shoulder. They said nothing, letting the hum of the fan take the place of words. After a while, Lisa sat up, bringing Rachel with her, kissed her friend's hand and wiped the single tear that had streamed down the side of her own nose.

"Brennan's right," Rachel said. "I'm always amazed how you never ugly-cry. I mean, could you sort of *try* to be weepy and bloated, just once?"

"Too much work done. I think my original tear ducts are on the back of my head."

"Yeah, nice try, blondie."

"All right." Lisa exhaled. "Enough wallowing. Let's put on the finishing touches."

She went to the dresser to show Rachel the accessories she'd picked out. The gold pieces, like a pirate's booty, were lined up in front of Rachel's cherry wood jewelry box, organized from the head down—earrings, necklace, bracelet, ring. She handed Rachel the gold hoops, not the ear huggers, but bigger—for drama, as Joanie liked to say. A simple gold chain encircled her neck, and an open-weave cuff magically attached itself to her right wrist.

The ring, Rachel didn't recognize—a textured circle-shaped love knot with a wide, polished band. It was beautiful. She put it on her right ring finger and held her hand out to admire it.

"That's one of mine," Lisa said. "This way, a little bit of me can be with you tonight. And it will remind you how fabulous I think you are." She wrapped her arms around Rachel in a tight hug.

"Okay, okay." Rachel smoothed out her gray jersey dress as Lisa released her. "Let's not be all female about this."

She checked herself in the mirror. *Not too bad.* The Spanx were doing their job, although they were holding in the chub so efficiently Rachel was afraid that when she sat down, she might fart out of her ear. Her dark hair was hanging in ringlets, no frizz, and her makeup was subtle, but expertly applied. They compromised on the shoes. Lisa wanted her in high heels but settled on a black wedge. Rachel was confident she could hold this together for an evening, like a cranky Cinderella.

"Am I presentable?" she asked her friend, who was happier than Rachel had seen her in days.

"Oh, honey." Lisa clasped her hands to her chest. "You look like a *person.*" She held her arms out wide.

"I'm not hugging you again."

"Fiiiine." Lisa dropped her arms. "Is what's-his-name picking you up? What does he drive? A Vespa?" Her mouth half-curled into an impish grin.

Lisa couldn't let her go without a sting on her evening companion. She'd been doing it since college.

"Is he bringing his mother?"

"He's taking you out? Is it double coupon night?"

"Two tickets to the hackeysack regional championships? Score!"

"Maybe he'll serenade you on his air guitar."

"I can't read these directions to the party. Did he write them in Klingon?"

Rachel chose not to engage. "Yes, he is. In about," she glanced at the clock on her nightstand, "fifteen minutes."

"Good. Time to sit and relax. Want a glass of wine?"

"Better not. Need to stay sharp."

They went downstairs, Lisa in her slippers, Rachel navigating in her new shoes. Rachel sat at the kitchen table, and Lisa opened the refrigerator to get the bottle of chardonnay. Pouring herself a glass, she leaned against the counter. After a few sips, her shoulders relaxed. She drummed her fingers on the table, the clock ticking the seconds away.

"Don't worry," Lisa said. "Dating is like riding a bike. You never forget how."

"It's *not* a date. Christ. I'm taking a new friend to a work thing. End of story, please. I'll introduce him to my colleagues, and we'll see if he hates all the same people I do."

"You're protesting awfully hard. There's got to be something wrong with him. Bald guy with a ponytail? Triple cleft chin? Builds droids in his basement?"

"You're thinking of drones. And that's enough. He's a nice, normal guy who has a little trouble matching his socks."

Lisa gulped the last of the wine from her glass and placed it on the counter with a flourish. The doorbell rang and Rachel got up to answer it. Lisa trailed behind her, making a quiet *ooooh* sound. The wine had definitely kicked in. Rachel opened the door, revealing Nathan wearing a blue suit.

Before he could get a word out, she cut him off. "All right, let's go."

"Now, let's not be rude," Lisa said. "Invite him in for a minute. You must be Nathan." She extended her hand. "I'm Lisa."

He clasped her hand, placing his other hand on top of hers. "Nice to meet you. I've heard a lot about you, Lisa."

"Believe only the good stuff." She winked. "Oh, my. You have big hands. Did you ever play football?" She grasped his hand.

"Baseball. A little, in college. Strictly second string. I mostly fetched water."

Lisa regarded Rachel admiringly. "Smart, handsome, *and* athletic. Talk about a triple threat."

Rachel turned her back on Nathan and gave Lisa a look, widening her eyes and pursing her lips.

She spun around. "All righty, time to go." She guided Nathan to the door.

He held it open.

"Oh, shoot, I forgot my purse," Rachel said. "Hold on a minute."

Nathan closed the door and stepped back into the foyer. Lisa moved closer to him.

"What position did you play?" Rachel heard Lisa say, as she dashed up the stairs as fast as the Spanx and new shoes would allow.

Picking her purse up off the dresser, she could hear Lisa's lilting laugh float up to the hallway. *Boy, she just can't help herself.*

"...and from this little blog, this big magazine wants to give me a column. *And* an award. Can you believe it?"

The hairs on Rachel's neck bristled at the sound of Lisa's boast. As she descended the stairs, she saw Lisa had her hand on his arm and had taken her hair down. *Like riding a bicycle.* Rachel's cheeks got warm, and she couldn't get to the bottom of the stairs fast enough.

"Got it?" Nathan said.

She held it up. "Right here."

"Shall we be off?"

"Yes, please."

She took her coat from the rack, and Nathan opened the door and let her step out of the house first. She locked it behind her and dropped her keys in her purse.

"Are you ready for this?" she said.

"Bring it on."

Nathan opened the passenger side door of his car for her, and she slid into the seat, put the purse in her lap, and clicked the seatbelt. The car was warm and smelled faintly of coffee. She found the culprit—a travel mug nestled in the front cup holder. Nathan got into the driver's seat and fastened his seatbelt. He noticed her glancing at the mug.

"Yeah." He moved the mug to the backseat cup holder. "That's three days old. I keep forgetting to dump it out."

"No problem. Better than one of those pine air fresheners."

"Those give me a headache. I figure I don't smoke or eat in the car, so I can maintain that new car smell as long as possible."

Are we really talking about smells?

"Do you know where we're going?"

"GPS. Even did a trial run to make sure the directions were correct."

"Seriously?"

"That was a joke. Hmmm. The GPS voice thought it was funny."

"Male voice or female voice?"

"Female."

"She's an easy audience."

Nathan laughed and made a right turn when the light turned

green. The car had warmed up and Rachel loosened the collar of her coat.

"Lisa's a hoot," Nathan said. "I didn't know she lived with you."

"She doesn't. She's staying over for the weekend. She broke up with her gentleman friend. Turns out he was married."

"Twist!"

"She's being very *Lisa* right now. She likes to wrap herself in a cloak of fabulousness, but she is having a bumpy time of it. She'll be fine, though. She always is."

"She mentioned the blog thing. I wouldn't have pegged her for the writer type, but it sounds cool."

Rachel paused and bit her lip. She tasted blood. "Yes, we're quite proud of Lisa. She likes to talk about it. A lot. Sometimes we have a hard time getting her to stop."

"You have high-maintenance friends. I mean, they're great, but they do expend a lot of energy."

She inhaled. "Without them, I'd probably spend my free time sitting on my couch, eating cheese. It's worth it."

"That actually sounds kind of amazing."

On the road ahead, the white lines disappeared under the car one at a time—*zip, zip, zip.* The light at the upcoming intersection turned red and Nathan slowed the car to a stop. The moon was in front of them, a bright crescent.

"You want to get me up to speed on these co-workers of yours?" Nathan shut off the radio.

"I'll try not to scare you too much."

The light turned green, and he pressed the accelerator.

"Dr. Collier is the department chair. He's fine, but don't get him going on a story. He's in love with the sound of his own voice. You'll be stuck for an hour. And no one will help you out because we know better."

"No one's willing to take one for the team?"

"Hell, no. His wife, Mrs. Collier, is short, very thin, very pulled."

"Huh?"

Rachel pulled the sides of her face back and pursed her lips. "And it wasn't done well, P.S. We can keep the chitchat with her to a minimum, but we do have to pay our respects. Keep the topics of conversation to the décor and the food. She loves me despite that all I've ever said to her is, *Thank you for having me,* and *Nice armoire. Is it new?*"

"If I compliment the positive Feng Shui of the room?"

"She'll probably kiss you on the lips. And Dr. Van Hewson is probably the most boring person ever. His wife, however, is a delight. Her name is Betsy. Don't know how they're a couple."

"Opposites attract."

"He also comes from money. That helps. Oh, oh, oh, and Dr. Householder is always selling things for her kid's fundraisers. I made the mistake of buying wrapping paper one year, and now she won't leave me alone."

"Where does her kid go to school? Our Lady of Perpetual Shakedowns?"

"No doubt. Okay, I think those are the major players. Wait. There is Cindy McPherson. You met her, I think. She is Dr. Collier's administrative assistant. She will hug you and kick you in the knees at the same time. Avoid her."

"Noted."

They arrived at their destination, and Nathan parked on the street. Rachel opened her door and he dashed around the side of the car.

"I was going to do that for you," he said.

"I've got it. Do I lock, or do you lock?" She shut the door.

Nathan clicked a button on the key remote, and the car answered with a brief *beep*. He held her elbow as they trod the gravel between the cars, but she gently eased away as they got onto the paved road and she felt steadier on her feet. She glanced at him out of the corner of her eye. He had a small smile on his face as he watched the other guests in front of them.

The house was festive, even from the outside. The moonlight glimmered through the mature trees in the front yard, covering the roof with interesting shadows. In each window on the second floor and on either side of the front door were white flameless candles illuminating the drapes behind them and wrapping the front façade in a cool, flickering glow.

"Crud! I forgot the wine." Rachel slapped her forehead.

"Hold on." Nathan jogged back to the car.

Halfway there he slipped, but caught himself at the last minute, and gave her the thumbs up. He opened the rear driver's side door and held up a bottle of wine.

"Ta-da!" He trotted back to the house, then came up the steps in two bounds and presented her the bottle. "I got this just in case."

She peered at the label in the porchlight. "Wow, this is…red. I don't know anything about wine."

"Me neither. I went to the mid-priced section of the wine area and hunted for a nice label."

"Good man."

Nathan rang the doorbell. It chimed with a simple, elegant tune.

He leaned in and whispered in Rachel's ear, "It would have cool if the doorbell was *Turkey in the Straw*."

She stifled a giggle as the large oak door opened, revealing Mrs. Collier in a beige silk dress. Light jazz music was playing, and Rachel wondered if it was live or recorded.

"Rachel! I'm glad you could make it." Mrs. Collier's smile sparkled, reflecting the light from the crystal chandelier hanging in the entryway.

She stepped aside to allow her guests to enter.

"Thank you for having us, Mrs. Collier. Is that chandelier new? It's beautiful."

"Oh, you're a dear. Yes, it is. And look—you brought a friend." She waved to her husband. "Darling, Rachel brought a friend."

"Will wonders never cease?" Collier approached them and stuck out his hand. "William Collier. Department chair."

Nathan shook his hand, smiling graciously as Collier held his grip too firmly.

"Nathan Fletcher. Division ottoman."

Collier and his wife tilted their heads.

"It was a joke," Nathan said. "I, um…have wine."

"This is for you." Rachel handed the wine to Mrs. Collier.

"Thank you, dear. Will, look what they brought." She showed it to her husband, who examined the label.

"Ah, I've had this." Collier nodded. "Scents of tobacco, licorice, and grilled herbs, as well as cherry and floral notes. It's a fairly mild red, fewer tannins in favor of a tad more finesse."

"That's totally what I was going for," Nathan replied. "Herbs and finesse."

"Will, why don't you take their coats?" Mrs. Collier took the bottle from her husband while Nathan helped Rachel out of her coat before handing them to Dr. Collier.

"Thank you." Rachel hoped she didn't have cat treats in the pocket.

"Come in, come in. Almost everyone is here. We have food there," Mrs. Collier pointed at the buffet table, "and the bar is over there. Won't you excuse me? I think Audra needs something." She flitted off to a woman in a gold sweater dress with talon-length fingernails.

"Do you want to mingle or eat?" Nathan put his hands in his

pockets.

"I see these people every day. Let's go for the food."

The buffet table was expansive, covered in a burgundy tablecloth with gold embroidered leaves running up and down each edge. There were a few chafing dishes full of hot appetizers, and serving platters featuring cold ones.

Nathan and Rachel picked up plates from the end, as well as small forks and equally small napkins. There were placards in front of each dish, displaying the name in a ruffled script—*Escargot in Tomato Crowns, Curried Quail Eggs in Herbs, Grapes Wrapped in Goat Cheese,* and *Radish, Boursin, and Chive Tartines.* They took their time, examining the varied fare. Rachel would have been happy with Chex Mix or queso dip.

When in Rome...

"Some paté du pretentious, madame?" A raised eyebrow accompanied Nathan's faux French accent.

"I'd rather have the pompous fromage, monsieur." Rachel's accent was worse than Nathan's.

He put a tartlet on her plate.

They found an open spot in the corner of the living room and staked their claim. The room was tastefully decorated with glass lamps, gold accent knickknacks, and beige brocade draperies. If the items were less expensive it might have been tacky, but it cost just enough to put it over the line into posh. A lot of the items came from Mrs. Collier's family—department chairs made a good living, but not Italian-hand-made-coffee-table good.

Nathan stared at his plate. "I don't even know where to begin. It's the barbecue burger all over again."

"Start with the big things, then work your way down. That's what I'm doing." Rachel speared a mini-meatball with her tiny three-pronged fork.

He picked up the tartine and bit into it. He made an approving grunting noise and finished the rest of it in the second bite.

"Pretty good," he said.

"Did you try the figs with goat cheese?"

"I have something with goat cheese."

"There's a lot of goat cheese. I guess that's her thing this year." Rachel popped the fig into her mouth.

"My mom was big on marshmallows. Her favorite was sweet potato casserole with mini-marshmallows on top."

She grimaced. "She was probably big on mayo, too."

"How did you know?"

"Easy. You're not Jewish."

The group in the living room mingled and drank, and made something resembling merry—at least, as much as a group of academics at a forced gathering could muster.

Nathan nudged Rachel and pointed out two fellows near the fireplace. Dr. Grant taught sociology, and the other man with the paisley vest and beard that went halfway down his neck was an instructor from the biology department, who Rachel had never formally met.

"What do you think they're saying to each other?" Nathan said.

"Probably some sort of collegiate pissing contest."

"Greetings, Professor," he said, imitating the first man. "Do you mind if I give you a lecture on a subject I clearly believe myself to be the world's leading authority?" He changed his voice as the other man started speaking. "Why, no, Dr. Neckbeard. I could listen to your feckless meandering all night."

Rachel laughed as she popped a baby quiche into her mouth. With the timing of a seasoned restaurant wait staffer, Cindy appeared mid-chew and squeezed Rachel's elbow.

"Oh, good, you found the buffet table," Cindy said.

Rachel swallowed the quiche and forced a smile.

"Hi, I'm Cindy," she said to Nathan, batting her eyelashes. "Haven't we met before?"

"Cindy, this is Nathan Fletcher. Nathan, this is Cindy."

"Nice to see you again, Cindy."

"So this is your invisible boyfriend." Cindy leaned in conspiratorially. "Some people thought you didn't exist. But here you are."

Rachel's back stiffened, and she grabbed a flute of champagne from a passing waiter.

"Nope, nope. Not my boyfriend, not a date. We're just friends." She was speaking faster and louder than she'd planned.

She patted Nathan on the arm and gulped the champagne.

"That makes more sense." Cindy gazed at Nathan. "I mean, no offense, Rachel. I just couldn't see you two...you know...together." She smiled a wan, thin smile. "One can never have too many friends."

"I think Mrs. Collier is looking for you," Rachel said. "Isn't that her over there?" She pointed in the opposite direction. "Let's go get you a drink, *friend*."

She dragged Nathan toward the bar while Cindy went in search of her boss's wife.

They stopped in the hall across from the kitchen, and Rachel tossed the contents of her plate into the garbage. She placed the plate on the counter and pressed her index finger under her right eye to stifle the twitch.

"You were right," Nathan said. "She's a piece of work."

"I've been working with her for four years. I should be used to it, but it's hard to build up a tolerance."

"You should smack her. That'd do it."

"The college frowns on giving tenure to pugilists."

"They'd be too afraid to say no." He placed his plate on the counter next to hers and straightened his tie. "Are you ready to get back out there?"

She took a deep breath and finished the last of her drink in one sip. "Yes, but we need to avoid Householder. I saw her making the rounds with an order form. Cookie dough."

They rejoined the party, maneuvering from group to group, making brief small talk. Nathan was a master of the nod-and-pass, asking just enough questions about the other person to make them feel interesting, and then passing them on to someone else. It was like ballet.

Rachel was fascinated. He was able to move among these people, people who were stuffy and elitist, without a hint of awkwardness or self-consciousness. And she noticed she got a few envious glances from other women.

Of course. He's the Homecoming King, and I'm head of the decorating committee.

Nathan lightly touched her lower back. "You want another drink?"

She gasped, startled. She was still buzzed from her earlier inhaled champagne. "No, I don't think so. What time is it?"

He checked his watch. "Nine o'clock."

"Only?"

"You seem a bit worn out. Do you want to go?"

"Do you?"

"I can go anytime. I'll get our coats."

Rachel was relieved at how well the evening went. In the past, party couples greeted her with a hint of sympathy, the lonely spinster. But tonight, with Nathan, it was different. She was one of them, their social equal. She had been figured out.

It was nice not having another round of the professor's spouses patting her hand and saying helpful things like, *Don't worry, dear. At least you have your career.* Or the female professors extolling the challenging of balancing family and academic life, and wasn't Rachel lucky not to have to worry about that? Their sympathies had lessened, she guessed.

Too bad it wasn't real.

The cold air embraced them as they left the house. Rachel put her purse under her arm and put her hands in her pockets to retrieve her gloves. She stumbled and Nathan took her elbow in support.

"Thank you." She righted herself. "Did you have an okay time?"

"Better than expected. Although, you were right. That Van Hewson guy is unbelievably dull. I considered jamming a toothpick into my palm just to stay awake."

"I usually start humming whenever he tries to talk to me."

"Good call. I'll try that next time." He opened the door for her.

He started the car and fired up the heater. She shivered, but the front seat warmed rapidly. They drove in silence for a few minutes, the hum of the heater filling the space.

"Do you date much?" he said.

Rachel paused, trying to formulate an honest answer that wouldn't make her sound too sad.

"It's that obvious, huh? No, not much. Although, I did have a blind date recently. It...didn't go well. We didn't have much in common. Why do you ask?"

"No reason. Just curious."

He flipped on the radio and lowered the volume of the NPR announcer discussing politics with his co-host. In her head, Rachel began an autopsy of the evening, dissecting moments to detect any missteps. She also managed to squash any implication that they were on a date, and not scare him off.

"There was a lot of goat cheese at that party, eh?" For the life of her, this was the only thing she could think of to say. "I like goat cheese. Not as much as Gouda, but you know...cheese." *Stop talking about cheese.*

"I like a good Muenster. Tangy."

"Do you date a lot?" The question popped out before she could self-edit.

Nathan eased the car to a stop at a red light. He gripped and released the steering wheel twice.

"Not really," he replied. "I tend to be a serial monogamist. I prefer to see one woman at a time."

"Any serious relationships?" *Shit. Stop asking!*

"A few. I broke up with a woman a few months ago, before I moved. We were together for two years."

The light turned green, and he eased the car forward.

"Why'd you break up?" *Are you insane?*

Nathan exhaled audibly through his nose, and Rachel was afraid she'd hit a nerve.

"She was a nice woman. Had her own catering business." He ran his hand through his hair. "But there was something missing. We never connected on…a meaningful level, I guess." He scratched the back of his neck. "She was perfect on paper, you know? But she didn't make me laugh. And she didn't like to eat, which I thought was weird considering she was in the food business. She worked out like a fiend, too, which I found tedious, although my friends thought it was awesome. I guess for me, there was no *there*, there."

From the window, Rachel watched the cars passing or falling back, the lights on the street bending and glowing in the night air. This was intimate, more than she was used to dealing with. It made her feel itchy and weird. She shifted in her seat and cracked the window.

"You all right?" he said.

She closed the window. "Yes, I'm fine. Just wanted a breeze for a second."

He turned onto her street and slowed as they approached her house. The living room light was on, the flickering glow indicating Lisa was awake, watching TV. He pulled into the driveway and parked the car. After unlocking the doors, he got out and came around before Rachel could step out. He opened her door and offered his hand.

"Got you this time." He smiled.

"Yeah, yeah, you're a gentleman. Noted." She gave a sheepish smile.

She took his hand and exited the car. He shut the door behind her, waiting as she straightened her coat and rebuttoned the two top buttons. She got her keys out, jingling them as she located the one for the front door. They climbed the steps, side by side, and he held the storm door for her as she put the key in the lock.

"Why don't you come in for a second? I'll get that book I mentioned to you earlier."

Nathan followed her inside. Rachel hung her coat on the rack and placed her purse on the end of the wooden staircase railing. She entered the living room, where Lisa was curled up on the couch. Rachel went to the bookcase and scanned the shelves for the wanted book.

"What are you doing?" Lisa adjusted the blanket that covered her legs.

"I'm looking for a book to lend Nathan. I'm not finding it. Must be upstairs."

"He's here?" She perked up as she brushed the blanket off her legs.

"Yes, he's by the front door."

"Why didn't you invite him in?"

"I didn't think we were going to hang out."

"Maybe he wants to. Go ask!"

"Hold on." She went back to the foyer.

Nathan was holding his coat and studying a painting next to the door.

"Nice print. Monet?" he said.

"Manet."

"I get them confused."

"Everyone does. Listen, why don't you go have a seat in the living room? It's that way, and to the right. I have to run upstairs to get the book."

As he went into the living room, Rachel headed up the stairs. Her feet were sore—even the wedge heels had taken their toll. She went into her room to check her bookcase. If it wasn't downstairs, it had to be here.

Bingo. She removed it from the shelf and flipped through it to make sure there were no stray notes or pieces of paper in it. As she came down the stairs, she heard Nathan and Lisa laughing from the living room. She found them sitting on the couch, watching the end of *Some Like It Hot*. She stood in the doorway, motionless.

"Rachel, Rachel! It's your favorite movie." Lisa pointed to the screen, where Jack Lemmon and Tony Curtis were hiding from the mobster. "I wanted to be like Marilyn Monroe when I was in high school. You know, all *boo boop be do*." She put her hand on Nathan's arm.

"She was my first crush, honestly," he replied. "I mean, the shot of her from behind when she's walking down the train platform? Wow. Talk about perfection. She could fill out a dress." He regarded the women. "I'm sorry, does that sound sexist?"

"No, it's honest," Lisa said. "She'd probably never make it in Hollywood today, to be frank. They'd tell her to lose thirty pounds."

"That would be a shame," he said. "Ooh, ooh, wait for it. Best closing line of any movie, ever."

"Well, nobody's perfect," Lisa and Nathan said in unison, as she repositioned her hand on his shoulder.

"Here's the book." Rachel held it out. "I found it."

"I think I'll like this." He examined the front and back covers. "Thank you for lending it to me."

He looked Rachel in the eye, but she glanced away.

"You're welcome. Take your time with it. I don't use it in class or anything." She alternated between staring at his shoes and at Lisa.

Her cheeks were flushed, either from the wine, the movie, or the company.

Nathan checked his watch. "It's getting late. I'd better head out."

"Oh, it's early." Lisa shifted her feet onto the floor. "Why don't you stay and hang out?"

"Maybe next time," Nathan replied.

"I'll walk you to the door," Rachel said, as Lisa got up from the couch.

Rachel flashed her a look, and Lisa sat back down.

They paused at the door as Nathan put on his coat.

"I had a good time tonight," he said. "Thanks for bringing me. You're right. Those folks are an interesting bunch."

"They are a motley crew, yes. You were a big hit. Well done."

Nathan stepped closer, and she became aware of the scent of his coat. It was a blend of wool and soap—clean, sweet, and spicy. He leaned in, and a wave of panic swirled around her stomach.

Oh, God, what's he…he can't be…

He leaned in more, and at the last second, she turned her face as his lips brushed her cheek. As she took an awkward step back, he hung his head for a moment before meeting her gaze. She couldn't identify the expression on his face—disappointment? Relief?

"Well, good night," he said, quietly.

He squeezed her elbow, opened the door and stepped out into the night. Rachel returned his wave as he got into his car. He backed out of the driveway, the tail lights growing dim as he drove away.

What the hell just happened there? Nothing. Nothing happened. He was being polite. You behaved accordingly.

She kicked off her shoes with great relief and went back to the living room. She sat on the couch, pulling the blanket from Lisa and placing it over her legs.

"Is he gone?" Lisa took back half the blanket.

"Yes."

"Did he kiss you goodnight?"

Rachel paused. "Cheek."

"He's very nice."

Lisa adjusted her legs under her and rested her arm on the back of the couch. "Is he, you know, boyfriend material, do you think?"

Rachel leaned her head back on the cushion. "He's great. Just out of my league, I think."

"You think so?"

"Definitely. At the party, people were thinking, *What's he doing with her?*" She tucked her hair behind her ears. "I mean, nobody actually said it. Well, Cindy kind of said it, but they were all thinking it." She sighed. "He's a good guy. We clicked. Definitely will be great friends." She rubbed her eyes, trying not to flake the mascara.

"And he's not seeing anyone else?" Lisa picked at the cording on the edge of the upholstery.

"No, he's single." Rachel uncovered her legs and tucked the rest of the blanket under Lisa's feet. "I'm going to get ready for bed. I'm tired. You going to watch another movie?"

"Yes. Do you mind?"

"Not at all." She kissed Lisa on the forehead and got up.

"I'll be heading home tomorrow," Lisa said. "After breakfast. I said I'd stay the weekend, but I should get back to real life, I guess."

"Okay. I'd love it if you stayed, but whatever you'd like. I'll make waffles before you go."

Lindsey the cat met her at the foot of the stairs, and they went up together.

"Good night!" Lisa yelled from the living room.

Once in her room, Rachel removed her jewelry, piece by piece, and placed it back in the box. She put Lisa's ring off to the side and made a mental note to give it back to her in the morning. After a quick shower, she put on her pajamas and got into bed, where Lindsey had staked out her usual spot at the foot. Rachel patted her as she slept, feeling her silky fur and that little spot on the back of her ear where the black fur turned white. She snuggled under the covers, bringing the blanket to her chin and nestling into her pillow. She rolled onto her side and turned off the light on the bedside table.

Her eyelids were heavy, weighed with her usual anxiety, and as she drifted off, the faint sounds of Tony Curtis wooing the voluptuous Marilyn wafted through her memory, and the sound of Lindsey's nearby purr relaxed her as the last of the day fell away.

Chapter Nine

Rachel slept in later than usual and awoke around ten. The house was quiet. She went downstairs and found that the cat had been fed, the dishwasher had been run, and there was a note in Lisa's flowing handwriting taped to the refrigerator.

You owe me waffles.

She'd signed it *L*, as if to clarify it was she who'd written the note, and not a disappointed burglar who'd broken in during the night, found nothing of value to steal, but found himself feeling a bit peckish.

Lisa had also set up the coffee maker. As it brewed, Rachel retrieved her favorite *Far Side* mug and poured a splash of creamer in it. Was it lunchtime? Brunchtime? She sat at the kitchen table as the coffee brewed. The steam rose, bringing with it that familiar comforting smell whose promise of caffeine would soon endow her with the will to move around and do things.

Her cell phone rang. She picked it up from the table and checked the caller ID. It was Brennan. She tapped the accept button.

"Are you watching that house show?" Brennan said, breathlessly.

"No, and you shouldn't either. It makes you crazy."

"Another woman rejected a house because of the wallpaper."

"People have weird standards."

"Somebody should tell her about his new invention called paint!" He paused. "Helloooo?"

"Oh, sorry. I thought there was more."

"No, I'm done. So you're coming to my parents' house with me for Thanksgiving, right? Yes? Say you will. Say it. Say it."

Rachel sighed heavily, and the cell phone echoed static feedback. "I guess. You owe me."

"Thank you, thank you, thank you."

"I mean it, Bren. This is not like I'll-buy-you-a-coffee owing. We're talking a Godfather-level favor."

"I'm fine with that. I'll email you the deets."

"Deets?"

"It's just something I'm trying out."

"Stop trying. You're not twenty."

That settled things. Rachel was going to Brennan's family for Thanksgiving, in three weeks. After a few more of his *thank you's* and myriad promises to do an appropriate level of ass-kissing for the next six months or so, they ended the call. She wasn't sure she should leave town so close to the *Charmé* awards ceremony at the beginning of December, but she decided that since she didn't have to do anything other than show up, she might as well. Might be good to get away for a couple days.

Rachel's coffee was ready, and she poured the carafe and filled her mug too much, requiring a big slurp off the top before bringing it to the table. After putting the mug down, she plopped into a chair and stared at the ceiling. She had much to do and didn't feel like doing any of it. Rachel figured she should at least change out of her pajamas, although the flannel was comfortable and the ice cream cone pattern was festive. Maybe she'd wear them all day.

She changed her mind after five minutes. After placing the mug on the dresser in her bedroom, she opened the second drawer and selected a pair of black knit pants and her purple fleece V-neck shirt.

At least they're not technically pajamas.

After dressing, she decided she was indeed hungry, and headed back to the kitchen, where she made an English muffin with peanut butter. The phone rang and she answered with a mouthful of muffin.

"Hello?"

"Hank called me." Joanie's voice sounded hopeful.

"That's great. Is he coming home?"

"Yes, but he has conditions."

"What kind of conditions?"

"Could you just come over? My phone battery is dying. I'll make you lunch."

"Do you have food? Or are we going to snack on potpourri?"

"That happened *once*. Could you stop and get a few things? Something lunchy. And cereal for Jason. And milk."

"Got it. See you in a bit." Rachel hung up and glanced at the half a muffin sitting on her plate, alongside her half-empty coffee cup. Deciding she'd finish it in the car, she dug out plastic containers and a travel mug. She put on her shoes and jacket and went to the supermarket.

After picking up the groceries, she made her way to Joanie's house. She greeted Rachel at the door and took the bags from her hands.

"Thank you for doing that," Joanie said. "I don't want to go out right now, in case Hank calls."

"That's what cell phones are for."

Joanie shook her head. "And get into a shouting match in the dairy aisle? No thanks." She put the bags on the counter and the milk in the refrigerator.

"That bad?"

"Oh, God, Rachel, it was awful. He called me last night, and it was the most awkward conversation we've ever had."

"Did he yell?"

"Not at first." She gestured for Rachel to sit. "First he told me how disappointed he was, and how he couldn't believe I'd gone ahead and accepted the acting job when he asked me not to. Want a sandwich?"

"Sure. Can you multitask?"

"We'll see. Anyway, things got more heated, and he said how my continuing to work was an affront to our marriage, and how I was putting my ambitions before him and Jason."

"An affront? Wow."

Joanie handed Rachel a cheese sandwich. "Want me to grill it?"

"I'm good. Continue."

"He said—can you believe this—that I clearly didn't place a priority on our marriage anymore, and that he didn't know if he could live like that." She leaned against the counter and put her hand on her forehead. "It just floored me. I couldn't believe what I was hearing. I told him I wouldn't quit the show, that it was too late. Then he said...maybe it was too late for him, too." She moved her hand from her head to her heart.

Rachel was speechless. They always seemed like the perfect couple.

"Is he coming home?" she said, tentatively.

"He said he would, on one condition. He wants us to go to couples counseling. He said it was the only chance we had to salvage our relationship."

"How do you feel?"

"I don't want to go! We don't need it!" Joanie's voice was shrill. "He needs to come home. I'll finish the show, and then I won't do anymore. It will be fine."

"If Hank wants it—"

"Hank doesn't know what he's talking about!" Joanie stabbed the air with her index finger. "He just wants someone else to tell me how selfish I am." She turned away, placing her elbows on the counter.

"Maybe you *are* wrong. I mean, you should do whatever you

want, but you did go behind his back."

Joanie spun around, her eyes blazing. "What the hell do you know? You've never been married. All you know are your books and your papers and your precious Ph.D. You do everything you can to keep people at arm's length so you don't have to deal with anything!"

Joanie had never spoken to her that way before. She stared at Joanie with her mouth hanging open, trying to harness the swirl of words and feelings.

Joanie folded her arms and stared out the window at the orange and red leaves in her backyard, floating on the light breeze. She breathed in and out, her auburn hair catching the sun.

Rachel waited for Joanie's breath to slow.

"What're you going to do?" Rachel whispered.

"I will go to counseling. It's the only way to get him to come home."

"Call him now. I'll leave so you can be alone."

Joanie turned around and relaxed her brow. "You don't have to. Stay. Have lunch."

"No, I think I'd better go." Rachel slung her purse over her shoulder. "I'll talk to you later."

Joanie stopped her. "I'm horrible."

"I shouldn't have said anything. You're right. I don't know." Rachel shrugged.

"I shouldn't have yelled. I asked you for your help. I'm kind of at a loss here."

"It'll be all right." Rachel kissed her on the cheek and went to the front door, leaving Joanie in the kitchen.

Rachel drove home in silence, gripping the wheel. Joanie's words sat in the pit of her stomach, churning, like two dogs playing tug of war with a rope toy.

Joanie was right. Nathan sure as hell wouldn't want an overweight, frizzy-haired, nerdy college instructor with low self-esteem as a girlfriend. The world didn't work that way.

At least, it never had for her.

As she pulled into her driveway, she allowed herself, just for a second, to consider the possibility. And in that second, as much as she hemmed and hawed and protested vociferously to herself, it became clear that she did have feelings for him. Weird, gnawing little feelings trying to poke their heads up and peek around. Like Joanie said, she had been working to keep him at arm's length and she hadn't even considered the possibility that she might possibly...maybe...someday be able to fall in love. With Nathan.

Shit.

It was one thing to realize this, and another thing entirely to act on it. If she told him, she'd risk losing him, running and screaming as far away from her as possible. Or worse yet, she'd receive the dreaded, *Thanks, pal,* with the requisite light punch on the arm. The absolute worst thing would be the *I just want to be friends* speech, one she'd heard too many times. And she couldn't bear hearing it from him.

She needed time to mull this over. She entered the house, shaky, but not yet down for the count. She would sit on this, and maybe if she quieted the negative voices in her brain for a little bit, the universe would tell her what to do. In the meantime, she needed to eat. She was still hungry, and she decided that life-altering paradigm shifts required a snack. And definitely more coffee.

As she waited for it to brew, she caught her reflection in the microwave door. She turned this way and that, and then held up an imaginary microphone.

"I'd like to thank *Charmé* for this award. Writing the blog began as a fun exercise, but helped me realize that although times change, and fashion might evolve, people are, at their core, as they have always been…"

She stopped. She was embarrassed, despite being alone in her own kitchen.

Oh, please. This is ridiculous. No.

She shook her head, poured herself the coffee, and removed a bagel from the breadbox.

Chapter Ten

Autumn was marching on, the days getting shorter, the jewel-toned leaves making their last exodus from the trees. Nathan had become a full-fledged member of Rachel's crew, bringing new energy and points of view to their interactions. He even joined them occasionally for lunch in the faculty cafeteria, although he made it clear he came for the company, not the cuisine. Rachel kept her feelings to herself, but secretly she was thrilled to have the chance to get to know him better.

Joanie and Hank had started couple's therapy, although Joanie dragged her feet the whole way. Rachel didn't understand her reluctance, especially if this was going to help them get through this difficult time. Joanie's stubbornness and refusal to admit her portion of the blame was a hindrance.

One Sunday, they decided to meet for the Autumn Festival on the school campus. It was happening later in the year than usual, and expected attendance was lower, but Rachel was looking forward to it. Stands filled with local artists' work, book sales, and plentiful hot cider came pretty close to her vision of nirvana. The fair itself, located between the science building and the fieldhouse, boasted stands covered with colorful canvas awnings, serenaded by the sounds of an indie rock band playing in the distance.

It was chilly, but not overly so. Rachel wore a wool coat, a scarf, and a smart cloche hat she hoped wouldn't smash her hair too much. Fortified with a nice pair of gloves, she soldiered on to face the day.

She took Brennan's arm, and they played their old game of *What's Her Problem?* It was an excuse to comment on the bad behaviors of others, wrapped in a bit of snark, but it did offer them a reminder on what not to do. A short course on *Don't Be That Person.* They didn't have to wait long for their first contestant. A middle-aged woman at one of the first booths was arguing with the vendor over his selection of knit hats.

"Why don't you have this in yellow?" The woman shook the cap at the man behind the table. "People like yellow. I want to buy this hat, but you don't have it in yellow!"

"We have one in orange," the seller said.

"Orange is not yellow, is it? *Is it?*"

Brennan and Rachel walked past the booth and gave the vendor a sympathetic glance.

"What's *her* problem?" Rachel said.

"Yellow fever."

"That must be it." She laughed and snuggled into his shoulder.

Joanie caught up with them and took Brennan's other arm.

"What's *her* problem?" She gestured with her head, toward the yellow hat lady.

"Let's go there." Rachel pointed to the book booth featuring a *40% Off Everything!* sign.

"We will not be your enablers," Joanie said. "You have a real book-hoarding problem. We're going to go shop the jewelry. Brennan said he'd buy me something shiny."

"I thought you were going to buy *me* something shiny," Brennan replied.

"We've got shopping to do," Joanie said.

"Hey, Joanie, have you seen Nathan or Lisa?" Rachel said.

"Nathan was parking the car. I haven't seen Lisa," Joanie replied, over her shoulder. "See you in a bit!"

As they set off in search of the shiny things, Rachel turned back to the book booth. This store, one of the few indies left in the area, had a nice collection of antique books, which they wisely didn't bring today, given the changeable weather. But they had a good selection, from Ernest Hemingway to Dan Brown.

She had gone through a Hemingway phase in grad school, mostly because a young man she'd had a crush on fancied himself Ernest reincarnated. He tried his best to be a man's man, like his idol. But the moment she beat him in Scrabble, he fell to pieces like a child who'd lost his favorite toy. The appeal wore off after that.

Rachel was acquainted with the owner of the shop, so she went to say hello. He fit the description of a stereotypical bookstore owner to a T, with his round wire glasses, gray, receding hairline, and tweedy vests. But he was no shy, retiring bookworm. Karl Pinkus possessed razor-sharp wit and an encyclopedic knowledge of late nineteenth century British literature. He wrote for *The New Yorker* many years ago, and even taught literature at a boy's prep school in England for a time. And this was after escaping the Nazis as a boy.

Rachel shook his hand. "Mr. Pinkus, I'm surprised to see you here. I would have thought you'd rather send an employee to do this sort of thing."

"What, and miss a chance to see my favorite customer in such a lovely hat? Wait. I have something for you." He bent under the table, his elongated, striped scarf dangling close to the floor.

"I do wear a hat well, don't I?" She laughed.

"It is a skill." Pinkus handed her a hardcover book.

"Oh, my goodness. How thoughtful." She ran her finger over the front of the book, a copy of Dorothy Parker's *After Such Pleasures*, a collection of short stories.

"It's not a first edition, but it's a nice reprint," he said. "I thought you might enjoy reading it during the holiday break."

Rachel held the book to her chest. "Thank you. How much do I owe?"

"My gift to you, young lady. For a person who appreciates the greats."

"Now you'll never stay in business giving it away. I insist on paying you."

"I know better than to argue with you." He touched his chin. "Fifteen?"

"Twenty-five."

"Eighteen."

"Twenty-two. And that's my final offer, Mr. Pinkus."

"Done."

Rachel handed him the cash.

I must be the only Jew in history to have purposely haggled for a higher price.

"Come in next week," he said. "I have new stock coming in."

"I will. I'd better catch up with my friends. Thank you for this." She held up the bag.

He gave her a friendly wave as she left, and though she purported to be in a hurry, she found herself dawdling, browsing the stalls as she searched for Brennan and Joanie. There was a necklace that Lisa would love—a gold rope chain with a green glass pendant. *Where is she?*

Rachel wandered past a few more booths selling miniature sculptures, paintings, and even one that featured a sign saying they'd cornrow your hair for ten dollars. A familiar voice called from a stall ahead, and another familiar one laughed in response. She got closer, and in the caricaturist's booth were Lisa and Nathan sharing a stool and getting their picture drawn.

"Rachel, hi!" Lisa smiled and waved, her hair artfully arranged under her cream cashmere beret. "Look what we're doing."

Rachel's eyes widened as she spotted at the artist's pad, and she hoped it wasn't noticeable.

"Riding...skateboards, apparently. Something I've never ever seen either of you do."

Am I smiling sincerely? Is that the face I'm making now? I totally can't tell.

Lisa laughed again, and her cheeks flushed a perfect shade of pink. "We wanted a picture that showed us being active. It was either skateboards or hang gliding."

"I have trouble drawing bicycles," the artist said. "It's the spokes..."

"Okay, thank you," Rachel said.

"I voted for hang gliding," Nathan said.

Lisa smiled yet again and playfully swatted his shoulder.

"There we go, folks. All finished." The artist handed the drawing to Lisa.

"Oh, it's cute. Don't you think so, Nathan?" She showed him the picture.

"My head's awfully big," he replied.

"It's drawn to scale," Rachel retorted.

"I walked into that, didn't I?" He handed the artist a ten-dollar bill.

"I'm going to keep this," Lisa rolled the paper. "Do you mind?"

"Be my guest," he said. "I already have one at home where I'm riding an elephant."

Lisa held out the drawing. "Rae, can you fit this in your bag? It's too big for mine."

"You want me to hold on to that?"

"Would you mind? Thanks!" She clapped her hands. "Want to go check out the paintings now? You, too, Rachel."

"Why don't you go ahead," Nathan replied. "I want to see what Rachel bought."

"I'll see if I can find Joanie and Brennan. Maybe we can get something to eat?"

Nathan and Rachel agreed, and Lisa set off to poke through the nearby art booths.

"What did you get?" he said.

"A collection of short stories by Dorothy Parker. The owner of Pinkus's Books set it aside for me. She's one of my favorites. Her, and Douglas Adams. Odd combo." She removed the book out of the bag and handed it to him.

"This wasn't just plain terrible, this was fancy terrible. This

was terrible with raisins in it. Didn't she say that? Or something to that effect?"

"*We have normality. I repeat, we have normality. Anything you still can't cope with is therefore your own problem. Adams.*"

Nathan handed her the book. "You have good taste."

As she put the book back in her bag, Nathan put his arm over her shoulder. To her surprise, she didn't flinch.

"You want to skip the shopping and get food?" he said. "Something to tide us over until lunch?"

"Sure. Maybe there's a cupcake stand. Dessert first."

"Sounds good."

They neared the fieldhouse, weaving around the people around them. She was never totally at ease in a crowd, stifling a long-dormant childhood fear of being lost and unable to find her parents. Rachel adjusted her hat with her free hand, and then stuffed her fist into her pocket. She found an old tissue and wrapped it around her fingers.

"So that drawing is fun." She attempted to sound breezy. "She stayed with you when you parked the car?"

"Yeah. Lisa said she didn't mind the extra walk. We spotted the booth when we were searching for you. She thought it would be a *hoot.*"

"I see she's warming up to you. A little faster than I expected." The pocket tissue was now in shreds.

"She's fun. Nice girl."

They entered the fieldhouse, full of food vendors selling a selection of cuisine to appeal to tastes from common to exotic. Booths were lined up snugly, and there was a huge piece of industrial rubber padding on the floor to protect the basketball court, like a big car mat. Generators were running with a low hum, and cords were plugged into the outlets, as many as the fire codes would allow. The smell of vegetarian kabobs to BBQ, Cuban pork to meatball subs, rather than being cacophonic, was intoxicating, like being in a dozen grandmother's kitchens at one time.

Joanie and Brennan waved from the seating area.

Rachel spotted her prey. "Sue's Cupcakes. Best in town. I'm not much of a sweets person, but I will make an exception for these."

She ordered a chocolate with caramel frosting. Nathan got red velvet. They joined Joanie and Brennan in the seating area and brought their bounty. Nathan stared at his cupcake for a moment, overwhelmed by the dense layer of frosting. Rachel expertly peeled the paper off hers, broke it in half horizontally, and put the bottom half on top of the icing, creating a cupcake sandwich. She bit into it, savoring its rich, velvety perfection.

"You did that like a boss," he said.

He followed her lead, made the sandwich, and bit into it. His eyes rolled back into his head.

"You were right," he said. "These are *amazing*."

Joanie and Brennan pointed to their empty paper cupcake liners on the table and nodded.

Out of nowhere, Lisa plopped down in the chair next to Nathan. "Oh, my God. Sue's Cupcakes. They're the best!"

"Why don't you go get one?" Rachel said. "They're right over there."

"Wow, I don't think I could eat a whole one. Could I have a bite of yours?" Lisa gazed at Nathan, her blue eyes sparkling.

She guided the hand holding his cupcake to her mouth. She took a small bite, closing her eyes as she did so.

"Yum." She chewed delicately. "Thank you."

Lisa batted her eyelashes, and Rachel felt butterflies in her stomach. Lisa was being Lisa, of course, getting over a breakup, and trying to boost her self-esteem by flirting with a nice single guy. Besides, Nathan wasn't her regular type, being neither rich nor worldly.

Rachel did a cleansing breath as Lisa continued to *ooh* and *ahh* over the cupcake but didn't eat any more of it.

I have no claim to him. He's a free agent.

She reminded herself of this several times as Lisa delicately dipped her manicured finger into the frosting and licked it off coquettishly.

Chill.

"Oh, look, falafel." Rachel made a beeline for the appropriate cart, across the gym floor, then *zigged* and adjusted course to land in front of the sandwich stand.

Joanie caught up with Rachel as she was perusing the menu board.

"Rachel Bathsheba Simon. What the hell was that?"

"What? I was still hungry."

"No, I mean Miss Hot Pants over there. She's practically feeding him icing with her tongue."

"I think I'm going to get the turkey. On rye."

"You can eyeball the food all you want. You need to go protect what's yours and tell blondie to back off."

"What's to protect?" Rachel approached the counter and ordered her sandwich.

The kid in the apron blinked at her. "You want lettuce?"

"Okay."

"Tomato?"

"Sure."

"Cucumber?"

"I didn't know that was an option. Lay it on me."

"Onion?"

"Why don't you give me all of my options, and then I'll tell you what I want."

"That's it." The kid narrowed his eyes and crossed his arms, indicating Rachel had interrupted his train of thought.

"All right, then," Joanie said. "Sandwich ordered. Go forth." She swooshed him away, and the kid turned around and assembled Rachel's lunch. "You can order whatever you want. But remember, food won't make it better."

Rachel peered over the top of her glasses. "Wow, you're being super helpful right now."

She paid the kid for the sandwich, wrapped in crisp white paper and taped shut, like a culinary present.

"Speaking of which, how's therapy going?"

"It's going to be an extended process," Joanie said. "I wish the doctor could just go in and fix it. Bing, bang, happy marriage."

"She's not a mechanic, Joanie. It's a process."

"It's supposed to be give and take, a lot of listening, Hank saying, *I feel this*, or *I feel that*. But it's just a laundry list of what I'm doing wrong. This is not what I signed up for. And then I have to go into rehearsal after that? Hank has never talked about his feelings before. He keeps everything bottled up. It's one of the things I love about him."

She stopped and accepted a sample of chocolate gelato from a young lady holding a tray. She finished it in one bite and took a second despite the girl's mild protest.

"Hang in there. I'm sure it will get better." Rachel removed the tiny cup from her friend's hand and threw it in a nearby trash can.

"The thing is, Rachel," Joanie stared at her feet, "I'm not one hundred percent sure I want to hang in there. I love Hank, but this is getting much too hard." She started walking again.

Rachel jogged to catch up with her. "Of course you do. You and Hank are a family."

"Maybe it's not enough for me anymore. I know that makes me a bad person…"

"But…" Rachel stopped herself. Who was she to give advice? Her longest meaningful relationship was with her cell phone carrier.

They returned to their group. Lisa was sitting close to Nathan, with Brennan two chairs over, his arms and legs crossed.

"Well, if it isn't the fourth and fifth wheel," Brennan said. "Welcome back." He smiled too broadly.

Joanie and Rachel sat. No one else was eating, so she put her sandwich in her bag for later, hoping the chilly weather would keep it cold enough until she could get it home and in the refrigerator. They sat there, staring at each other.

"So Joanie?" Lisa said. "How are you and Hank doing?"

Brennan and Rachel gave her the *shut up* signal, making a back-and-forth gesture over their mouths.

"Yikes, okay," she said. "I'm sure you'll be fine."

"This is *fun*." Brennan stood. "Who's up for a drink?"

No one moved.

"There's a bar about a block from here. I'm buying."

"That decides it," Joanie said. "Mama needs a cocktail."

"Sounds like fun," Lisa said. "Nathan?"

"Sure, what the hell." He stood, putting on his black leather gloves. "Looks like we have a holdout." He pointed at Rachel, who remained seated.

"No, I'm going to go home, I think."

"Do you need a ride?" Brennan said.

"There's a bus stop close to here, and the route goes right by my house. I'll be fine." She paused, waiting for resistance.

Since the expected, Oh-no-you-simply-*must*-come protest from Joanie and Brennan were not forthcoming, she gave them each a hug.

"Don't worry," Brennan whispered in her ear. "I'll take notes and report back."

He ran to catch up with the others, and Rachel headed for the bus stop. She checked her bag to make sure she had enough money for the fare.

She was the only one waiting. Glancing at her watch, she noted it would only be a few minutes until the bus arrived. She swapped out her glasses for her prescription sunglasses and tucked the case back in her purse, then tapped her foot and checked her watch more times than necessary.

The bus approached, the number *425* displayed in the front window. There were empty seats in the back and she made her way down the aisle, trying not to bump anyone or trip over the bag that the older woman in the middle insisted on keeping in the aisle. Rachel landed in the second to last row, thankful to have space to herself. As the bus departed, she decided to eat her sandwich. Rachel wasn't hungry, but she needed something to do.

Carefully unwrapping the paper, she laid each end out and smoothed them as much as possible. She bit into a half, noting the tang of the mustard and the saltiness of the sliced turkey. She chewed slowly as she watched the buildings pass by through the windows. The increasing fullness in her stomach was comforting, and as she continued to eat, her brain calmed and her stomach relaxed. The sandwich was finished in short order, and Rachel wadded the paper into a ball and gripped it in her fist. It was now only a few blocks until her stop, so she pulled the cord.

Her walk home was filled with thoughts about Nathan. And Lisa. And Joanie. And *Charmé*. And...pancakes. She unlocked the front door of her house and entered. She relieved herself of her bags, then hung her coat on the rack, headed straight for the kitchen and searched the cabinets for pancake mix, but was disappointed to find none.

Plan B? As if on autopilot, she went to the freezer.
Waffles. That'll do.

Chapter Eleven

Thanksgiving break was nearly upon them, and Rachel's students were getting restless. It was her Friday afternoon class, and the ones that did manage to show up were annoyed that Rachel hadn't canceled class like some of the other instructors. It was a rough crowd.

She trudged on, but she didn't want to be there, either. She had too much on her mind to focus on the likes of Thomas Hardy, and she'd rather be reading a *People* magazine on her couch than discussing *Jude the Obscure*. Or writing her column for *Charmé*.

"What is one of the major themes in *Jude*?"

Three students raised their hands, three more than Rachel expected. She called on the one who appeared the least distracted, a brunette in the front row.

"Caitlyn? What do you think?"

"Love?" She brushed her cheek with her pink pencil-topper.

"Yes, but can we get even more specific?"

"Marriage?" Caitlyn pushed strands of hair away from her face.

"I agree," Rachel said. "I think the institution of marriage could be considered one of the book's major themes. Jude and Sue are married, unhappily, to other people, but are drawn together. Their relationship is full of tragedy, not just because of the family curse, but because society won't accept their relationship as legitimate."

"Like gay people trying to get married." Steve, a round-headed boy in the third row, held up his hand, a case of the late autumn sniffles making his voice nasal.

"Sure. Society, especially at the time the book was written, condemned the rejection of convention." Rachel flipped forward in her notes. "Sue and Jude were eventually drawn into an endless cycle of self-imposed oppression and could not break free." She blinked a few times. "In this book, Hardy attacked the institutions Britain held in the highest esteem—higher education, social class, and marriage. Hardy does not necessarily suggest that marriage is automatically a bad thing to be avoided at all costs. He just makes it clear that he believes people should be able to step away from a marriage if things do go sideways and get divorced. This was a big deal at the time. He also implies that love doesn't necessarily equal marriage, so a decent, understanding society should accept Jude and Sue's relationship because they truly love each other, no matter if they're married or not. It was hot stuff at the time."

"Did people get mad? Like, boycott the book and stuff?" Steve's congestion dampened his voice and he had to strain to get enough volume.

"They sure did. The backlash was bad enough to make Hardy never want to write another book." Her shoulders were tight, and she wanted to sit.

"Have you ever been married, Dr. Simon?" Caitlyn waved her fuzzy pencil in the air.

"Nope, never have." Rachel closed her notebook.

"That's sad, especially at your age. Why not?"

At my age. Harrumph.

"No one's asked yet, Caitlyn. Why, do you know somebody for me?" She forced a smile, and the class laughed. "Look, why don't we call it an afternoon? I'm sure you've got plans, and I have to go home and put on my sad spinster sweatpants. Have a good break, everyone."

The class collectively sighed in relief as they packed their backpacks and purses, shoving in books and putting their laptops away. Rachel sat at her table as they filed out, murmuring amongst themselves with excitement and the requisite nineteen-year-old energy which Rachel definitely did not possess. She returned their waves and gave a courtesy *You, too!* when a few of them wished her a Happy Thanksgiving.

When the last student excited, after verifying there was no over-the-break reading assignment, Rachel stared at the empty classroom. The tiered desks were neat and orderly, the rows straight, nothing left behind. This contrasted with the chaos in her head and the millions of thoughts jockeying for position.

She glanced at the poster hanging on the wall to her right.

"Have a nice holiday, Emily." She saluted Miss Dickenson, picked up her overstuffed bag, and headed for her office.

The halls were less crowded than usual, though they bristled with the excitement of a week off from school. Rachel made her way down the hallway, turned left, then right at the ceramic bust of Thoreau, rummaged around for the keys in her briefcase, and unlocked the door.

She noticed a quote from Keats that she'd pasted on the front had gone askew and put it back into place. After closing the door behind her, she sunk into the floral print couch she'd managed to fit in her shoebox-sized office and covered her eyes with her arm. She had paperwork to hand in before she left, not to mention the packing she hadn't even started yet. She had time—she didn't leave until Wednesday morning, and it was only Friday. Still, she didn't like to wait until the last minute. That was a recipe for being unprepared, and she wanted to make sure she had everything she needed to get through the visit with Brennan's family. She regretted agreeing to go.

My parents went on a cruise, and I have nothing else going on. That's why I'm going.

Not that she hadn't sat down to an enormous bowl of mashed potatoes and watched the Macy's Thanksgiving Day Parade alone before, but it didn't hold the same allure this year. Her stomach ached. She wished she had mashed potatoes right then and there.

There was a knock on the door, and Brennan poked his head in. "You decent?"

"I don't know about that, but I'm dressed."

He entered and looked down at her. "I have a few things for you."

He handed her a printout of their flight itinerary. She placed it on the arm of the couch without looking at it.

"And this is for our car rental, which I'm putting you in charge of." He handed her another sheet of paper. "And this is the gift card for the spa thing that I promised. And here is a list of the relatives and family associates who could be there, their major issues, and a list of conversation topics you should definitely stay away from. Also, I would avoid my Uncle Werner. He's pretty much a raging anti-Semite."

"Do you also have an extra key to the liquor cabinet?" she said.

"Key? You're assuming there's a lock on it? Please. That's for amateurs." He crossed his arms. "Um, are you all right?"

"I'm fiiine." She sighed heavily.

Brennan sat in her desk chair and swiveled around. "There's a chance Werner won't show up."

"Why do you invite him if he's so terrible?"

He shrugged. "Family." He raised an eyebrow. "Is there anything else? It's going to be a long plane ride."

"We're going to Ohio. It will take an hour."

"I was speaking metaphorically. What's the matter? You look weird."

Rachel covered her face with a throw pillow. "Mffn mrfms lrfmsm Nathan."

"Come again?" Brennan leaned in.

She removed the pillow from her face and slammed it on the couch. She leaned in to meet Brennan halfway.

"I...have..." She gestured emphatically, but vaguely, hoping Brennan would receive her intention telepathically.

"Is this some sort of game of emotionally stunted charades?"

"Well, for lack of a better word, certain..."

"You couldn't find a better word than *certain*?"

"Particular..."

"Oh, for the love of Judy, just spit it out!"

"Feelings. I'm trying to say, feelings.'"

"Feelings? For what?"

"You know, when you...and you just...but—"

"For Christ's sake, Annie Sullivan had an easier time working with Helen Keller."

"Nathan," Rachel shouted. "I think I'm in love with Nathan! Maybe." She grabbed the pillow again and put it over her mouth.

"*No!*" Brennan leaped out of his chair. "This is huge. I mean, maybe not for normal people who can express their feelings, but you know, for you this is *huge!*"

She brought the pillow down a few inches. "It's not that huge."

"This is *huge*." He paced the length of the office. "Have you told him? Does he know? Does anyone know? Am I the first?" He loomed over her, looking like the Jolly Gay Giant. "Huge!" He plopped down next to her on the couch.

"Okay, relax there, Sparky. We're not talking about trading secrets with North Korea. It's a crush."

"We both know it's more than that. Have you considered, you know, telling him?"

"I could barely tell *you.*"

"But you did."

"This doesn't go any further than you and me. I've been down this road before. I tell him, he freaks out, it ruins our friendship, and he runs away so fast I have to wave away the dust. Besides, I'm not even totally sure how I feel. Maybe it's indigestion."

"Or maybe—"

"No maybes. It's not happening. Can't do it." Her eyes watered.

Brennan brought her hand to his lips and kissed it. "It's all right, doll. We'll leave it be."

"I wish I hadn't said anything. Please don't tell anyone until I figure this out. Especially Joanie. She's such a yenta."

"I won't. I wish you would, but I won't push it."

"Thank you." She kissed his hand in return.

"I've got stuff to do and information to process. I'll call you

Tuesday night and quiz you on that list." Brennan opened the office door, then paused. "Oh, and you know Werner the bigot? His wife likes opera. Specifically, singing opera. What she lacks in talent she more than makes up for in volume. Be prepared for selections from *Götterdämmerung*."

Rachel threw a pillow, narrowly missing him as he slipped out and shut the door. The pillow fell to the floor with a sad thud.

She was in love or had heartburn. Either way, she needed some Tums. There was no way she was telling Nathan. Like in *Jude the Obscure*, no one would accept them as a couple. On television, fat guys had hot wives all the time. An ugly man with a beautiful woman? Most people wouldn't think twice. They'd assume he had a wonderful personality, or at least tons of money. But she had never seen the reverse. Handsome fellow with a chunky gal? She's his sister. Or a blind date gone bad.

Rachel picked up the pillow, reset it on the couch, and fixed the angle to make it just right. She closed the curtains, blocking out the late-morning sun. She re-shelved a couple books and put a stack of papers in an accordion folder. Gazing around at the posters of her favorite writers and artists—Whitman, Parker, Van Gogh, Hughes, Asimov, Adams—she calmed down. Life would proceed as usual. And, as Douglas Adams had advised, she had her towel, metaphorically speaking.

~ * ~

A few days later, she arrived at the airport earlier than she needed to, even given the holiday rush. She had no bags to check, and the lines to get through security were moving along at a reasonable pace. After she was properly screened, x-rayed, and determined to probably not be a terrorist, she bought a coffee and bagel, then stopped at a newsstand to pick up a few magazines. She refused the offer of a plastic bag and put the magazines in the outer pocket of her gray tweed carry-on.

She got to the gate, and since she already had her boarding pass, there was nothing else to do but wait. She was tired. She hadn't slept well and her brain was working overtime despite every measure to keep it mellow, like counting sheep, bunnies, and Colin Firth movies.

After thirty minutes of sipping, drumming, and waiting, she dug into her carry-on and broke off a piece of her bagel that she'd been saving for the flight. She nibbled it, aware of the growing knot in her stomach that always appeared before flying. She'd flown dozens of times, and before every flight, she became convinced that that was the time Peter Graves and Kareem Abdul-Jabbar would be piloting the plane and it would not end well.

Finally, Brennan showed up. She gave him a barely perceptible nod.

"You made it," she intoned, trying to work the residual poppy seed from her back tooth.

"I did. And I met a cute flight attendant at the Starbuck's stand." Brennan took her coffee and had a swig. "I need this. I was distracted and forgot to buy coffee. I mean, I'm not going to call him, but it's nice to know that I could." He held out the coffee cup.

"You keep it. I'm good."

"You get some carbs?"

"All set." She patted her bag.

He shrugged. "Most people take Valium to fly. Not pastry."

She grasped his coat lapel. "Did you bring any?"

"Valium or pastry?"

"Either."

Brennan shook his head, wistfully.

After a bumpy start to the flight—sky potholes, Brennan called them—the rest was uneventful. The man in front of her even fell asleep, his nasally ragged breath coming in a loud, *huh huh huh shooo*. She opened her laptop to work on her column for the magazine. Soon the captain announced their decent.

After getting the rental car, the drive to Brennan's parents' house was easy since the traffic was light. He was insistent on referring to her as his girlfriend, and she was not to correct him in any way or roll her eyes. He was determined to carry out this ruse, and no amount of sighing or sarcasm would sway him.

Twenty minutes later, the Cleveland Inquisition completed, they arrived at the Donaldson family estate. Brennan came from means, but this house was much more than she'd expected. A brown brick Tudor house that might qualify as a mansion greeted them, and as they drove around the front circular drive, it spanned her entire view. Manicured bushes ran the length of the façade, with rose bushes dotting the front path. Rachel pressed her nose against the passenger window to take it in, like a street urchin being brought to the palace of the Duke of Fancy.

Brennan parked the car and jumped out to pop the trunk. Rachel followed suit, never taking her eyes off the house.

"Just a modest pied-à-terre, right?" She unloaded her travel bag.

"It's not much, but it's home." He closed the trunk.

"I had no idea your family was like the Rockefellers of

Cleveland."

"I'm an adjunct at a small private college. How else do you think I maintain my fabulous lifestyle?"

Rachel laughed. He lived in a modest one-bedroom apartment in a four-floor walkup.

"Now don't be offended if my mom doesn't warm up to you right away. That's just how she is."

"I feel like I should go around to the servant's entrance."

Before Rachel could finish her thought, the grand double doors opened, revealing a brightly lit entrance and a tiny blonde woman in a pink cardigan, with a tight bun. Her pursed lips morphed into a big smile as she opened her arms wide to bring Brennan into the fold. As he entered the house, he put his bags down and enveloped the petite woman in a big hug.

"Hi, Mom!"

Rachel closed the doors behind them, expecting a booming sound, like the closing of a castle, but it latched quietly. She held her bag in one hand, purse slung over the other, like a chauffeur waiting for a tip. All around her were rich thick fabrics, crystal, and lots of polished wood. Her gaze caught on a marble statue in the middle of the foyer—an image of a woman in a toga, holding a string instrument. Rachel estimated it cost more than her car.

"You must be Rachel." Mrs. Donaldson stopped hugging her son. "I'm very happy to meet you. Brennan has told me so much about you." Her eyes were warm and brown, like her son's.

"Thank you for inviting me for the holiday."

"Let's get you settled," Mrs. Donaldson said.

As if by magic, a man in a black suit appeared and took their coats and collected the bags.

"Hoynes will bring your things upstairs and show you to your room. I'm sure you'll want a few minutes to freshen up."

"Um, room?"

"I'm not as old-fashioned as Brennan might think. I have no problem with two adults sharing a room. *My* mother, however, was another matter. Walter and I couldn't even be in the same wing until we were married." Mrs. Donaldson laughed, brightly. "We'll see you two in a few minutes. You're just in time for lunch." She glided out of the foyer and down the hall, leaving a faint trail of Chanel No. 5 in her wake.

Hoynes cleared his throat and proceeded up the grand staircase. Rachel punched Brennan on the arm.

"We're sharing a room?" she whispered, her lips barely

moving.

"It'll be fun," he said. "Like a sleepover."

"I'm drawing a mustache on you the moment you fall asleep."

"Relax. It's a suite. We won't even see each other," he whispered back.

They followed Hoynes through the expansive hallway, dotted with white doors and paintings of flowers and landscapes. He opened the double doors on the end, revealing their suite. The room was enormous, with plush, cream carpeting and embroidered draperies that pooled under the windows. The furniture was heavy, solid, enameled wood, with embroidered runners over the top of the large dressers. In the center, against the far wall, was a king-sized, incredibly deep canopy bed, its duvet edged in thick lace and covered in a large English rose print. It was like something out of a Jane Austin novel, and Rachel was speechless.

"If you need anything, Master Brennan, please let me know." Hoynes stood at attention.

"Thank you, Hoynes, as always."

Rachel whispered in Brennan's ear, "Are we supposed to tip him?"

He ignored her. "Let my mother know we'll be down shortly."

Hoynes nodded curtly and left the room, closing the doors behind him. Brennan grinned widely and made a running leap for the bed. He landed with barely a sound, momentarily disappearing into the bedding. He made a snow angel in the duvet, hands and feet moving over the rich fabric.

"Happy, are we?" Rachel positioned herself at the foot of the bed, arms akimbo.

"I always wanted to sleep in here when I was a kid." He sat up and regarded her sternly. "It's kind of a *big deal.*" He put air quotes around the last words in case Rachel didn't glean their importance.

He flopped back. She took in the room, getting her bearings. To her right was her own private bathroom. Peeking in, she spied marble countertops, his-and-her sinks, and what was either a tub or an Olympic-sized swimming pool. She clapped in glee.

"See? Not bad." He peered over her shoulder and pointed at a set of doors. "My room is right through there. We share the bathroom, though."

"The accommodations are nice, I'll give you that. You really grew up here?" She placed her bag on the bed and removed her toothbrush.

"Yup. Rode my skateboard up and down these halls every day

after school. Hoynes hated that, but he never ratted me out to my parents."

"He was your Mr. Carson."

"That would make me Lady Mary. Awesome." He laughed again.

Rachel went to the bathroom to brush her teeth, studying her face in the mirror as she swished the water in her mouth, squinted, and spit. She fluffed her curls with her fingers and took a tinted lip balm out of her travel bag. Dotting it on her lips, she wondered how Nathan's holiday was going.

Hopefully he won't be alone too much. I can't wait to tell him about my visit to Donaldson Abbey.

After she washed her hands, Rachel and Brennan went downstairs to have lunch. At her parents' house, they would have had cold cuts and bagels. She was not prepared for what she discovered upon entering the dining room.

The table was set with beautiful china, each plate had at least four spoons, and what she was pretty certain was a finger bowl. She hoped all those Colin Firth period dramas would come in handy. At least she knew not drink out of it.

She stood in the doorway, feeling like she had, indeed, been raised in a barn. Someone *ahem-ed* behind her, and her shoulders jumped like a frog on a hot plate. Moving swiftly to the side, a black-suited form glided past her. Noting that there was a lot of gliding done by people in this house, she stared at the man holding out the chair for her, as if neither of had them any other place to be and anything else to do.

"Rachel, sit." Brennan pointed to the chair.

Visions of Colin Firth gave way to the patient, wan smile of the man in the black suit. She slid into the chair next to Brennan and folded her hands in her lap.

"Relax. You're not having tea with the queen," Brennan said.

"Just the Countess of Lake Point." She gave him a sideways glance.

"Yes, but there's much less curtseying involved."

"Oh, I much prefer a formal salute." Mrs. Donaldson's smooth voice startled Rachel.

She was standing at the head of the table, one hand poised on the back of the chair. "Why don't you both come here to my end? It will be just the three of us."

Holy crap, how did she enter so quietly? My mother announces herself two rooms away.

The table seemed to go on for miles. Rachel stood behind the last chair on the end, waiting for Mrs. Donaldson to take the lead and sit.

She must have sensed Rachel's hesitation as she pointed to the seat next to her. "Sit, dear."

Rachel sat and once again folded her hands in her lap. The light was shining through the dining room windows, the morning clouds having given way to clear sky. Mrs. Donaldson was casual and elegant, like a WASPy elfin princess. Her pink turtleneck matched the subtle lacquer on her manicured hands. Rachel decided she wanted to be her when she grew up.

"I ordered bagels in honor of your visit," Mrs. Donaldson said. "I've never had one before. Such fun to try new things."

"Thank you. That was quite considerate," Rachel replied, very aware she was in a place where bagels were considered exotic cuisine.

"We'll keep it casual. Just sandwiches and soup."

"Rachel does love a good sandwich," Brennan said.

"That sounds lovely." She vowed to eat carefully so the aforementioned soup didn't wind up in its usual place on the front of her shirt.

"Brennan tells me you also teach at the college. How do you like it?"

"It's challenging but rewarding." Rachel attempted to match Mrs. Donaldson's perfect posture. "Tough to compete with movies and video games, but I try. I think a familiarity with classic literature is the base of a well-rounded education. I work hard to show my students the value of it."

"I agree," she replied. "I was a comparative literature major at Vassar, so I share your enthusiasm. I never finished my degree, as I left at the beginning of my junior year to marry Brennan's father."

"He whisked you off your feet?" Rachel said.

"Something like that." She took a vodka tonic from the tray that materialized in front of her. "I was knocked up."

"Mother!" He choked and spit out his iced tea.

"Oh, dear, please. Don't be shocked. You've seen photos of your sister as a newborn. She was nine pounds. Did she look like a preemie to you?" She winked at Rachel whose spine relaxed.

The gentleman serving their lunch appeared with a large tray filled with bread and plates of sliced meats, and different salads in glass bowls. One by one, he arranged them on the table, per Mrs. Donaldson's direction that they'd be *casual*. Their end of the table was covered with plates of carved turkey, ham, and roast beef, and bread that smelled fresh from the oven, along with the promised bagels. Rachel spotted the coleslaw, obviously made from scratch, and she wanted to kiss Mrs. Donaldson on both cheeks.

"This is amazing!" she said.

"Good, I'm glad you approve. I've been looking forward to it myself. If I had to face one more cucumber sandwich at the club I would cry."

I love this woman more by the minute.

"I'm glad Brennan has found a nice girl for himself. His father and I feared he'd never settle down."

Oh, yeah. I forgot about that.

"Rachel is a great gal," Brennan said. "It's like dating my best friend." He squeezed her on the knee.

"How long have you been a couple? You were a little vague on the phone."

"We met, of course, when I started at the college," Brennan said, his voice quickening. "But it didn't get romantic until...when would you say, hon?" He placed his hand on Rachel's arm.

"It's hard to say," Rachel replied. "It just sort of snuck up on us." She patted his hand twice and then smacked it.

"She was reluctant to get together, because of the age difference."

"Yes. That's the reason. My age."

Brennan clamped his hand on her bicep.

"There's nothing wrong with finding a woman with life experience, dear." Mrs. Donaldson gave Rachel a knowing look. "As long as they make you happy."

"Oh, she does, Mother. She does." Brennan kissed Rachel's hand. "She's a keeper."

"I'm a keeper!"

"Goodness, why don't we eat?" Mrs. Donaldson said. "Let's not let this food go to waste. Please pass the, uh, what do you call that, dear?" She pointed to the basket of bagels.

"Bialy," Rachel replied. "It's kind of like a bagel with no hole." She passed the basket.

"How unusual. I didn't know they came with and without." She placed the bread on her plate. "Brennan tells me you're a writer, too?"

"Sort, of. Well, yes, actually. I started a blog on my own, just for fun, but a magazine spotted it and offered me a column. It's been surreal."

"But she lets her friend take credit for it, because she doesn't think they'd want her as is," Brennan said.

"That's ridiculous. You're a lovely woman," Mrs. Donaldson replied.

"Lisa is lovelier," Rachel muttered.

"What was that?"

"Nothing. Sorry. It's complex."

Mrs. Donaldson sipped her drink. "What publication?"

"*Charmé*. Lots of young girls wearing very expensive clothes. But they're trying to *smarten* up their writing."

"That's where Rachel comes in," Brennan said.

"Indeed. Glad you're in there somewhere." Mrs. Donaldson peered around the table. "Hmmm, I don't see the butter. Darling, could you go to the kitchen and get it for me?"

"Ask Gerald to bring it in." Brennan piled roast beef and coleslaw on his plate.

Rachel leaned in. "Put the coleslaw *on* your sandwich. Trust me."

"Oh, God, you're a genius."

"He's busy with the Thanksgiving preparations, dear," Mrs. Donaldson said. "Why don't you go get it? Please?" She raised her eyebrows and gave him a closed mouth smile that indicated this was more of a command than a request.

His hand stopped mid-air, and he placed the serving fork back on the tray. He picked up his napkin from his lap, dabbed his mouth, and placed it next to his plate. His gaze darted from Rachel to his mother, and back to Rachel, giving her a pleading glance. She sipped her water. He kept her gaze as long as he could until he was out of the room.

She held the water glass to her lips and took a sip, then another, finishing the glass in hopes of avoiding the conversation until he returned.

"Brennan is a lovely young man, don't you think?"

Rachel placed the glass on the table and smoothed the tablecloth. "I do, indeed. He's very special."

"He obviously thinks the world of you, Rachel."

"Thank you. He is important to me as well." Rachel spread stone ground mustard on a piece of rye.

"You two are quite close."

"Absolutely."

"Then obviously you know Brennan is a homosexual."

Rachel forgot how to chew. *It's a trap! It's a trap!*

Her sandwich lodged in the pocket of her cheek and refused to budge. Feeling like a chipmunk storing nuts for winter, she chewed as best as she could, thoroughly, trying to buy some time.

"Yes," she replied. "You know?"

"Of course I know. We all know. He just doesn't know we know. Or maybe he does. He must, on some level."

"I don't think he does. He's never said anything to you?"

"He didn't have to. Despite this," she waved her delicate hand around the room, "we're a close family. We noticed the signs."

"You've never talked about it?" Rachel was floored.

In her family, they examined and argued over every feeling, every idea, down to the barest bit of minutiae. But the Donaldsons apparently chose the *suppress and ignore* option of family management.

"We thought it best he come to us." She picked up her glass and clinked the ice back and forth. "He never did."

"He loves you."

"I know. I'm sure that's why he brought you, to spare us having to deal with what he thinks we can't accept." She leaned in. "We can."

"Would you like me to leave?" Rachel was trapped, caught in the ruse.

"Of course not. You're his friend. And a good one, at that. Anyone who obviously loves him as you do is welcome here." She patted Rachel's hand, much as Brennan had done. "We'll keep this our secret, yes? He's clearly not ready to talk to us."

Brennan returned with the butter. He placed the butter dish next to his mother and sat, crossing his legs and sucking in his cheeks. "What are you two gals chatting about?"

"Your mother was telling me how lovely the garden is in the spring. Perfect for a wedding." Rachel pinched his knee under the table.

Brennan reached for more food. He plopped the meat onto his plate and cut it into pieces. He scooped it up and shoved it into his mouth in one bite.

Chuckling, she picked up her sandwich, and in her peripheral vision, Mrs. Donaldson winked. She wondered how Brennan could misjudge his family so much. Or perhaps he wasn't ready to be himself with them, to change what he viewed as the normal dynamic. But it would be a change for the better.

After lunch, Brennan and Rachel departed for the spa. Rachel was expecting a shop in a strip mall, but the facility itself, like Brennan's house, was a surprise. It was a large freestanding structure with marble Corinthian columns on either side of the front entrance. Even in November the landscaping was pristine, with fountains and bushes carved into twisting manicured designs. Rachel half-expected a drawbridge to be lowered and flying cupids to zing arrows at them, greeting their arrival. She had to settle for valet parking.

Brennan pulled open the wrought-iron handles and held the door for Rachel. The light bamboo flooring shone under the diffused, recessed overhead lights. Pots of delicate orchids lined the reception desk, staffed by neatly coiffed young women in pale peach coats. It smelled faintly of lavender, vanilla, and money. Rachel was thankful Brennan was paying, as she wasn't sure she could even afford to sit in the lobby.

"Appointments booked under Donaldson," Brennan said to the pretty brunette at the computer.

"Ah, yes. Donaldson. Party of two. We've been expecting you. Do you know your way into the spa area?" She handed them rolled towels and plush peach robes, the same color as her coat.

"Yes, we do," Brennan replied. "Thank you."

"You've been here before?" Rachel ran her hand over her velvety robe.

"Not my first time at the rodeo, kid."

"I'll let Renee and Pearl know you're here." The brunette picked up a white and crystal French-style phone and pushed a button.

Rachel followed Brennan past the reception desk, took a left, then a right down the pastel-painted hall. They passed through the frosted glass doors and were surrounded by whispers, the clinking of glasses, and the gentle *drip-drip-drip* of moving water. She relaxed for the first time in a long time, and her eyelids became heavy.

If heaven exists, it will look and smell like this. And have mimosas.

Brennan and Rachel entered their individual dressing rooms. Folded on the table was a terry cloth turban that matched the robe, and a pair of slippers in a sealed plastic bag. Rachel turned up her nose for a second, imagining rented bowling shoes, but upon further inspection saw that these were brand-new. After opening the wooden locker door, she undressed and hung her clothes inside. *Socks on or off?* Throwing caution to the wind, she tossed them into the locker and removed her jewelry for good measure. She put on the plush robe, snapped up the robe ends like a wrap dress, and tied the belt around her waist.

Nice touch with the snaps. No chance of wardrobe malfunctions in this spa.

Rachel gathered her hair into a loose topknot and put on the turban, tucking in any stray locks. She held the locker key and placed the elastic keychain around her wrist. She was armed and ready for pampering.

Rachel and Brennan exited their rooms at the same time. They admired their matching spa ensembles, although he was not wearing the turban and had tied the belt like a cummerbund.

"Where's your little hat?" she said.

"I thought it would be a bit too much. But otherwise, I make this work." He laughed. "Although, I would have preferred some marabou trim on the footwear."

"Because that wouldn't be too much. I'm confused about your standards." She caught a glimpse of the two of them in an ornate gold-framed mirror on the wall. "Oh, yeah. We're a convincing couple." She picked up a glass of lemon water from the stand.

They followed a serene white-coated lady to a pair of overstuffed recliners, surrounded by lotions, potions, mini-whirlpools, and artificially-lit candles, with the ever-calming plinky-plunky music oozing from the overhead speakers. Rachel sat in the chair and put her feet up, letting out an almost-silent *aaah*.

She let the technician massage her shoulders, worried that it would be a two-person job and she'd have to call for backup. She placed her feet in the whirlpool, allowing the warm water to permeate her joints. But when the technician went after her feet with practiced hands, she meant business. At once painful and enjoyable, the therapist worked knots out of her soles, kneading the muscle and digging a knuckle into a pressure point that made Rachel's legs twitch, then relax.

Once her feet were properly serviced, the aesthetician took over. Rachel and Brennan both got facials. Him, an avocado-based mask that made Rachel hungry. And she got a thick, creamy concoction that the aesthetician said would be stress relieving and anti-aging and smelled like mint. She spread the cream on Rachel's face, like a pastry chef icing a cake. Then, like the proverbial cherry on the sundae, she placed a cucumber slice on each eye, which Rachel had only seen in television sitcoms.

"Reduces puffiness," the facialist said, as if reading her thoughts.

"Do I get the rest of the salad later?" Rachel said. "Or are you saving the lettuce for my neck?"

The facialist gave a polite laugh and adjusted Rachel's turban. "Just relax now. Let the ingredients do their magic."

"Magic? So I'll leave here looking like Heidi Klum?"

"She's a facialist, Rachel," Brennan intoned. "Not Professor Dumbledore."

She ignored him and closed her eyes under the cucumbers. This was a new experience—the pampering, the indulgence, the total lack of anything that had to be done *right now*. She let her lower back unclench and touch the curve of the reclining chair as she drifted off with the music. She did her best to let images of school, her mother, of everything, pass by like boats on a river, until nothing was left but the sound of the harp…and Nathan.

Rachel gave a start and adjusted a cucumber. She focused on his face, his green eyes that crinkled at the corners. For the first time, she lingered, wrapping her thoughts into and through the crevasses of her mind, taking just enough hold and giving off a glimmer of hope.

I hope this isn't the lavender talking.

She let out a sigh with such force it emptied her lungs.

Her reverie was interrupted by the sound of Brennan's voice.

"You need to come clean."

Rachel pointed to her face. "I thought they were going to come in and remove this stuff?" She took the cucumbers off her eyes and placed them on the table next to her.

"I mean, about the blog. And the column. And the awards. Lisa's starting to believe she's the one responsible for your work."

"And they will cancel it immediately. You didn't see this place, Bren. Everyone there was thin and perfect and confident. It's the whole reason I used Lisa's picture in the first place."

"Maybe they will. But isn't that better than letting someone else take credit for your work? Honestly, kiddo. It's the way to go." He rested his hands on his chest. "And yes, I'm seeing the irony here, but let's call it a do-as-I-say thing."

"I can't—"

"You use that word a lot. You can. Lisa, who, don't get me wrong, I love dearly, is slowly taking this away from you. Put your foot down. If you don't, what else is she going to take?" His robe pocket buzzed.

"You're not supposed to have that in here," she whispered.

"What can I say?" He took out his phone. "I am an iAddict." His eyes widened as he saw the caller ID. "It's Lisa." He accepted the call and held the phone an inch from his face. "Hello, gorgeous. Why are you bothering me?" He handed the phone to Rachel. "She wants to talk to you."

"I can't talk. I have goop on my face."

"I'll put it on speaker."

"What's going on?" Lisa said.

"We are in the middle of having facials," Rachel replied.

"Both of you? You let a stranger touch your face?"

"What do you need, Lisa?" Rachel was irritated by the interruption.

"Can the whole place hear me?"

"No, we're in a private room," Brennan said.

"Fancy!" Lisa said.

Rachel tensed, from head to toe. "What's up, hon?"

"Oh, yeah. I have great news for you, and I wanted to share right away." Her voice sounded light and youthful.

"Okay, but make it quick. I think the woman is going to come back in here in a few minutes to add another layer of spackle."

"First of all, I've spent lot of time thinking about things since you left, and I'm totally over Bruce."

"I've been gone a day but continue."

"I thought about the things you said to me, and you were right, as usual. I need to stop chasing the glamour men, the unattainable men—"

"The married men," Brennan said.

"That was an error, yes," Lisa replied. "But remember, I didn't know he was married—"

"All good so far," Rachel said. "Is there more?" She glanced at Brennan, who had taken a bite from each cucumber slice and repositioned them on his face.

"Can't you wait for lunch?" Rachel whispered.

"Lean over. Your face looks like dip."

She waved him off. "Lisa, what were you saying?"

"That I heeded your advice. I found a great guy, and we're officially dating."

"That's great. I'm happy for you. I'm sure the duchess and Brennan will enjoy putting him through the ringer."

"That's the great thing," Lisa replied. "They don't have to. It's Nathan!"

The music on the overhead speakers sounded warped, as if a rip had occurred in the fabric of time and space right there in the day spa. Rachel's mouth went dry.

"I figured you'd be cool with us seeing each other," Lisa said. "I mean, you did say you're just friends, right? You said it over and over, and I figured, what could be better? Two of your best friends getting together. It's been almost two weeks now, but I wanted to wait before I told you, to make sure."

Rachel stared at Brennan, who had frozen in place with the last half cucumber slice hanging out of his mouth.

"Rae? You there?"

He grabbed the phone from Rachel's hand before she dropped it. "She's here. The technician came in to take the mask off. Listen, that's great news. We'll talk more when we get home. Bye." He hit the end button with such force it almost slipped out of his hand.

He placed it on the table furthest from Rachel and cocked his head, offering the silent sympathy people have when they don't know what to say.

She focused on the painting of posies on the wall, blinking and trying to bring it into focus. She couldn't breathe. In a heartbeat, the thing that she'd allowed herself to hope for had been ripped away. And she had brought it all on herself.

"Rachel, I—"

"All righty. Let's get those hands done." A new technician burst in, carrying a crockpot full of wax.

"I don't think we're—"

"Oh, you want this treatment," the woman said. "Makes the hands baby soft!"

She was like a tornado in a peach smock, a paraffin-pusher of the highest order, and she wasn't taking *no* or the proffer of immanent heartbreak as a deterrent. She placed a pot on each table and positioned herself on a wheeled stool between Rachel and Brennan. She dipped each of Brennan's hands in his pot of wax and held them up to let the excess drip off. After wheeling over to Rachel, she repeated the process. It happened so fast Rachel couldn't protest.

"We'll let that harden for a few minutes, and I'll be back to peel it off."

"What about our masks?" Brennan said.

"I'm just hands, sweetie. I'll tell Mirabel you're ready to have that cleaned off." She blew out of the room as briskly as she had appeared.

Brennan and Rachel remained immobile, like statues with their hands up, ready to fight imaginary opponents.

"I can't believe this," Rachel said.

"We'll get the goop off us and go back to the house."

"No, not this." She waved her wax-enveloped hands. *"This."*

"Everything will be—"

"Don't say everything will be okay. It's not okay." She took a towel from the table and wiped her face. "But I should have known." She threw the towel on the table. "I waited too long, too afraid to say anything." She clawed at the wax on her hands, trying to peel it off, but it mushed around her hands like thin Silly Putty. "What the hell!"

"I think you have to wait until it's dry."

Rachel slunk into her chair. "What. The. Hell." She slouched so low she was in danger of sliding off.

She shimmied back up without using her hands. Brennan got up to help her, offering his arms as a counterbalance. She linked her arm through his and continued to shimmy. It didn't help, and she sunk back into the base of the recliner. Her heart thumped and her breath came in heaving waves. After an eternity, the wax solidified and she peeled it from her hands. Then she helped Brennan with his, piling the wax onto the middle table, where it sat like gobs of sad melted candles.

Rachel's eyes welled, the tears burning as she wiped them, getting bits of leftover wax on her lashes. She stared at her feet, her robe hanging and her terry turban askew. She was lost, deflated, and sticky.

He held her face in his hands. "You'll be all right."

"But...but...I..." She took a halting breath. "Who could have seen this coming?"

He hugged her. "We all did, Rach," he whispered. "We all did."

Chapter Twelve

They drove back to the house in silence. Rachel leaned her head against the headrest, the late autumn foliage rushing by in a blur. She was lulled into a waking coma, hovering in the place between consciousness and daydream, and wanted to occupy neither. She closed her eyes to block out the trees and the rain and the passing cars. She breathed deeply, inhaling the remnants of the spa treatment—lavender, peach, rose and something that smelled like cake frosting—which intermingled with the pine car freshener that hung on the door handle of the rental. It was an odd combination, as if the cast of *Steel Magnolias* decided to have a picnic in the forest.

Rachel was glad to be out of the spa. She was sure the final technician had been surprised to find her covered in tears and lumps of wax, holding on to Brennan for dear life. She followed him out of there glassy-eyed, but aware of the worried stares of the incoming clients.

"She got the Brazilian," he told one woman, who was regarding them with pursed lips. "First time. She's a little out of sorts."

Rachel hadn't spoken a word since she scraped the paraffin off her hands. Not because of the staff at the spa, or the onlookers, or even Brennan. It was because going beyond her own self-imposed façade was too much to bear. She had lowered her wall, just a bit and just for a moment, and it had caved in on her.

She hadn't even had the chance to admire the view before it crumbled like one of those dry, overly sweet granola bars the next-door neighbor always gave out at Halloween in her childhood memories. Her tongue felt two sizes too big for her mouth, and she didn't want to open her eyes, even after they arrived back at the house and Brennan shut off the ignition.

"Are you ready to go in?" He rubbed her arm.

She opened her eyes slowly and gripped the door handle. "I'm fine. I had a moment back there, but everything is fine."

"I'll get the door." He exited the driver's side.

His footfalls crunched on the gravel, and the brisk rush of air filled her lungs as he opened her door. The cold air was crisp and invigorating, and she breathed in through her nose, letting the chill spread over her face and throat. Brennan took her hand, his leather gloves encircling her wool mittens like a father escorting his tired daughter back home after a busy day.

"You want to eat?" he said.

"No." She shook her head and stopped walking. "That has never happened to me before. Even at my uncle's funeral, I went back for seconds."

"This is different. It's not like there was a death."

"Wasn't there?" She laughed, darkly.

They trudged on, the driveway looking like an airport runway.

"Let's go in the back," Brennan said. "Avoid the crowd."

"Seriously, I'll be fine. There's no need to—"

He pulled her hand like a puppy on a leash. They headed around the house, and the grass squeaked with moisture as their boots hit the ground. They jogged past the landscaped topiaries and the few leaves the gardener missed on his last visit for the season.

The house loomed above them, the lights from inside dancing on the cold ground. They entered a storage area filled with appliances, a few lamps, bolts of velvet, carved wooden chairs, ceramic vases, at least twelve different silk wreaths in varying colors, and on the other side, organized shelves full of canned goods.

"C'mon," he said. "We'll go in through the laundry area and take the back stairs to our room."

He poked his head in, checking both ways before entering. Rachel followed him and stopped to wipe her boots on the thick mat. After going up the staircase, they padded down the hall to their room. Brennan shut the door behind them, removed her mittens and gloves, and laid them on the overstuffed chair by the door.

After leading her to the bed, he sat her down and pulled off her boots, and took them into the bathroom. He brought back a warm, damp washcloth and dabbed at her forehead and her cheeks, removing any last trace of her facial. She accepted the cloth and held the length of it over her face.

Brennan sat next to her, one arm over her shoulder, the other on her leg as she breathed in and out through the washcloth.

"You want to take a bath?" he said.

"That would be nice."

Brennan went to the bathroom and turned on the faucets. Through the partially open door, he went back and forth from the linen closet, laying out large, fluffy towels and a pink terrycloth robe with pockets so deep they could carry a toddler. Music spilled forth from the bathroom, strains of Vivaldi dancing and looping through the room. He handed her the stereo remote and kissed her hand.

"It's all yours, kid. Take whatever time you need. You'll feel better after a good soak." He paused. "Hey, you want to stay up here? I'll make an excuse to mother. The others will be drinking. They won't notice."

"No, I'll come down. I don't want your mother to think I'm ill. I'll have a nice bath, and I'll feel better."

"I'll be downstairs when you're ready." He squeezed her fingers. "Trust me. It'll be fine. We're a bit past cocktail hour. It'll be very mellow down there."

After Brennan left, Rachel prepared her bath. She ran her fingers through her hair and went into the bathroom, her toes sinking into the deep pile of the bath rug. She found that Brennan had left a piece of chocolate for her on the counter. She popped the sweet into her mouth, savoring it and letting it coat her tongue. She turned off the faucet of the extra-large oval tub and ran her hand over the selection of scented oil perched on the edge. After choosing the vanilla lavender, she took off her clothes and eased into the tub, allowing the warm fragrant water to surround her.

"Never forget self-care," her old therapist had said. *"You can do better than a donut."*

Rachel leaned her head against the green inflated pillow, and hot, fat tears welled in the corners of her eyes. She shut them tight, her lids squeezing the droplets onto her face, which joined the scented water bit by bit. For the first time, she didn't fight it. She let the tears come.

She wasn't sure how much time had passed, but the water had become tepid, and her fingers pruny. She unplugged the tub and removed a fluffy towel from the pile. She caught a glimpse of herself in the mirror and was startled. Her shoulders were rounded, and her eyes more sunken and shadowed than before. Her skin, however, was none the worse for wear, as the facialist at the spa had thoroughly cleaned her pores and buffed her cells anew.

At least I have a low-grade glow on the outside.

She went into the bedroom and removed some clothes from her suitcase. After changing quickly, she removed the elastic from her hair and gave it a spritz of detangling spray and a fluff, then put a coat of mascara on her lashes. Blinking in the mirror, she felt removed, as if she recognized the woman staring back at her but was compelled to silently judge anyway.

The mascara wand fell from her hand, clattering on the marble countertop, before falling onto the pink rug. She grabbed a tissue and swooped to pick it up and dab at the black flecks, and as she glanced at herself on the way up, the silent judge made one more pronouncement.

Idiot.

She stuffed the mascara in her makeup bag and went back into the bedroom to put on her shoes. She teetered a bit and found her footing in the two-inch heels on the plush carpet. She smoothed out the creases in her trousers and inhaled deeply.

Time to face the family.

Rachel turned the crystal doorknob and exited the safe haven of the bedroom. She eventually found the long, curving staircase with the elegant carved wooden banister. She grasped it, giving herself a secure anchor, and carefully placed one foot on each stair, concerned with crushing the pile on the carpet runner and turning an ankle in the new boots. She had a moment of grandeur—*Jew Descending a Staircase.*

Then her heel went rogue and she had a flash of Bambi on the ice as her arms jerked and her torso bent in an attempt to remain vertical. After the danger passed, she adjusted her shirt and checked if anyone noticed. She was relieved that the moment appeared to have gone unseen.

That would have been quite an entrance.

The sound of clinking glasses and a light melody on a piano indicated that cocktail hour was nearby and still in full swing. When she found the salon, there was a full bar, with a bartender in a green vest and bow tie, and cater waiters circulating with silver platters full of delicate finger food no one was interested in. There were only twelve people in the room, but these people took up space. They were to the manor born, cocktail glass in hand, cashmere sweater on back.

As Rachel's awkward blinking returned, a black-clad figure gracefully appeared next to her.

"First thing to do is to get a drink. That will give you something to do with your hands." Hoynes gave her a slight, professional smile.

"Is Brennan here?" she said.

"He is. However, he is currently cornered by his Uncle Bertram. He might be a while."

"Would it be unseemly to eat?"

"It would be unusual. I believe the hors d'oeuvres to be merely for show. That's my working theory. Ask the bartender for an extra olive." Hoynes smiled again and winked.

"Thank you, Hoynes." She went to the bar, found space on the end, and leaned on it to promote an air of casualness.

"Can I get you something, miss?"

"Um, gin and tonic, please." She stole a few olives from the bowl when the bartender's back was turned.

Then she turned away and stuffed one in her mouth.

"You're Brennan's lady friend?"

The voice startled Rachel, and she inhaled a pimento. She coughed as delicately as she could, trying to dislodge the red pepper before responding.

Rachel found herself face-to-face with a tall brunette, late middle-aged, with a pixie cut, too much eyeliner, and nude lipstick. She was also sporting a peacock brooch with ruby eyes that Rachel swore followed her as she turned back to the bar to retrieve her drink.

"I am," Rachel said. "Rachel Simon. How do you do?" Her voice caught in her throat, but it was probably the pimento.

"Maxine Donaldson Reardon. Pleasure." She held out a limp hand.

Rachel wasn't sure if she was supposed to shake it or kiss it. She hedged her bets and shook the woman's hand lightly. It felt like a piece of boiled chicken that had been left on a plate for several hours.

"Did you have a nice trip here?" Maxine said. "You're from where? Milwaukee?"

"Chicago. I grew up in Oak Park. Suburb. Have you been to Chicago?"

"I haven't, no. But my husband has done business there." She waved toward him, catching the attention of a white-haired man in a blue blazer.

When her head was turned, Rachel popped another olive in her mouth.

"He's the managing partner at Cook & Reardon," Maxine continued. "He's set to retire next year. We plan on spending at least a year abroad."

Seeing no chance of eating the last olive in her hand, Rachel covertly placed it in the potted plant.

"Abroad, you say?"

From across the room, Brennan disengaged himself from his uncle.

"He's a sweet boy," Maxine said, noticing Rachel's gaze. "But I do believe you'll have a tough go with him."

"What do you mean?"

Maxine touched Rachel's arm and leaned in. "You do know he's a homosexual, yes?"

Rachel widened her eyes. Had Brennan ever actually met his family?

"Don't worry, dear. You just need to pull yourself together and find a nice, appropriate fellow." She squeezed Rachel's brine-tinged fingers. "It's not too late for you. I'm sure there's a man out there. One who doesn't mind a few years and a couple of extra pounds on a girl." She gave Rachel a close-lipped smile. "Excuse me, won't you?" Maxine turned and joined another group.

Rachel felt like she had been punched in the neck. The bartender slid a carved glass bowl of mixed nuts toward her.

"Thanks," she said. "But I think I need something stronger."

She tried to flag down one of the cater waiters, but they appeared to be stuck on a circuit around the room, never stopping to offer food, strengthening Hoynes's theory that the appetizers were for display purposes only. She followed a waiter with a tray back to the kitchen, like a hunter tracking her prey. She treaded lightly, lest anyone discover that a guest had escaped and corralled her back to the party to attract more baleful stares from Maxine.

The kitchen was expansive, and much less busy than Rachel would have expected, given the number of guests in attendance. Rachel hoped to find finger food, a crustless sandwich, mini-gherkins— anything to pad the lining of her stomach so she wouldn't be done in by a second gin and tonic. Running her finger along the black granite countertop, she was mustering the courage to ask the chef straight out for something to eat, when she spied the pantry.

Screw it. I'll take care of it myself.

She sidled up to the pantry door, opened it enough to accommodate her width, and closed it behind her. She gave the string hanging from the overhead light a tug and took inventory. The pantry was the size of her college dorm, and filled floor-to-ceiling with canned, jarred, and boxed items, half of them with labels in a foreign language.

Although she felt a guilty about pilfering food, she nonetheless scanned the shelves for something, anything, to nosh, nibble, or otherwise cram down her throat. She eliminated those God-awful water crackers that were on every single cheese-and-cracker tray she'd ever encountered.

She spotted Saltines, which would have been an option if they had any kind of jam or jelly other than mint. This was definitely not the pantry of a person who liked food. It was full, but full of those foods that no one had eaten since 1952.

Rachel was desperate now, like a junkie trying to score a hit to take the edge off. She was about to give up hope when she spotted her old friend. It sat on the third shelf from the bottom, like a beacon in the harbor. It called to her, beckoning with its screw on lid and colorful label. Ah, peanut butter. It was even chunky.

She snatched the item from its perch, glanced behind her to make sure no one saw, despite the fact that she was alone. Peanut butter. She would indeed survive.

She needed a utensil. She'd eaten it out of the jar with her fingers before, but she was a guest stealing food in another person's house and she figured she shouldn't be a total savage about it. But none was to be found. Smoked salt, sure. Anchovies, yes. Pine nuts, couldn't miss them. There were even piquillo peppers. Rachel didn't know what they were, but she was surprised that Mrs. Donaldson could have them in her pantry, yet have no idea what a bialy was.

Rachel decided she shouldn't be surprised. Mrs. Donaldson ran a tight ship and this was her pantry, not a utensil drawer, which Rachel was sure held at least seven different types of forks. She was ready give up hope and scoop out a lump of peanut butter with her thumb when she spotted an option—chopsticks.

That'll do.

They weren't even ivory with gold Chinese characters on them. They obviously came from a takeout bag, probably tossed in the pantry by a kitchen assistant who wanted to go home for the night. She tore the paper, removed the wooden sticks, and sat on the stepladder she'd spied in the back of the pantry.

After taking off the lid, she peeled the silver inner liner, put it on the shelf, and scooped the unseparated chopsticks into the smooth top of the peanut butter. She pulled out a huge, mountain-shaped dollop. She put her mouth over it like a soft-serve ice cream cone, practically slurping the thick, chunky paste over her tongue. She double-dipped into the jar, breaking her own rule, so enamored by the salty, fat-filled bounty that it took her a moment to notice the pantry door had opened and she was no longer alone.

The familiar, silhouetted figure stood in the doorway like a Ferragamo-clad sheriff with a fluorescent light halo. Rachel froze, irrationally hoping that her stillness would render her invisible.

"That's a unique approach. I usually scoop my peanut butter out with a Hershey bar."

Mrs. Donaldson entered the pantry, immaculate in her cream wool skirt, pale yellow cashmere twin set, and double set of pearls perched around her neck. She regarded Rachel with without a trace of pity or contempt, either of which Rachel would have expected, given the situation.

She continued chewing the mouthful of peanut butter until she was able to swallow in a big, sticky gulp.

"I'm sorry, Mrs. Donaldson. I just..." She had no words to explain her situation, and she simultaneously wondered if she tried to remove the chopsticks, would the entire content of the jar come out at one time, like a big peanut popsicle? "I-I'll, um, replace the peanut butter."

Mrs. Donaldson closed the pantry door behind her and pulled out the other stepstool. She said nothing, just sat with her ankles crossed and her hands folded in her lap.

Rachel's cheeks got hot, like a child who'd gotten her hand caught in the cookie jar after being told she couldn't have any snacks.

"Don't worry, Rachel," she said, gently. "Is the food that bad, or is there something else going on?"

"I wouldn't know. The waiters moved very fast." Rachel squeezed the plastic jar with surprising force.

She was on the verge of tears, and she stared at the floor in embarrassment.

Mrs. Donaldson removed the jar from her hand and placed it on the shelf. She moved her stepladder closer and held Rachel's sticky hands in hers. They were delicate, yet strong, and their warmth was comforting.

"Who's the fellow?" she whispered.

"There's no fellow."

"Bullshit."

Rachel gasped.

"What? We swear in Lake Point. It's just not always audible. It usually takes the form of a withering glance."

The corners of Rachel's mouth turned up. "I'm familiar."

She disengaged her left hand and wiped the tears that ran down her cheek. With her free hand, she reached for the peanut butter jar.

"No," Mrs. Donaldson said. "I'm cutting you off."

Rachel drew back her hand and attempted to gather the swirling vortex of thoughts racing through her mind and form a coherent response, lest she make a mad lunge for the Nutella. She tapped her fingers on her thigh, squeezed her eyes shut, and hummed *Auld Lang Syne*, for no logical reason.

"Well, I..." she managed to squeak out. "There's this...well, when you...um, it's just..."

"It's all right, dear. If you're not ready to talk about it, I completely underst—"

"I'minlovewithaguywe'refriendsbutInevertoldhimnowhe'sdatin gmybestfriendLisawhoisblondeandgorgeousandIthinkIblewmychanceca nIhaveacookieplease?"

Rachel gasped for breath and put her hands on either side of her face, like the painting *The Scream*, only much sweatier. She expected Mrs. Donaldson to recoil in horror, but the woman was smiling.

"It's like I'm back in high school," Rachel said. "It's embarrassing."

"Don't be embarrassed. I imagine this will affect your engagement to Brennan, however." Mrs. Donaldson chuckled. "Tell me about him."

"He's gay and teaches accounting. Likes argyle vests, inexplicably."

"Rachel, you're deflecting. Do you do this a lot?"

"On occasion."

"Listen, I don't like those people out there in my living room any more than you do. I would be happy to stay here all night. Talk."

Her eyes were kind, her face reassuring, unlike Rachel's mother, who probably would have told her to buck up, go to the gym, or buy a new purse.

She stared at Brennan's mother, trying to find a reason to leave, to say never mind and go back to her room. She couldn't find one.

"I met Nathan a few months ago." Rachel's voice sounded scratchy. "He was like someone went to central casting and read off a description of *The Perfect Man for Rachel Simon*. I mean, he's not perfect. He likes reading Westerns, follows hockey, tends to crack his knuckles in the middle of movies, and hums when he eats soup."

"And this Nathan, he likes you, I assume?"

"It would appear so. I mean, he likes to do things with me, and he hangs out with us."

"Us?"

"Me and Brennan and Joanie."

"I'm not seeing the problem. He likes you, and you like him."

"No, there's more to it than that." Rachel glanced at the shelves. "I've just—I've…never done well with men. Never had the knack. I don't know if it's my looks or personality, but I've spent a lot of time on the sidelines."

"That sounds like a personal choice, dear."

"I don't remember choosing this. I just can't get it synced. The ones who seem to be interested view me as low-hanging fruit. And the ones I want, well, I get terrified that if I say anything, I'll scare them away. I force myself into the friend zone. I tamp down everything, because if I give any indication of how I really feel, they won't want anything to do with me." Rachel gave an exasperated sigh. "And how sad is that? I'm a grown woman, for God's sake, acting like a stupid teenager. Pathetic."

"So you're in love with a man, you never told him how you feel and have kept him at arm's length, and now you're devastated because he's dating Lisa, I'm assuming?"

"Pretty much. But there's more."

"How is that possible?"

Rachel snorted. "As if I couldn't get more pathetic, Lisa is also posing as me at the magazine that offered me a column, and is giving me, via her, an award. An award." She met Mrs. Donaldson's gaze. "And it was my doing. I talked her into it."

"And Lisa ran with it."

"Apparently. I'm not sure what else I expected, though."

"I think you have a couple of choices here. You can scrape together a bit of self-esteem and tell him, and also come clean with the magazine."

"Yikes."

"Or you can move on. Brooding will do you no good. But I still think you should be honest with those people. You're better than that."

"That's the thing, Mrs. Donaldson. I don't think I am."

"Call me Anne. And it's distressing that you think that way. You think that's part of the problem?"

"Probably. Old habits die hard."

"You're a grown woman. I'm not going to judge you." Mrs. Donaldson handed the peanut butter back to Rachel. "Here." She pulled a bag pretzel sticks off the shelf and passed them over. "They go surprisingly well together."

Rachel placed the bag in her lap. "Thank you."

Anne smoothed out the faint creases in her tailored skirt.

"Dear, here's how I see it. You can take a few more minutes to wallow. You've earned it. But you need to take time to think about who you want to be. You should be playing the star in your own life, not taking the supporting role all the time. You are smart, funny, and kind, and you should always express that." She put her hand on Rachel's shoulder. "Don't get in your own way anymore. Tell him, or don't, but don't let the past define you. You are more magnificent than you know."

"Thank you," Rachel whispered.

"You're welcome. Take your time and come join us if you're up to it. Goodness knows I could use a friendly face."

"Do I hug you now? I feel like I'm supposed to hug you."

"You can. It's not mandatory, however."

"Maybe later."

"I don't think you're giving this fellow enough credit." Anne smiled and placed her manicured hand on the doorknob. "The good ones value substance over sizzle." She opened the door, then turned back to Rachel. "Eventually, anyway. Some take longer to get there than others." She waved and closed the door behind her.

Rachel gazed at the food in her lap. She was staring down the barrel at forty, and she was sitting in a pantry, stuffing her face and thinking, *poor me*. It was not her finest hour. She took out a pretzel rod and held it over the peanut butter jar.

"What the hell am I doing?" she yelled.

She put the pretzel back in the bag and folded the top, then placed both food items back on the shelf.

I will not cry in the pantry. I will not cry in the pantry. Shit.

She clicked off the overhead light, then took in the silence, the dry smell of the room, and the reality of the situation. What was she supposed to do? Go home and proclaim her love to Nathan, and say to him, *Hey, I know you're dating my friend, who is gorgeous and perfect and will pretty much worship the ground you walk on, but I can make jokes about nineteenth-century British writers?* She shook her head.

"And *Charmé* will dump me faster than a cook holding a handful of hot soup," she murmured.

Rachel fumbled around for the door handle and poked her head out. The coast was clear. She slipped out of the pantry, left the kitchen, and headed straight to her room, where she kicked off her shoes. Without changing into her nightgown, she fell into the plush mattress, enveloping herself in the lace-trimmed cotton sheets, and threw the floral comforter over her head. She rolled over and turned off the bedside lamp, plunging the room into a restful darkness. She would do her best to sleep, and hopefully in the morning, she'd have a clearer idea of what to do.

~ * ~

Rachel opened her eyes again around ten in the morning. The room was bright with the morning sun, and she groaned, rolled over, and pulled the cover more tightly around her head. She was falling back asleep when the duvet was yanked from her face.

"Wakey, wakey, eggs and bakey." Brennan ducked as Rachel gave a start and nearly punched him in the face. "Whoa, watch it there, Sugar Ray!"

She put on her glasses and blinked a few times to bring Brennan into focus.

"Sorry," she croaked, her voice heavy with sleep.

She slumped back into her pillow. He perched himself on the edge of the bed.

"I brought coffee." He pointed to a silver tray with a matching coffee serving set. "Believe it or not, it tastes better when it's not in a travel mug."

Rachel scooted into a seated position and held the sheet to her chest, despite being fully dressed.

"Thank goodness." She moved to get out of bed, but Brennan stopped her.

"I'll get it." He crossed the room to the tray and filled two china cups with the steaming brew.

He brought her one, and she accepted it eagerly.

"Missed you last night," he said.

"I was detained."

"By a jar of peanut butter. In a closet. My mom told me."

Rachel's face got hot. "It wasn't discussed over a round of Manhattans, was it?"

"No. And why would we be drinking Manhattans? Do we live in 1960?"

"I pictured everyone with Manhattans. Or Tom Collins. Or a Rob Roy!"

"Scotch, Rachel. We are Scotch people. In libations, not ethnicity."

Rachel sipped her coffee. "This is very good."

"It's terribly expensive. The beans were hand-picked and pooped out by the Asian palm civet."

She almost choked on her coffee and struggled to get it down, hoping it wouldn't come out of her nose.

"What?" she said.

"Just kidding. I think it's Folgers."

Rachel was skeptical, but sipped it again, nonetheless. The caffeine began its happy dance in her brain.

"Ohhh. You missed the drama," Brennan said. "My sister came home late and drunk as a skunk."

"I never understood that saying. I didn't think skunks were known for their alcoholism."

"Can I continue?"

"Go on."

"Sharon makes her appearance in the living room, coat still on, leaves in her hair. She's got her train case in one hand, and a bottle of merlot in the other. She plops the train case down in the middle of the room, takes a swig from the bottle, and yells, *Hey, boring people. Bring on the turkey. This is Jared."*

"You named the turkey *Jared?*"

"No, that's the name of the man she was with."

"I thought her husband's name was Steve."

"It is."

"Oooh."

"She met Jared at the airport bar. He's got a neck tattoo." Brennan sipped his drink.

"Charming. What happened to Steve?"

"Sharon was vague. Dad was not pleased. Anyway, she went on and on about how marriage was stifling her *inner self*, and how she needed to be her own person, and quoted either the Koran or Oprah. It was weird. And the guy didn't say a word. He just kept eyeing the bar. Eventually, Dad had the chauffeur come in and usher them off to the guesthouse. Hopefully they're sleeping it off." He put his cup and saucer on the nightstand. "I hope you don't mind, but I rescheduled our flight to tonight. With the Nathan and Lisa thing, and now the touring company of The Sharon Show, I thought it might be better to leave sooner rather than later."

"I'm not sure I want to go back sooner. Can I stay here?"

"You'll run out of peanut butter eventually."

"You don't want to let that one go, do you? Okay. What's on the schedule for today?"

"You up for it? You've had quite a twenty-four hours."

"I said I was fine. And I am."

"Good soldier. Dinner is at one, but people will be hanging around starting at noon. Don't feel the need to make an appearance before then. We'll eat, have dessert, perhaps a brief nap, and head to the airport at five-thirty."

"Now at your Thanksgiving, do people eat or do they just pass around cocktails? I'm fine either way, but I want to be prepared."

He laughed. "No, there's food. Mom puts on an apron and pretends that she cooked the whole thing. Just go with it."

Anne's *apron* was probably taffeta with hand-sewn pearls, and Rachel couldn't help but grin.

"And we're still going ahead with the whole boyfriend-girlfriend façade?"

Brennan hung his head. "Yes."

"Brennan—"

"Not yet. Not…yet." He got up and put the saucers back on the tray. "It's not something I can come out and say. We don't do that." His shoulders slumped. "I'm afraid it will change the way they look at me."

Rachel desperately wanted to tell him, but kept her mouth shut. This was his story, not hers.

She swung her legs over the edge of the bed. "I don't think you're giving them enough credit." *That sounds familiar.*

"Maybe when I can show them I'm in a steady relationship, show them I'm not a promiscuous stereotype."

"That would be a lot to spring on them. Hello, mother, father. We've never discussed this in any meaningful way, but meet my lover, Rupert."

"Rupert?"

"It's a name. Besides, maybe they'll be offended you lied to them."

They weren't, but she wasn't above playing the guilt card.

"Offense I can handle. You just ignore it for a few months, and everyone pretends to forget." He sat next to her again. "I'll tell them. In my own time. But I'm not going to do it on a major holiday, in front of their friends and business associates."

"Would make a hell of a toast, though."

Brennan shot her a look that told her the discussion was over.

"All right," Rachel said. "Why don't you go do something while I pull myself together? I appreciate the coffee, but I've got prep work to do."

"Might take you longer than you anticipated." He handed Rachel her cell phone. "You've got texts."

She groaned. "Oh, God. Did you read them?"

"One or two. I needed to know what you were in for. I've got your back."

She let out another groan and flopped back on the bed.

"If it helps, not all of them are from Lisa. Joanie got in a few, too."

"Why would that help? Is she back with Hank?"

"No, but misery loves company."

"Does she know about Nathan and Lisa?"

"Oh, yeah. Lisa's been busy spreading the news."

"Great."

"You'll survive." He put his hand on her knee. "Just nut up."

"You first."

Brennan walked to the door separating their suites. "There's more coffee if you want it. See you downstairs in a bit." He shut the door behind him.

Rachel stared at the cell phone in her hand. *Like ripping off a Band-Aid.*

The first three texts were from Lisa.

I'm so happy! It's like a fresh start.

I'm cooking Thanksgiving dinner. Do I have to defrost the turkey first?

I bought yams? I think?

Joanie was having dinner with her son, without Hank.

Made appointment with new therapist. Not much progress with old.

She kept gazing at me over the top of her glasses, like my mom.

Then another from Lisa.

You are the smartest person I know. I'm glad I listened to you and found a totally different type of guy to be with. Things are great!

Rachel deleted them without responding. *They can wait.*

The last text was from Nathan.

I miss you.

She closed the text message app and placed the phone on the nightstand. In one swift movement, she tucked her feet back under the covers and pulled the blanket over her head. She steadied her breath and focused on her stomach rising and lowering with each inhale and exhale.

She shut her eyes for an hour, more dozing than sleeping, periodically peeking through the covers, at the clock. At 11:30 she willed herself to exit the warm comforter. She shuffled to the bathroom, her glasses perched atop her nose.

I've seen worse.

Under closer inspection, the dark circles under her eyes proved to be mostly mascara. She used a shower cap to hold her hair from her face and dragged a cleaning wipe across her face.

That's a look.

Rachel washed her face. The smell of the creamy white foam reminded her of her mother, with her myriad lotions and potions stacked on her bathroom countertop, things that Rachel was never ever allowed to touch. Her mother was a firm believer in a rigorous skin care regimen—cleanser, eye cream, night cream, day cream, wrinkle serum, firming lotion. Rachel would be in awe as her mother applied these magic beauty tonics in just the right order, using her ring finger to tap in the eye cream, and adding a dab here, a dab there. Always outwardly secure in her beauty, using the tips and tricks women were supposed to do to *maintain*, as she put it.

She, on the other hand, was a minimalist. She washed, she dried, and she put on moisturizer when she remembered. Her mother would wince at her daughter's routine. She had no patience for laziness, and less for self-indulgence.

What would she tell me to do right now?

Rachel rinsed the soap from her face.

Nut up.

Rachel decided to take a shower. She disrobed and got under the running water, letting it rush over her, washing away the day and the last of her self-indulgent wallowing.

That's it. That's enough, now.

She got out of the shower and dried off. If anyone was in the wrong, it was she. Lisa's instincts were right—Nathan was a good guy. And if he wants to be with her, more power to him.

Maybe it's better I never said anything. Better a case of unrequited love than to be dumped for your best friend.

At least that was how she decided to rationalize it.

Rachel put on her clothes, choosing a gray wool skirt, a burgundy sweater, and black tights. After slipping on a pair of black loafers, she assessed her image in the mirror. She smoothed her hair and her skirt and pushed her glasses to the top of her nose.

Showtime.

Heading out the bedroom door, she steeled herself. It couldn't be any worse than Thanksgivings with her family—the times her mother locked herself in her bedroom, overcome with stress, not allowing anyone to help, then admonishing them because she had to *do it all herself.* Her father wouldn't let them eat dinner until she came out, but then she'd be upset because the food had gotten cold.

Or the time her father and uncle got into an argument about Reagan's economic policies, which Rachel didn't understand, but caused everyone to ignore her requests to please pass the peas.

Or even the time they ate a ten-minute Thanksgiving meal because they were going to her Aunt's house for dinner and Rachel's mother hated her cooking, and then Rachel got sick in the car on the way there and vomited in her mother's purse.

The bar was set pretty low.

Hoynes was at the bottom of the stairs, staid and steady in his black suit, hanging an obviously expensive fur coat in the front closet.

"Hello, Dr. Simon," he said. "The guests are in the dining room. Can I get you a drink?"

"Isn't it a bit early?"

"One would think. But no."

In the dining room, people were sipping cocktails, and with their rigid stances and forced polite laughter, appeared at least three levels removed from festive.

She recognized a few faces from the night before, as well as Brennan's Aunt Maxine and her husband. There was another man standing uncomfortably next to the sideboard and scratching his neck tattoo. Rachel assumed it was Jared.

Brennan made a beeline to Rachel, drink already in hand. "You made it!"

"Barely. Where's your mother and sister?"

"Mother is in the kitchen, supervising. Sharon hasn't made an appearance yet."

"Jared has."

"Yeah, that's kind of weird."

The dining room was elegantly set, with floral china, shiny silverware, and etched crystal glasses. The table itself was covered in a thick brown and gold tablecloth, with an elegant, intricately patterned runner down the center. Arrangements of lilies in decorative vases dotted the room, with a centerpiece of glass beads in the shape of a turkey. The smell of sage and rosemary wafted through the dining room, confirming that food would indeed be served. There were even place cards with names written in a floral script.

Brennan and Rachel were seated near the end of the table, next to Anne and across from Sharon and her guest. Jared's placard said *Steven*, further proof that his appearance was a surprise and was passively-aggressively put on the table, anyway.

"Do we sit, or just stand around?" Rachel said.

"Hover until Mother gives us the go-ahead."

After a minute or two, Anne Donaldson came sweeping in, yellow apron over her light blue Chanel suit. The apron was pristine, of course, indicating, as Brennan had suggested, more of a supervision role in the kitchen.

She certainly isn't making a pie.

"Let's be seated." Anne circled the room, herding folks from their groups to the grand maple table in the center.

Rachel was impressed that not a drop of gin was spilled. She and Brennan sat, with William, Brennan's father, sitting in the captain's chair at the head of the table. Mr. Donaldson might have been the figurehead leader, but Anne was definitely at the helm, steering the guests like a seasoned guide negotiating the hostessing terrain.

They were seated, and Rachel noticed that one chair was empty—Sharon's. Everyone pretended not to notice. Jared, however, seemed to feel her absence as he unfolded his napkin and dabbed at the beads of sweat forming on his brow. The unbuttoned sleeves on his obviously borrowed button-down shirt inched toward his elbows.

Rachel wondered why he hadn't gotten up and left. He had a lot of patience for a guy with a chin beard and a tattoo of a dragon on his neck.

"I'm glad you're here on this happy occasion," Anne said. "I was wondering if anyone would like to share something they're thankful for? It's a bit corny, but I think it can be excused this time of year."

"She's expecting a corny-copia," Brennan whispered in Rachel's ear.

"Brennan, would you like to start?" Anne said.

"Busted," Rachel whispered back.

"I'm still working on it, Mother. Maybe come back to me?"

His uncle raised his glass. "I'm glad business was good. Three new accounts."

A smattering of polite applause.

Maxine went next. "I'm glad to be here with you lovely people, in this lovely home. Also, Brittany got accepted to Vassar, and we are over the moon."

Rachel busied herself by folding and unfolding her napkin, trying to get it back in the shape of a swan. It eventually took the shape of a deformed turtle.

"We know what Brennan is thankful for." Maxine's voice broke Rachel's napkin trance.

It's now or never, buddy. Rachel bored her gaze into the side of his head. *Just say the words.*

But he was gazing at his lap, his fingers running over the knuckles of his other hand. He lifted his chin, inhaled, and opened his mouth.

"I dumped Steven and skipped out on rehab! Happy freaking Thanksgiving!"

Sharon was in the doorway, leaning on the doorframe for support, with a bottle of wine in one hand.

She pointed the bottle at Jared. "Oh, good, you saved me a seat. We start yet?"

She plopped down on the polished wood chair and leaned her elbows on the crisp tablecloth. Jared grimaced at her. She didn't notice and popped the cork out of the bottle. She poured the contents into a glass and noticing there was a bit left after filling the goblet, remedied the situation by chugging the bottle. He winced again, placing his hand on his stomach. She continued to ignore him and picked up her wine in a mock salute.

"Hey, Brennan," she slurred. "You still keeping up the straight show?" She took another deep swig and pointed at Rachel. "You know he's gay, right? Going to be a pretty dull honeymoon."

The stunned silence gave way to a roomful of throat clearing, chair shifting, and silverware clinking as drinks were refilled. Brennan's jaw hung open, and Anne held her face in her hands.

Brennan's father rose and retrieved the wine glass from his daughter's outstretched hand. Brennan took a deep breath, smoothed his sweater vest, and opened his mouth to speak. Jared moaned, held his stomach, and keeled over, passing out on the floor with a loud thud.

"Oh, you have *got* to be kidding me," Brennan muttered.

~ * ~

"I can't believe they already know!" Brennan threw a sweater into his suitcase, with an unusual lack of care. "How could they not tell me?"

"I guess they figured you were already aware." Rachel picked up and refolded his sweater. "Isn't this easier?"

"They deprived me of my moment. After all that, I was supposed to get a moment. It was in the brochure."

"You got a drunk sister and an unconscious man on the floor. That's pretty dramatic."

"It's not the same." He tossed socks into the suitcase, which bounced off the top and landed on the rug. "I was hoping to sing a selection from *Yentl*, for Pete's sake!"

"You weren't going to sing."

"I could have sung."

She removed her suitcase from the bottom of the closet and tossed items into it, ignoring every one of her mother's Seven Rules for Efficient Packing, which did not include standing at a dresser and tossing underwear over her shoulder.

Why did I bother to unpack? I was only going to be here for two days.

"Rachel, where'd you go? You almost done?"

"Mother flashback. I'll get my stuff from the bathroom." Rachel proceeded to gather her things and shove them into random pockets, violating Packing Rules four and six.

Brennan and Rachel met Anne at the bottom of the stairs.

"Oh, dear, you should have told me you were ready. I would have had someone bring your bags down."

"That's all right," Rachel replied. "It's just the one, and it's pretty light."

Anne kissed Brennan on the cheek and gave him a gentle hug. "It was wonderful to see you, sweetheart. I'm sorry it ended on such an awkward note."

"It saved me from having to hire an accompanist."

Anne smiled warmly and placed her hand on the side of his face. "We love you, Brennan. Always, and no matter what." She sighed. "So one child is gay, and the other is an alcoholic. It won't keep us out of the country club." She chuckled and turned to Rachel. "It won't even make the gossip rounds. It's not like anyone's in jail for embezzlement." She leaned in. "Like the Henderson's son," she whispered.

"Thank you for inviting me," Rachel said. "I had a lovely time."

"I'm glad to have met you," Anne replied. "I'm happy Brennan has such good friends."

"And thank you for the peanut butter. I made note of the brand. I'll send a replacement when I get home."

Anne smiled again and embraced Rachel gently. Caught off-guard, Rachel tensed for a moment, but relaxed into the cashmere and the smell of Chanel No. 5.

"You are a star," she whispered in Rachel's ear.

She released Rachel, then kissed Brennan again. "Have a safe flight back. Do you have your boarding passes?"

"Yes, Mother. Right here." Brennan patted the pocket of his jacket.

Anne opened the door, and he and Rachel stepped through, onto the porch.

"Dad's okay with it, right?"

"Don't worry about your father, dear. He's more open-minded than you think. He may even have owned an Elton John record at one time."

Brennan laughed. "I love you, Mom."

Rachel and Brennan made their way to the rental car and stowed the bags in the trunk. Once inside, he gripped the steering wheel with both hands.

"Well, that was quite a show, even without my musical number." He started the engine. "But composure was maintained. Especially you. I wouldn't have blamed you if you had locked yourself in your room for two days."

"You had enough going on without me adding more to it. Didn't want to freak out the goyim."

Rachel leaned her head on the headrest. She was determined not to wallow. She didn't want to be one of those sad, pathetic women, grasping at the last memories of *The One Who Got Away,* a modern-day

Miss Havisham in her elastic waist jeans and a sweatshirt with an appliqué turtle on it. There wasn't anything she could do about it now, anyway. She was too slow, too reticent, too unwilling to believe. Lisa wasn't. Good for her. Rachel would have to swallow it, tamp it down, and everything would be fine. She'd move on. She'd done it before.

She gently rubbed her stomach and removed a couple of Tums from her purse.

In a few short hours, she was getting out of a taxi at her house. They dropped Brennan off first, the spring in his step contrasting to the lead-footedness of hers. He hugged her before he got out of the cab, promising to call tomorrow. She gave him a half-hearted punch on the arm.

"Not too early," she intoned. "I'll be quite hungover."

"You mean, you'll be sleeping off a food coma?"

"You know me too well."

She paid the driver, with extra in the tip as a reward for not being one of those drivers who felt the need to chat with their passengers. Trudging to her door, she fumbled with her keys, her fingers sausage-like in her new leather gloves, a gift from Brennan's parents. After unlocking the door, she went inside and closed it behind her, and let her bags fall with a thud next to the stairs. She let out a cleansing sigh and went to the kitchen, turning on lights as she went.

Lisa had been in to take care of the cat. Rachel noticed Lindsey's bowls were filled with food and water, and she plucked a note from the refrigerator door.

Yes, I cleaned out the litterbox. You're low on dry food.

Kitty missed you. Me too.

Love, L.

As if on cue, Lindsey appeared and curled around Rachel's ankles, purring up a storm. She stretched down to scratch her ears, and the cat looked at her, emerald eyes wide.

"I'm glad I'm home, too, sweetie. Did you have a nice time with Auntie Lisa?"

Rachel laid her cell phone on the kitchen table, accidentally swiping the screen. She had a voicemail from Lisa. She debated deleting it without listening since she wasn't sure she wanted to hear Lisa's voice right now. Instead she put aside her phone, saving the message for later.

She spent the weekend cleaning her house and working on her writing. Back in class on Monday, she regained whatever semblance of a groove she might have had and fell back into her routine. Other than a few texts from Brennan checking up on her, she kept to herself and went from school to home, stopping only at the grocery store to get blueberries, bread, and Swiss cheese. And a coffee cake.

By Thursday, things were nearly normal. The swirling in her head had stopped, no doubt stilled by a looming sense of resignation and the remainder of the coffee cake. She made herself a salad with her dinner and opened a bottle of merlot she had in the cabinet. Then and only then, with glass in hand, did she listen to Lisa's message.

"Hi, dolly, it's Lisa!" Her voice sounded chipper. *"I hope you had a great time at Brennan's home, and you simply must tell me every single thing as soon as possible. In fact, why don't you come to my house Saturday night? I'm cooking dinner, if you can believe that. I'm totally a domestic diva now, and I'm sure Nathan would love to see you. He talks about you all the time. I'll even invite Joanie. Hopefully she'll be able to come."* Her voice got muffled as she called into the distance. *"Nathan, sweetie, put that over there. No, by the lamp."* Her voice came back to full volume. *"Call me when you can. See you Saturday."*

Rachel hit the end button and stared at her phone. She could be a bitter old hermit and not go, or suck it up, slap a smile on her face and be Rachel The Great Friend. As long as they were happy, she could be happy for them, too.

Or whatever other lies she could get herself to believe. She felt like a warm, damp blanket had been wrapped around her head, heavy and foggy. She shoved the phone into her pocket.

I might be too chickenshit to say anything to Nathan, but I need to tell Charmé. *Even if I lose the job, at least they'll know it was me. I'm calling Brittany tomorrow. I promise.*

The doorbell rang, and Rachel gave a start. It rang again, the bong-bong echoing through the house with more urgency, like the person on the outside was in a hurry to be seen.

Seriously. I have to do at least this one thing.

She jogged to the front door and looked through the peephole. The person on the other side was like a ghost, an aura of light from the front porch silhouetting a figure that was at once familiar and foreign.

One thing.

She opened the door, slowly, willing her brain to absorb what she was seeing. Familiar blue eyes, peering at her from the handsome face topped with effortlessly styled jet-black hair. Then there was the voice.

"Hey, baby cakes. Got room for a visitor from the east?"

Alex.

What was that thing again?

Chapter Thirteen

All Rachel could hear was circus music in her head. It was a few seconds before the language-translating Babel Fish from *The Hitchhiker's Guide to the Galaxy* kicked in, and the *wah-wah* sound that was coming out of the apparition's mouth morphed into a vaguely intelligible language.

"You look like you've seen a ghost," he said. "You going to let me in?"

"Sha, uh, well, yes." Rachel opened the storm door to let him slide past her.

He smelled of lime and sandalwood and hair product, the same as he had years ago, and she found herself unable to move, locked in a memory, until the scent of him disappeared into the air.

They stood in the foyer, the silence becoming more deafening with each passing second. Rachel gingerly closed the door, locked the deadbolt with a thunderous clunk, and pressed her head against it. Turning her head, then shoulders, she caught sight of the perfectly scuffed black boots standing in the hall, with their thick lug soles and shiny buckles that hung below the hem of his dark-wash jeans, then inched her gaze upward, taking in the sight of a smooth gray T-shirt underneath a fashionably distressed black leather motorcycle jacket. Chin. Cheeks. Eyes.

As she met Alex's gaze, he smiled, put his bag down and spread his arms out in greeting. Rachel was unable to blink. He strode toward her and enveloped her in a wrap of leather, muscle, and memories.

"It's amazing to see you, Rachel." He let go of the hug and put his hands on her shoulders. "I probably should have called. But hey, there are so few surprises left in the world, and I knew you wouldn't mind."

"It's been a long time." She was relieved she could string a sentence together.

"I know." He released her shoulders and ran a hand through his hair. "I'm just glad you're living in the same place. I called a few mutual friends, but no one would give me your address. I took a chance you were still here. You had just moved in the last time I saw you, what, seven years ago?"

"Eight."

"Wow." He whistled. "Eight years. How the hell have you been, kid?"

"Fine. Uh, great. Why don't you come in? Do you want something to eat?"

"Taking care of me already. Same old Rachel."

Alex followed her into the living room and sat on the couch, crossing his long legs at the knee. He stretched his arms over the back of the couch and flashed that grin that had zapped her all those years ago.

"No, I'm good," he said. "Are you going to sit?"

Rachel's hands were foreign objects that had somehow attached themselves to her arms. She folded them, put them on her hips, and then folded them again.

"I guess, ahem, yes. I shall sit." *I shall?*

She sidled between his knees and the coffee table, realizing she could have gone around the other way. She lowered herself onto the couch too fast, resulting in her landing with a bounce. After resting her hands on the cushion to steady herself, she touched her hair, and put on what she hoped was a confident smile. *Smooth.*

"So what are you doing here?" Her voice was pitched too high to be cool and casual.

"I'll be honest, Rae. I've had a tough go of it lately. I lost my staff job at *Features* magazine, and freelance gigs have kind of dried up. I mean, everyone with a smartphone thinks they're a professional photographer."

"I'm sorry to hear that."

"Yeah, thanks. I mean, I'll bounce back. Talent is rewarded in the end, you know?"

"Of course. You do amazing work."

"You think so?" His eyebrows shot up. "What do you like best about it?"

She had the words at the ready. "The way you use the light. And you always have a good sense of the depth of field, and that gives your pictures a real impact."

It was like being back in college.

Alex hung his head and sighed. "You always did get me."

"How is…um, Shanna? Are you still with her?"

"No, we split three years ago. Good thing, too. I dated a bunch of other women after her, like one after the other. But then I met this girl, Hope, a few months later. It was crazy. We were living together after about three weeks. It was like it was meant to be. It blazed, you know?"

"Where is she right now?"

Alex focused his gaze on the corner of the room. "I'm not sure. She, uh, she left me."

"That's a lot to deal with at one time—the job, and your girlfriend."

"No kidding." Alex turned his toward Rachel and leaned in. "That's what made me think of you. If I came here, if I saw you again, you would make everything better. Like you used to." He held her chin between his thumb and forefinger, and brushed her cheek with his other hand, knocking her glasses askew. "You made *me* better."

She met his gaze, and she was entranced. *Oh, boy...*

Her cell phone dinged, startling her and breaking the moment. She adjusted her glasses and touched her hair. Realizing the sound was coming from her pocket, she fumbled for it and checked the screen.

Do you have time to discuss menu options for Saturday night? Need your food expertise.

She put the phone on the table. "Sorry about that. It was Lisa."

"Lisa! How's she doing?"

"She's…fine."

"Do you want to text her back?"

"No, it's okay. It can wait."

"Oh, go ahead. I don't mind. She has her minor dramas from time to time."

"Thanks." Rachel picked up the phone, opened Lisa's text then typed her response. *Not a good time. Alex here.* She hit send and placed it back on the table. "I said I'd call her tomorrow."

The phone rang.

"Wow," Alex said. "Lisa must really need to talk to you."

"I'm sure it's nothing."

"Go ahead and take it. I can check my messages in the meantime. Tell her I said hi." He got up from the couch and retrieved his phone from his bag.

Rachel answered the phone. She didn't have time to say hello before Lisa jumped in.

"You mean *Alex*-Alex? Oh, my God, what's he doing there? Are you all right?"

Rachel had to hold the phone away from her ear and made a beeline for the kitchen.

"I'm fine, I'm fine," she whispered. "He showed up out of the blue."

"You must be floored. You holding it together?"

"Of course. Why wouldn't I"

"Oh, please. Tell me you have amnesia. That man destroyed you."

"He didn't destroy me. Besides, that was a million years ago."

"If you say so. Hey, I have to go. Are you bringing him Saturday? I don't want you alone with him any more than you have to be. Is he staying with you?"

"We haven't discussed it yet. He literally just got here."

"Rachel."

"Lisa, I'm fine. I'm a grown-up, not a college girl. There is an Alex wall. He will not scale it."

"I'll see you Saturday, then. Be good."

"I will. Bye."

Lisa was right. She did have a pattern with Alex—a push-pull, hot-cold samba step that usually ended with Rachel being left alone. But that was years ago. She was thirty-eight, not twenty-one. Besides, even if she couldn't have Nathan, she certainly wasn't going to settle for the Casanova with the telephoto lens.

She checked the cabinets and refrigerator for something to offer her guest. She'd cleaned out her stock of perishables before she left for Ohio, so her only choices were a bottle of white grape juice, a box of mango nectar she didn't remember buying, and a plastic pitcher of iced tea.

Maybe the mango juice was for a recipe? Seriously? That's what I'm thinking about now? Mango juice?

She closed the door and stared at the magnets dotting the front. Cupcakes, cats, a quote from Gandhi, and one from the local cable company. She opened the door again and pulled out the tea and a couple of glasses, poured, then placed the pitcher back into the refrigerator with more force than was necessary.

She went back to the living room. Alex was engrossed in his phone and didn't look up when she offered him the tea. He merely raised his index finger, signaling her to wait. He gave his phone a final swipe and returned it to his bag. Rachel once again held out the tea.

"Scotch?" He took a sip and winced. "Tea. No, thanks." He handed her back the glass. "Do you have anything stronger?"

"I have a half-empty bottle of Riesling." Rachel poured the contents of his glass into hers, placed the empty glass on a week-old copy of *Newsweek,* and sat on the end of the couch. "This is...well, it's been a while. Catch me up."

They sat and talked for the next hour and a half, and Alex

caught Rachel up with the events of the last few years. She listened and nodded. Every so often he'd run his hands through his dark hair and gaze at her earnestly with his blue eyes, and she was transported to another time, another place. His words floated away, losing meaning, and there was only his gaze, darting here, there, at her and past her. At last he wrapped up his stories, and she brought herself back into the moment.

"...and that's when I decided to settle in New York for good. That's the place for me. Or so I thought."

"I think it's great you found a home. I have a great time whenever I visit there. I went to this great storefront gallery—"

"I think I'd like to turn in now. You have a place for me to crash?"

"Oh, sure. Of course. You can have the spare bedroom. I'll have to make up the bed."

Alex took out his phone, stuck it in his pocket, and handed her the bag.

"Great. Thanks. Let me know when you're done. I'm going to send out a few emails." He shifted his focus to his phone, his fingers passing over the screen.

"Hmm. Okay. I guess I'll just..."

His thumbs tap-tapped over the keypad.

She edged her way past the coffee table, holding his bag as she headed upstairs. "When you're ready, it's the first door on the right at the top of the stairs."

Alex gave a quiet grunt and continued typing.

She tossed the bag in the guest room and got linens from the hall closet then made the bed quickly. He couldn't care less about hospital corners. She got an extra blanket from the closet and placed it on the foot of the bed. When she turned, she found Alex in the doorway, watching her. She gave a start.

"Looks amazing." He neared her.

"Doesn't get much use. I mostly use it as an extra closet."

"Sure is nicer than a hotel. And you can't beat the turndown service."

"I hope you'll be comfortable."

He placed his hands on her waist. "I already am."

His gaze was steady and direct. He stepped forward and smiled. She closed her eyes, and after a moment, opened them as he was taking off his jacket. He threw it over the back of the desk chair and rubbed his shoulders.

"Well, I'm beat. Thanks for putting me up, kid."

"You're welcome. The bathroom is across the hall. Sleep tight." She turned on her heel and left the room, closing the door behind her.

She went to her room and latched the door. Then she remembered Lindsey liked to camp out on her bed at night, and she opened the door a crack. As if on cue, the cat stuck her tiny pink nose through, came in, and hopped on the bed. Rachel scratched the cat's ears, staring at the slits of darkness between the vertical blinds. She got ready for bed, picked up her book, and slipped under the coverlet.

The next morning, she awoke later than usual. She had slept fitfully, plagued with strange dreams she couldn't remember. Her book was still open, laying on her chest. As her eyes adjusted to the morning light, she threw on a robe and went down the hall. Alex's door was open, and his bed had been made. She went to the kitchen to make coffee, where there was a note underneath one of the cupcake magnets, scrawled in his even hand.

Went out. Will be back.

Figuring his loose concept of time was intact, she set the coffee pot to brew and went back upstairs to change. By the time she came down, Alex was sitting at the kitchen table, having helped himself to coffee, and was toasting a bagel from the local bakery.

"Morning, baby cakes. Thanks for the brew. Want a bagel? Brought cream cheese, too. You were out."

"Maybe later. Just coffee now."

There was only enough left for half a cup. Her shoulders tensed as she made another pot.

"Do you have plans for the day?" She leaned back against the counter.

"Don't you have classes?"

"Not today. There's a campus thing."

"Thought we'd hang out together." He winked. "If that's okay with you, of course."

"I've got a couple errands to run this morning, but I'm sure you can entertain yourself. I've got a party at Lisa's tomorrow night, if you want to come."

"Sounds like tons of fun."

"I don't mean to be a rude hostess, but will you be staying here, or—"

"One step ahead of you. Reserved a room at the motel down the road. It's not what I'm used to, but it will do."

The smell of coffee filled the room again, and she put two packets of sweetener in her mug, in anticipation. She did her best to pour her coffee casually.

She caught his eye as she took her first sip. "Can I help you?"

"Were you always this pretty?" Alex set his mug on the table and wiped a smidge of cream cheese with a napkin.

"I'm not sure how to answer that." Rachel pushed her glasses back up her nose.

"You're more attractive than I remember. I mean, physically."

"I, um, thank you?"

"How come we never dated?"

"You couldn't get past my looks."

"That makes me sound unbelievably shallow." He cleared his throat and shifted in his chair.

"You'd be attentive and affectionate when we were alone, but the moment others were around, it was if you didn't know me."

She was in a discussion she'd never planned to have but could no longer avoid.

He stared at the table. "I didn't know. Honestly."

He got up and approached her, removed the mug from her hands, and placed it on the counter. He took Rachel in his arms and held her firmly. She could hear his heart beating, off-sync with hers, in a relay *boom, BOOM.* She froze, her arms stuck to her sides. She was trapped. His embrace made her claustrophobic. Then, as if on their own, her arms moved up his torso and rested beneath his.

"I didn't mean to make you feel ugly," he whispered.

They were words she never thought she'd hear. A warm tear rolled past her nose. She was angry, as she had long ago determined she would never waste any more tears on him. But this wasn't an angry tear. It was a tear of relief, validation after years of disappointment.

He held her at arm's length and wiped the solo tear. "What do you say we finish our breakfast, then spend the day together? Errands, shopping, whatever. We have time to make up for."

She agreed and sat at the table. He placed her coffee in front of her and offered the main section of the paper. He took the sports section for himself.

Maybe he's changed.

After dismissing that thought, she remembered she needed to jot down a few ideas for the next column, so she grabbed her laptop and exited the kitchen. As she sat on the couch and opened the computer, her phone pinged with a text from Lisa.

Meeting with Brittany. Didn't want to bother you with it. Just talking plans for the awards. She loves my ideas, btw.

Rachel felt the blood rush to her face. *Oh, hell no.*

It had been a partnership until then, albeit with a false front, but they had appeared to be on the same page. She couldn't believe Lisa's audacity. She didn't actually *do* anything. The work was Rachel's and Rachel's alone. She was the one who spent hours on research, on crafting the essays, on making sure they said exactly what she wanted them to say.

How stupid she had been to try to fool the magazine. They were behaving exactly as she'd feared, and it made her stomach churn. In a split second, she knew what she had to do.

"Alex," she re-entered the kitchen, "I have to pop into the city for a bit. There's something I need to take care of."

"Where you going?"

"I have to go to the offices of *Charmé* magazine. Can't explain why right now. You can stay here, or I can drop you off somewhere until I get back." She gathered her purse and briefcase from the kitchen chair.

"Oh, no, I'm coming with you. You, at a fashion magazine? Staging a protest?"

"In a manner of speaking." She tapped her foot impatiently.

"No, seriously."

"I'm writing a column for them," Rachel said, hesitantly.

"At *Charmé*? Lisa must be jealous."

"Not as much as you might think."

"I'm definitely coming with." Alex put on his coat and patted his back and jacket pocket. "Phone, sunglasses, wallet. I'm good. Let's roll." He took a big swig from his coffee mug and set it on the table with a flourish. "Adventure awaits!" He breezed past her and made a beeline for the front door.

She was momentarily stunned, then dashed after him with the car keys.

~ * ~

"You let her take credit for your work?" Alex's voice got higher at the end of his sentence. "That's wacky, even for you." He drummed his fingers on the car's armrest as they headed north into the city.

"It's more complicated than that. They're this high-end fashion magazine—"

"I've freelanced for them."

"Then you know there's no way they would want to hire me if they knew what I really looked like. So I used Lisa's face. Things…sort of got out of hand."

"Hmm. Maybe you're right." He checked his hair in the visor

mirror. "I knew a girl who worked there. She was smart, like you, but they put her to work in subscription services. I think she lasted a month or two." He gazed out the window. "The editor-in-chief is great, but she's less hands-on these days. She's been letting her senior staff run the show. They don't want to work with us old-timers."

"Lisa's our age." Rachel glanced at Alex, his sharp jawline brushing the collar of his jacket.

"Yeah, but she looks like an ex-model. They probably thought they hit the jackpot."

Rachel gripped the steering wheel, the traffic on the Stevenson Expressway beginning to slow, undoubtedly due to another round of constant construction work.

"Yeah. Jackpot," she said.

Once downtown, she found overpriced parking and marched up to the front of the *Charmé* building. Alex entered first and waited for her in the lobby, watching as she got too much momentum going in the revolving doors and rotated through them three times before flinging herself into the main lobby.

"Did you forget how doors work?" He patted her shoulder.

"I'm fine," she said, tersely. "Let's go up."

As the elevator arrived at desired floor, she let out her breath in a forced stream. She had no idea what she was going to say to these people. Each scenario ended by her being removed by security, news of which would make it back to the college and would most definitely not be good for her chances of being awarded tenure.

It's hard enough getting a decent academic job these days. I don't need to add a criminal record to the mix.

The doors opened, revealing that now-familiar mix of high-end perfume, self-tanner, and...floor wax? Rachel recognized the scent from her youth, when she had been banished from the kitchen or dining room because her mother was *having the floors done.*

She gingerly stepped off the elevator. The receptionist's face fell upon seeing Rachel but brightened after catching sight of Rachel's handsome companion.

"You need to get back to that Brittany person's office, right?" he whispered.

"Yes, that's going to be the first hurdle."

Her foot slipped on the polished floor, and she stumbled. She concentrated on keeping herself upright and kept moving.

"Leave it to me." He sidled up to the desk and ran his hand through his hair as he leaned on the counter. "Hey," he said to the young woman, who took no more notice of Rachel. "Alex Hunter.

Photographer. Has anyone told you that you have amazing bone structure?"

Rachel rolled her eyes, but his opening line worked. She slipped past the desk, down the short hallway, and opened the glass doors to the magazine's office. She decided to adopt an air of confidence and pretend she belonged. Her façade cracked, however, when the worker bees realized she did not resemble a queen.

"Excuse me. Excuse me!" A voice behind her grew louder and more urgent.

She kept going, searching for an office that might be Brittany's. A hand touched her shoulder, and she jumped in surprise.

"Are you the juice girl?" A spritely brunette smiled at Rachel.

"Pardon?"

"The juice girl. A lot of us are juicing this week, and we need to place a new order."

"Uh, sure. Juice. Hey, Brittany Ekberg wanted to do a special request. Do you know where her, um, office is?" Rachel was beginning to sweat.

"Right there." The brunette pointed to a door about fifteen feet from where they were standing.

Rachel's eyes opened wide.

"Why don't you take care of her first? We'll write down what we need and catch you on the way out."

"Cool. Great. Good. Thanks." Rachel's heart beat faster.

She neared Brittany's office, feeling as if she was moving through water, and paused outside with her hand ready to knock. The sound of women's laughter emanated from the other side of the glass door, and Rachel froze.

"This is such amazing work, Rach. I think we're going to be brilliant working together…" Brittany's voice sounded excited, like she was talking to her new best friend.

Rachel's pulse pounded in her ears. Without knocking, she turned the handle of the office door and propelled herself inside. She was greeted by two sets of eyes staring at her—one showing surprise, the other worry and shame.

"You! How did you get back here? I didn't put you on the list." Brittany pursed her lips and crossed her arms.

"Lisa! What are you doing here?" Lisa jumped to her feet.

"I have something I need to say."

All eyes were on Rachel, like she was stuck in a million-watt spotlight.

"No, no you don't." Lisa gripped Rachel's shoulders. "You

should run things by me first, remember?"

"I can't do this anymore. We are not who we say we are."

"What are you talking about? Rachel, what is this woman talking about?" Brittany's voice grew more irritated.

"I am the one responsible for the writing. Me." Rachel wiped her forehead with the back of her hand.

"What Lisa means to say is she's my muse and helps me develop my ideas."

Lisa clamped her hands, vice-like, on Rachel's shoulders, and she winced.

Lisa leaned in close to Rachel's ear. "Don't do this. Please. I've got it."

"This is not yours. You can't take everything," Rachel hissed back.

"What do you—"

"What's going on?" Brittany said. "Rachel, keep your assistant in line, please. This is not how we do things here."

"Let me tell you how you do things *here*." Rachel's voice had evened out, although the words came out louder than she planned.

"I don't have time for this," Brittany said. "Rachel, deal with her, or I'm afraid I'll have to rethink our working relationship. This is not the appearance we want to have."

"And it's all about appearances, isn't it?"

"Out. Now." Brittany's face grew impassive, and she picked up the receiver on her phone. "Don't make me call our people."

"Go, Lisa. Please. We'll talk about this later." Lisa stared at her friend and mouthed the word *please*.

"I think we'll talk about it now." Rachel replaced the fear in her stomach with a pool of courage, ready to be drawn from. "You have a perfectly smart and capable young woman working at this publication, who has been relegated to the mailroom simply because of the way she looks. I'm sure if her aunt knew exactly where she's been spending her time—"

"We're done here, Lisa." Brittany picked up the receiver again and pressed a single button. "I don't need you telling me how to staff my department. Rachel, do we need to have another conversation?"

"No, no." Lisa let go of Rachel's shoulder. "I'll take care of it. Lisa, you're fired. Go home." Lisa turned her back on Brittany. "I'm sorry. I'm sorry," she whispered. "We'll talk later."

A large man in a blue uniform appeared at the office door and took Rachel by the elbow. "Let's go, miss. We don't want to make a scene."

Rachel tried to appeal to Lisa one last time, but her friend's eyes were squarely focused on the carpet. Turning in defeat, Rachel let the security guard lead her out of the office. As the doors closed behind her, Brittany scoffed.

"You did the right thing. You don't need some fat helper following you around…"

Rachel's legs felt like lead as she walked down the hall. She was lightheaded and swayed, and the guard touched her other arm to steady her.

"I didn't realize we were taking hostages," a voice said.

Rachel glanced up at the unlined, ageless face of Elizabeth Burns. The editor-in-chief held a stack of files and was looking at Rachel askance.

"I'm seeing this woman out," the security guard said. "She's been asked to leave."

"Certainly she doesn't need an armed escort. You're not going to run off with the light fixtures, are you?" Ms. Burns peered closely at Rachel. "You're Rachel Simon's assistant, yes?"

"Former assistant," the guard said.

"Thank you," Ms. Burns replied. "I think I can see our guest out." She waved him off. "Had a bit of a moment, did we? They only call out Mike for the big situations."

"I was trying to talk to Brittany. I had…something to say."

"I'm sure you did."

Rachel looked Ms. Burns in the eye. "Did you know Amy is working in the mailroom? Because certain people here didn't think she fit a certain profile?"

"No. That's not true. She works in marketing. She tells me all the time how well it's going."

"She doesn't want to get anyone in trouble."

Ms. Burns paused and squinted. "Sounds like she's a pretty good storyteller, too. Like someone else I might know." She shifted the folders in her hands. "What did you come here to tell Brittany? Anything that might interest me?"

Rachel wanted to tell her everything, every fib, every cover story, every reason why she'd lied.

Say it, say it.

Out of the corner of her eye, she caught Lisa poking her head out of Brittany's office, and her resolve waned.

"No," Rachel said. "Just a misunderstanding."

"Good. Let me see you to the lobby. I think I need to call my niece and get the straight scoop."

They stepped into the lobby, where Rachel noticed Alex chatting up an assistant holding an armful of scarves.

"Don't worry," Ms. Burns said. "You're not in trouble. Brittany's just having a snit. She likes things a certain way, and when a piece or two doesn't fit she gets a little bitchy." She turned on her heel and headed back to the executive offices. "Keep helping Rachel with her columns." She stopped and turned her head. "They're very good. Rachel is a talented writer." The doors closed behind her, leaving Rachel leaning on the receptionist's desk.

"Excuse me? I heard you were taking juice orders?" The receptionist smirked and pointed to the elevators.

Rachel yanked the handle of her bag higher on her shoulder and stood up straight. She went over to Alex and tugged on his jacket.

"Alex? Let's go. I'm done."

He continued talking to the assistant, who was enthralled.

"Alex? *Alex?*"

"Oh, hey, hi, you done?" He just then noticed her presence.

"We need to go."

"One minute." He turned back to the assistant. "You pick out the bracelets all by yourself?"

"Now!" Rachel marched to the elevator and jammed her finger into the button.

"Okay, okay." He jogged to meet her. "How did it go?"

"Swimmingly. Everything is fan-fricking-tastic."

"Awesome. You want to get a coffee? I could go for a coffee."

The doors opened, and they got on.

"I'm upset, Alex. I don't know what I'm doing with my life right now. I'm rethinking everything. Nothing makes sense anymore."

"It's a no on the coffee, then?" Alex selected the button for the first floor as the doors closed.

It was a long drive home.

~ * ~

After breakfast the next day, Alex and Rachel headed out to run errands. For late November it was warmer than expected. It was what her mother used to call a *cinnamon day*, with a plethora of reds, oranges, and browns, and a crisp, spicy tinge in the air. People milled about, trying to shake off their recent holiday binges and make small talk about being sick of pumpkin spice everything.

Rachel kept herself busy, trying to keep the loop of yesterday's events from replaying in her head like a cheap B-movie. The evening was spent in her living room, reviewing pictures from Alex's recent gallery show in New York. He was not enthusiastic about the photos at first, but with each picture she reminded him of the good things about his work. She felt like a middle-aged cheerleader.

"You know what?" He shut his portfolio with a flourish. "I'm going to make you dinner."

"You cook?"

"Not really. But I can make chili. Hope always liked my chili, and she said it was the best she'd ever tried."

"Hey, if it was good enough to get a supermodel to eat, go for it."

As Alex cooked, Rachel set the table in the dining room, using the *good* dishes and cloth napkins. He insisted she light candles, and they sat together at the end of the table, toasting each other with the red wine he'd picked up that afternoon.

"To you." He clinked her glass. "You always know what I need."

She gave him a slight smile. Alex had apparently decided to forget the whole thing. She wanted to call Nathan, who'd know just what to say, but remembered that was no longer an option.

After dessert, which she ate with great relish, she drove Alex to his motel. When she got back, she threw herself into cleaning the numerous pots and pans he used to make his *one-dish* meal. Bending over to turn on the dishwasher, she felt lightheaded, and leaned on the edge of the counter. She attempted to dry the pots but gave up and went straight to bed.

She picked him up the next morning and gave him a tour of the campus. The buildings were mostly empty, save for a few staff members and custodians, and their footsteps echoed down the hallways of the main building as she pointed out pictures and rooms of interest.

After heading downtown, they stopped for coffee at the Java Hut. He opened the front door, and she found herself blocked by Alex's arms as he proceeded to go in first. He didn't hold the door open and she nearly walked into the glass. They got in line behind three college-aged girls, who made eyes at him and giggled.

"Hey, how's it going?" he said to the girls.

"Awesome," said the bravest of the three, a pretty redhead with a russet pea coat and a matching knit headband.

The other two smiled and batted their eyelashes as only nineteen-year-olds could.

"I like your gloves." He motioned to the shortest of the girls, who was sporting pink fingerless gloves with yellow hearts.

The line moved, and the girls gave their orders—mocha frappe thingies—and giggled when they were asked the obvious question of whether they'd like whipped cream on top.

Before Alex stepped up to order, the redhead approached him. "Hey, you wanna sit with us? We're gonna hang out."

She had a dimple in her left cheek that deepened with her shy, coy smile. Her friends laughed, half-embarrassed, half-emboldened by their friend's request.

He was caught up in the co-eds' attention, laughing with the group. "That'd be great! Lemme get my coffee."

The girls squealed a bit as they sat at a square table by the side window.

"Medium-dry cappuccino, please."

The kid behind the counter rang him up and started on his order. Alex appeared to remember he wasn't alone and regarded Rachel out of the corner of his eye.

"Hey, is there room for my friend here?" he asked the girls.

One of the girls sighed, and the other two shook their heads as they gave Rachel the up-and-down. The redhead appointed herself their new spokesperson.

"The table's kind of small. I don't think there's room for five."

He took his coffee from the barista and addressed Rachel. "I'll be over here."

He turned back to the girls before she could answer. He leaned on their table, the dashing older man holding court with the young maidens. They hung on every word, laughing too loud and piping in with bon mots like, *You're so funny!*

Rachel paid for her coffee and headed for the door. "Alex? Alex?"

This was becoming a theme.

One of the girls pointed at her. "Your mom is calling you."

The other girls exploded in a fit of giggling. He held up his hand in a cool wave.

"See ya," he said to the girls.

He swaggered as he met Rachel at the exit.

"Made new friends, I see." She pushed the door open, not waiting for him.

The air outside was cooler, as was she.

"Oh, come on. I was just having some harmless fun."

"Yeah, yeah, yeah," she replied, as they proceeded down the sidewalk. "Just remember the band Nirvana."

"Why?" He matched his pace to hers.

"Because you *can*."

He put his arm around her shoulder. "Don't be grumpy. They

were flirting. It was nothing."

It was an interesting choice of words. Like the Christmas party during their junior year. Alex had asked her to dance, despite the bottle-blonde in the strapless blue dress who had been hanging on him since they got there. It was a magical night for Rachel, with them dancing, drinking wine, and having deep conversations about their lives after they graduated. They even hit the all-night diner a few hours later, sharing a cinnamon roll that was easily the size of a child's head. She drove home, alone, in a romantic daze, sure her charm and personality had won the day.

Until she found out a few days later that upon leaving the diner, he had gone back to the party and hooked up with the blonde in the blue dress.

"It was no big deal," he said, after she had mustered the courage to confront him. *"You're the one I like to talk to."*

By the time they got to the car, she had brushed the memory away. Alex tossed his cup in a trash can and slid into the passenger seat. At the first stoplight, she rummaged around in her purse for something, anything…moving her fingers around the wallet, house keys, old receipts, and four tubes of lip balm…bingo. She opened the wrapper on the who-knows-how-old piece of butterscotch and slipped it into her mouth. She sighed, the sweetness melting on her tongue.

After unlocking the door to her house, they went inside. Rachel held open the storm door as Alex opened the main door and entered first. She hung her coat on the rack and held out her hand for him to hand her his.

"Do you want something to eat?" she said. "Want to wash up?"

"Nah, I'm good. I'll change my shirt and run a comb through my hair before we go." He paused and cocked his head. "When are we leaving?"

"In about two hours."

"Great. Mind if I stretch out on the couch and take a quick nap?"

"Suit yourself. I'll try not to bother you."

"Hey, thanks." He kicked off his boots and swung his legs onto the cushions of the couch. "Make sure you give me fifteen minutes to clean up before we go, okay?"

"No problem." Rachel remembered she'd left the dry cleaning and groceries in the car. "I'm just going to run out to…"

His arm was flung over his eyes, and he was fast asleep. She removed her keys from the bowl next to the door and ran out to the car then attempted to haul everything in one trip, probably not the best of plans. She had her wool pants in the plastic bag hanging over her shoulder, two fabric grocery bags in the crook of each elbow, the coffee in one hand, and a bottle of wine in the other. She managed to open the door with the three remaining fingers, but not being used to carrying this many things, she tripped over the dry-cleaning bag. After placing the bunch down, she hung the pants in the hall closet.

"Hey, you need any help?" Alex mumbled from the couch.

"Got it. Thanks."

Rachel picked up the bags again and hauled them from the foyer to the kitchen. She emptied the bags and put things away. Wasn't she was supposed to bring something to Lisa's house tonight? Rachel had no time to make anything. She slapped her forehead, and then opened each cabinet, searching for party-appropriate food. Crackers? No cheese, though. Bruschetta? She had tomatoes, basil, and garlic, but no Italian bread.

A light went on in her head. She whipped the freezer door open and shoved aside a few bags of frozen broccoli. Success! Two boxes of mini-quiche. She glanced at the baking directions, got a plastic container from one of the lower cabinets, and dumped in the contents of the boxes.

She went to her bedroom to figure out what she was going to wear. Not wanting to disturb Alex if she made any noise, she closed the door behind her. She pulled a pair of black pants and a black sweater from her closet, her basic uniform. Before changing clothes, she decided to follow Alex's lead and have a short lie-down.

She tossed and turned, putting her hand under her head, then by her side. She decided the nap wasn't going to happen and picked up her book from the nightstand. As she did so, her phone dinged with a text from Joanie.

Rachel   Theodocia   Simon.   Lisa   said   you're   bringing someone???

Rachel typed her reply. *An old friend. No biggie.*

Joanie responded immediately. *Is he cute?*

Rachel rolled her eyes. *He would be if we were in the seventh grade. See you later.*

She placed the phone down, and it dinged again.

Bring food. Lisa never has enough. Gentiles.

Rachel chuckled. She leaned her head against the wall and shut her eyes. She didn't intend to sleep, but must have drifted off because after what seemed like a few minutes, she woke with a start. Glancing at the clock, she was relieved she had a few minutes to get ready. She changed into her party clothes swiftly, put on a touch of pressed powder, and swiped on a touch of lipstick.

Sometimes being low-maintenance has its benefits.

She went downstairs, expecting to have to wake Alex, but he was standing in the living room, ready to go. He was wearing a pair of black jeans, collared shirt, and a jacket. He'd also shaved. The effect was striking.

"You look great," he said. "And hey, actual makeup."

"I've been wearing *actual makeup* for years. Just not a lot of it."

"You've got natural beauty. Don't need much."

"You're just saying that so I'll make you pancakes tomorrow."

"We're having pancakes tomorrow? Awesome!" He gazed at her more intently. "I mean it, though."

The eye contact made Rachel nervous, and she broke away.

"Let me get the quiches from the fridge, and we'll go."

Hors d'oeuvres in hand, they stopped at the front door for their coats. Before she could don hers, he picked up her coat from the rack and helped her with it.

"Thank you," Rachel said. "You've, er, I mean, you've never done that before."

"I'm full of surprises, I guess." He shrugged. "There's a lot of things I should've done before."

They arrived at Lisa's condo, and Rachel found a spot in Guest Parking and put the visitor's pass on the dashboard. They walked into the lobby and hit the elevator button.

"Rachel, I've been thinking."

"That's good. An active mind is a healthy mind."

"I'm serious. What would you think about me, you know, hanging around here?"

"Define *hanging around*. And *here*." She tapped her foot, waiting for the elevator.

"I'm serious. It's been super being with you these last couple days. I had forgotten how great you make me feel. Like I could take on the world."

The elevator doors opened, and they got on. She hit the button for the seventh floor.

"Isn't it a bit fast?" she said. "What about New York?"

The elevator began its ascent with a little hop.

He took her by the shoulders. "That's just it. It is fast. I was meant to be here. I need you, Rae. Nobody can do what you do." He leaned in and kissed her.

It was a gentle kiss at first and deepened with passion and

intensity.

Her head swam as memories came flooding back, of him, the attraction, the disappointment, and the pain. The doors opened, and she pulled away. Straightening her coat, she tried to ignore the wobbling in her knees and get herself together before they got to Lisa's door.

Lisa answered the doorbell, resplendent in a light blue dress and matching belt that accentuated her tiny waist. Her blonde hair was done in an effortless sweep, pinned up in the back with artfully arranged tendrils on the side and nape of her neck. The sparkle in her light blue eyes dimmed as she glanced at Alex.

"You're here." She hugged Rachel. "Yay!"

Like Alex, Lisa had obviously decided to ignore the events of the previous day, and Rachel could not have been more relieved.

"Yay!" She held out the container of mini-quiches.

"Oh, thank God." Lisa sighed. "I was afraid I didn't have enough food."

Joanie, standing about six feet behind her, mouthed, *See?*

Lisa accepted the plastic box. "Come in."

The place was immaculate, as usual, her professionally decorated rooms filled with the perfect accents and colors. The living room, with its light blue and white trim, was decorated with lit candles and silver trim around the mantle and side tables, with plain silver and blue ornaments scattered in a pre-holiday festive scene. She was going all-out for the group of friends who were happy to settle for popcorn and cheap wine.

Rachel wondered how much was for their benefit, and how much was designed to impress Nathan, who didn't care much for decorative artifice.

"Alex, how nice to see you again. So glad you could come." Lisa's smile was forced as she took their coats. "I'll put these in the spare room and get the quiches in the oven. Make yourself at home."

She was off, leaving the scent of her designer perfume in her wake.

Alex and Rachel went into the living room, where everyone else was already assembled.

"Making your grand entrance, I see." Brennan gave her a hug.

"We're not late. Lisa said seven."

"We arrived early, hoping to catch her off guard. Didn't work, dammit." He kissed Rachel's cheek and squinted at her.

Joanie had reseated herself and was halfway through a large sip of wine. She waved. Nathan sat on the chair adjacent to the couch, striking in his dark gray slacks and a light gray sweater over a blue and gray plaid button-down, which Lisa had most likely picked out for him.

Rachel glanced at his shoes. He was wearing multi-colored striped socks, which Lisa would hate.

Snuck that one by her, didn't ya, pal.

Brennan squeezed her shoulders before she could greet Nathan. "Oh, my God. You have to meet Jon."

In the hallway stood a handsome young Asian man in slim pants and an even slimmer tie. His hair was tousled with just the right amount of product, and he wore an earring in each ear.

"Rachel, this is Jon. I finally got the nerve to call him yesterday. This is our first date. He's a children's book illustrator." Brennan ran out of breath and gasped for air before continuing. "He's a lot of fun, really smart, and you'll get to be the best of friends."

Joanie patted his hand. "Breathe, Judy." She took another sip of wine.

"Very nice," Rachel said. "Does he speak?"

"I get a word in occasionally." Jon shook Rachel's hand. "Nice to meet you."

"Come, dear. Sit by your Aunt Gladys." Joanie motioned toward Jon, and he sat next to her.

"For more introductions, this is Alex," Rachel said. "He's an old friend from college."

Nathan got up and shook his hand. "I'm Nathan. Nice to meet you."

"Same here, man."

Nathan embraced Rachel tightly. "Good to see you. Missed you. You look pretty."

"Missed you, too. Nice sweater."

"Oh, yeah." He patted the front. "Gift from Lisa. You know, I—"

"Sit down, sit down." Joanie motioned, assuming her role as Queen Bee. "Either of you want a drink?"

"I'm good." Rachel sat on the arm of the couch. "Alex?"

"I could go for a Scotch."

"Brennan, go get Alex a glass of red wine, would you?" Joanie said. "I don't think there's any Scotch."

"I'll get it," Jon said. "I can check on the popovers while I'm up."

"He's very domestic," Brennan said. "I mean, I guess he is. He brought popovers. That takes effort."

"So Alex, what do you do for a living?" Nathan said.

Lisa entered with Alex's wine. "Jon's arranging the buffet

table. What a sweet guy. Well done, Bren." She handed Alex the glass. "Rachel, could you help me in the kitchen? I need to know how long to bake the quiches."

"Just put them in the oven at three seventy-five, for twenty minutes."

Lisa's expression told Rachel she wasn't interested in the baking directions. Rachel followed her into the kitchen.

"I can't believe you brought him!" Lisa said.

"Shhh. You said it was fine."

"Fine for me. I'm not the one whose heart he broke fifteen years ago."

"A little louder, Lisa. I don't think they heard you in Paraguay."

"Why is he still here?" She folded her arms across her chest. "Isn't there some skank he needs to be hooking up with in New York?"

Rachel picked up the baking sheet and put the food in the oven without checking the temperature. She closed the oven door and paused to carefully choose her words.

"He's, ah, thinking of staying around for a while."

"And when did he make this grand announcement?"

"In the elevator. On the way up."

"Ugh! Rae." Lisa stomped to the refrigerator and flung open the door, then grabbed a bottle of tonic water and slammed the door shut. "This is not, I repeat, *not*, a good idea."

Rachel took the tonic water from her and put it on the counter. "I guess I'm full of bad ideas these days."

"I don't want to talk about that."

"Okay, *that* you don't want to talk about. Apparently with Brittany you couldn't shut up."

Brennan and Joanie appeared in the doorway.

"Need any help?" Joanie said. "I can peel limes or something."

"I think you're making a huge mistake. Again." Lisa put her hands on her hips.

"I think we came at just the right time," Brennan whispered to Joanie.

"What's going on here?" Joanie said. "Lisa's got that one frown line that the doctor didn't Botox out."

Lisa threw up her hands. "Go ahead. Tell them."

"There's nothing to tell. Alex is thinking about staying in Chicago. He wants to, um, see how things go. With me."

"And she almost blew the job with the magazine yesterday. Got tossed out by security."

Brennan put his hands over his mouth, and Joanie lifted her eyebrows about two inches.

"And he kissed me in the elevator." Rachel gave Lisa one more jab.

"The security guard?" Joanie said.

"Alex."

"That is a lot to unpack." Brennan stared at Rachel, his gaze boring into hers.

She met his gaze, but only for a second, before turning away.

"Brennan, could you please give us a moment?" Lisa said.

"Oh, I'm not missing any of this. I'm staying right here."

She gave him a look that could've wilted daisies.

"Fine," he said. "But I need a reason to go back in there." He glanced around. "I'll take...this." He picked up a pair of tongs and held them vertically in front of him. "But I think I can add a different perspective to the situation."

Three sets of female eyes locked on to him. He held out the tongs and left the kitchen.

"Joanie, would you please talk sense into her?" Lisa said.

"About which thing?"

"Either," Lisa replied. "Pick a battle."

"I don't think either is a huge deal. Dating? Pssh. She should have a little fun. And I mean, you guys didn't lose the gig, despite Rachel showing a spine for the first time in, I don't know, *ever*—"

"I just think Alex is a bad idea," Lisa said.

"Fine, you're on the record." Rachel was beginning to resent being lectured.

How many times had she warned Lisa not to go out with a particular guy? How many more times had she talked Lisa down after a bad relationship ended? And now, after Rachel had basically handed her the perfect man, Lisa was going to lecture her? Rachel felt that familiar gnawing in the pit of her stomach. She had to get away from this.

"Let those things bake for another ten minutes," Rachel said. "I'll be in the living room."

She left Joanie and Lisa in the kitchen and went to the living room. *Maybe I'll have some wine, after all.*

She stopped short at the sound of men's voices.

"Yeah, Rachel's not the kind of girl I usually go for." It was Alex. "I mean, she's great and all, but I usually date models, actresses, those types. But I'm at a place in my life where I think, what the heck. I can get past her looks."

Nathan's voice was quieter. "How big of you."

"It might not work back in New York, but out here, at least no one will think I'm a chubby chaser, you know? Besides, she's the smartest girl I've ever met. Always knows what to say to make me feel better."

"There's more to her than that. And some people might find her attractive."

Jon breezed past them and narrowly avoided bumping into Rachel, who was hovering in the hall. "Hey, Rachel, I'm going to get drink refills. You want anything?"

Rachel was so startled she had trouble finding words. "Um, uh, white wine, please."

Her cover had been blown. She walked further into the living room, greeting Alex and Nathan.

"Hi, guys!" she said, too brightly.

"Everything all right in the kitchen?" Nathan said.

"Absolutely." She gestured at the side table holding the hors-d'oeuvres. "Alex, do you want anything?"

"Sure. Whatever you think looks good. I trust your judgment when it comes to food." He went back to the couch, sat, and crossed his legs.

Nathan followed her to the buffet table. "He's, uh...yeah. College friend, you said?"

Rachel picked up a plate. "It's complicated. The friendship was kind of off and on. Hot and cold." She noticed a plate of pastries, marked with a card that said, *Jon.* "Obviously Jon wanted credit for bringing those," she said. "He must be very proud."

"Or that's the name of the dish. You never know. Maybe he calls the pita chips *Dave.*"

"As one does." Rachel put a popover on the plate, just for emphasis. "You eating?"

"Yeah, I think I will. Lisa had me running around today, helping her set up. I don't think I've eaten since this morning."

"You're going to want *two* Jons, then. And perhaps one or two Stanleys. They're fresh."

He laughed. "Stanleys always hit the spot."

"Speaking of Lisa," Rachel placed a crab cake on the plate, "how are you guys doing? 'Cause this is...new."

Rachel wanted to know, and she didn't want to know.

Nathan paused and lifted a plate from the stack. He picked up the silver tongs and put two of the bacon-wrapped shrimp on his plate.

"We're, uh, good," he replied. "We're good. Lisa's great.

Surprised me what she first asked me out, but it's going, uh, good."

Rachel put a crab cake on his plate.

"But it's only been a few weeks," he said.

As if on cue, Lisa appeared next to Nathan, holding a tray of the mini-quiches in one hand, wrapping the other arm around his waist.

Rachel internally cringed.

"How's it going?" Lisa purred. "Nathan, honey, you want one of these? Rachel brought them. They smell wonderful."

"Oh, sure, I'll—*mmrmph.*"

His words were cut off as Lisa fed him one of the appetizers.

"Why don't you two join us over here?" Joanie called out.

Lisa brushed a few crumbs from the side of his mouth, playfully tapped him on the nose, winked, and left to tend to her guests.

"I think we've been summoned." He cleared his throat. "Hand me a few more of those shrimps, please."

"You mean a few more of the Liams."

"Of course."

They returned to the group. Rachel sat next to Alex, who had sagged against the back of the couch and was staring glassy-eyed at Brennan and Jon. She held out his plate, but he just took a shrimp from it. Rachel wondered if she was supposed to keep holding the plate or not. Nathan leaned forward, took the plate from her hand, and placed it on the coffee table.

Drinks and food were refilled, and Lisa suggested they play charades. She went to get notepaper and pens, and they wrote down their suggestions. Jon volunteered his hat, and into it went all the book, movie, television show and song titles they could come up with. Lisa and Nathan were a team, along with Joanie and Brennan, and Rachel was paired with Jon. Alex, nursing his third glass of wine, volunteered to keep score.

Joanie and Brennan were an unstoppable force.

She made one undulating gesture, and Brennan veiled out, "*Gentlemen Prefer Blondes!*"

"Amazing!" Jon flashed him an admiring smile.

"What do you expect, darling?" Joanie demurred. "I'm royalty."

"Yeah, yeah, have a seat, duchess," Rachel said. "Nathan, you're up."

Lisa elegantly arose from her perch on the arm of Nathan's chair as he selected his clue.

"You ready?" he said.

She sat on the chair and crossed her legs. "Ready." She glanced at Rachel.

Nathan looked at the clue and put it on the table. He held up his index finger, made the gesture for *movie*, and mimed tying a knot.

"Rolling. *Rolling Thunder. Rolling in the Deep!*" Lisa guessed.

Nathan shook his head and kept miming the knot.

"Tie. Tying the knot!"

"That's not a movie, Lisa," Joanie said.

Lisa waved her off.

Notting Hill.

Nathan held up two fingers. He moved his hand up and down, indicating high to low.

Notting Hill. It's Notting Hill.

"Flying." Lisa was clearly grasping at straws. "Sailing. *Titanic.* It's *Titanic!*"

"Time's up," Alex said.

Notting Hill.

"It was *Notting Hill*," Nathan said.

"Oh, I love that movie!" Lisa said. "I should have gotten it."

They played a few more rounds, and every time Alex would put his hand on Rachel's shoulder, or his hand on her leg, Lisa would purse her lips.

When they had a break in the game, she followed Rachel to the bathroom. She entered the room right after Rachel and shut the door behind her.

"We have to stop meeting like this," Rachel said.

"You need to end it."

"I have to pee first."

"I'm not kidding. Is he staying with you?"

"Why do we always fight in the bathroom?"

"Oh, come on. Is history repeating itself? Is he going to take advantage of you again?"

"He's not taking advantage."

"Please. He's going to barge into your life so you can mend whatever psychic wound he has going, and when he's feeling on top of the world once more, *poof!* He'll be out of there."

Rachel pushed past her and stood at the sink. "Are you just annoyed that you lost at Charades?"

"People don't change who they are."

She turned on the water to wash her hands. "Lisa, why don't you mind your own business for once and let me mind mine?"

"What do you mean by that?"

"I mean that you can't stand for me to have anything nice for myself." Rachel rinsed her hands and shook off the excess water. "And my writing thing? You were very eager to take credit for that, weren't you?"

"You asked me to!"

"I asked you to be the face. I didn't ask you to take the initiative and start taking meetings without me."

"I'm helping you. I know the lingo."

"Any time you see me have something good, you want to take it away. You want to keep me sad and alone so I'll always be available to take care of you." Rachel dried her hands on the rose-patterned guest towel.

"Name one time I've done that." Lisa sat on the lid of the toilet.

"You want to get into this?" Rachel put her hands on her hips. "Michael? That sweet boy from my dorm? You flirted with him and ignored him. He didn't want to be near me anymore in case he ran into you. And how about Spenser? I'm pretty sure you told him I was a lesbian. Oh, and Marc? I told you I liked him, and you swooped in and asked him out before I had the chance. And my twenty-third birthday? You threw me a party but made it all about you because you couldn't stand to see me the center of attention for *one day*."

"You didn't have a chance with any of those guys. They weren't into you. And that party was turning into a dud. I was helping you out."

"We'll never know, will we? You sure saw to that."

"I'm sorry you think I'm such a terrible person." Lisa got up. "But if Alex breaks your heart again, don't come crying to me. I don't want to hear it." She swung open the door and stormed out.

"Are you freaking kidding me with this?" Rachel followed her like a laser beam, caught and dragged her by her elbow into the spare room. "*You* don't want to hear it? What about all those times I picked you up off the floor after a tragic breakup? I was there for you every single time, and now you pelt me with an ultimatum?"

"Uh, hi, ladies." Brennan was standing at the side of the bed, fishing for something in his coat pocket.

"Hi," they said in unison, never breaking eye contact with each other.

"When I said you should get back in the game," Lisa said, "I didn't mean with him."

"I didn't plan it. He showed up. Maybe you're jealous Alex paid attention to me and not you, for once in your life. And that I have a talent you don't. That must be killing you."

"Are you sure about that?" Lisa folded her arms and jutted out her hip.

"Why don't you go out to the living room and pee a circle around Nathan in case there's someone who doesn't know you trapped your prey."

Lisa hung her mouth hung open, wordless. Her eyes welled up, and she made a beeline for the door. Rachel's hands were shaking.

"You okay?" Brennan said.

"What the hell was that?"

"You tell me. You didn't tell her about Nathan, did you?" He pulled her down to sit next to him on the edge of the bed.

"Are you kidding?"

"Are you going to let Alex stay?"

"It's a free country. He can stay, or he can go back to New York."

"I mean, stay with you."

She leaned over and put her head on his shoulder. He put his arm around her, steadying her still-shaking arms.

"Nathan's not available. You saw Lisa. She's not letting him go. Even if I said something, I think it's too late. And maybe Alex has changed. I'm so tired of being alone. Tired of being the odd man out. Just tired."

"I understand." Brennan kissed the top of her head. "Alex is kind of a dick, though."

"Yes."

"Does Nathan know you write the column for the magazine? That you're the one who really won the award?"

"No. I've let him think it's Lisa. It's just…easier."

They sat in silence for a moment.

"Jon is very nice," Rachel said.

"Oh, good, we're back to me. He wants me to pose for him."

"Nude?"

"Of course. He's an artist. But I'm not that kind of boy."

"Yes, you are."

"Yes, I am." He was almost giddy. "Now give me a hug."

Rachel hugged him hard. "I think I need to go now." She picked up her coat and slung Alex's over her arm. "I'll be fine. I'll figure it out." She took a big breath.

In the living room, Joanie was deep in conversation with her new nephew, Jon, and Lisa and Nathan were standing by the coffee table, arms around each other's waists. Alex waited by the chair, tapping his foot and looking at his watch. Rachel handed him his coat.

"Well, we're off," Rachel said. "Thank you for having us."

Nathan smiled, but Lisa wouldn't meet her eyes.

"You're leaving already?" He sounded disappointed.

"Yeah," Alex said. "It was a great time. Thanks."

He put his arms through the sleeves of his coat, then shook hands with Nathan, who followed them to the door.

"I'll go get the elevator." Alex strode down the hall.

Nathan took Rachel's hand. "It was nice to see you. I'll save you some Leonards for next time." He smiled, his eyes crinkling in the corners.

"Yeah, you too. Maybe we can get coffee sometime—"

"Elevator," Alex shouted.

"That would be nice," Nathan said. "I'd like that."

"Nathan?" Lisa called. "Can you help me?"

"Guess I better go back in. Had fun with you tonight. You totally would have gotten *Notting Hill*." He touched her lightly on the arm. "Good night."

Rachel held her hand up in a wave and joined Alex, who was holding the elevator. She held back a tear as the doors closed.

"That was fun," he said, as they got into her car. "That Joanie is a character. What do you call her? The countess? That fits."

"Duchess."

Rachel turned the heater to high, letting the air into the cabin with a whoosh. The wheels screeched as she pulled out of the parking lot.

"Nathan's a nice guy, too," Alex said. "Bland, but all right." He buckled the seatbelt over his jacket. "Did you two ever, you know, go out?"

"No. Why do you ask?"

"Just asking. Probably good that you didn't because I think Lisa's got her claws in him good."

Rachel stayed silent as Alex talked of parties he'd been to in New York. After a few minutes, she interrupted his stream of talk.

"Do you want to go right to your motel, or do you want to come back to my house and watch a movie?"

"I'd like to go back to your place. But can we stop at the motel first? I need to pick up my charger."

When they got back to Rachel's house, she was suddenly tired. She didn't even hang up her coat, just tossed it on the back of the wing chair in the front room.

"I'm not up to watching a movie," she said.

"Me neither."

"You can watch something if you like, or I can take you back to the motel."

"Okay."

"I'm going to get a book from upstairs. You want something to read?"

"Sure."

Rachel trudged up the stairs. She wasn't sleepy, but drained. She went to the spare bedroom, where she kept a bookcase for the overflow.

"I've got a variety of genres here." She motioned to the shelves. "I've even got back copies of *The New Yorker,* if you'd prefer."

Alex walked up behind her and kissed her neck.

"I'd prefer you," he murmured. "You never did give me an answer before." He turned her around and held her by her waist.

"Alex, I'm confused. You were never this clear about your intentions before."

"That was years ago when I was young and stupid. I cared too much what people thought. I need to be with you. You *get* me." He kissed her gently on the lips. "I can get past your size. You could get some fancy lingerie, you know, that hides a bit here and there. I could deal with that." He kissed her again, deeper and longer. "C'mon, let's go for it. We make such a great team, you and me."

Rachel said nothing. He drew her in tighter, gently running his hands up and down the ample hips and thighs she was supposed to dress in lace and silk to become more acceptable to him—the same body he'd dismissed many years ago.

He leaned in again, and his warm breath was on her cheek, then her neck. She moved nearer to him, taking leave of her senses, of her truth, of everything that was good and right, and she surrendered.

"You can stay."

They laid on the bed, his hands greedily exploring her curves, unbuttoning her sweater, his supple lips caressing her neck, her breasts, her stomach. She closed her eyes and drifted away, to another place, another time, another person…

Alex's phone rang, the tone startling and shrill. He removed one hand from her hip to take the phone from his pocket and glanced at the screen before hitting the accept button.

"Hey, man, what's up?" He released her from his hold. "You hear anything about that freelance gig?"

"Alex, I—"

He held up his index finger and got up from the bed. "Hey, that's good news. Did you talk to Serge?"

Rachel clutched her sweater, holding it together as she sat up in disbelief. He paced the room, engaged in his conversation. She got up from the bed and went to the door.

"Rachel? Give me a minute, okay?"

She waited another few minutes, but he had forgotten her. She padded out of the room and went to her own bedroom and closed the door behind her. She sat on her bed and petted the cat. Alex's phone rang again, and she fell asleep to the sound of his low murmurs from the other room. He would not be coming back.

She woke the next morning with a cat paw on her forehead. Rachel reluctantly opened her eyes and found herself nose-to-nose with Lindsey, who was making her Oh-God-I-haven't eaten-in-forever-I'm-starving noise.

Rachel rolled over and ignored her, but the cat wasn't having any of it. She meowed and placed her other paw squarely on Rachel's nose. She sat up and realized she'd slept in her clothes. She took them off, threw on her bathrobe, and washed her face. She wondered if Alex was still here, perhaps asleep in the spare room. They had unfinished business to attend to.

I will not.

Something clicked in her brain, something primal, and she would not accept being *less than.* She was not to be settled for. She was not a condolence prize.

Don't let the past define you, Anne's voice said.

The door to the other bedroom was open, the bed unused, save for a few wrinkles. She went downstairs and looked around the kitchen, finding only Alex's cell phone charger. Then she spied her to-do list hanging from a magnet on the refrigerator. There was no mistaking his handwriting, sharp and angled, and obviously written in haste.

Had to leave early. Got a text from Hope. She wants me back. Called for a car, flying to NY ASAP. Sorry.

She stood there, barefoot, holding the note. One moment she was thinking about Alex. The next, about how she needed coffee. She thought about their kiss, and two seconds later she was noticing dust under the cabinet door. She should be mad. Flat-out, dead-on, spit-in-your-face pissed.

Lindsey was doing laps around her ankles. Rachel put out a bowl of wet food, petting her fur as she placed the bowl on the floor.

She sat in one of the chairs, note clutched in her fist.

Sorry.

She read that one word over and over again, until it lost meaning.

Sorry I showed up unannounced after a decade.

Sorry I ignored you in public.

Sorry I thought you were never good enough for me, unless I was feeling like crap.

Sorry I led you on, multiple times, told you I wanted to be with you, and then left when my supermodel ex-girlfriend snapped her fingers.

A strange feeling developed in Rachel's throat. It grew larger, traveling up her neck and into her mouth, until it demanded to be released—as a long, loud laugh.

By all reasonable accounts, and every woman's magazine article she ever read, she should be crying her eyes out. She should be wailing and moaning, shuffling around in her sweatpants and slippers, and inhaling ice cream. But it wasn't in her. She laughed until she cried, wiping the tears away with a dish towel, and removed a bagel from the bag on the counter. She took a huge bite but spit it out.

Blueberry? Who the hell buys blueberry bagels? I dodged a bullet on that one.

She laughed again, holding the dish towel to her face. It was absurd. She had spent plenty of energy on him over the years, making sure to be supportive, helping him to pick up the pieces of his psyche each time he faced failure or a girl dumped him, just so he could get back out in the world and deny he knew her. And despite being older and wiser, she'd nearly done it again. A part of her hoped he had changed, and that maybe this time he could accept her.

Except this time, she didn't want him to.

Fuck you, Alex.

Rachel's phone dinged. She groaned, as her brain had turned to gelatin and was not ready to deal with the world before a cup of coffee. She picked up the phone, Alex's text on the front screen.

What on earth could he want? I swear to God, if he's asking for money I will drive to the airport and kick him in the nuts.

She opened the text message.

Hey, Rachel. Did I leave my charger there? Can't find it. Thx.

She shook her head in disbelief. *Are you kidding me with this? These are his final words to me?*

Rachel threw his charger in the garbage and typed her response.

Sorry, no. Haven't seen it.

She deleted the text and blocked his number. Her stomach clenched, and she stopped laughing. She got a box of chocolate chip cookies from the cabinet and opened it as she made her way back to the table. She was shaky and raw now, like she had landed on the surface of an alien planet, armed only with a travel mug and a handful of cookies.

One by one she ate the cookies, chewing and swallowing, but barely tasting them. She didn't care about the chocolate melting on her fingers. Didn't care about the crispness of the outer edges as she bit through it. She kept eating the cookies, waiting for the numbness that would inevitably follow.

She focused on eating so she wouldn't have to think about Nathan, who was with someone else. Or Alex, who found it easy to get up and leave as if she was an afterthought. Or how she had possibly lost her best friend over a magazine job. She couldn't, however, avoid the thought that she had made a mess of things, and how yet again she was *The Girl Nobody Wanted.*

I can't do this anymore.

She finished the package of cookies and threw the empty container in the trash. After wandering into the living room, she sat on the couch, pulled her legs up under her, and focused on her stomach. She had eaten until she couldn't think anymore. Eaten until she was truly done. And at that moment, only one thought was able to make its way to the surface of her food-numbed brain.

What the hell do I do now?

Chapter Fourteen

Monday arrived abruptly. It was two weeks before Christmas break, and the students had burned through their Thanksgiving respite and were antsy for another break. Rachel was, too. But they had finals to get through, about which more than a few students complained mightily.

She ignored the academic whining, sleepwalking through her days, her patience as short as the hours of daylight they had this time of year. She put them in discussion groups so they could review amongst themselves the material to be covered on the final. She assigned a written portion to keep the class from turning into a gabfest. That day, as most days recently, she minimized her interaction with others.

Her life continued in much the same fashion—get up, get through classes, go home, grade papers, work on her writing for the magazine. It was a routine that was rapidly and easily honed, punctuated with takeout containers and trips to the store for wine and cookies.

Her students, who didn't usually notice anything past their phones, looked at her askance, as if she were a porcelain doll who had been played with too roughly and was beginning to show the hairline cracks.

"Are you mad, Dr. Simon?" A student hovered at her desk, the typical vocal fry grating her ears, as the rest of the class was starting to pack up.

"I'm not mad, Kim."

"Yah, you seem mad." She handed Rachel her group's work, her wrist stacked with charm bracelets. "It's making us, you know, sad."

Rachel seized the papers from her and slammed them on her desk. "Maybe if the class did their work instead of discussing utter nonsense and using their phones to find other people's ideas and pass them off as their own, I might be less irritated."

Kim's eyes grew wide as the other students stared at Rachel's outburst.

The girl hugged her backpack to her chest. "Yah, okay, whatever."

"Forgive me, Kim. It's been a bad day. Have a good...I'll see you Wednesday."

Rachel just wanted them to leave. She pretended to busy herself with her planner as the students left class, whispering to each other and keeping a wide berth.

The following week, after her last morning class, she went to the faculty cafeteria to meet Brennan and Joanie. She hadn't seen either of them since the party, and her absence had become conspicuous. Rachel had neither the energy to keep up with them, nor the desire to talk. Texts had been deleted, phone calls ignored. It wasn't until a handwritten letter was delivered that morning that she could no longer avoid them. She opened the thick, peach paper to reveal Joanie's elegant script.

Rachel Henrietta Simon. Put down the Mallowmars and
get your ass to the cafeteria for lunch, stat.

Underneath was Brennan's contribution, in his typical cuneiform scratch.

We've left a trail of peanut butter cups in case you forgot your way.

She had been summoned. She tucked the test packets into her tote bag, displacing the baggie holding a squished almond butter and banana sandwich she had been saving for the drive home. She picked up her coat and briefcase, slung the tote bag over her shoulder, and trudged to the cafeteria.

Peering through her tired, squinting eyes, she spied her friends at their usual table. Joanie waved her over.

"She lives!" she said, as Rachel slipped into the chair and dropped her stuff on the floor. "We had our doubts."

"So did I," she replied.

"The food here is inedible," Joanie said.

"And she's planning on seconds," Brennan said.

Rachel said nothing and rubbed her coat between her fingers.

"We wanted to see you." Joanie picked a piece of lint from a curl in Rachel's ponytail. "We wanted to make sure you were all right."

Rachel shrugged. "I'm fine. I've been busy."

"You want to talk about...anything?" Brennan said.

She shook her head, her mouth forming a thin line. She shifted from side to side as if there were pins in her chair.

"There's nothing to talk about. Seriously. Lisa and I have had fights before. It's no big deal."

"You don't have to talk." Joanie patted Rachel's hand. "But I have something to tell you that will hopefully cheer you up, at least a little bit." She paused and held Rachel's hand. "Hank has decided to move back in."

Rachel felt a pulse of energy run through her torso. "Joanie, that's wonderful. Therapy did the trick, then?"

"Oh, hell no. He got tired of paying a hundred dollars an hour to *bitch about our problems*, as he delicately put it. Figured we could work it out at home, for free."

"And the play?"

"We open January sixth. Hank said he'd be at the opening. Then I'm taking a break. All will be well, I think."

"I'm very glad." Rachel squeezed her hand.

"Shall I put you down for two?"

"Two what?"

"Two tickets," Brennan said. "That's her subtle way of asking if you'll be bringing Alex."

Rachel sighed heavily. "Yeah, there will be no plus-one. Alex is no longer with us."

Brennan and Joanie's eyes widened, and Joanie put her hand to her mouth.

"No, no, he's not dead. He's just…no longer with us."

"He dumped you?" Brennan poked at the tater tots on his tray.

"He left."

"What did he say?" Joanie asked.

Rachel paused. "He didn't say anything. He left me a note. On my to-do list."

"On a to-do list? Like, buy eggs, pick up dry cleaning, break up with Rachel?"

"Well, there wasn't a relationship to *break up*, but yeah, pretty much." Rachel picked up one of Brennan's tater tots and popped it into her mouth.

"What a dick," Joanie said.

"That's what I said," he said.

"Agreed," Rachel said.

"Did you sleep with him?" he said.

"No. Threw away his phone charger, though."

"Rachel Clarabelle Simon, I'm proud of you." Joanie pinched Rachel's cheek. "It's not a burning effigy, but it's a start." She gestured toward the salad bar. "Brennan, sweetie, can you get me a fruit salad?"

"It's all the way over there. And there's kind of a line. You really need fruit salad?"

"I really do. Here's five dollars. Treat yourself to pudding." Joanie handed him the money.

"Fine. If I'm not back in half an hour, send a Sherpa to search for me. I'll be posed dramatically at the base of the ice cream machine."

Joanie shifted her chair closer to Rachel.

"You still don't know my middle name." Rachel stiffened as Joanie grasped her hand. "Ow. What's the matter? Did somebody die?"

"How long have you been in love with Nathan?"

Rachel disengaged her hand, picked up a sweetener packet and shook it back and forth. She debated whether to confirm or deny, as neither felt like the right way to respond.

"How did you know?" she said.

"I had my suspicions. I knew you liked him, but I didn't know if it went deeper than that. Then you told us about Alex, and I knew that's not what's been bothering you. He was a jerk." She paused. "There's something there, right?"

"Obviously not, because he's with Lisa."

"Oh, that."

"Yeah, *oh, that*. Kind of a big deal." Rachel tossed aside the sweetener packet, which slid off the Formica tabletop and hit the floor.

"Did you tell him how you feel?"

She squinted at Joanie, as if her friend had grown a third arm out of her forehead. "No, because he's with Lisa."

"That's not a good answer. Why didn't you tell him?"

"Because life has shown me that I am meant to be alone. Men like Nathan do not fall in love with women like me. It just doesn't happen. Assholes don't want me either, P.S., but that's another story." Rachel swallowed hard. "If I had said anything to Nathan, I'd have gotten the speech about how he likes me as a friend, and everything would be awkward, and we wouldn't even be friends anymore. I couldn't bear that. And yes, I sound like I'm in the eighth grade. Stop looking at me like that."

"Listen, let me tell you something." Joanie rotated her chair toward Rachel. "When I met Hank, it was love at first sight. For me, anyway. Hank was a straight arrow, honest as they come. He didn't want anything to do with a crazy redheaded actress prone to bursting into song at the drop of a hat. It wasn't in his plans. He began seeing a friend of mine. Nice girl, very Midwestern. A tad dull, in my opinion, but she had a great rack. Anyway, I decided I wasn't giving up unless they were walking down the aisle. I told him, in no uncertain terms, that he and I were perfect for each other, despite our differences. I *fought* for him, Rachel."

"Basically, you stole him away from his girlfriend."

"Maybe. But you can't steal a guy who doesn't want to be stolen. My point is, I didn't give up on love. He took a chance on a loud drama-bitch with crazy curly hair, a pear-shaped ass, and a borderline drinking problem, and we've been together twenty years. We've had a few bumps in the road, along with some ginormous potholes, obviously. But we're still here. I didn't give up. And neither should you." She clenched Rachel's hand. "Whether you believe it or not."

She fought back the hot, fat tears that were forming. She would not cry over this because she was fresh out of the will to cope with feeling sad and pathetic. That was not who she was anymore. She had polished her new armor.

"It doesn't matter, anyway," Rachel said. "Lisa—"

"Screw Lisa. Listen, I love her, too. Don't get me wrong. But she and Nathan aren't right together. She got dumped, and then got desperate, and Nathan was a good option. That's all. And also, believe me, she can't keep up the writer façade forever. She doesn't have the chops." She placed her hands on either side of Rachel's face and gazed into her eyes. "Don't give up. Please."

Brennan reappeared at the table, holding a tray in one hand.

"You would not believe the drama going on at the salad bar. It's like *Gone with the Wind* over there, with Dr. Steinketz as Rhett Butler, and half the custodial staff as the Confederate Army." He sat, closed his eyes, and sighed, pressing his palms onto the table. "Not my circus, not my monkeys." He opened his eyes and passed a white bowl to Joanie. "Here. Enjoy."

Joanie took the plastic container, then gave Brennan the side-eye. "This isn't fruit salad."

"It's tapioca."

"I asked for fruit salad."

"They didn't have any."

"Did you ask?"

"I hinted. I gestured."

"This is *tapioca*. Did you *ask* for fruit salad? Out loud?"

"Listen, Scarlett O'Hara at the cash register was distracted. Eat your tapioca, Gladys."

Rachel picked up a spoon from Brennan's tray and took a scoop of his chocolate pudding, then took another. She was reaching for a third when Brennan put the bowl in front of her.

"Here. This will be faster," he said.

"We were talking about Nathan," Joanie said, as Rachel shoved another spoonful of pudding in her mouth.

"You know?" he said.

"*You* know?" Joanie looked at Rachel, accusingly.

"I was there when she met him," Brennan said. "Right place, right time. Did you talk sense into her?"

"I'm going to need more pudding," Rachel said.

"Let's go easy on that." Joanie took the spoon from Rachel's hand. "Desserts can only fix so much."

After talking Rachel out of wiping the remnants of the pudding from the bowl with her finger, Joanie went to teach her last class of the day, and Brennan walked Rachel to her car. He carried her briefcase and tote bag, and she held his arm as they trudged through the snow. He placed her bags in the back seat of her car and hugged her.

"Thank you for the help," she said. "I appreciate it. I'll try to be more present. I've been out of sorts. But I'm fine."

"You're using that word a lot."

"It's true."

"How's your eating been?"

"Normal."

"Please. You inhaled that pudding like someone was going to take it away from you."

"Yeah, *you* were." Rachel scratched her ear. "It doesn't matter."

"*You* matter," he said, his mouth close to her ear. "I love you." He kissed her cheek. "And Alex..."

"I love you, too," she replied. "Alex didn't break me. He didn't even dent me. And it wasn't him. I think it was sort of the idea of him. Like if I tried hard enough—"

"It would never be enough. He is a tourist, stopping just long enough to take pictures and ruin the local scenery."

"You're right. You're right." She laughed, wistfully. "Even though I didn't want him, I guess I wanted to be wanted."

Brennan squeezed her hand and kissed her again before she got into her car. Rachel drove home, resisting the deep need to run away from her life, to be anywhere else, to find a spot in the world where she could leave herself and not face the stinging vulnerability she always sought to avoid.

At the next light, she rooted around her purse and glove compartment, eventually nabbing a bag of goldfish crackers she had saved for an emergency. Eating gave her a way of pretending to feel everything without having to actually feel anything. Hand to mouth, hand to mouth, she was living both in the present moment and in the past, trying to numb the pain of both. She feared a life of her own undoing, of being unable to give herself over to the idea of love, because no one would truly love her, and at some point it was just another thing that would go away. All her life she'd feared being broken, so she had broken herself first.

Finishing the goldfish crackers, she made her way home, quiet and full, yet with a dull, indefinable hunger she felt would never be sated.

Chapter Fifteen

Rachel stood in front of her last class before winter break, the room full of students working on their final exam. The room was silent, save for the sounds of shuffling in seats and tapping of erasers on the desks. The afternoon sun shone through the back windows, casting lengthy shadows between the rows of chairs. A few students scribbled furiously. The left-handed students twisted themselves around, trying to keep their papers on the right-sided desks. Others stared at the clock or at the posters on the wall for inspiration.

One by one, they finished the questions and flipped their test packets over, gathered their things, and deposited the tests on Rachel's desk before exiting. She kept looking about the room as students wrote and pondered their answers, but she was thinking about shoes. Her new shoes, specifically.

Before classes that afternoon, she stopped at the shoe boutique downtown and spied those beautiful black satin strappy heels in the window. This time, however, she didn't try to talk herself into the sensible brown shoes in the back. She went in, tried them on, and bought them. She would have to practice walking in them, and they cost more than her first car, but they were pretty, impractical, and most importantly, she wanted them.

They currently sat in a festive shopping bag with lots of pink tissue paper, in the trunk of her car. She wanted to tell Lisa, who she imagined would insist they go shopping for a new dress, asserting that one could not wear shoes of that caliber with elastic waist pants.

And even if Rachel reminded her that she only owned one pair of said pants, Lisa would retort that was one pair too many, unless she was auditioning for the road company of *The Golden Girls: The Musical*.

Rachel smiled inwardly but felt a wave of sadness. She and Lisa had fought before, but it usually lasted no more than a couple hours, before one of them caved and they made up over a Sara Lee frozen cake. But it was different this time. She hadn't caved, and Lisa had gone silent.

Finally the last student submitted his packet, then shuffled out in his green hoodie and baggy sweatpants. He breathed a sigh of relief and greeted his friends in the hall with a hearty, "Done, bro!"

Once Rachel was alone, she, too, breathed a sigh of relief, and straightened the stack of papers she now had to grade during the break, along with submitting a column to *Charmé*. She didn't have to do any of that right away, though, and she was looking forward to going home and putting her feet up. And wearing her new shoes, of course.

She got her coat from the rack behind her desk and went to put her arm in.

"Glad to be done?"

Startled, Rachel missed the sleeve. At the sight of Nathan leaning against the doorframe, her breath caught in her chest and her face felt warm. She dropped her coat on the floor, picked it up and reminded herself to breathe. As she stood, she responded with what she hoped was a not-too-forced smile.

"Sure am!"

"Mind if I come in?"

"Oh, yes, sure. I was just getting organized before I go." She shuffled papers around, willing her shoulders relax.

"Nice room. Are the pictures yours?"

"Yes. I've collected them over the last few years. Some of my favorite writers. Keeps me inspired, I guess."

They both noticed the poster of Emily Dickenson, peeling off the wall.

"Looks like Emily is trying to make a break for it," Nathan said.

"I suppose I should have had them laminated." She cleared her throat and sat at her desk.

"That would slow them down. How have you been? Haven't seen you in a while."

"I'm fine. Busy. The usual." She picked up a pen. "Are you sticking around here for the holiday?" She recapped the pen and put it in her desk caddy.

"No." Nathan leaned on her desk. "Going back to New Jersey for a few days to see my folks. And my sister had her baby a few months ago."

"That'll be nice for you. Especially since you didn't get home at Thanksgiving."

"How about you? Your family doesn't celebrate Christmas, but are you going to see them?"

"Nope. My parents are going on another cruise this year. They'll be gone through the New Year. And Joanie is doing Christmukkah with her family, and Brennan is taking Jon to meet his parents. I'll be on my own."

Nathan looked like he was sucking on a lozenge, his *tell* for when he was trying to find the right words. "So...no Alex?"

Rachel's spine stiffened. "Alex is...no longer with us."

"My God! What happened?"

"Oh, no, no, he's fine. He went back to New York."

I have got to stop phrasing it like that.

Nathan let out a loud breath. "I can't say I'm sorry. He was kind of a dick."

"That's the consensus, yes."

"I didn't want to say anything before, but he is. He's definitely not good enough for you."

"I guess not."

"Did you break up with him? Please tell me you had the good sense to dump him."

She paused. "It was a mutual thing."

"*Pfft.* That means he left you. How did he do it? On the phone? Text? Or did he just up and leave? Lisa told me that's his M.O."

Rachel bristled. "He left me a note."

"Classy. Probably on the back of an envelope, right?" Nathan got up and went to the window, with his back to her. "Lisa and I both think you deserve better."

"Oh, really?" she said, icy tone.

She felt her shoulders tense, and indignation filled her.

"The two of you do? You've been together, what, two months? And now you're experts on all the relationships in the world? The Law according to the Perfect Couple. Great."

His shoulders sagged. "We're not the perfect couple."

"Could have fooled me. Throwing parties, she's picking out clothes for you—"

He spun and threw up his hands. "She asked me out, and I said yes. She's emotionally available, which is more than I can say for—she's nice. I like her. But we're not perfect."

"I'm happy for you, anyway. I'm sure your parents will love her," Rachel snapped.

He pointed at her, and then ran his hands through his hair.

"I don't get you. You close yourself off at every opportunity to people who genuinely care, but you have no problem making yourself a doormat for a guy who uses you to prop himself up, treats you like crap, then drops you as soon as he thinks he has something better. And the funny thing is, it doesn't even faze you!"

"Stop it." Her heart pounded louder and louder.

"No, seriously, Rachel. What is it? I thought we were getting close. I thought there was something between us. I mean, I could feel it, couldn't you? But you always shut down." Nathan was pacing, one hand on his hip, the other on his head. "And then to see you with that asshole. God!" He turned to her. "Maybe you deserved Alex. I hope that on some level he did hurt you, just so that you, for one minute, could feel the pain I—" He put his hands to his side and hung his head. "I'm sorry," he whispered. "I didn't mean to yell."

Her throat tightened and tears welled in her eyes, the kind of fat, hot tears that refused to be wiped away.

Tell him. Tell him now.

His face was still red, and his breathing was ragged. "What? You want to tell me something?"

"You...have...no...idea..." Rachel whispered.

"Idea of what? Idea of *what*, Rachel?"

She stood there, her mouth agape.

Where's that newfound self-esteem now, Rachel?

If I tell him, he will go away.

"Why am I with Lisa?" He moved closer to Rachel. "Because she says what she feels. She puts herself out there and doesn't hide behind her glasses and her books and her jokes. She took the initiative and wrote a blog that got her noticed by a big-time magazine, and now she's got a second career and an award. She doesn't live in fear, Rachel. Not like you."

With those words, more tears came, and Rachel couldn't stop them. She had to get out. She needed to run. She snatched her coat and bags and pushed the door to the classroom open with such force that it banged on the wall next to it.

"Rachel, wait!"

Nathan called after her, his voice growing distant as she dashed down the hallway, jostling past students saying their goodbyes to their friends before heading home. Around her was white noise, and she kept going, opened the main doors and inhaled the cold air like a diver breaking the surface of the water. She proceeded across the quad with tunnel vision. Getting to her car was her only mission, and she would not be stopped.

"Dr. Simon! Dr. Simon! Wait, please!" The shrill voice was unmistakable and was getting closer.

If she could make it to her car before...

"Dr. Simon! Are you doing speed walking these days? My goodness." Cindy McPherson was out of breath as she caught up with Rachel.

She grasped Rachel's arm to stop her. Rachel faced her, reluctantly.

"I wanted to see if you're coming to our final Secret Santa Swap. You don't have a family, so you're probably on your own for the holiday. I wanted to make sure you didn't miss this last chance to socialize. There will be punch and cookies," she said, as a final selling point.

"Cindy, shut up." Rachel surprised herself with the surety and strength of her voice. "We are grown-ass adults. We don't need to stand around the office handing each other keychains and scratch-off lottery tickets."

"But everybody is—"

"For once in your life, just put a sock in it, would you?" Rachel walked away.

Cindy's mouth hung open as she looked around for witnesses, then turned on her heel and went back inside in a huff. Rachel made a beeline for her car, drove home, and dragged herself into the house. She shut and locked the door behind her. She sat on the couch, in the dark, still in her coat, and her beautiful new shoes in the trunk.

For the next few days, Rachel avoided the normal hustle and bustle of the early holiday season by staying in her house. She'd been back on autopilot since school let out, going through the motions as if in a daze. But she had much on her mind, and somehow things were beginning to change.

She thought about her friends. Joanie hadn't called her in several days, but Rachel decided it was a good sign that her family was knitting itself together again. Brennan's texts had been entertaining, as he had brought Jon home to Lake Point. And despite it being early in their relationship, Jon was weathering the Donaldson's well. They'd even visited Sharon in rehab, and she'd given her blessing on their relationship, although they hadn't asked for it. But she insisted it was part of her process, so they stayed and ate Santa Claus cookies with tea.

Rachel had never gone this long without talking to Lisa, and she missed the sound of her voice, chattering on about clothes and movies, and criticizing her shoes. She wasn't mad anymore. The anger had melted away. Lisa had said hurtful things, but Rachel wasn't sure she was totally off the mark.

She missed Nathan, too, but his was a more wistful absence, a lilting whisper of an ache signifying what might have been. It was a strange sort of isolation, and she pretended it was self-imposed, but she really was alone. And for the first time, she let herself feel it.

To her surprise, she survived.

Chapter Sixteen

The following Saturday afternoon, Rachel awoke from her nap to find two pairs of eyes leaning over her bed and staring at her.

"Holy crap!"

"Why aren't you dressed yet? Ceremony is in two hours."

Joanie's face came into focus as she stepped back from Rachel's bed.

"C'mon. Up and at 'em, George McFadden." Brennan opened the closet doors and rifled through her clothes. "What are you, Amish?"

Rachel sat up halfway, willing her brain to focus on what was happening. Joanie was wearing a silver sequined pantsuit, and Brennan was clad in a sharp navy suit.

"Is that today?" Rachel said.

"Yes, it's today, genius," Brennan replied. "We need to go watch Lisa accept your award. It will build character."

"Why do people always say that about things that are terrible?" Joanie said to him. "No one ever says, *Here, have cake. It will build character.*" She pulled Rachel out of bed. "Yes, it's terrible. But we're going. We're going to support Lisa, come hell or high water."

"She doesn't want me there." Rachel sat back on her bed and face-planted into her pillow.

"Rachel Cleopatra Simon," Brennan said. "Of course she does. You two are best friends. BFFs. Besties. Cheese muffins. Okay, that was too much. But my point stands."

"I don't have anything to wear."

"That's why we brought something." Joanie dashed into the hall and returned with a garment bag. "This is for you."

Rachel unzipped the bag, revealing a black cocktail dress with a lined lace front.

"Wow." She pushed her glasses up her nose. "This is gorgeous."

"Yes, it is," Brennan said. "So put your hair up, get dressed, spritz some perfume, and let's go already!" He pulled her sweatshirt over her head and was poised to make a go for her T-shirt.

"I got it, I got it." She shooed him away. "But I'm doing this under protest."

"This is nothing new," Joanie replied. "You've got twenty minutes."

After Rachel got dressed, the trio sat in the back of the town car Joanie rented for the evening. The driver had made sure the limo was stocked with liquor and a few snacks, though Rachel only found the will to sip on bottled water. Joanie and Brennan clinked their glasses in a toast to themselves as the Chicago skyline grew closer and closer. Rachel was cold, even with the heater on, and she held her coat shut.

"Want a pretzel?" he said.

"No thanks. Salty," Rachel replied.

"Good idea," Joanie said. "Save room for when we get there. I'll bet there will be appetizers floating around. I love a good appetizer."

"Yeah, I think I'm appetizered out." Rachel recalled the mini-quiches from Lisa's apartment, and her stomach lurched.

The driver let them out in front of the hotel, and they headed in, bracing against the cold. The ballroom was opulent, filled with hundreds of beautiful people milling about. As Brennan checked their coats, a trio of young, slinky-clad ectomorphs sashayed past them.

"Probably going to split a dinner mint," Joanie said. "Ooh, that was mean. Shouldn't shame."

"Don't you feel intimidated?" Rachel said.

"By whom? *Them?*" Joanie pointed her thumb toward the models. "Why? Because they're young? Thin? Gorgeous? Successful? Desired by many? Okay, I get it." She shrugged. "But honestly, I don't."

"Lucky."

"Please. I bet they're home every night watching Netflix in worn-out PJs like the rest of us."

The gaggle of models floated by again, flipping their shiny hair and laughing at nothing.

"Well, maybe not. But I bet they're dumb as a box of rocks," Joanie whispered.

"Actually," Brennan said, "the middle one went to Dartmouth, I think."

Joanie and Rachel frowned at him.

"Just kidding." Brennan turned his head and watched a blonde woman in a white dress slink past. "I am reasonably certain that's the actress we saw in that movie that one time we went to that thing," he said.

"The one with the…" Joanie mimed, indicating a set of large

breasts.

"No, the one with the…" Brennan touched his nose.

"Oh, her. I like her," Joanie replied.

"Shall we go in?" Rachel tapped her foot and futzed with her dress.

She considered stalking the waiter with the bacon-wrapped shrimp, but her gurgling stomach made her think twice.

"I don't want a table too close to the front," she said. "I want to be able to make a getaway."

"Listen, we'll just watch you—I mean, not you—get the award," Joanie said. "Then we'll go hit a Sonic for cheeseburgers. I haven't had one in ages."

Joanie, Brennan, and Rachel's phones dinged at the same time. Rachel removed hers from her purse and rolled her eyes.

Tell Rachel to come backstage. Emergency!

"Did you two get the same message?" she said.

Joanie and Brennan nodded.

"I'm not going. She wanted all this attention for herself. She can have it."

"Rachel—"

"No, I'm serious. This was a bad idea to begin with, and that's on me. But I'll tell you, she ran with it. She did her best to nudge me out of the picture and pretend she was the one who did the work. She wanted the glory, so she can have it. I'm out."

"You're going to leave her alone back there?" Brennan said.

Rachel removed a champagne flute from a nearby tray and downed it in one gulp. "Yes."

"You can't—"

"I *know* it's all my fault." Rachel slammed the glass on the table. "I'm responsible for this whole damn mess. Me. Just me."

"Are you still talking about the magazine?" Joanie whispered.

"Yes! Maybe." Rachel held her breath. "Damn it. Here, hold this." She handed Brennan her purse. "How do I get backstage?"

"Probably over there behind the stage." He pointed.

Rachel took a deep breath. "Damn. It." She dashed off toward the stage.

She started to ask a young man wearing a headset for directions, when Amy, clad in a green satin gown, waved at her from the side door.

"Lisa! Lisa! Over here." She waved again, with more enthusiasm.

It took Rachel a moment to remember that here she was Lisa,

and she was being summoned.

"Amy, nice to see you. You look great."

"Thanks. My aunt got it for me. None of the designers wanted to dress me because of my size, but Aunt Elizabeth made a few calls."

She hugged Rachel, who was caught off-guard and stiffened her shoulders.

"Guess what? I'm not in the mailroom anymore. Aunt Elizabeth said she talked to you and decided to promote me into marketing. Isn't that exciting? Score one for the fat girls, right?"

"Right. That's great, Amy. You deserve it."

"Thanks. I do. And maybe things will work out for you, too. Maybe Rachel can help you get a writing job for yourself. My aunt says you're very smart and have a great take on things."

"I admire your confidence." Rachel glanced at the green pattern woven into the carpet. "How do you get backstage? Rachel was looking for me."

"Yeah, just go that way." Amy pointed to a door a few feet away in the hall. "Giving the boss a pep talk?"

"Something like that. Good luck to you, okay?" Rachel patted her young companion on the arm and headed for the backstage area, in search of Lisa.

The wings of the stage were dim and Rachel bumped into several technicians on the way in. Craning her neck, she scanned the area for her tall blonde friend. Onstage, she could hear the current honoree giving her speech, talking about science and advances in technology Rachel didn't understand. She stopped to let her eyes adjust to the lighting and leaned on the back of a chair.

"Listen, I need to wait for Rac—I mean, Lisa to get back here. She always helps me when I'm nervous. I don't know if I can do this."

Rachel sat up at the sound of Lisa's voice.

"That's not true, doll," Brittany replied. "You totally can. You don't need her. You got here on your own."

"Here's the thing, though. I—"

"Rachel, I know she's your friend, but she's…how can I put this…a troll. Seriously. She stands out like a sore thumb around the office, and she thinks she knows it all."

"She's not a troll. She's the smartest, best person I know."

Rachel stepped forward, wanting to hear better, but trying to remain unseen. Brittany's arms were folded, and Lisa's posture was hunched. She was also terrified, something Rachel could see, even in the low light.

"You've got five minutes to pull it together, Rachel. Or maybe

I'll have to rethink the offer we made you."

Elizabeth Burns approached them. She sucked in her breath.

"Brittany, can I see you for a moment?" Elizabeth took her arm and led her away.

Brittany gave Lisa one last point, for emphasis, and soon they were out of sight.

Lisa turned and spotted Rachel. "Rae! You're here." She gathered Rachel into her arms. "I've been thinking...I'm very sorry. About everything."

"It's fine. Things were said." Rachel gazed past Lisa, to the wall behind her.

She couldn't face her yet.

"Where's Alex?" Lisa said, hesitantly.

"He's gone. Took off the morning after your party."

Lisa opened her mouth to interject, but Rachel held up her hand.

"Yes, you were right. He hadn't changed. But I'm fine. No pieces to pick up. Turns out I didn't like him much, after all. I liked being needed. But that's not enough, is it?" She finally met Lisa's gaze. "Where's Nathan?"

"He's not coming. We...broke up."

Rachel's heart leapt to her throat. "Really?"

"I suppose I saw it coming, but I ignored the signs. I wanted it to work. He was so perfect on paper. But we never clicked. I mean, he watches World War Two documentaries." She leaned in. "He likes *hockey.*"

"You were only together for a little while. Those things take time."

"Not for you guys. You clicked right away."

Rachel shrugged. "We had no paper."

"It wasn't me Nathan wanted. I mean, he was wonderful to me, but I never felt like his first choice." Her voice was raspy.

"Sweetheart, look at you. You're always everyone's first choice. That's why we're here."

Lisa took Rachel's hand. "You love him, don't you?"

"No! I mean, no. It's just..." Rachel looked away.

"My God, you do. How could I not have seen it? You told me you didn't, and I believed you. That's the only reason I pursued Nathan. I never would have done anything, otherwise."

"I would rather have seen him with you, who I love, than some random woman."

"That's a bunch of bullshit, isn't it?"

"Yeah, I knew it when I said it."

"How have you gotten through this?"

"I ate a lot of Oreos."

"My favorite." Lisa laughed. "But at some point you're going to have to stop being afraid. You need to stop talking yourself out of things before you even try. It's a sure way to live a small life, Rachel." She noticed Rachel's feet. "New shoes? Pretty."

"Hard to walk in them."

"Makes it tougher to run away." Lisa pointed at the woman on the stage. "She's talking about edible glassware. She figured out a way to make a wine glass you can eat with cheese and dip when you finish your wine. I don't belong here. You do."

"It's a little late now, Lisa."

"No, it's not. I'm going to do something I should have done from the start. You're going out there."

The wine glass inventor left the stage to thunderous applause, replaced at the podium by Elizabeth Burns. Rachel listened to her origin story, from her work at the college, to the discovery of her blog, and her first meeting at *Charmé*.

Rachel's knees buckled, and she swayed. "I am not. No. No way. I can't."

"You speak in public all the time."

"No, literally, I *can't*. They'll know what we did."

Lisa hugged her again, too hard for Rachel's limited comfort. "It's the right thing."

Elizabeth's voice got louder as Rachel panicked.

"And now, as one of our Women to Watch, I'd like to introduce—"

"Lisa, no, I—his can't happen—"

"Dr. Rachel Simon!"

Lisa released Rachel from her stronghold and shoved her onto the stage. Rachel tried to leave, but Lisa blocked her way. "Go." She motioned to the microphone that was placed center stage.

Rachel inched toward Elizabeth, who appeared less surprised than Rachel expected. She turned again to Lisa, who was arguing with Brittany and restraining her from rushing the stage.

Facing the spotlight, Rachel felt the floor start to wobble like the deck of a sailboat.

Don't faint, don't faint.

She kept her eyes on Elizabeth, who was holding out the microphone.

"Give 'em hell, Rachel," she whispered, winked, and passed

off the mic, leaving Rachel alone on stage.

She could hear the murmur of the crowd as they tried to reconcile the large picture of Lisa on the overhead projector, with the round, sweaty brunette in front of them.

"Hi. I, um—"

"Talk into the mic," a man in the audience shouted.

"Oh, right. Of course." She held the mic to her face. "Hi." She gazed at the huge picture of Lisa, looming over her. "So, yeah. I photograph well, don't I?"

The crowd twittered with laughter.

She turned back. "Camera adds ten pounds. I was being photographed by a team of six."

Rachel scanned the audience, shielding her eyes from the bright light, trying to locate Joanie and Brennan. She noticed a glass of water on the podium and picked it up, her hand shaking. *I wonder if it's edible.*

"So you might be wondering what's up right now." Her voice quavered less. "I am Rachel Simon. This gorgeous lady," she pointed to the screen, "is my best friend, Lisa. She's such a good friend that she agreed to go along with this hare-brained scheme of mine." She gave a half-hearted laugh. "You see, it started when…"

Out of the corner of her eye, and just under the edge of the light, she spotted Nathan, who was standing by one of the side doors, holding a wrapped package. He stared back at her, and her mind went blank.

"Rachel!" Lisa stage-whispered, from her spot in the wings. "Keep talking."

Rachel managed to force her gaze back to the audience in front of her. "I shouldn't be here. I'm not what *Charmé* had in mind. They found my blog and thought I was Lisa. Because I used her picture. Wouldn't you? I mean, come on."

She was pacing, hoping it would help her find the words that were not forthcoming.

"I did it because I was afraid. I'm afraid of a lot. When you grow up looking like me and you aren't one hundred percent secure with yourself—and let's be honest, how many of us are, except maybe that table over there—the world lets you know, on a daily basis, that you're *less than*. Which is ironic because I'm actually larger than is ideal." She paused, gripping the mic with both hands. "I let *Charmé* think what they wanted. I was convinced there was no way they'd want me, so I didn't give them a chance. Happens a lot."

She turned back to the podium, trying with every fiber of her being not to focus on Nathan.

"It was just easier. In my mind, Lisa hasn't lived with rejection. She hasn't lived with being constantly reminded that she's not enough. She hasn't had to live with *this*." She gestured up and down her body. "She doesn't know what it's like to be the girl nobody wanted. Who nobody sees. The one who can't please her mother because she's not beautiful like she is. Every time I'm passed over for somebody a little prettier, a little thinner, it cuts me a little bit more. Every. Time." Her words were coming faster now, a sense of breathless urgency behind them.

She glanced at Nathan, who was standing there with his mouth agape.

"I've missed a lot. Why do we do this to ourselves? I'm not the only one. We accept being hungry because we think we shouldn't enjoy our food. We accept being with someone who doesn't really love us, because we think we don't deserve more. We accept the job in the mailroom because someone we don't care about told us that's where we belong."

Rachel walked to center stage and put the microphone in its holder.

"And I'd like to apologize. I'm sorry for lying about who I was, and to my friends, for putting them through this. And I'm also sorry to myself because I've missed so much."

She walked a few steps stage left and faced Nathan. He shook his head, opened the door and walked out of the ballroom. Rachel lost her breath and felt lightheaded. Taking a deep breath, she marched back to the mic.

"Sometimes you just need to have the cake, you know? So have a piece of damn cake!"

The audience was silent. Then, from the back of the room, her friends cheered.

"Woo-hoo! Yeah! Rachel!"

The audience clapped and chanted, "Cake! Cake! Cake!"

Lisa, who had been joined by Elizabeth, was cheering from the side. Lisa was beaming, and Elizabeth placed her hand over her heart in approval. Rachel smiled, tentatively, and then smiled with embarrassment as she noticed the picture of Lisa on the screen had been replaced with one of her.

Not bad. She gazed up at her faculty directory photo.

She left the stage, with the audience still cheering.

"Good job! I'm so proud of you," Lisa said. "I'm going to hug you again. Deal with it."

"Nice speech, Rachel," Elizabeth said. "Although, it's too bad you felt you couldn't be honest with us."

"I understand if you want to fire me."

"Oh, no, we're running your article. It's good work. And I think our readers will appreciate it even more coming from you. The real you." Elizabeth placed an assuring hand on her arm. "Let's talk Monday, okay?"

Rachel got off stage and led Lisa back to the table where Joanie and Brennan were beaming.

"That was amazing!" he said.

"I am over the moon for you. I am *verklempt*. Literally *verklempt*." Joanie cupped Rachel's face in her hands. "You want to get that cheeseburger now?"

"I do. I really, really do."

It wasn't cake, but she would enjoy it, nonetheless.

Chapter Seventeen

Six weeks into the new term, once again whatever energy students and faculty had regained over the holiday break was beginning to dissipate. Blankets of snow coated the trees and grass, rendering it see-your-breath cold, with a lot of wet brown slosh being mucked about. People moved with a sense of purpose, and their eyes shone brightly, not due to any positive attitude, but because of a deep desire to get back inside. Especially the ones who didn't have the sense to dress properly for the weather.

That was The Great Age Divide. The adults, who wore big hats and scarves, appearances be damned. And the students, who held onto the belief that walking around in nine-degree weather in a sweatshirt and baseball cap was cool.

As for Rachel, she had no need to be cool. She had regular discussions with the head custodian on the appropriate classroom temperature level, which she maintained did not allow her to see her breath when she discussed *Leaves of Grass*. Most days they agreed to disagree, hence the extra three sweaters Rachel kept at her desk.

Her last class ended, and as she was erasing the whiteboard, Brennan entered the room.

"Want to get a coffee?" he said. "Holy crap, it is cold in here! Should I build a fire?"

"You know how to build a fire?"

"Sure. I was a Boy Scout. For a week." He sat on the edge of her desk. "I could probably earn a couple retroactive badges by helping Joanie cross the street."

"Don't let her hear that. She can kick your ass six ways 'til Sunday, in high heels, singing selections from *Hello, Dolly!*"

"No doubt." He laughed. "Speaking of which, are you going?"

"Wow, is that this weekend?" She brushed the non-existent chalk from her hands. "Yes. I said I would. Are we supposed to bring gifts?"

"Not unless there's a registry for couples that have been married for twenty years, separated, went to therapy, and are now more in love than ever and are rubbing it in our collective faces. With a festive Valentine's theme."

"That is very specific. Maybe at Target?"

"I'm bringing booze. One size fits all."

"Aren't they going to have an open bar?"

"It'll be for later."

"Sounds like a plan. And I'll have to take a rain check on the coffee. I'm behind on grading."

"I won't see you until the party, then. Jon and I are going skating tomorrow, and we have a Skype date with my mother over dinner on Friday."

"I'm glad he was a hit with your parents."

"Oh, please. I think they like him better." Brennan hopped off the desk. "See you Saturday." He waved and blew her a kiss as he left.

Rachel wasn't lying about the grading. She did have a stack of papers in her bag. But she had been keeping a low profile, focusing on herself in a positive way. It had worked out for the best, as Joanie was spending more time with her family, and made a deal with Hank that she would only do two shows a year on top of her teaching load.

Brennan and Jon were attached at the hip, basking in the new-couple glow. She did see Lisa from time to time, although Lisa had landed a promotion at her firm, and threw herself into her work.

As for Rachel, her house had never been cleaner, her closets more organized, and she had been seeing a therapist since after the new year. She didn't tell anyone about that, as she decided it was good to have something that was just for herself.

Saturday came, the day of Joanie's party. Rachel called her in the afternoon to offer help, but Joanie refused, saying, "I have professionals on the case, dear." Joanie was a born party planner, and Rachel had no doubt she kept those professionals on their toes.

Joanie sounded sharp and energized, with lightness in her voice that she hadn't had in a long time. A few weeks prior, she told Rachel she now had her priorities in place, and fortunately her priorities still included entertaining in high style.

With her therapist's encouragement, Rachel decided to try to look forward to the evening's festivities despite her general disdain for Valentine's Day. Except for the chocolate. She always liked the chocolate.

Rachel took her time getting ready for the party, even going so far as to put in her contact lenses, which she rarely wore. The plum eye shadow brought out the green flecks in her irises, and she went crazy and put on two layers of mascara.

What the hell. It's a party.

The night was clear and it hadn't snowed in a few days, so the roads had been plowed clean. She pulled into the parking lot of the golf club and followed the signs to the LAWSON VALENTINE'S NIGHT ROMANCE EXTRAVENGANZA. The sign even had silver cherubs with bows and arrows, causing Rachel to seriously consider going home.

The ballroom was spectacular. Joanie had managed to procure the room with the fireplace and the enclosed patio with glass doors overlooking the pond. Not that anyone would be going outside, but the view of the night sky was beautiful. The room was festooned with silver and varying shades of red, dark rich drapes and sparkling accents, like a Valentine's fairyland. A large crowd milled about. A few guests were wearing angel wings, some with halos topping their heads. A six-piece band played in the corner. Rachel was transfixed.

"Rachel! You're here." Lisa landed at her side, decked out in a tight dark dress and her trademark pearls. "Let's check your coat and get you a drink."

A few minutes later, they were at the bar, glasses in hand. Rachel spotted Joanie across the room, Hank by her side, working the crowd like a pro.

"She seems really happy," Lisa said.

"So does he, surprisingly. He hasn't been a party guy, historically."

"At least one person in our group is in a healthy relationship." Lisa sipped her martini.

"Don't forget Brennan," Rachel spied Brennan and Jon on the dance floor. "Our little boy is doing quite well for himself."

"Very true." Lisa squinted at Brennan. "Is he vogueing?"

"I didn't teach him that."

Lisa laughed. "It's nice to be out like this."

"Or like *that,*" Rachel indicated Brennan. "Did you bring anyone?"

"Nope," Lisa played with the plastic spear holding the two olives in her glass. "I'm trying something new. Dating myself."

"I do that whenever I make a *Love Boat* reference." Rachel took a fig stuffed with goat cheese from a passing waiter.

"I'm serious. I'm taking time to be on my own." Lisa snatched the fig from Rachel's hand and put it in her mouth. "I haven't been without a boyfriend for more than a week or two since I was thirteen. I think I need a break." She chewed and pointed to her mouth. "This is *good.*"

"Yeah, food. Who knew?"

The band changed songs, moving from an up-tempo piece to a ballad. The dance floor population changed, a few dancers exiting to get a drink, others moving in to enjoy a relaxed turn with their partner. The glitter ball hanging from the ceiling threw sparkling light throughout the room like large snowflakes.

"I'm proud of you." Rachel snagged another fig from the waiter, who was making a return trip. "It shows real growth. I'm sure that when you're ready, the right guy will be there for you." She popped the fig in her mouth before Lisa could take it. "These *are* good."

Joanie was across the room, introducing Hank to a few people, some who had a lot of ear piercings, two who had green hair, and a few who wore colorful scarves. She waved at Rachel and Lisa.

"Who is that Joanie is standing next to? The one in the purple tie? He's gorgeous." Lisa put her drink down and pulled her lip gloss out of her purse.

Rachel rolled her eyes.

Joanie excused herself from the group and joined Lisa and Rachel at the bar. Her red dress shimmered in the light, the bottom part floaty and ethereal, swirling around her legs as she moved. Her matching red hair was arranged in an artful low bun, and her eyes matched her diamond earrings in fire and intensity. Rachel thought she was a vision. She embraced both of them, giving Rachel an extra kiss on the cheek. She smelled of wine and Shalimar.

"Lisa, you look gorgeous," Joanie said. "I'm so glad you're here. Listen, I have someone you'd like to meet."

"Lisa is off the market," Rachel said. "She's only dating herself these days."

"Yes, I'm taking a bit of a hiatus."

Joanie pointed to the handsome man in the purple tie. "Gavin works in fashion. He's a buyer for Saks, I think. Well-off. Very cosmopolitan."

"Hmm, I don't know—"

"He's straight, single, wealthy, and works in fashion. He's a unicorn. Go."

"I wouldn't want to be rude." Lisa snapped her purse shut. "The one in the purple tie, you say?" She picked up her drink and zoned in on the target.

Joanie chuckled. "Like shooting fish in a Birkin." She turned to Rachel. "You coming for Passover this year? I'm having it catered. Brennan and Jon are doing it. It was a tough negotiation, but they only had two general questions."

"In addition to the usual Four Questions."

"Yes. Jon wanted to know if eggs had to be certified Kosher, and Brennan wanted to know what the hell my problem was."

"Wouldn't miss it for the world. I'll bring bail money."

"Smart." Joanie got another drink from the bar. "Just FYI, Nathan is here."

"Okay."

"I think you should talk to him tonight. It's time."

"I don't think he wants to talk to me. He left the awards thing without saying anything. I guess he was shocked to find out Lisa didn't write the blog."

"Oh, please. He knew. Talking to her, talking to you, it's kind of obvious."

Rachel said nothing and sipped her wine. Joanie took the glass from her and placed it on the bar.

"Rachel, I love you, but stop acting like a twelve-year-old girl who burped in front of the boy she has a crush on. Because if I have to kick you in the ass, I will. And you don't want that because I'm wearing my big girl shoes tonight." She turned Rachel around to face the windows, where Nathan was standing, alone. "Make this one count," she whispered in Rachel's ear.

Rachel caught Nathan's eye. Joanie gave her a nudge, and Rachel began what felt like a mile-long trek across the room. He smiled as she approached, but she found herself avoiding his gaze—looking at the floor, at the other guests, at the ceiling—and almost caused a collision with two other guests and a bartender carrying a case of wine.

After the commotion, she found herself standing next to him, and she stared out the window at the stars.

"Pretty night," Nathan said.

"Yes."

"Come on. I got you a present." He opened the screen door and stepped onto the patio. "It's okay. It's enclosed. We won't be cold."

She followed him onto the patio, encircled with glass windows that went from floor to ceiling and curved over their heads like a large skylight. He handed her a package and she accepted, gingerly, like it was a crystal bird. She untied the string, letting it fall, and unfolded the paper.

"I meant to give it to you at the awards thing, but—"

"Yeah." She turned it over and read the title embossed on the dust jacket.

Nathan pointed at the book. "It's a UK first edition of *The Hitchhiker's Guide to the Galaxy.* There's some fading on the spine, and a bit of wear on the corners of the flap hinges. But the owner assured me it was a good find."

She held the book to her chest. "This is amazing. Thank you. How did you—"

"I remember you mentioned once that Douglas Adams was one of your favorites. I saw it and thought of you."

Rachel was speechless. She ran her fingers over the cover and the spine and flipped through a few pages when she spied a flash of dark handwritten lettering in the front pages.

"It's signed?"

"Oh, is it?" Nathan said, with mock incredulousness. "I had no idea."

She embraced him, then backed away after a few seconds.

"Thank you again. This is…" She took a deep breath. "This is the best present I've ever gotten. Better than the Barry Manilow tickets I got in the fourth grade."

"High praise."

Together, they gazed at the sky. She had never seen such a clear night, every star glimmering as sharp points of light.

"There." He pointed diagonally across the sky. "Full moon."

"Pretty."

"If you get a second full moon during a month, that's called a blue moon. They're special because they don't happen very often." He took Rachel's hand. "Like some people."

The music from the dance floor hung in the night air, along with the sound of people *ya-hooing* to the tune of *Celebration*.

"I'm sorry I lied about the whole magazine thing," she whispered.

"I'm sorry I left. I needed time to think."

She pointed at the sky. "Is that a shooting star?"

"I think it's an airplane."

"Oh. Would have made for a nice moment."

"Hey, I'm going to come right out and say this, because hinting and implying doesn't get us anywhere. I have never had this much trouble getting a woman to notice me, even with my matching sock issues and questionable taste in documentaries." Nathan lifted his pants legs to reveal striped socks, each with mismatched colors. "I'm employed. I'm tall. I have all my hair. I'm a nice guy. I usually don't have to work this hard. But you've been a real challenge, Rachel Miriam Simon."

"You know my middle name. Can you tell everyone else?" She laughed. "And I noticed you. Believe me."

"Then what is your deal? Please?"

She sighed. "Deep down, I couldn't figure out what a man like you would see in someone like me."

"You said in your speech that you're the girl nobody sees. I see you, Rachel. I see more than you could ever know. I see kindness. I see intelligence. I see someone who puts other people ahead of herself without a second thought. I see a woman with killer curves, a beautiful face, and a fierce wit. And when it comes right down to it, I'd rather spend my time with you than anyone else. Plus, you can do Julius Caesar jokes off the top of your head. That's pretty cool."

"That's what works for you?"

"I'm a maverick. In a sweater vest."

"Wow. Talk about a blue moon."

Brennan appeared in the doorway, panting. "Rachel, you have got to get back in here. Jon has Hank doing the Electric Slide, and it is the best thing I have ever seen." He came in through the glass door and stopped short. "Whoops!"

"Bren, can you give us a minute?" Rachel said, her eyes never leaving Nathan's.

Brennan turned on his heel, exited, and slid the glass door closed behind him.

The music changed, and the din from the dancers disappeared. The band transitioned into a slowed-down version of *For Once In My Life*.

"May I have this dance?" Nathan held out his hand.

Clutching her book, she slipped her other hand in his, his arm encircling his waist. They swayed in time to the music, and after a few seconds, she relaxed. When she looked in his eyes, his expression was intense, as if he truly saw her, the *real* her, and for the first time, she wasn't afraid.

He leaned down and kissed her, gently. His mouth was warm, his breath smelling of coffee and dark chocolate. She tensed at first, just for a second, and then surrendered. Warmth spread through her cheeks as their lips touched, his hands gently cupping the sides of her face.

Yes. This is...yes.

"I'm going to ask you a question." His hands left her face and encircled her waist again. "And I want to be exceptionally clear so there's no question as to my intent." He cleared his throat. "Will you go out on a date with me? On a real, live, honest-to-goodness date? A no-kidding date-date?"

She smiled and offered her answer without hesitation. "I think we should just be friends."

Nathan's eyes widened, and he froze. He stared, unblinking,

with one eyebrow raised. Rachel put her hands up in mock defense.

"I'm kidding, I'm kidding. I would like that very much. I'd...love it."

"I'd love it, too."

Nathan held her close, and they resumed dancing, the sound of the music enveloping them. And it may have only been a run-of-the-mill full moon in the sky, but as far as Rachel was concerned, it was as blue as they came. Rare and special.

And for once, it was just for her.

Acknowledgements

Thank you to my father, James Inglis, for giving me the support I needed to finish this story.

Also to my agent, Amy Brewer of Metamorphosis Literary Agency, who believed in my work and has been a source of support and encouragement during the whole journey.

And a special shout-out to any woman out there, regardless of age or size, who is still struggling to love and accept herself just as she is. You'll get there. I believe in you.

About the Author

Jennifer Inglis has studied comedy writing at the The Second City training center and is a member of the Chicago Writer's Association. An alumna of Northern Illinois University and National-Louis University, Jennifer earned a bachelor's degree in Theater Arts and a master's degree in Education.

Most recently, she worked as a public school teacher, instructing her students in English Language Arts and Drama, and has worn a variety of hats in professional theater in suburban Chicago, including that of playwright, actor, director, and producer. She lives in Chicago with her cat, Daisy.

Jennifer loves to hear from her readers. You can find and connect with her at the links below.

Website/Blog: https://www.jenniferinglis.com
Twitter: https://twitter.com/Jennifer_Inglis
Facebook: https://www.facebook.com/JenniferInglisWriter/
Instagram: https://www.instagram.com/jennifer.inglis.writes/

~~~

If you enjoyed *Girls Who Wear Glasses,* we think you will also enjoy *Some Assembly Required* by Robin Winzenread. Turn the page for a peek!

OVERWORKED. UNDERSEXED.
EXASPERATED
A LOVE THAT STICKS BUT ISN'T STICKY

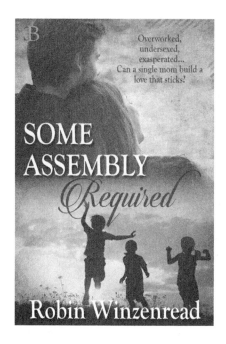

TURN THE PAGE
FOR A LOOK INSIDE!

Chapter One

As my young son's cries echo through this diner, I'm reminded again why some animals eat their young.

It's because they want to.

"Hey, Mom! Nick farted, and he didn't say excuse me!"

Normally when Aaron, my spunky six-year-old, announces something so crudely, we're at home, and his booming voice is muted by the artfully arranged basket of dirty laundry I've shoved my head into in hopes of hiding like an ostrich from a tiny, tenacious predator.

This time, however, Aaron yells it in the middle of a crowded diner in the small, stranger-adverse, southern Illinois town we're about to call home and, frankly, we don't need any more attention. Thanks to my semi-feral pack of three lippy offspring, we've already lit this place on fire, and not in a good way.

Despite our involuntary efforts to unhinge the locals with our strangers-in-a-strange-land antics, this dumpy, dingy diner, minus its frosty clientele, has a real comfortable feel, not unlike the ratty, stretched-out yoga pants I love but no longer wear because a) they don't fit any more and b) I burned them—along with a voodoo doll I crafted of my ex-husband (see my Pinterest board for patterns), after I forced it to have sex with my son's GI Joe action figure (see downward-facing dog for position).

Crap. I should have put the pictures on Instagram. Wait, I think they're still on my phone.

"Mom!" Aaron bellows again.

Right now, I'd kill for a pile of sweaty socks to dive into, but there's nary a basket of tighty-whities in sight, and that kid loves an audience, even a primarily rural, all-white-bread, mouth-gaping, wary one.

Frowning, I point at his chair. "Sit."

More than a bit self-conscious, I scan the room, hoping for signs of defrost from the gawking audience and pray my attempt to sound parental falls on nearby ears, earning me scant mom points. Of course, a giant burp which may have contained three of the six vowel sounds just erupted from my faux angelic four-year-old daughter, Madison, so I'll kiss that goodwill goodbye. I hand her a napkin and execute my go-to look, a serious I-mean-it-this-time scowl. "Maddy, say excuse me."

"Excuse me."

belch

Good lord, I'm doomed.

"Listen to me, Mom. Nick farted."

I fork my chef salad with ranch dressing on the side and raise an eyebrow at my youngest son. "Knock it off, kiddo."

"You said when we fart, we have to say excuse me, and he didn't." Finally, Aaron sits, unaware I've been stealing his fries, also on the side.

Kids, so clueless.

Nick, my angelic eight-year-old, is hot on his brother's heels and equally loud, "We don't have to say it when we're on the toilet. You can fart on the toilet and not say excuse me. It's allowed. Ask Mom."

Aaron picks up a water glass and holds it to his mouth. "It sounded like a raptor." He blows across the top, filling the air with a wet, revolting sound, once again alarming the nearby locals. "See?" He laughs. "Just like a raptor."

I point at his plate and scrutinize the last of his hamburger. "Thank you for that lovely demonstration, now finish your lunch."

Naturally, as we discuss fart etiquette, the locals are still gawking, and I can't blame them. We're strangers in a county where I'm betting everyone knows each other somehow and, here's the real shocker, we're not merely passing through. We're staying. On purpose.

We're not alone, either. My brother, Justin, his wife, Olivia, and their bubbly toddler twins kickstarted this adventure—moving to the sticks—so we're eight in total. Admittedly, this all sounded better a month ago when we adults hashed it out over too much wine and a little bit of vodka. Okay, maybe a lot of vodka. Back then, Justin had been headhunted for a construction manager job here in town, and I was in a post-divorce, downward-spiral bind, so they invited the kiddies and me to join them.

For me, I hope it's temporary until I can get settled somewhere, as in land a job, land a purpose, land a life. When they offered, I immediately saw the appeal—the more distance between me and the ex and his younger, sluttier girlfriend the better—and I decided to move south too.

Now I can't back out. I've already sold my house which buys me time, but I've got nowhere else to go. Where would I land? I've got three kids and limited skills. Plus, I don't even have a career to use as an excuse to change my mind or to even point me in another direction.

In other words, I'm stuck. Whether I want to or not, I'm relocating to a run-down farmhouse in the middle of nowhere Illinois to help Justin and Olivia with their grandiose plans of fixing it up and living "authentic" lives since, according to Instagram, Pinterest, and lifestyle blogs everywhere, manicured suburbs with cookie-cutter houses, working utilities and paved sidewalks don't count. Unless you're stinking rich, which, unfortunately, we, most definitely, are not.

Let's see, Justin has a new career opportunity, Olivia is going to restore, repaint, repurpose, and blog her way to a book deal, and me…and me…

Nope. I got nothing. No plans, no dreams, no job, nada. Here I am, the not-so-proud owner of a cheap polyester wardrobe with three kids rapidly outgrowing their own. I better come up with something, and quick.

Where's cheesecake when you need it? I stab a cherry tomato, pluck it from my fork, and chew. The world is full of people living their dreams, while mine consists of an unbroken night's sleep and a day without something gooey in my shoes. I take aim at a cucumber slice, pop it in my mouth, and pretend it's a donut. At least I don't have to wash these dishes.

Across from me, Olivia, my sometimes-vegan sister-in-law is unaware I'm questioning my life's purpose while she questions her lunch choice. Unsatisfied, she drops her mushroom melt onto her plate and frowns. I knew it wouldn't pass inspection. She may have lowered her standards to marry my brother, but she'd never do so for food. This is why she and I get along so well.

Olivia rocks back in her chair and smacks her lips, dissatisfied. "There's no way this was cooked on a meat-free grill. I swear I can taste bacon. Maybe sausage too." Her tongue swirls around in her mouth, searching for more hints of offending pork. "Definitely sausage."

Frankly, I enjoy finding pork in my mouth. Then again, I have food issues. Though, if I liked munching tube steak more often, perhaps my ex wouldn't have wandered. The bastard.

Justin watches his wife's tongue roll around, and I don't blame him. She's beautiful—dark, luminous eyes, full lips flushed a natural pink glow, cascading dark curls, radiant brown skin, a toned physique despite two-year-old twins. She's everything I am not.

She tells me I'm cute. Of course, the Pillsbury Dough Boy is cute too. Screw that. I want to be hot.

Regardless, I expect something crude to erupt from my brother's mouth as he stares at his lovely bride, so I'm pleasantly surprised when it doesn't. Instead, he shakes his head and works on his stack of onion rings. "What do you expect when you order off menu in a place like this, babe? Be glad they had portobellos."

Across from me, she frowns. Model tall and fashionably lean, she's casually elegant in a turquoise and brown print maxi dress, glittery dangle earrings, silky black curls, and daring red kitten heels that hug her slender feet. How does she do it? She exudes an easy glamour even as she peels a corner of toasted bun away from her sandwich, revealing a congealed mass of something.

"This isn't a portobello. It's a light dove gray, not a soft, deep, charcoal gray. I'm telling you this is a bad sandwich. I'm not eating it." She extracts her fingers from the offending fungus and crosses her bangle bracelet encased arms.

Foodies. Go figure. No Instagram picture for you, sandwich from hell.

Fortunately their twins, Jaylen and Jayden, adorable in matching Swedish-inspired sweater dress ensembles and print tights, are less picky. Clearly, it comes from my chunky side of the family. They may be dressed to impress, but the ketchup slathered over their precious toddler faces says, "We have Auntie Ro's DNA in us somewhere."

I love that.

Justin cuts up the last half of a cold chicken strip and shares it with his daughters, who are constrained by plastic highchairs—which I can't do with my kids any more, darn the luck—and, in addition to having no idea how to imitate raptors with half-empty water glasses like my boys or identify mushrooms by basis of color like their mother, they are still quite cute.

Love them as I do, my boys haven't been cute for a while. Such a long while. Maddy, well, she's cute on a day-to-day basis. Yet, they are my world. My phlegm covered, obnoxious, arguing world.

Justin wipes Jaylen's cheek and checks his phone. "We need to get the bill. It's getting late."

I survey the room, hunting for our waitress. Despite the near constant stranger stares, this place intrigues me. It feels a hundred years old in a good, cozy way. The diner's creaky, wood floor is well worn and the walls are exposed brick, which is quaint in restaurants even if it detracts from the value in Midwestern homes, including the giant moldering one Justin and Olivia bought northeast of town. Old tin advertising posters depict blue ribbon vegetables and old-time tractors in shades of red and green and yellow on the walls, and they may be the real antique deal.

They're really into primary colors, these farm folks. Perhaps the best way to spice up a quiet life is to sprinkle it with something bright and shiny. As for me, I've been living in dull shades of beige for at least half a marriage now, if not longer. Should I try bright and shiny? Couldn't hurt.

Red-pleather booths line the wall of windows to the left, and a row of tables divides the room, including the two tables we've shoved together which my children have destroyed with crumbs, blobs of ketchup, and snot. Of course, the twins helped too, but they're toddlers so you can't point a finger at them especially since all the customers are too busy pointing fingers at mine.

Bar stools belly up to a Formica counter to the right, and it's all very old school and quaint, although I would hate to have to clean the place, partly because Maddy sneezed, and her mouth was open and full of fries.

Kids. So gross.

Three portly gentlemen in caps, flannel, and overalls overflow from the booth closest to our table and, clearly, they're regulars. They're polishing off burgers and chips, though no one is sneezing with his mouth open, most likely because his teeth will fly out in the process. I imagine the pleather booths are permanently imprinted with the marks of old asses from a decade's worth of lunches. Sometimes it's good to make an impression. The one we're currently making, however? Probably not.

Nearly every table, booth, and stool are taken. Must be a popular place. Or it may be the only place in this itty, bitty town. It's the type of place where everyone knows your name, meaning they all stared the minute we walked in because they don't know ours, it's a brisk Tuesday in early November, and we sure aren't local.

Yet.

Several men of various ages in blue jeans and farm hats sit in a row upon the counter stools, munching their lunches. A smattering of conversations on hog feed, soybean yields, and tractor parts fills the air. They all talk at once, the way guys tend to do, with none of them listening except to the sound of his own voice, the way guys also tend to do, like stray dogs in a pound when strangers check them out and they're hoping to impress.

Except for one of them, the one I noticed the minute we walked in and have kept tabs on ever since. Unlike the others, this man is quiet and, better yet, he doesn't have the typical middle-aged, dad-bod build. While most of the other men are stocky and round, square and cubed, pear shaped and apple dumpling-esque, like bad geometry gone rogue, he isn't. He's tall with a rather broad triangular back and, given the way it's stretching the confines of his faded, dark red, button-down shirt, it's a well-muscled isosceles triangle at that. Brown cowboy boots with a Texas flag burned on the side of the wooden heel peek from beneath seasoned blue jeans, and those jeans cling to a pair of muscular thighs that could squeeze apples for juice.

God, I have a hankering for hot cider. With a great big, thick, rock-hard cinnamon stick swirling around too. Hmmm, spicy.

This Midwestern cowboy's dark-brown hair is thick with a slight wave that would go a tad bit wild if he let it, and he needs to let it. Who doesn't love surfer curls, and his are perfect. They're the kind I could run my fingers through forever or hang onto hard in the sack, if need be. Trust me, there's a need be.

His body is lean, yet strong, and beneath his rolled-up sleeves, there's a swell of ample biceps and the sinewy lines of strong, tan forearms. It's a tan I'm betting goes a lot further than his elbows. His face is sun-kissed too, and well-defined with high cheekbones and a sturdy chin. A hint of fine lines fans out from the corners of his chocolate-brown eyes and, while not many, there're enough to catch any drool should my lips happen to ravage his face.

Facial lines on guys are so damn sexy. They hint at wisdom, experience, strength. Lines on women should be sexy too, even the stretchy white, hip-dwelling ones from multiple, boob-sucking babies, but men don't think that way, which is why I only objectify them these days. Since getting literally screwed over by my ex, I'm the permanent mascot for Team Anti-Relationship. I blame those defective Y chromosomes myself. Stupid Y chromosomes.

Regardless, it's difficult not to watch as this well-built triangle of a man wipes his mouth with a napkin. I wouldn't mind being that white crumpled paper in that strong tan hand, even if I, too, end up spent on the counter afterward. At any rate, he stands, claps the guy to his left on the back, and I may have peed myself.

The sexy boot-clad stranger pulls cash from his wallet and sets it on the lucky napkin. "I've got to get back to the elevator, Phil. Busy day."

Sweet, a Texas accent. How very Matthew McConaughey. Mama like.

A pear-shaped man next to him raises his glass. "See ya, Sam. You headed to George's this afternoon?"

"I hope so. I need to get with Edmund first, plus we have a couple of trailers coming in, and I've got to do a moisture check on at least two of them." His voice is low, but soft, the way you hope a new vibrator will sound, but never does until the batteries die which defeats the purpose, proving once again irony can be cruel.

And what the hell is a moisture check?

I zero in on the open button of his shirt, drawn to his chest like flies to honey, because that's what I do now that I'm divorced and have no husband and no purpose—I ogle strange men for the raw meat they are. Nothing's going to happen anyway. Truth be told, I haven't dated in an eternity and have no real plans to start, partly because I've forgotten how; just another unfortunate aspect of my life on permanent hold. I've been invited to the singles' buffet, but I'm too afraid to grab a plate. At this point in my recently wrecked, random life, I would rather vomit. Hell, I barely smell the entrees. I'm only interested in licking a hunk of two-legged meatloaf for the sauce anyway. There's no harm in that, right?

Where was I? Right, his chest, and it's a good chest, with the "oood" dragged out like a child's Benadryl-laced nap on a hot afternoon. It's that goood.

Of course, as I mentally drag out the "oood," my lips involuntarily form the word in the air imitating a goldfish in a bowl. While I ogle this particular cut of prime rib, I realize he's noticed my stare not to mention my "oood" inspired fish lips, which is not an attractive look, despite what selfie-addicted college girls think. Our eyes lock. An avalanche of goosebumps crawls its way up my back and down my arms and, I swear, I vibrate. Not like one of those little lipstick vibrators that can go off in your purse at the airport, thank you very much, but something more substantial with a silly name like Rabbit or Butterfly or Bone Master.

That, my friends, is the closest I've come to real sex in two and half years. Excuse me, but we need a moisture check at table two, please. Not to mention a mop. Okay…definitely a mop.

For a moment, we hold our stare—me with my fish lips frozen into place, vibrating silently in my long-sleeved, heather green T-shirt and jeans, surrounded by my small tribe of ketchup-covered children, and him all hot, tan, buff, and beefy, staring at us the way one gawks at a bloody, ten-car pile-up. All too soon, he blinks, the deer-in-the-headlights look fades, and he drops his gaze.

C'mon, stud, look again. I'm not wearing a push-up bra for nothing.

Big, dark, brown eyes pop up again and find mine. All too soon, they flit away to the floor.

Score.

Damn, he's fine. Someone smoke me a cigarette, I'm spent.

I scan the table, imagining my children are radiating cuteness. No dice. Aaron imitates walrus tusks with the last of his French-fries, Nick is trying to de-fang him with a straw full of root beer, and Maddy's two-knuckles deep into a nostril. And I'm sitting next to Justin.

Figures. My big, burly, ginger-headed, lug of a wedding-ring-wearing brother is beside me. Does this hunk of burning stud think he's my husband? Should I pick my own nose with my naked, ring-less finger? Invest in a face tattoo that reads "divorced and horny?" Why do I even care? He's only man meat. After all, was he really even looking at me? Or Olivia? Sexy, sultry, damn-sure-married-to-my-brother Olivia? I whip back to the stud prepared to blink "I'm easy" in Morse code.

blink *blink* *bliiiink*

With a spin on his star-studded boots, Hotty McHot heads toward the hallway at the back of the diner, oblivious that my gaze is rivetted to his ass and equally clueless to the fact that I have questions needing immediate answers, not to mention an overwhelming need to scream, "I'm single and put out, no strings attached" in his general direction.

Olivia pulls me back to reality with her own questions. "I mean, is it that difficult to scrape the grill before you cook someone's meal?"

She's still honked off about her sandwich, unaware I'm over here having mental sex with the hunky cowboy while sending my kids off to a good boarding school for the better part of the winter.

"I didn't have many options here," she rattles on, "even their salads have meat and egg in them. Instead of a writing a book, I should open a vegan restaurant. I was going to give them a good review for the ambiance, but not now. Wait until I post this on Yelp."

Eyeballing the room, Justin polishes off the last of his double-cheese burger. "Sweetie, we're moving to the land of pork and beef. Vegan won't fly here, and I doubt the help cares about Yelp. Did you notice our waitress? She's got a flip phone. Time to put away your inner princess and stick with the book idea."

Long fingers with bronze gel manicured nails rat-a-tat-tat on the tabletop. She locks onto him with dark, intelligent, laser-beam eyes. "Would it kill you to be supportive, honey bunch? You might as well say, uck-fay u-vay."

Apparently channeling some weird, inner death wish, Justin picks up an onion ring, takes a bite, then pulls a string of overcooked translucent slime free from its breaded coating. He snaps it free with his teeth, then offers it to her. "Your book is going to be great, babe, and it will appeal to a larger audience than here. Remember the goal, Liv. As for me, I'm trying to keep you humble. No one likes high maintenance."

The limp, greasy onion hangs in the air. She ignores it, but not him. "Okay, this time, sweetie, I'll say it. Uck-fay u-vay with an ig-bay ick-day."

Jaylen looks up from her highchair and munches a chicken strip. "Uck-fay?" she repeats through fried poultry. "Ick-day?"

Behind her an older woman, also fluent in pig Latin, does a coffee-laced spit-take in her window booth. I hope she's not a new neighbor.

Justin chuckles and polishes off the offending string of onion. Olivia stews. Time to implement an offense. Clearly, we need an exit strategy.

Where's our waitress? I spy her delivering plates of food three booths down and wave. She nods, so I use these few moments to ward off any drama. "Suggestion, you two. Let's not piss off the help. This may be the only place where we can hide from the kids and eat our feelings. Not to mention drink. Agreed?"

Justin snorts, but says nothing. Olivia rolls her eyes, but also says nothing. Success, although it's tentative. Time to leave.

Water pitcher in hand, our waitress returns to our table. She surveys the left-over lunch carnage, unaware my sister-in-law is both unimpressed and pissed off, and it's fairly obvious that, if we're all going to be regulars here, a sizeable tip, different children, or the offer of a kidney is in order. A middle-aged woman in jeans, T-shirt, and an apron with short, no-nonsense, dishwater hair, she refills our water glasses, possibly so I'll have something with which to wipe the seats or drown our young. Or both. I can't be sure. But I'm open to options.

She sets the water pitcher on the table and starts stacking dirty plates. "Ready for dessert?" She's a bit harried, and, with the possibility of an eruption from Olivia hanging over our heads, I pick up a napkin and start wiping. "We have cherry cobbler."

An indignant cry erupts from the booth behind us. One of the three portly gentlemen hollers—this is the kind of place where you holler— "Save me a piece of cobbler."

"Yeah, yeah, in a minute, Ernie." The waitress scowls. "What else can I get you? Pie? Cake? The coffee's fresh."

"Yeah, but it ain't good though," barks the man named Ernie. A fresh wave of snorts erupts from his companions.

I stifle a laugh, but it's a challenge, especially since Aaron's been flicking my salad croutons in their general direction throughout most of the meal and, despite my scolding, he's getting quite good with his trick shots.

"I bet you've done this before," I say to the woman whose name tag reads "Anna."

She glares at the booth. "Yep, they're regulars. Of course, I call 'em a pain in the butt, myself."

"Good to know, Anna."

"Name's Sarah. This is the only tag we had left."

Of course. Naturally, the crusty old guys are regulars in a diner where everyone knows your name, so you wear a tag that isn't your own, presumably for strangers who rarely show up on a Tuesday. I like this quirky town, even if it doesn't like me.

"Where are you all from? Chicago?" pries the waitress formerly known as Anna.

Olivia avoids eye contact and spit shines her twins. "Is it obvious?"

Curious, Sarah takes in the dress, the earrings, the bright red shoes. "Yep. What brings you through town?"

Backs stiffen throughout the room. Heads swivel in our direction. The general roar of conversation drops a decibel or two, all the better to eavesdrop, I assume.

I confiscate Maddy's spoon and add it to the pile of flatware on my salad plate, then plunge on before anyone at our table offers an unwelcomed critique of the menu. "We're moving here. They bought a place on Stockpile Road, Thornhill."

Eyes stare from all corners of the diner. Bodies sit taller. Ears bend toward us, and whispers swim across a sea of faces.

"Thornhill?" Sarah cocks her head. "You mean old lady Yeager's place? I hope you're good with a hammer."

"It needs a bulldozer," shouts a voice from the back.

"Stick a sock in it, Ernie. Men," she mutters.

"I've got a toxic ex and a lot of frustration, so…" I imitate a manic hammering motion, but, getting no response from the masses, I load up Aaron's spoon with croutons and keep talking. "Justin's in construction—he's starting a new job here next week. He'll put us to work on the house. Should be fun."

Olivia stares at the hunk of sandwich left on her plate before looking pointedly at our waitress. "I plan to blog about the experience—articles on reclaiming the house, restoring the gardens, growing our own vegetables and herbs, recipes, homemade soaps. Think avant-garde Martha Stewart. It's what I do."

Sarah blinks rapidly as she digests Olivia's words. "Ah." She hesitates. "Want a doggie bag?"

Justin chokes on the last bite of his burger as he examines his phone. "Not necessary, but thanks. Can we get our bill though?"

A finger-painted, ketchup rendition of a farting raptor rambles across Aaron's plate. Sarah sets down her stack of dishes, rips our bill from the order pad in her apron pocket, and picks up my son's plate without so much as an appraisal. "So, you all are moving here. Good to know. I haven't been up there in years." She adds another plate to her stack, obliterating his finger art. "I hear it's a real project. Anyway, good luck, and welcome to town." She spins on her heels with arms full of dirty dishes. "You can pay at the register."

Justin tucks his phone in his pocket and wipes his mouth, pleased with his greasy, meaty lunch. "We need to get going. The movers will be here within the hour."

My heart does a double thump. Time to head to the new homestead. True, I'm a hanger-on in this adventure of theirs, just a barnacle on their barge, but I'm excited too even if I haven't been to the place yet. Desperate to reignite my life, the promise of a thousand potential projects, plans, and ideas leap to mind, calling out to me with hope. Maybe this is where I'll find myself. Or a purpose beyond wiping tiny hineys. Something. Anything, really.

Ready to settle the bill, I toss two twenties at Justin. "Here's my cash. Can you pay mine too? I'll run to the restroom, and then we'll get out of here. Sound good?

He grabs the cash. "Yep. Get going, sis. I got this."

My imagination whirls with anticipation as I rise. Roughly fifteen minutes from now, we should be there, home. Can a fresh start be far behind?

Oblivious to my growing excitement, Aaron considers me for a moment as I push back from the table, ready to roll. "Mom, if you fart in there, are you going to say excuse me?"

Nick polishes off his root beer and sets his glass on the table. "I bet she won't. I bet she'll sit there, fart, and say nothing."

Good gravy, will they get off this topic already? My stern gaze falls on blind eyes. Ignoring them, I make a hasty exit to the restroom, but Aaron once again sends shockwaves through the diner with his cry, "Will you tell us if you fart?"

sigh

Maybe I can outrun his voice. I rush away and turn the corner sharp, seeking sanctuary in the women's room. Instead, however, I spy something even better. Speeding toward me from an open door at the end of the hall is Hottie McHot-Stuff, the good-looking cowboy with moisture on his mind.

We both stop short. I sidestep right, as he sidesteps left into my path. We chuckle. Immediately we both dance the other way, blocking one another yet again.

I flash him a smile and grin. "Sorry about that. How about I stop, and you walk on by?"

Hints of vanilla, pine, and leather waft my way. He nods agreement, and our eyes connect. For a moment, we hold yet another stare.

Damn, he's even better looking up close and personal. I could get used to this. Heat rises in my face—where'd that come from? Moisture rises in my jeans—I know where that came from.

All too soon, he breaks our gaze and sidesteps around me. "Excuse me and thank you." Boots clack on the wooden floor, and he saunters away, dragging a steam cloud from my body in his wake. It's a wonder the candy-striped wallpaper in the hallway doesn't peel.

Happy to have a new hobby, I peek over my shoulder and gape at each swaying butt cheek. "You're welcome," I mumble as his blue-jean clad McNuggets disappear around the corner. "You are very welcome."

Into the diner restroom I go, daydreaming about hot cowboys and diner sex. A random inspection of my breasts, hoping they impressed, halts my midday revelry. Because, naturally, there's a hunk of crusted ketchup clinging to my left boob.

Perfect. At least there isn't a French fry in my cleavage. Or is there?

I scrape at the hardened blob with marginal success, preferring to study this fresh new stain on my old, dumpy T-shirt rather than the current flustered face in the mirror. I hate mirrors. The view always disappoints, even now after I've dropped a few dozen post-divorce, pissed-off pounds. But, as I de-crust and wash my hands, I finally look up.

Stain or no stain, I want to see what the cowboy saw.

A round, pixie face with a smattering of freckles that in twenty years when I'm pushing fifty everyone will assume are age spots. Bright green eyes with ex-husband anger issues and a twinkle of insanity. A hint of frown lines spreading across my pale, translucent forehead, explaining my new-found love of long, wispy bangs. Reddish blonde hair thanks to a box from the grocery store. A great big mouth built for yelling and eating. Yep. That about sums it up.

I pinch my cheeks for color because, nowadays, for sheer self-respect alone and in spite of my self-imposed dating ban, I'm making an effort. The truth is, in my full-time baby-making years, I'll admit I didn't most days. A relentless, nonstop tug of war between keeping it together or giving up and letting everything go to seed waged inside me as I confronted dirty diapers, dirty dishes, dirty underwear, and dirty socks. Clad in sensible shoes and something stretchy most days, I only wanted to be comfortable.

News flash. Husbands hate comfortable.

Which is why I am comfortable no more. Time to flush and flee. My old chubby life swirls down the crapper, and my new, uncomfortable, slightly less chubby, but even less focused one awaits. Halle-freaking-lujah, I'm a stalled work in progress.

Drowning in my personal funk, I toss a paper towel in the trash and bolt from the bathroom, far away from the mirror when—slam!

A tall, thin, elderly man sways, reduced to a sapling in a strong breeze, threatening to collapse to the floor under the weight of my rapidly advancing body. He's bundled up in a thick coat, and thank heavens, too, because his right lapel is the only thing that kept him upright.

I cling to it now, gripping with all my might as he steadies his skinny legs beneath himself. His dusty brown bowler hat tilts far forward on a patch of thin silver hair, and there's a spare quality about him.

A tired, watery stare falls upon me, and his initial alarm gives way to anger. "Young lady, watch yourself!"

Why couldn't I have slammed into the cowboy? I could have grabbed something more substantial than this old man's coat.

Letting go of the gentleman's lapels, I lurch backward. "Oh, my gosh, I'm sorry!"

He stands erect, but even with his dignity restored, his anger grows. "You, young people. You don't think, none of you. You have no concept of your own actions, no sense of responsibility!"

Holy crap. What do I say to that? I'm tongue-tied. After all, I did mow him down with my mom thighs. Plus, he thinks I'm "young people," and he sounds like he means it, possibly even enough to pinkie swear.

However, neither of us whips out a tiny digit. Instead, we stand there, locked in stony silence. "Sorry," I repeat for want of anything else to say.

Finally, he turns with a huff and disappears around the corner into the dining room.

Great. We've barely been in town an hour, and I am far from

making friends.

Shaken, I hesitate. Please let this move be the right decision. Please?

It has to be because, right now, I'm a freaking mess. Somehow, I managed to abdicate control over my life to a man who eventually chafed under the responsibility. Now? Now, post-divorce, I'm a rudderless ship, a floating piece of flotsam bobbing downstream, willy nilly, with no real goals or plans other than to make this move, which may or may not be a smart move. What if this proves to be a dead end too? I can't have any more dead ends. Wasn't my marriage enough?

Everyone else has it together. Why the hell don't I?

Desperate for hope, I settle for a plea to the universe instead. Alone in the hall, eyes closed, back against the wall, I give it a go.

Hey, universe, will you please let this move be the right decision for me and my kiddies? Please? With sugar on top?

No one answers, God, Karma, the universe, or alien overlords for whom I am a rapidly failing SIMS avatar, nothing.

Was I expecting an answer?

sigh

No.

I'm alone in the hallway. No skinny old men or hot, buff cowboys walk my way. Regrets, fear, and second thoughts burn behind my eyelids, threatening tears. Steeling myself, I open my eyes, ready to swipe them away before any should fall when I notice it.

A bulletin board anchors the opposite wall, demanding my attention. It's plastered with everything from hay for sale (first cut too, which I assume is the deepest) to pictures of mixed-breed puppies alongside notices for church chili suppers. Bluegrass music drifts in from the dining area, and I drink it in, savoring the ambiance, searching for a sign.

Wait, what's this? An employment ad? For an actual job? Who in the hell advertises on bulletin boards in this digital age? Better question, is it a sign from the universe? A random act of coincidence? A magical stroke of luck?

Who cares? It's an ad. I lean forward and read.

"Local businessman with multiple enterprises seeks organized, responsible individual to serve as part-time office manager with potential for full time available. Knowledge of basic accounting a plus. Requires good communication skills, customer service, and an ability to type. Pleasant office demeanor a necessity."

Oh my. It's a real job.

Snapping a picture with my cell phone, I give thanks to my

short-lived pre-baby history of minimum-wage, part-time jobs at gas-stations and mini-marts. Customer service? No one rang up a carton of Marlboro Lights faster than me. Responsible? The Circle K condom dispenser in the men's restroom was never empty on my watch.

Is this my sign? It sounds like a stretch. Can I really do all that? I, mean, I wasn't exactly bred for this job, was I?

Bred for it? Ick, parent sex. There's an early Saturday-morning memory from age ten I don't need to recall right now.

Scratch that. It's time to be bold and bring on the next chapter of my life.

Lord knows, I need it.

Chapter Two

My SUV hugs the road as we trail behind Justin and Olivia, headed to our new home. Our new home. Geez, that feels weird, false somehow. Is it my home too? I can't shake this notion I'm clinging to my brother like a used dryer sheet in a basket full of bath towels. At least I smell good.

Low, amber-colored hills undulate around us as we climb through the valley, hauling children and ass along the main road out of town, Poseyville, Illinois to be exact. These rolling hills are capped here and there with painfully neat farms, towering pines, and woods shedding leaves in clouds of red, brown, and yellow. Justin plows through a massive clump, and a storm of dead foliage whorls into my path, eclipsing me with color. I bust through it in six-cylinder glory, growing ever closer to our home.

Nope. Not happening. Still feels weird.

Justin's turn signal snaps on, and I follow him onto a gravel road next to a large red barn. Fat, docile cows hunch together under a large maple. Making the turn, I lower my window. "Moo!" A few black and white heads gape in my general direction, but otherwise they take no notice.

Olivia's voice calls to me from my cell phone on the dash. "Did you seriously moo at those cows?"

I back off Justin's bumper and continue to window gawk. "Yep. I've got to make friends somehow. Cows seem a good place to start. They feel like a judgment free zone."

She ignores my attempt at socializing with the locals. "Cows are so pretty. Too bad they smell."

Forget friendship and fragrance, now steak fills my thoughts. I step on the gas, wishing I burned calories as easily as my SUV. "Tasty too. My favorite cow color is medium rare."

Her sigh sizzles through the speaker. "You're killing me, Ro." My brother's laugh echoes in the distance too, but she ignores him. "You're not planning on eating Bessie, are you?"

"Bessie? You've already got her named?"

"I don't know, maybe, if we ever actually have a cow, which, honestly, I can't imagine. But Gertrude's good too."

Braking into another curve, I fly through a tunnel of trees. "Not Gertrude. I'm saving that for a goose."

Aaron kicks the back of my seat, possibly aiming for a kidney. "Mom, are we getting a goose?"

Maddy's eyes never leave SpongeBob on the DVD player. "And a cow?"

This is turning into a real pet parade.

Olivia interrupts with a dose of common sense. "I was kidding about the cow. What do any of us know about farm animals? I'm happy to start with herbs."

Wait, aren't animals a requirement in the country? I hope so. "Kids, we'll talk about pets later."

"If we get any," asks Aaron, "are we gonna eat 'em?"

"No!" yells Maddy before I can reply.

"No!" chimes in Olivia.

"Definitely," Justin remarks.

"Guys," I holler back, "there will be no eating of pets. At least not while Livy's vegan."

Justin's snort echoes from my cell phone followed by the distinct sounds of muffled arguing.

Nick catches my reflection in the rearview mirror. "Mom, can we get a guinea pig? They're small."

Aaron kicks the seat again. "They eat guinea pigs in Peru."

"Mom…," Nick whines.

"Aaron…," I warn, "and how do you know that?"

Soothing the rising tensions from one vehicle away, Olivia interrupts, "Maybe we should start with a cat. They can live outdoors, can't they?"

I glare at Aaron in the rearview mirror, and I cut him off before he can start. "Keep quiet, kiddo. Yes, they can," I bark at the dash.

The children chat on, excited about our future cow, goose, guinea pig, and cat. Maddy contemplates a flock of penguins, and I ignore the ensuing argument about where they live and if Aaron can eat one, should we coax some to Illinois. We pass another herd of cattle as we tear down the road and I can't let it go. "Maybe if we get a cow, I can milk her."

There's silence from the cell phone.

Should I sweeten this deal? Time to appeal to her inner blogger. "Wouldn't it be fun to make our own cheese?"

Ever the foodie, she takes the bait. "Good question. It might be fun. I'll try anything once."

"That's why I married you," adds Justin.

Oh, I love this. It's working. And ick. I ignore him and work on planting the pet seed. "Sounds fun, doesn't it? We can start our own cheese farm."

She laughs. "I believe the word is dairy."

Oh. Right. "Thanks, itch-bay."

Still, I don't think she's embracing my hopes of future cow ownership.

"We don't need a cow to make cheese," she explains, "only raw milk. Plus, I'm not sold on dairy. I wonder if we can make it with almond milk. Or soy?"

My pet dreams deflate. "Moo?" I press.

"Meow," crackles from my cell phone. "Let's start smaller. Think cat."

The left turn signal blinks in front of me, interrupting our conversation, and we grind to a halt under a canopy of leaves. A narrow gravel drive cuts through the hills, angling upward through a stand of trees, disappearing beyond sight in the dappled sunshine. A rusted metal gate, complete with chain and lock, clings to two wooden fence posts, barring our way as it thrusts a rusty sign declaring, "No Trespassing" in our path.

We're here.

A twinge of anxiety fills my chest. Am I trespassing? Should I even be here?

I don't know. Maybe?

Images I've memorized from Olivia's blog posts, pictures, and emails come to mind, the huge brick house upon a tree-lined hill, empty and forlorn. Massive shade trees hug its flanks. High-ceilinged rooms drip with woodwork and character. Wide-plank wooden floors tell a tale of paths traveled over time. Huge stone fireplaces anchor room after room, fueling my imagination as they once heated the home. A broken, forlorn greenhouse, locked in silence, calls out for glass and seedlings, cantaloupe, and care.

My heart beats a cry, "We're home, we're home," even if, technically, it's not my home. I clutch the steering wheel hard, desperate for a sense of stability in the whirling dervish of my life. Anticipation and anxiety overwhelm me.

Bright shiny stars pop into view, and a tiny ache materializes above my right eye. *You're holding your breath, Ro. Breathe, breathe, freaking breathe. One day at a time, remember? One day at a time.*

They've offered to sell me land—they have plenty, acres and acres of it—they've said so several times. I could build a tiny house, plant a garden, start a project of my own. I desperately need a real project, a substantial project, something beyond trying to fit into skinny jeans, though I have no clue what it might be.

Justin hops from his truck and fumbles with the rusted lock and chain. After a momentary struggle, he pushes the gate open with a bladder-piercing shriek and returns to his truck, pausing long enough to give me a wave, a grin, and, naturally, the finger. I flip the bird back. With a laugh, he climbs in then turns his SUV onto the lane.

Once more, I do what I do best. I follow.

My cell phone sparks to life. "Wait until you see it," Olivia's voice tingles. "It's so beautiful. You'll love what I want to do with the kitchen and the dining room? Oh, my, those floors! You can't find wide-plank oak anymore, at least, not in our budget."

Her plans filter through the air waves. It's thrilling when she goes into full-on air-raid mode. Sometimes, it's even contagious.

Will I ever be contagious?

Emotions overwhelm me. "Sweetie, thanks again for including us," I reply. "I mean it. I owe you guys big time for this. It won't be for long, I promise."

A hesitation. "Ro, stop it. We want you here. Don't forget it."

Justin's voice booms out. "Yeah, sis, we love free labor. Those floors aren't going to strip themselves."

smack

"Ow!"

Brothers. Such idiots.

I love those two.

Hallmark moment over, we drive single file up the narrow lane. Ruts mar the path, demanding my focus, but I'm desperate to catch sight of the house. The kids are silent, riveted to the scene as we crawl along the winding lane. It cuts through hills thick with trees, skirting a ravine laced with mottled tan and white sycamores. Tall, wide trees hug either side of a meandering creek, its bed carved between the hills, heading toward parts unknown.

"Mom," Aaron pipes up from the cheap seats, "this looks like a place where people disappear. For good. You know, like in those movies you won't let us watch."

I knew the silence wouldn't last.

Justin's voice crackles from my cell phone, "Good one, kid."

We climb the last hill under a canopy of yellow and gold when it emerges.

Thornhill.

A gray moldering hunk, the huge L-shaped house perches on a ridge, surveying the land below, a tired, old queen on her throne. She's massive, a three-story behemoth. I'm surprised she doesn't sport a flying buttress or two. A wide porch crowned with an equally wide balcony spans her broad front, overlooking the valley below. Large shuttered windows and a pair of French doors take advantage of the ample view.

Olivia wasn't kidding. It is beautiful, achingly beautiful. Haunting, proud, alone, yet, somehow, so beautiful. What did she say, again? Oh, right, the old gal's got good bones.

But battle scars mar the once proud home, etching her façade with the cruel, relentless markers of time. The high-pitched roof sags in spots—at least I can wear a bra—and the once white-painted brick gleams in faded shades of neglected pinks and browns. Clumps of thick weeds sprout between the porch boards, and the effect reminds me of my calves, which I no longer shave because winter's coming and what's the freaking point anyway? No one grabs them in the dark, and the friction keeps my socks up.

It hits me, then, a kindred connection to this poor, sagging gal, and it washes over me. Already, we have so much in common. Perhaps we need each other.

The west side comes into view, as we crest the hill. Another set of French doors overlook a courtyard behind the house, anchored by the sad, diminutive greenhouse of my dreams. Skeletal remains of wild rambling rose vines clamber over it and into it through absent panes of glass. Olivia's Instagram-inspired visions may be hijacking my imagination because if I squint, I can almost make out the plan—rows of lettuce, pots of tomatoes, beds of basil, thyme, and oregano, and a tall lemon tree bursting with bright yellow fruit. I'll plant a fig tree in a pot, and I'll keep it alive, I promise. Daffodils, too, I'll plant daffodils. My nana always grew daffodils, wide, yellow swathes of daffodils.

Thoroughly devoid of gardening plans, Aaron strains in his seat behind me. "Wow. What a dump. Are we really going to live here?"

Nick presses his face against the glass. "Is this it?"

Great. Me? I picture daffodils, but not my boys. Maybe I should set them up with a Pinterest account. Or make them read their aunt's blog, then quiz them afterward for cookies. Couldn't hurt. I focus on Nick in the rearview mirror and ignore Aaron. "Yep, this is home."

His sweet, sensitive face melts into a frown as he contemplates the giant, rundown house. "It looks haunted."

Sensing an opportunity, Aaron stretches across Maddy pinned in her booster seat all the better to torment his brother. "I bet there's ghosts in there that'll rip our faces off."

Her gaze whips away from the house to the rearview mirror, catching my attention. "Are there ghosts, Mommy?"

Geez, that kid. Don't blame me, he gets it from his father.

I flash my foulest stink eye at Aaron but answer the other two. "No ghosts. Would Justin buy it if it had ghosts? You know he's a big old wuss about that stuff."

"Hey," echoes from my brother.

Ignoring his protests one-car away, I plunge on. "There are no ghosts, ghouls, or monsters, just plenty of room. Not to mention history, lots and lots of history."

Another kick lands on the back of my seat. "Yuck," Aaron moans. "History sucks."

Clearly, not a good selling point, though great punishment material. "Keep it up, kiddo, and I'll make you memorize the Constitution."

Addressing my cell phone, I holler at Olivia, "The charm of the place is lost on the rug rats."

She chuckles. "Makes me glad the girls are too young to have an opinion. I'm hanging up now. Let's go explore."

"You got it."

Nick studies the house, his curiosity piqued. "We get to go exploring?"

Oh, I can work with this. "Of course. We're on an adventure. That big, old house is full of nooks and crannies. Don't you want to take a look?"

A tempered smile lights his face. "Yeah. I guess so."

Okay, we're getting there. I channel my inner confident mom voice. "Good, so, let's go exploring."

Ghosts forgotten, Maddy squirms in her booster seat, ready to roam. "I want to go exploring too."

Aaron stares through the window. "I bet there's rats in there. I'm gonna catch 'em and train 'em."

Heaven help me, train them to do what? I can almost picture it—large, well-skilled rats in tiny argyle sweaters and itty, bitty hard hats run through an obstacle course of children's books, hunting for hunks of processed cheese. Embracing the sweet bliss of occasional parental ignorance, I shake off that intriguing, but disturbing, mental image and don't pry for details.

Cresting the last knoll, I park and release my three rabid hounds. They break into a run, erupting into banshee squeals, no doubt sending any would-be ghosts far into the distance hills. The rest of us follow in hot pursuit.

The excitement is palpable. Justin and Olivia talk over each other, imagining future garden plots here and future orchards there, discussing priorities and making plans. They're one step closer to their dream. Must be intoxicating.

The air is fresh, crisp, with no hint of the ever-present smell of exhaust coming from the nearby highway overpass of my former home. Crickets and bird song fill the air. A gentle breeze rustles the trees overhead, sending yellow and gold falling before us. We amble up a wide flagstone path past a clump of large blue spruce when I notice my kids standing motionless in front of the house. I pick up the pace, break free of the trees, reach the front porch, and gasp.

High upon the landscape we stand. It's deceptive, this prominence, its height disguised by the rolling elevation around us, not to mention the plentiful trees. An expansive view of the valley stretches before us, and we gawk, all of us, even the children. I want to drink it in. I want to watch the sun rise from this spot. I want to twirl around in the yard and sing about how the hills are alive with the sound of music, I want—

"Mom?"

"Yes, Aaron?"

"Can I have a rocket?"

"No."

Hill after tumbling hill sprout up to the south, each capped with tidy farms and gold and burgundy trees. A glimpse of the creek sparkles below us in the sunshine, and beyond it lies an orchard, long since relieved of its harvest, near the turnoff with its substantial red barn anchored alongside the road. The pasture corner is empty now, but in the distance, more cows stroll in grass-filled fields. Poseyville remains out of view, though the water tower winks its flashing red light in the afternoon haze. Farther past it, the tip of the Methodist Church steeple hugs the edge of town a few miles distant, pointing toward heaven.

Nick scans the horizon. "This is cool." He swivels my way. "Isn't it neat, Mom?"

Boy, is it. I ruffle his hair. "Yep. No wonder they put the house here."

Aaron clears his throat. "I bet I can spit really far from here." He works on a loogie, ready to fire one off into the valley below.

Ugh. I've said it before, and I'll say it again. Kids, they're beyond gross. They're disgusting. "No spitting, Aaron."

Naturally, he swallows it.

For the love of God...

I stifle a gag. Olivia stifles a gag. Leave it to him to make it even grosser.

Justin gives his nephew an appreciative stare. "Dude." My six-foot-three brother offers a fist bump, and my youngest son reciprocates.

Guys. Also so gross.

My equally disgusting brother steps behind me and bumps me with his shoulder, getting my attention. "Penny for your thoughts, sis."

Good question. What am I thinking beyond gross, disgusting, and, finally, back to wow? I look left, then right. What a view. "You got a great place, little bro. Pictures don't do it justice. What are your thoughts?"

A smirk swims across his face. "Honestly? Now, I'm thinking about getting a bottle rocket."

Olivia turns Jayden loose, sending leaves scattering under her tiny toddler feet. "Nope." She laughs.

He puts his arm around his wife and pulls her in for a hug. "Ah, come on. Party pooper."

Uninterested in public displays of affection, Nick kicks at the ground and squirms in his shoes, desperate to burn energy after our lengthy road trip. "Can I throw rocks down the hill?"

First spit, now rocks. What next? Sticks?

Justin scans the valley, probably wondering how far he can throw too. "Sure. I might give it a try myself."

Yep. Thought so. They're gross, but not complicated.

Establishing parameters, I point at a large stone and ward off Nick. "Not that one. Small ones only. And only down the hill."

He pivots on his heels, ready to rock. "Thanks, Mom."

Aaron spins after him. "I want to throw some too."

"Wait a sec." I snatch his collar before he can take off, stalling his progress. "Small ones, kiddo. I mean it. Be really careful. Don't throw them at your brother. Or your sister. Or your cousins. Or the house. Definitely not the house."

So many disclaimers with that child. My conversations with him are walking footnotes dripping with asterisks.

Nick sprints to the drive, leaving a trail of swirling leaves behind him. "I bet I can throw further than you!"

Released from my grip, Aaron dashes after him, pumping his arms as he flies after his older brother. "Bet cha' can't!"

Content they have a plan, but wary of its outcome, I brace myself for the unknown, preferring to take in the view. It's easy to do, this letting go of responsibility, even for the briefest of moments. I want to savor this—I would paint it if I knew how.

Instead, I settle for my cell phone. At least it can zoom, and Olivia's been after me to be more active on Instagram. I open my camera app and snap picture after picture—Maddie cavorting with the twins, Justin kissing his lovely wife in the dappled sunshine, the long-distance view beckoning with its palette of reds, oranges, yellows, and greens, a true technicolor force of nature.

Circling around, I hunt for my boys, ready to capture them in action as they hunt for rocks, preparing for their epic throwing contest on the hill. Instead of finding them hunkered over the gravel drive, however, I spy them between the blue spruce trees, laughing, bending, chatting, and petting. Because they're not alone.

A cat, plump, yellow, and happy to meet them too, headbutts Aaron's knees. The fat feline leans into my son with his wide-angled head and glides across his legs. A long, swishing tail flicks back and forth in pursuit. Running out of boy, the fluffy kitty turns and tucks into another rub in the opposite direction, sliding back across Aaron, headed straight for Nick. Back and forth it goes, rubbing, spinning, and swishing across my boys' legs.

Nick catches me watching them with their new four-legged friend. All innocence and joy, he points at the kitty. "We found a cat."

"Cat?" Olivia and Justin grind to a halt in mid kiss, their happy-homeowner dance suspended.

Livy's mouth drops open, the word barely off her lips, no doubt reliving our pet conversation during our drive minutes ago. Who knew it would be so prophetic?

Justin squints at the boys, an eyebrow arches up, and a hint of tickled wonder blooms across his grizzled cheeks. "What'd you know? Looks like we got ourselves a cat."

Blinking in slow motion, she scrutinizes her husband. "Did you plan this somehow?"

He raises calloused hands in the air, "Honest, hun, I had nothing to do with it."

"Mom," Aaron interrupts, "can we keep it?"

Ah, the inevitable cry for kitty-cat ownership, right on schedule. He sits now, cradling the fat feline. Nick hovers alongside him, scratching an ear. From here, it certainly smells like adoption.

Tiny girl ears catch the word cat on the breeze. Maddie and the twins brake to a halt, then launch headlong at the boys, squealing. To its credit, the chubby kitty remains undisturbed and, rather than bolting for the weeds as any sane creature should do, it sprawls across Aaron's lap, soaking up the attention, ready for more.

My youngest reaches the cat and drops to her knees, swooning with instant love. "Oh, you, poor baby, I'll take care of you. Mommy, we've gotta keep him. He'll die if we don't."

Oh goodie, a guilt trip too. It's not even my birthday. How generous.

We join the children and study the cat. Shushing Maddie with a finger to my lips, I bend over my son and visually inspect the feline rump fluff from a safe distance. "Are you a fella?" I make eye contact with Olivia. "Should we peek under the hood?"

She tilts away avoiding its bottom. "Probably, but you do it. Quick, Ro, take a peek."

"Nope, sorry." I shake my head. "We haven't even been introduced yet. I feel like we should get to know each other first, maybe have dinner together."

"Oh, for heaven's sake." Justin squats between the children and examines the cat's bottom. "Congrats. It's a boy."

I lean over Aaron to the sound of purrs. "You sure?"

Standing straight, Justin wraps his long gorilla arms around his wife and rests his chin on her head. "Yeah, I can tell the difference between the naughty bits, sis. You may have forgotten, though."

Ouch. What a turd.

Olivia interrupts our squabbles, eyeballing the cat. "He can't be a stray; he hasn't missed many meals. Lost, maybe, but not a stray."

I kneel beside the kids and search for a collar, but find none, although I do find ample evidence of fat rolls. "Boy, he is a butterball. Do you think someone dropped him off?"

My sister-in-law, however, holds her ground. "What if he got out on accident? What if there's a kid crying right now because he can't find his pet? We should probably call the shelter. If he's lost, someone may have reported it."

An avalanche of no and why can't we pour from the mouths of children who only want to love this fur ball. Is that so wrong?

With that chub, however, he probably does belong to someone. Ah, reason, why must you suck so?

Justin and I deflate. He steps around his frowning wife and pets the purring pussy. "I guess we should probably call the shelter. Maybe tomorrow. We're too busy to deal with this today, what with the movers and all. He can sleep in our room tonight. You know, so we can keep an eye on him, make sure he stays out of trouble."

Flailing her hands in frustration, Oliva fails to take the bait. "Oh, good grief. Are you already attached to this cat?"

"Look at him, Liv. What's not to love?"

Determined, Maddie digs in, ready to fight the good fight.

"Please, Mommy, can we keep him? Please?"

Nick takes up the gauntlet too, ready to impale my guilt-tripping, parental heart. "Yeah, please?" he implores. "You said we could get a cat"

I shoot a glance at Olivia who shoots one back.

Growing increasingly tired and cranky, my daughter whines even louder. "We'll be good if we can keep him, we promise. Even Aaron."

"I'm not making any promises," Aaron back tracks, ever the politician. "I can catch mice for him, though. I bet there's plenty in the house. Look at it."

"Hey," Justin yells for the second time in ten minutes.

My boy rambles on, making plans. "I'll make traps to catch them and everything. Please?"

Sporting a mischievous grin, Justin aims it at Olivia with a pretend pout, "Yeah, please, Mom? Can we?"

"Please?" repeat Nick and Maddy as they take up their uncle's rallying cries.

"Pwees?" Jaylen and Jayden coo in sync, radiating their personal brand of precious toddler charm.

"Yeah, 'cause Dad isn't around to sneeze anymore," Aaron insists, going for the kill, expertly playing the child-of-a-recent-divorce card. "Mom, you always said we couldn't have pets 'cause of Dad. He's not here now. Can't we at least keep the cat?"

Ah, that boy, he has this guilt thing down to a science.

Sensing the children need reinforcements, the cat rolls onto his back and displays his ample white tummy, declaring in his own kitty way, "Scratch me, minions." Our babies giggle and comply, under the magical spell of homeless kitty cuteness.

I attempt to impart reason into this conversation, careful not to wreck any teeny, tiny dreams or piss off any large, grown adults in the process. "Listen, kids," I begin, "we'll get a pet eventually." I will them to understand, but the looks on their faces are so hopeful. I falter. "...I want to keep this guy too." I hesitate. Tiny chins quiver and tiny eyes turn to glass. Sniffles penetrate the air. "He probably belongs to someone. He's too fat and happy to be a stray. We need to find his owner."

Ratcheting up the darling factor, the four-legged interloper paws at my daughter's pig tails, putting on a show as she hugs him, sprouting tears. He catches one pigtail between his paws and chews the end. The children laugh, even Maddy, and she teases him with strawberry blonde curls. "He wants to play with me."

Resolve melts. Plans go astray. I dissolve into lukewarm gelatin.

Parenthood, it's such a badass kick to the head.

Fortunately, Olivia isn't immune either. Giving in, she sighs. "Okay, he can stay for a few days. We'll call the shelter on Friday and," she caves, "if no one claims him, we'll keep him."

Squeals of delight erupt on the hill, including the loudest from Justin. She shakes her head, laughing. "If it does belong to someone else, we'll all take him back, and then we'll get another cat. Deal?"

"Deal," we all agree.

I lift the cat from the swarm of children and hand him to Justin, who cradles him close. "Now how about we go explore the house? Did you forget we haven't even seen it yet?"

My children swivel toward the gray form hulking behind us. Nick fidgets in the grass. "Can we bring the cat?"

Instantly we all face Olivia. She looks from child to child to husband. "Oh, all right. You can bring the cat."

"Yay!" fills the air.

Happy, excited, and, finally, curious, the kids make for the house. Nick hip checks Aaron and sprints to the porch, determined to be first. Never one to be beaten, Aaron tears after his brother yelling louder than a high-school cheer block at a championship game. When God handed out inside voices, that kid must have slept in and missed it.

The rest of us trail behind them, ready to explore, but already I'm slipping back into daydream mode. First a cat but what next? A dog? A hamster? No guinea pigs though.

Cat crisis momentarily resolved, we stroll through the lawn, making plans. Olivia points to a spot for lilacs. Justin mentions a grape arbor. I imagine scooping litter boxes. Can we use it as fertilizer? I could sprinkle it around the roses.

Maybe I can learn to garden. They both offered to show me. I'll eat fresh vegetables for a change, not canned. Surely, I can manage that.

Summers filled with tomatoes, wouldn't that be nice. Come autumn, we'll be knee deep in a pumpkin patch. Winter? Sledding parties and snowball fights—won't that be fun. I'm starting to see the vision now. It's fuzzy and foggy, but at least I'm cleaning off my glasses and peering at the furry, weedy future.

I'll ask Olivia to give me cooking lessons that go beyond opening a box, adding water then stirring until ready. I can learn to grow herbs, cook with them, make pies from scratch, simmer homemade stocks—all that good stuff she goes on and on about in her blog. Justin can teach me to be handy around the house. Surely, I can beat stuff with a hammer.

Maybe I will buy a few acres, build a modest house, plant my own garden, get a cat, and start new traditions. I'll put down roots too, and not merely the vegetable kind. Better rooted than rootless, right?

They say when one door closes, another opens, but lately too many of those closed doors slammed in my face, and the only ones I've opened since I had to pry at with a freaking crowbar. Now I have the chance to build a new life here, and it's becoming more concrete with every passing second.

I join my family on the porch of our new home, ready to start our adventure. Things are starting to look up.

I think.

Out Now!
http://champagnebooks.com/store/213_robin-winzenread

What's next on your reading list?

Champagne Book Group promises to bring to readers fiction at its finest.

Discover your next
fine read!
http://www.champagnebooks.com/

We are delighted to invite you to receive exclusive rewards. Join our Facebook group for VIP savings, bonus content, early access to new ideas we've cooked up, learn about special events for our readers, and sneak peeks at our fabulous titles.

Join now.
https://www.facebook.com/groups/ChampagneBookClub/

Printed in Great Britain
by Amazon